DUBIOUS FORT DUBOIS

BY

MICHAEL McINERNEY

Also By Michael McInerney
The Wackentute Diary

www.greenmousepress.com

Look here for the author's website for "Tuesday is Muse Day" "This Week in History" & "Relax : Things Can Always Be Verse"

Published by Green Mouse Press
PO Box 442 Belmar, New Jersey 07719
ISBN: 978-0-9905679-1-2

Cover Art by Jacqueline Quatse

Disclaimer: This is a work of fiction. Names, characters, places, and incidents either are a product of the author's imagination, or are used fictitiously. Any resemblance to actual persons, living or dead, events, or locales is entirely coincidental.

ACKNOWLEDGEMENTS

The picture of the struggling writer, cloistered in his den working alone for long hours . . . days . . . weeks . . . months, etc., staring at a blank sheet of paper (or computer screen) is misleading. At least it is where I am concerned. What I do; what I produce; is the result of the many contributions I have received over the years. Most recently that would include the Lee County and Monmouth County Library Systems; the patience and the diligence of my editors: Laura Ginsburg and Nancy M. I am very grateful for the electronic perseverance of Katharine & Jason Irizarry. And I am indebted for the inspiration and art of Jacqueline Quatse. I thank the genetics I inherited; the schools I attended (by that I mean the teachers who struggled to educate me); the many friends throughout my life who shared with me their sense of humor and keen wit – especially the New Breed. I thank the incredible, wonderful serendipity that landed me among my siblings; and the colossal good fortune of finding, winning, and holding on to Nancy.

Dedicated to
Rob – Kate – James – Andrea
For the encouragement, faith, and love

Dubious
Fort Dubois

Chapter 1 - Prelude

The Scotch Highlands are cold and hilly,
And oft times wet (or wetter!).
The troops did not like it there.
They thought anywhere else was better.

And the locals did not like them much,
They wished they'd all go away.
They wished they'd pack up their gear,
And go back home to England and stay.

Since the dawn of time it seems that royalty has found it difficult keeping their throne "in the family", so to speak. The principals - those royal (sometimes ruling) families around the world, and Europe in particular - are a rather close knit sort of group often due to arranged marriages between and within families for political reasons. And, sadly, these unions of limited gene pools all too often result in offspring who have sometimes been found wanting in certain areas. Not the least of which is their decision making abilities. This has had many unfortunate results. Remember that these people are responsible for the welfare of their subjects, and make crucial decisions concerning economics, law, foreign relations, religion, etc. for the populace. This lack of sound judgment frequently manifests itself after some monarch has expired.

Kings, or queens for that matter, have never thought it necessary to leave a will. And somewhere back in the fog of unrecorded history the concept of Primogeniture took root. This simply meant that the eldest son would ascend to the newly vacant throne. "The

King is dead …. Long live the King!" Old is out – New is in. Sounds simple, no? This practice of Primogeniture provided a simplified process at a time of grief and stress for all concerned. Unfortunately this process did not sit well with second sons, or thirds, or fourths either. Daughters often thought it heinous. Brothers, sisters, uncles, nephews and aunts, just to name a few, also found it wanting. Spouses, generals, popes…..ah, the list goes on. Sad to say, a satisfactory solution to this problem has escaped European Royalty to this day. (On a brighter note there are far fewer Royals in Europe (as well as elsewhere) concerned with this enigma in this day and age.)

In the year of 1714 AD this process was, unfortunately, in full bloom. Anne from the Scottish House of Stuart, Queen of Great Britain, died on August 1st. Her husband, Prince George of Denmark and Norway, and also Duke of Cumberland, had predeceased her, and they had no surviving children. Despite a prearranged plan of succession, put in place by the Act of Settlement (passed by Parliament in 1701) that had decreed that her crown would pass to George I of the House of Hanover, there were objections from the House of Stuart. Loud ones!

The House of Stuart was still very upset about how the last Stuart king, James, had been forced out by the Hanover forces of William of Orange in 1688. They wanted their throne back. The people from the House of Hanover demurred. The squabble between the two houses ran intermittently from that initial ouster in 1688 almost until the middle of the next century.

In August of 1745, Charles Edward Stuart (Bonnie Prince Charlie), the last legitimate Stuart heir to the British crown, sailed from exile in France to Scotland with a small army to press his claim. They were known to history as The Jacobites. Rallying many Highland Scottish clans around him, as well as an assorted batch of English Episcopalians and Irishmen, he marched south from Scotland toward England. The English forces were slow to respond, and the rebels, The Jacobites, scored a few small, but impressive victories. At Prestonpans (east of Edinburgh) they won their most impressive victory that September. However, in the following April of 1746, the rebels ran into the House of Hanover forces of lowland Scots and English regulars, commanded by the son of King George II, Prince William, Duke of Cumberland

("Sweet William" or "Stinking Billy" depending on which side you were on) at the Battle of Culloden. The battle was a rather one-sided affair with the Stuarts coming in a distant second. Bonnie Prince Charlie narrowly escaped with his life, and little else, and scurried back into exile in France. Thoughts of restoring the Stuarts to the throne were permanently shelved by Bonnie Prince Charlie. Henceforth he occupied his time with one love affair after another (including one with his married first cousin!). Oh, those Royals!

The House of Hanover, in an effort to put this Stuart claim to rest once and for all, came down rather heavily on the Scots after their victory at Culloden. The treatment of the disloyal Highland Clans was brutal and unrelenting. The harshness ranged from heavy taxation to the confiscation of the private property of suspected Stuart loyalists. Many were arrested, jailed, deported, or even executed. Soldiers roamed the countryside for years afterwards attempting to extinguish the Stuart flame forever. They even went so far as to ban the wearing of the Scots' beloved tartans. The Scots did not take to this kindly.

Two and a half years after the Battle of Culloden, British troops were still in the highlands. And in the isolated, desolate lake district of northern Scotland a twenty man detachment of the Royal West Essex Dragoons was patrolling, village to village, trying to ferret out any remaining "traitors" in the area. Despite being Dragoons, they were on foot. All their mounts, except their commanding officer's mount and the horse pulling his baggage cart, had been reassigned to a more favored unit. The men were not pleased. Trudging the highways and byways of this inhospitable hilly country in the winter had worn their boots, and their patriotic fervor, to the nub.

This evening found them waiting out the daily blustery rain storm in their makeshift quarters. The barn they currently called 'home' had a roof that leaked, and its walls only partially protected them from the gusting wind outside. Their evening meal, which they had confiscated from a nearby farmer, hadn't been enough to go around, and they were all still hungry. Their commanding officer was Colonel Oliver Highcross, a mean spirited, inept tyrant whom all the men hated. He had achieved his high rank, with its prestige, privileges and various material rewards, the same way many of his peers had achieved theirs. He had inherited it. Courageous and daring forebears had earned the prizes of riches, and pensions, and lands that victory affords. In this case that referred to his father, the Duke of Nunch, and former Admiral in His Majesty's Navy. The famous, and oft decorated, Admiral had obtained the commission for his obnoxious son, and then had him sent off to the far north of Scotland. Out of sight - Out of mind.

As usual, Colonel Highcross had left the sergeant-major in charge of the troop when he had earlier ridden ahead to the next village. Sergeant Major Bottoms, who had eaten his full before allowing his men to join in, assigned Corporal Westport to take charge of the troop, and then bedded down in the driest corner of the barn. Corporal Westport and the soldiers made the best of what was left for dinner.

All but Private Wilbur Smith, that is. He was "Blinking Willie" to his comrades, due to his constant nervous twitch, and he was the lowest in rank, with the least seniority, and the last in line for any consideration in the company. He had been assigned to accompany Colonel Highcross as his personal guard in this hostile country. As he jogged alongside the mounted Colonel they made their way to the next village. They made an odd pair.

Private Smith was taller than Colonel Highcross, by about a foot. The colonel weighed more, by about 80 lbs. The colonel had very small round eyes, placed very close to the sides of his arching nose. His small mouth was unusually far from that nose, and his chin was non-existent. All these smallish features were at the center of his large round face. These facial traits were in sharp contrast to his impressive military bearing; and his attire was tailored and immaculate despite the travel in the rough terrain. He carried extra uniforms in his large baggage cart.

The private's face and body were alike. Both were long and narrow. His incessant blinking caught and held any onlooker's attention so thoroughly that most were unable to describe any other physical features he had. His uniform was filthy and didn't fit him, and hadn't since the day it had been issued to him. And the private slouched as if he was a foot taller than he actually was.

The colonel had decided to spend his evening, after his long day in the saddle, in the local tavern. He almost always did. He had discovered early in his deployment to Scotland something the locals called "the water of life". We know it as Scotch. Private Smith was assigned to accompany him to the tavern, as far as the door, and to stand guard against any local ruffians.

Upon entering the tavern Colonel Highcross took stock of his surroundings. The only two people in the room were a barmaid and a barman. The combination of the overcast sky, and the small windows in front provided very little light. The fireplace along the side wall was empty, and thus provided neither heat nor light. Three candles provided what other little light there was. One was just inside the front door; the second was on the bar which was positioned along the back wall. And a third candle was on one of the small tables in the room. Before closing the door behind him, the Colonel turned and had a brief conversation with Private Smith. Neither the barman, nor the waitress standing nearby heard exactly what was said. The waitress, however, thought she heard one of them say "Stinkin' Willy".

The colonel closed the door behind him, and sat down on a bench at the only table with a candle. He only glanced for a moment at the barman, but then gave the barmaid a long measuring look. She was, perhaps, past her prime, and a tad overweight, and there was no smile on her face. Because it was her job, she reluctantly approached the officer. She didn't like the English in general, and she especially hated the ones in uniform. She had lost a husband and a brother in the recent war; but of the two, she only mourned her brother.

The squat English officer greeted her with a smiling face. It seemed a lecherous grin to her. "Good evening, Mrs." he said, barely above a whisper. She was unable to muster a reciprocating smile. He took a long look at her, head to foot and again smiling, said to her, "I want something to eat." And a moment later, "And drink. What have you got?"

The barman, and owner of the tavern, stood 5 feet 4 inches tall and weighted 120 lbs soaking wet. But despite his diminutive size he ruled his roost. But he also knew very well the animosity that his barmaid harbored for the English military "I'll take care of the gentleman, Kenna," he said to her, and quickly positioned himself between the two. He then turned immediately to the British officer. "I have some very good stew, Sir. Just made it up this mornin'." He smiled and lied. He went on to add that the ale he had in stock was the very best, and the local whiskey was even better. The officer was hungry, but his attention stayed on the barmaid as she sashayed out of the room into the back kitchen. Disappointed to be deprived of her company he told the barman to bring the stew, and added that he better be 'damn quick about it'.

In no time at all the barman returned with a plate of the five day old stew made up of some local vegetables and vegetation, with some parts of various animals. He had added a splash of whiskey and spit in it for good luck. He was no fan of the occupying British Army either, but a customer was a customer. He added a chunk of stale bread and a tankard of ale, and placed it all in front of the colonel.

"That woman? You called her 'Kenna'. She's your wife?" the colonel asked.

"Oh no, Sir. Her name's Kenna MacBride." He said, "She works here for me, I own this place. I'm Tom Kilgore. The poor dear is a widow twice over." He added. "I pay her what I can to help feed the little ones at home."

Colonel Highcross was going to ask how her husbands had died, but then realized he didn't care, so he asked, "Where'd she go?"

"Just to get a breath of air, Sir. She's been workin' the entire day for me. I'm sure she'll be back in a moment." He answered without the foggiest notion of where she was.

"Good." said the officer. "Tell her to come and sit with me. I don't like to dine alone."

The barman went back into the kitchen to retrieve her for the colonel, but Kenna wasn't there. "Damn!" he thought to himself. "Now where's she off to?" Kilgore returned to the front and sadly told the officer she had gone off to take care of one of her children, but would be back in no time.

Annoyed slightly, Colonel Highcross told him to send her out the minute she returned. "And take this ale back. It's piss. Bring me some whiskey."

When she burst in the back door 10 minutes later she was out of breath and flushed from running. She tried catching her breath as her boss started to pepper her with instructions. "Get out there right away, "And be nice, damn it. And push him on the whiskey. Get him to buy you some of it. I think we . . . ."

"Shut up and listen!" she hissed at him just louder than a whisper. She leaned in close to him; her breast heaving with heavy breathing; perspiration glistening on her face. "Do you not know who that bastard is?" she asked in disbelief. He looked at her in silence, and then shook his head. "That's Prince William, you ninny. 'Stinking Billy' himself!" Her eyes were bulging out of her head.

He started to disagree with her, "Nah, it can't be. I don't think that's the Prince…." But she cut him off.

"It is, I tell ya." She said. "I heard him saying 'Stinking Willy'." She paused, and then corrected herself, "Stinkin' Billy." It had to have been "Stinkin' Billy" she thought.

The owner was skeptical, to say the least. "You heard what? I think it's supposed to be 'Stinkin' Billy'. Not 'Willy'. Isn't it?" And do ye think a soldier would call the Prince by that name, anyway? Do ye? And he's only got one guard out front? Don't you think that the Prince would have…."

She cut him off again. "It's him. I know it. I saw him once. That's a general out there. And that general is Prince William himself." She was certain, and she wasn't going to debate the point. She whirled around, wiped her face and breast with a rag, and went out into the dining room. She was right that the man in front was an English officer. And she had seen Prince William, in the flesh, several years ago in Edinburgh. But she hadn't been very close to him. And, truth be told, this fellow out front was certainly no 'prince' (on any level). And he was not even a General. The uniforms were similar, but the differences were just too subtle for her eye. But in her mind she was sure, and that set the wheels in motion for the calamities that followed.

Owen Dundoon stood very still, trying hard to stay out of the misting rain. He was under the only patch of roof still above the abandoned stable, but the gusting wind sprayed the rain around. He peered out the partially open front doors, and watched the sleeping guard on the covered front porch of Kilgore's tavern across the street. The guard had a blanket tightly wrapped around him; his long musket, with the bayonet attached, leaned against the building at his side.

Owen heard a commotion behind him from probably fifty yards away as it approached the rear of the stable. Heavy footsteps, grunting and cursing preceded Dick MacGrooty's entry through the long gone back door of the stable. "Jaysus, Mary and St Joseph! Could you make any more noise than that? You could wake the dead!" Owen growled at the rain soaked, panting Dick.

"Holy Mother of God!" was all Dick could say, at first. He repeated it several times. A moment later, with some wind restored, he looked at Owen, who hadn't taken his eyes off what he had been looking at, and said, "Where's the riot? Norman come racing up the lane like a madman, told me to get my gun, and get here as fast as blazes." He paused, and tried to see what Owen was focused on. Then he added, "What in the hell is goin' on?"

"Thank Christ you didn't wake that damn guard. He must be half dead. Or maybe half deaf? I don't know which!" He turned slowly to Dick. He towered over him. Owen was over six foot tall, and was thick everywhere. Behind his back he was described by friends and foe alike 'as strong as an ox, and only a wee bit smarter'. He was nearly bald on top of his large head, and his arms and hands were huge. He tended the livestock on the estate of a wealthy landowner in the area, and had, at one time or another, been bitten, kicked, scratched, or otherwise assaulted by every one of them. He didn't particularly like animals.

Dick, on the other hand, was smaller and not nearly as strong. But he considered himself very much smarter. That was open to debate. He spent his days avoiding work of any kind, and usually was very successful at it. He spent most days fast asleep, and wandered through the neighborhoods at night looking for anything not nailed down. Both had been recruits in the failed Jacobite Rebellion; but neither had seen any fighting. Disappearing from the ranks when danger was in the air seemed to be a skill both possessed in abundance.

"Ya know who's sitting in Kilgore's at this very moment?" Owen asked Dick. Dick shook his head. With a gleam in his eye, and a broad grin, Owen said while nodding slowly, "Stinking Billy!"

"Whaa?" was Dick's first response. Owen smiled, knowing he had stunned his friend. "Ya daft!" Dick said, "Prince William? Prince William, son of King George? Have ya been drinkin', yer big fool? What in the name of God would he be doing here? And without an army around him for protection!" Owen explained to him, in a soft voice so as not to alarm the guard across the street, that Kenna had come to him in a mad dash not twenty minutes ago, to tell him that the Prince was, indeed, in Kilgore's at that very moment.

The fact that Kenna said she was sure it was the Prince was all the certainty that Owen needed. Owen was madly in love with Kenna MacBride. In his eyes she was the perfect woman, and despite her rough demeanor and girth he wanted very much to be her third husband. When she had come charging down the lane that short time ago to his stable, and grabbed him by his shirtfront, and issued him her instructions he never uttered a word. Instead, he flew into action.

Dick wasn't so sure. Owen kept saying that Kenna was certain. Dick processed the information again, this time more slowly. He came to the conclusion that it was possible . . . remotely possible . . . that Prince William . . . son of King George II of Great Britain . . . "Stinking Billy" . . . might . . . *possibly* . . . a very remote chance . . . be across the street in Thomas Kilgore's Tavern. "So what?" he was finally able to say.

"'So what?' 'So what' yer say? Here's our chance. Here's our chance on a silver platter, lad!"

"'Our chance for what? Whaddya talkin' about?" Dick was confused. He always felt uncomfortable when Owen came up with ideas.

"To kill him, of course! Why'd ya think I told Norman to tell yer to bring yer gun?"

Dick was shocked. A million thoughts raced through his overburdened brain. The only thought he was able to communicate was, "Just mine?"

"Jaysus, Mary, and St Joseph! No, yer fool. Norman's getting' his too. And both of mine! I told him to bring some knives too, just to finish the job if we have to." Owen was bursting with pride that he had, without a moment's hesitation, hatched this entire plan. It was actually Kenna's plan, but Owen left that fact out. Dick would have been only slightly more confident had he known that, but he didn't. Dick's lack of confidence was not based solely on the source of the plan, however. As he thought it all over it occurred to him that he had never shot a man before. In fact, he had never shot **at** a man before!

The two men stood in silence for the next ten minutes. Owen peered out through the doors and watched the sleeping guard and for any sign of movement at the doorway of the tavern. He began to worry that Norman wasn't going to get back in time with the three extra guns before Stinking Billy left. He hoped that Kenna would be able to stall him until Norman arrived.

He didn't have to worry. At that moment Kenna was sitting on the English Colonel's lap, encouraging him to finish his fifth cup of whiskey. Kenna (with Tom Kilgore's encouragement) was running up the man's bill by drinking water and charging for whiskey. She was also thinking that in about one hour this 'son of a bitch' would be dead in the street. The officer, oblivious to this planned scenario, was enjoying himself immensely with a lady on his lap, and getting progressively drunker. They were both feeling very good.

Dick was not so gleeful. His less-than-admirable track record of petty pilfering, laziness, and general antisocial behavior was about to take a major step upward with the assassination of Prince William. He had come up with at least fifty reasons why they shouldn't do it, but Owen wouldn't listen. "Jaysus, Mary, and St Joseph! Are yer forgettin' what this bastard's done? Are yer fergettin' what he done to Kenna? Made her a widow! Killed Timmy MacBride."

"I never liked Timmy, you know." Dick said quietly, to no one in particular. Then turning and looking right at Owen said, "Besides, Timmy was probably shot by one of our men. He was shot in the back. Remember?" Another possibility occurred to Dick, and he added softly again, "Or he might have been running away when he got shot?"

Owen didn't want to argue the point. He switched gears. "How about Niall then? Her brutha. You knew him, and everyone who knew him, liked him. He was a good soul." Owen didn't think Dick would argue that point. He was right; Dick didn't want to argue that point. Dick wanted to go home.

Just then a huge man came crashing through the rear of the stable carrying two rifles, a blunderbuss pistol, and a scythe. Tucked into his belt were two long knives. "Mother of God! You're a regiment!" said Dick. Norman MacMulveigh was even bigger in size than Owen, and still in his teens. The two older men were heroes to him for opposite reasons. He admired Owen for having a steady job. And, as a bonus, that job was tending to animals. Norman thought that was his life's goal. On the other hand, he admired Dick because he had no job. He lived, apparently to Norman, a life of perfect leisure. This apparent contradiction went a long way in explaining how Norman's mind worked. Or didn't.

"Quiet!" ordered Owen. The three men silently went about divvying up the guns and knives. The scythe was left leaning up against the wall. All three men had flintlock muskets that Owen and Dick had stolen from a battlefield several years before. Finally curiosity got the best of Dick. "Why did you bring the scythe?"

The still panting Norman said, "I could only find two knives."

"I think that one without the handle is a bayonet." Dick corrected.

Norman looked back at Dick, and said defensively, "Owen wasn't very specific, you know."

"Quiet!" Owen said again. "Now listen; we may not have much time." The other two men looked at him. "When Stinking Billy comes out the door, we'll be ready for him. But we'll wait till he moves away from the door. Kenna said she'll wait till he's out, and then shut it and lock it behind him. We don't want him dodging back in there for cover. Once the door closes . . . we'll race out from here .... screaming like the bloody witches of Hell . . . halfway across the street . . . we'll halt, stand, and fire . . . all three of us! Then you two drop your rifles and charge him with the knives to finish him off . . . if it's necessary. While you two are charging the rest of the way across the street I'll pull my pistol, and fire again. Four shots. Two knives. That oughta do the job."

Dick saw a flaw immediately. He had no desire to do the up close work that a stabbing would require, so he suggested, "I'm a good shot. Why don't I do that second shot, and you take the other knife."

Owen disagreed, "Who the hell told you that you're a good shot? You're a terrible shot. Besides, the pistol is mine. I ought to shoot it."

Dick took a new tack. "I don't feel so good about running in front of you while you're firing off that blunderbuss." He shook his head, "You just might get me in the back, like poor Niall."

"It wasn't Niall that got hit in the back. It was Timmy. Niall got hit by a cannon ball. Stop yer fussin'." chided Owen. ""If it'll make you feel any better I'll shoot the pistol first, and save the musket for last." That did not, contrary to Owen's opinion, make Dick feel any better. Norman chimed in saying that he ought to fire the pistol because he was the fastest runner. The two older men looked at each other in confusion. The conversation continued to meander from one topic to another as Dick looked for an honorable, or at least viable, way to avoid involvement.

After what seemed like an hour's worth of bickering back and forth, the three assassins fell silent, each with his own thoughts. Owen was imagining how his participation in this would enhance his standing in Kenna's eyes. Dick was staring at the door hoping it would never open. Norman chuckled when he thought about how frightened that guard was going to be when they raced across the street at him.

Dick heard him, and asked what was so funny.

Norman gestured with his head toward the tavern, and whispered, "He gonna pee in his pants when we coming roarin' at him.

In a painful hoarse voice Dick said, "Jasus Christ! What if he shoots back?"

That broke Norman's reverie, and he turned to Dick. "Who?" he asked.

"The bloody guard, yer twit. He's got a musket!" This wrinkle caused another long animated disagreement between the three conspirators. They took turns proposing that the guard would be so flummoxed by their screams and shots that he'd be no factor at all. And each took a turn suggesting that this guard might be an experienced, hardened British soldier fully capable of shooting the three of them dead in seconds. Dick was sure the latter was true. They weren't finished discussing the possibilities and certainly nowhere near a solution to their dilemma when a flurry of motion at the front of the tavern caused them to freeze. The door had swung open.

Only moments before, in the tavern, the owner had suggested to the now very drunk colonel that they should settle accounts. The colonel, who was accustomed to running roughshod over the locals he dealt with on a daily basis, dismissed the idea out of hand. He wanted to prolong the evening's festivities with the now wildly attractive Mrs. MacBride, and thought perhaps, if anything, he would leave a few shillings or maybe even a half a crown ("if Mrs. MacBride is nice to me!"). This angered the barman who had tallied up the inflated tab to nearly two crowns. He came around the bar, after picking up his 'Billy stick', as he called it, a short club wrapped in leather he kept back there for occasions such as these. He was not going to be denied.

The colonel didn't see him approaching, but Mrs. MacBride had and she was not about to let a dispute over the bill derail her plan for the evening. In a flash she leapt onto the colonel's lap, and put her face only inches from his. In the softest voice she could muster she told the colonel he had to pay the bill, "Cause I'm in the mood, right now." She let the last word ease ever so slowly out of her mouth. The colonel staggered to his feet, nearly dropping the barmaid to the floor. He fumbled quickly through a pocket of his coat and spilled several coins onto the table, some fell to the floor. He had no idea what the amount was; he didn't care. He had unbuttoned his pants after his second plate of stew and had not re-buttoned them. He somehow got his coat back on, and buckled his sword belt around his lower chest.

Kenna MacBride and Colonel Oliver Highcross made their way to the front door. He wobbled; she walked. He leaned; she bore his weight. She quietly opened the front door to the early evening light, and cooed to the officer, "Sssssshhhh. Don't wake your guard. We don't need him for what we're gonna do!" The drunken officer giggled. The guard stirred. Kenna froze. She watched as the guard shifted his position on the stool slightly, but then resumed his nap. She motioned to the officer to be quiet, and led him out onto the porch. Glancing across the street she spied the three faces in the stable doorway.

Kenna was staring at them. They thought she was nodding. The officer was staggering. The guard was still asleep. Owen gripped the two others by the arm, and said "Wait for her to get inside." And he had no sooner said it when she suddenly whirled around, nearly knocking the officer off his unsteady feet. She jumped back inside the door and slammed it shut.

That startled Tom Kilgore, who was oblivious to the unfolding plan, and was on his knees collecting and counting the coins the Colonel had dropped. When he heard the door slam, he looked up and said, "Huh?", and then immediately returned to his coin retrieval.

Outside, the Colonel attempted to regain his balance. The guard stirred. And Norman, Dick and Owen all emerged from the stable and raced across the street toward the tavern hollering like mad men.

Colonel Highcross, who had initially turned around confused by Kenna's sudden departure, whirled back around again to the noise in the street. The guard jumped to his feet, sending his stool spinning away, and stumbled slightly when his feet got tangled in his discarded blanket. His musket, leaning against the wall, got jostled by the stool and fell over. When the weapon hit the ground it discharged. Private Smith had loaded and cocked his weapon before settling down to his nap ('in case I need it in a hurry' he had rationalized) and had left it leaning against the building. Inside the tavern Kenna was hoping that the shot she heard was from one of her compatriots, and that the ball had found its mark. Kilgore, who was once again crawling around on his hands and knees searching for the colonel's coins, rose to a kneeling position confused about the commotion.

The three assassins racing across the street halted immediately at the sound of Smith's discharging weapon. Each one turned to the other to see if there was any damage done, and if they were all still in unison. Their shoulder to shoulder formation reaffirmed their resolve, and the three men raised their muskets and pulled the triggers.

Dick, who was standing in the middle, was the only one to fire a shot. To each of the five men present, it sounded like a cannon. Dick, inexperienced with firearms and a tad nervous, may have put a little too much powder in the pan when he loaded it. The flash nearly blinded him, and the recoil almost threw him to the ground. The ball hissed between the two Englishmen, and through the front window of Kilgore's Tavern.

"Someone's shot my winda?" Kilgore asked himself. Then in a much louder voice yelled, "What in hell is going on out there?"

Kenna, who was standing with her ear to the front door, didn't answer him.

Back out in the middle of the street Owen, on the left, knew exactly why his gun didn't fire. In the excitement of the charge across the street, he had forgotten to cock back the hammer. He now corrected his mistake, and again began taking aim.

Norman, on the right end of the line, was baffled when his hadn't fired. He took the weapon from his shoulder and looked down at it, inadvertently pointing it right at Dick. Dick would have screamed at him for doing that, but having the muzzle of the musket three inches from his nose took his breath away. He took a step backward, away from the muzzle, and inadvertently bumped into Owen just as he pulled the trigger. The shot was well off the human target, but dead center on the other front window of the tavern.

For Dick the unexpected blast and flash of the musket firing inches behind his head, after just having Norman's musket inches from his nose took their toll. That combination of events took the wind out of his sails, and the resolve out of his knees. Dick dropped to a kneeling position.

Up on the porch the two British soldiers were in a state of panic. When the screaming first began neither man had any idea what was going on. The guard had been in a deep sleep only seconds ago, but was now wide awake after his musket had fallen and fired. The consumed alcohol had the colonel two steps behind the private in understanding the situation. Dick's musket shot became, in a manner of speaking, a serious wake-up call to them both. And they had both very clearly heard that ball sail between them and crash through the window in the wall behind them. They both turned toward the now missing glass and realized it hadn't missed them by very much. Private Smith, now clearly in fear for his life, bent over to retrieve his weapon. The colonel, now aware he was a target, contorted his body in an attempt to make himself smaller. This action caused his still unbuttoned pants to slip from his hips and drop to his ankles. He looked out into the street, and saw the other two assassins preparing to fire. And with Private Smith bent over, Colonel Highcross correctly assessed he was to be the only, and therefore likely, target. His instantaneous assessment of the situation called for allowing his pants to remain down, but he felt Smith needed to be raised right now! Grabbing Private Smith by the shoulders he yanked him back into to an upright position, and slid in behind him. The Colonel correctly guessed that the slender Private did not provide total coverage for him, but 'something was better than nothing'. For the Colonel the transition from drunken stupor to sobriety was progressing quickly.

The discharge of Owen's musket (judging by its effect on the other window it was wide by 10 feet) gave the two British soldiers increased motivation to improve their situation. As the Colonel peeked from around the private's shoulder at the assailants again, Private Smith once again tried to reach his fallen musket. Jerking himself free of the officer's grip, he bent over. And with him doubled over, Colonel Highcross realized that he was once again fully exposed to the attackers so he began to scream. (There were so few other options he thought he had.) Private Smith heard him, and thought that the colonel might have been shot.

That's the scene that Norman saw as he once more lifted his musket to his shoulder and took aim at the porch. The soldier, bent over at the waist, was directly in front of the officer whose pants were down around his ankles! That just doesn't look right thought Norman, and again he hesitated. But he dismissed it an instant later, and tried again to focus his aim on the officer.

Moments after the shot had shattered the first window; Tom Kilgore got up off the floor and made his way cautiously to his broken window. Disbelief and dismay were what he was feeling. It would be expensive, and take a long time to replace the broken window because there wasn't a glazier within miles. As he peeked out the now *open* window he took in the scene. In the dim evening light he saw three men with guns out in the street. In this fading light and haze of gun powder smoke, he couldn't make out who they were, but they looked somewhat familiar. Right outside the window were the two English soldiers on his porch, jostling around. "What in hell's goin' on out ….." he started to say. Before he could finish his question another musket fired, and his other window now exploded into the room. He whirled around to see his other window in a thousand pieces on the floor. That ended the "disbelief and dismay" phase of Kilgore's involvement in this episode. More spitting out the words than speaking them, he roared, "MOTHER OF CHRIST! ....WHO'S SHOOTIN' AT MY FOKKIN' WINDAS?"

Out in the street, Owen had dropped his musket and was now struggling mightily to free his pistol, which was apparently stuck in his belt He did not know at this moment that the private was fighting furiously to free himself from his commander's grip. Owen was under the impression that the guard was probably now taking aim at them, or more importantly, *him.* Finally pulling the blunderbuss free, he got his bearings and realized that, as he had struggled to free his gun, he had somehow turned around and was now facing down the street. He whirled around to get his bearings. And at that moment, Norman fired his shot.

Only a moment before, Kilgore, fit to be tied at the annihilation of his precious windows, strode toward the front door currently being held shut by Kenna. In his hand was his Billy stick, and he had every intention of going outside and bashing a few heads. "Get out of my way!" he thundered at Kenna, intent on bringing havoc to the transgressors outside. Kenna knew him, and she knew that tone of voice. She got out of his way.

He flung open the door and stepped out onto the porch. Here he had a fateful momentary hesitation. It was initially caused by the indecision about who he was going to hit first with his Billy stick. But then his recognition of what was actually going on, and his sudden recollection of the age old adage concerning the rash stupidity of "bringing a club to a gunfight" froze him in his tracks. Although too smoky in the fading light to recognize the people in the street, he could clearly see the huge pistol, held by the man on the right, pointing in his direction, and alas, the muzzle of that weapon seemed only a few yards away.

Norman had his sights set right on the screaming colonel. But the sudden opening of the door just to the right of the colonel, and the emergence of the raging barman completely unraveled him. Involuntarily, he shifted his aim to this new target, closed his eyes, and fired.

This sudden jerking movement by Norman's gun muzzle caught Kilgore's eye, making him glance in that direction. He saw the flash of powder and heard the musket fire. He would always remember the puff of smoke at the musket's mouth and the musket ball emerging out of it in what appeared to be slow motion. And on that musket ball he saw the smiling face of Beelzebub himself (he swore to this until his dying day) as it came straight at him.

Had Kilgore been 5 foot 7 inches tall that ball would have gone directly between his eyebrows. But at 5 foot 4 he was merely left with a slight scratch on the top of his bald head, and a pair of pants he could never wear again. The musket ball, after tickling the top of Kilgore's skull, continued on its way through the open door and hit a cask of ale sitting on the bar at the rear of the tavern adding it to the victims list of today's proceedings at the Kilgore Tavern.

Kilgore's knees appropriately gave way when he fainted, and he collapsed in the doorway. Kenna, just inside the doorway, grabbed the now unconscious barman by the collar and pulled him back into the tavern. Again, she slammed the door shut.

Norman watched as the bottom of Kilgore's feet receded back into the bar. He felt torn between the elation of a nearly perfect shot, and the dismay that it had been the wrong target. Dick was still struggling to regain his feet. Owen was trying to steady his outstretched arm, which held the heavy pistol. He knew only too well that this was his last chance at getting Prince William.

Up on the porch, Private Smith took advantage of the momentary lull when he saw the colonel's sword in front of his chest. A handy sword is better than a missing musket he correctly assessed, and snatched it from its scabbard. He turned to the assailants in the street, and raised the sword above his head. He would have charged them had he not jammed the blade into the overhead of the porch, where it stuck fast.

The colonel, now without even his sword, knew he was totally defenseless. He looked out into the street. The man on the extreme right had pistol in his hand, and was aiming it. The man in the center was on one knee, and probably reloading. And the man on the left had a musket in one hand and a knife in the other. For the colonel the exertion of manhandling Smith, the adrenaline rush of being shot at, the long expulsion of breath by screaming, the food poisoning effects of the stew, and, of course, the alcohol he had consumed, finally took their toll. Colonel Oliver Highcross passed out.

Private Smith continued to struggle with pulling the sword out of the overhead without success. Both Owen and Norman stood mesmerized as Smith, gripping the handle of the upraised sword with both hands, danced with his feet in midair as he attempted to yank it free.

At this exact moment the half-dressed, but fully armed, remainder of the troop raced around a corner into the street, not 50 yards away. They had heard the very first shot, and although most of them would have preferred not running to the rescue of the colonel, Sergeant Major Bottoms had insisted. What they saw as they turned into the street were the armed assailants in the street; and they also saw Private Smith, with the sword held high over his head, his feet dancing in midair, and the prostrate Colonel on the porch.

As the first ten of the twenty men rumbled into the street, Owen saw them out of the corner of his eye; he calmly stepped around his two comrades, raised his pistol at them and fired. The blunderbuss, a notoriously inaccurate weapon at this distance, sent its load of lead buckshot out in a wide pattern, and hit a great many things; windows, walls, etc. None of those things were human, however.

But the flash and noise of the pistol shot, as well as the resulting ricochets and breaking glass, was impossible to ignore and caused the first two ranks of hard charging soldiers to halt dead in their tracks. This resulted in the men in the next few ranks crashing headlong into their mates up front. This human pileup brought the pursuit to a temporary halt And that confusion allowed Owen, Norman, and the suddenly coordinated and fleet-footed Dick to retreat back into the stable from which they had come, and to continue on through the back door (without slowing down to pick up the scythe), and on into the woods beyond. In a very impressive display of stamina the three men didn't stop running for thirty minutes.

Chapter 2 - The Quest Begins

On the shores of Susquehanna,
In the shadows of Fort Royal,
Stood young Highcross, the bold Major,
Pointing with his finger westward,
Pointing with his finger westward,
He asked the troops, the settlers,
"Do you know this place called Dubois?"
They looked at him as if struck dumb!

(Apologies to H. W. Longfellow)

Somewhere over 3200 miles southwest of Kilgore's Tavern (and twelve years later) sat the small isolated British outpost known as Fort Royal. Located in the gentle rolling hills of what is now central Pennsylvania, the outpost was almost equidistant from New York City and Philadelphia, and was the jumping off point for settlers and soldiers heading into the newly acquired Ohio Territory.

Since the early 1700's the French and British had debated over who 'owned' the Ohio Territory. The Native American Indians, already occupying this land for the past millennium plus, were not invited to the debate. In 1753 Governor Dinwiddie of Virginia sent an armed detachment of the Virginia militia, under the command of a young George Washington, to tell the French to depart the area. The French replied, "Non".

These French, aka "The Whitecoats", then proceeded to use superior numbers, firepower, and accuracy to send Washington's militia scurrying back to the governor. Hostilities began to escalate and finally resulted in the subsequent outbreak of war in what became known locally as The French-Indian War; and when it expanded to Europe, was known there as the Seven Years War. In the early going, at least in the North American theater of operations, the French pretty much had their way. That is until 1758, when William Pitt became the British Prime Minister and he decided on a new policy. Win.

Pouring men, money and munitions into the fray, the tide turned and the French were pretty much sent sailing home by 1760. The entire Ohio Valley was now firmly in British hands and the former French military bastion known as Fort Duquesne (the original site of what was to become Pittsburgh, Pennsylvania) was re-christened Fort Pitt in the Prime Minister's honor. While the hostilities between the two countries would continue in Europe (the Treaty of Paris - one of the 500 or so, peace treaties signed by European leaders in the second millennium CE - finally ended the hostilities worldwide in 1763) the vast Ohio Territory was now declared open for settlers. The many Indians already occupying this land were, again, not consulted.

In central Pennsylvania the British had built a fort in 1752 on the Susquehanna River, and called it Fort Royal. It was situated about midway from the large English settlements of New York and Philadelphia on the east coast and the French fortress of Fort Duquesne to the west. The French were forced to abandon and destroy their fort in 1758 in the face of an advancing large English force. That large English force rebuilt the fort and occupied it with the garrison from Fort Royal moving *en masse* to the newly christened "Fort Pitt".

A small detachment was left at Fort Royal to maintain it as a way station for those travelling west. And like most military outposts in the New World, it was surrounded by settlers and farmers of one kind or another. There was a small village adjacent to the fort, and over fifty farms in the vicinity. The population in the immediate area was nearing 600.

Fort Royal, far more spacious than necessary for the small detachment left to man it, was commanded by Captain Phillip Wallingford. It was supported, through a clerical error, in equal measures from both New York and Philadelphia. That included rations, supplies, munitions, and *pay*. This over-abundance was greatly appreciated by the troops at Fort Royal, and thusly, they did not correct the error. The official roster said that there was a captain, a lieutenant, a sergeant, and 20 soldiers stationed at Ft Royal. That was, in fact, an exaggeration. The actual number of soldiers at the fort was twelve. That included both the captain and the lieutenant. There was no sergeant. He had retired to a nearby farm and was living with a widow half his age. And through dysentery and desertion the roster of soldiers on duty had dwindled to only ten.

Captain Wallingford spent a great deal of his time in New York and Philadelphia, tending to official business. By 1760 both New York City and Philadelphia were growing rapidly. New York had a population of over 110,000 people, and Philadelphia had nearly 140,000 inhabitants. And the captain was quite content to partake of the nightlife these burgeoning metropolises had to offer. He was never in a hurry to return to Ft Royal. The lieutenant, under strict instructions from the Captain to do nothing while he was away, followed his orders precisely. The lieutenant, when temporarily in charge, was from the laissez faire school of command. He asked very little of his troops other than to not bother him, and they obliged. They did have two responsibilities. One was to man the front gate at the post, and the other to man the headquarters office. Both jobs required the soldier to remain at his post from 7 AM to 5PM every day. There wasn't anything to do at either place, just be there. The ten soldiers still 'present and accounted for' split the duty, so it worked out 'one day on – four days off'. Most of them had a served for several years prior to this assignment in various military expeditions on the continent, or worse, in India, and found this arrangement as close to ideal as any soldier's lot could be. A few of them took up part-time jobs in their ample free time to augment their already above par salaries. It is safe to say that this was probably the most contented lot of soldiers in the entire British Army.

Duty was also very good for the lieutenant True, his career as an officer hadn't seen any recognition or improvement since receiving his commission 12 years ago; and he was buried in this backwoods post with little likelihood of that ever changing. But, as he saw it, he was never being shot at either. He was never ordered around by anyone, except on those rare occasions when the captain was around (almost never). The men of the troop left him pretty much alone.

The lieutenant rose every morning whenever he woke up. After he made his own breakfast (the troops told him they were soldiers, not cooks) he would stop by the post's headquarters to tend to any official business. Any incoming mail was forwarded, unopened, to wherever the captain currently was. He was under strict instructions not to do anything in the captain's absence. If he had any inkling to do such a thing he was to pass it by the captain, via the mail, before acting. He would normally spend his day wandering around the country side enjoying nature and naps. He also enjoyed fishing, and had become quite good at it.

He awoke on the morning of April 30th to a hard knock on the flap of his combination lean-to/tent that served as his quarters. (There had been at one time expanded quarters for all the junior officers stationed here before that large troop had moved on to Fort Pitt. But those facilities had been systematically diminished as the men required firewood for their barracks.)

"Hey, Wilbur!" said the voice on the other side of the flap, "You in there? Open up!" He had always kept the flap fastened securely on the inside ever since that infamous ice water raid of several winters ago. The soldiers at Fort Royal didn't place much stock in formality, and used first names, unless it involved Captain Wallingford. It sounded like Private Purpley to the suddenly awake lieutenant. He, himself, used last names for the men in order to maintain some modicum of military formality. The lieutenant opened the flap and the private rushed in. He explained that some officer was at the headquarters door looking for the officer in charge. "That'd be you, right?"

The private was sent back to the office to tell the stranger that the 'Officer in Charge" would see him presently. He dressed quickly, and headed to the two room cabin that served as the commanding officer's quarters and fort's HQ. The room serving as the office had the only outside door and window. Approaching it he thought that being at his desk when he first met this stranger would give him some measure of authority. "Not to worry" he thought, and made his way around the back and climbed through the window. He fell hard to the floor when the heel of his boot caught the sill. The crash was heard clearly outside.

Purpley opened the door and stuck his head in, "Are you okay?" Assured by the lieutenant, as he struggled to his feet and stumbled into the chair behind the desk, that he was, Purpley was instructed to show the officer in. The door swung open, and in walked a tall, broad shouldered, immaculately attired British officer, with nearly imperial bearing. He was a sight to behold, and the lieutenant remained glued in his chair. At first mesmerized by the furious blinking of the lieutenant, the officer simply stared back.

Because British officers did not wear rank insignia on their uniforms in 1760, neither saluted the other as they were both a little confused on the protocol. The junior officer should, under most circumstances, salute first, and hold it until the senior officer returns the salute entirely. But the lieutenant was the acting commanding officer of the post, and therefore felt he should be saluted first. They both stared at each other waiting for the other to salute. The standoff lasted a painfully embarrassing ten seconds. Then the visitor flinched, and that caused the sitting lieutenant to begin a salute. That small movement then prompted the visitor to snap up his hand in salute. They both started and stopped several times in this military pas-de-deux. The lieutenant even started to stand up a few times. When they finally came to a halt, both men had their hands raised in a salute, and the lieutenant was half-standing. He was finally able to blurt out, "Please be seated."

The visitor took a seat on a small bench opposite the desk. He took a long slow look around the office. The mystery crash he had heard a few moments ago was solved when he saw no rear door, and the open window. He finally settled his gaze on the name plate on the desk. It was a piece of paper wrapped around a triangular block of wood. "Lieutenant Wilbur Smith" was penciled on the paper. "You are Lieutenant Smith?" he asked.

"Smythe" corrected the lieutenant

"I beg your pardon"?

"Smythe. It's pronounced Smythe."

"But it's spelled," he gestured toward the name plate, "S-M-I-T-H. That's Smith, is it not?"

"It's my name. I should hope I know how to pronounce it" said the lieutenant, somewhat indignantly.

"But not, apparently how to spell it" said the major under his breath. "My name is Highcross. Major Highcross of the Royal Northwest Sussex Foot Guard. I am here on orders from King George. I'm terribly sorry to come barging in on you like this on the Sabbath, but I only arrived late last evening. Tried knocking on the gate, but apparently no one heard me." He waited a moment to allow the lieutenant to offer an explanation for the absence of any guards on the gate. The lieutenant offered none, and just sat silently blinking at him. He went on, "I hope I can count on your assistance." Then, almost as an afterthought he asked, "You are in command here?"

Smith ignored the question, or the mention of the Royal Northwest Sussex Foot Guard, or orders, or duties, or even King George, he zeroed in on something else the Major had said.

"Highcross?" asked the Lieutenant, now leaning forward. Turning his head slightly to the side as if he wanted to whisper to him, he asked, "Are you related to a certain Colonel Highcross?"

"You must mean my dear uncle, Oliver. Deceased, I'm afraid. Caught one in India fighting the French a few years back."

The lieutenant said nothing, but thought to himself, "Yeah, 'caught', all right. If he caught anything, it was syphilis."

"Did you know him? Serve with him?" asked the Major interrupting the Lieutenant's revelry.

"Yeah, back in Scottish Highlands in '48. That Jacobite thing. Nasty work." But he stopped short there. He had actually arrived there after the Battle of Culloden, and as such, missed almost all of the hostilities. He had no intention of going over the specifics of his service, especially with a relative of Colonel Highcross. Rehashing the history of the Battle of Kilgore's Tavern would do no one any good.

Despite the efforts of Colonel Oliver Highcross at that time to bury the entire episode, too many people had witnessed it, and a report had to be produced. The Colonel, of course, did not want the actual details of the incident to be made public. The fact he had left his troop for women and whiskey; the fact he had performed shamefully during the attack; the fact his pants fell down and he had passed out had never made it into the official report of the incident. But to keep them out he had had to swear to the laundered details provided by Sergeant Major Bottoms. The Sergeant Major had his own agenda when he wrote the official report. He had been with the troop when most of the action had occurred, so he was unable to paint himself as the singular hero. But Smith was a willing co-conspirator, and had leapt at the chance. The final report stated, in so many words, that the colonel, while pursuing traitors in this small village, was attacked by a gang of ten assassins, and wounded almost to the point of death. He fought gallantly, but ultimately fell unconscious due to his wounds. While he lay unconscious, Private Smith singlehandedly defended the stricken officer by first using his musket . . . and then when he ran out of ammunition . . . he used the colonel's own sword to ward off the attackers. At the last moment Sergeant Bottoms arrived leading a rescue party that made a desperate charge into the ranks of the murdering horde, and drove them off. For the colonel this version was far better than the truth. For Bottoms this version earned him a marginally better pension, which he enjoys currently at his cottage by the sea.

As for Smith, he was granted a commission for his heroic actions! Colonel Highcross had told Smith that he would give him his highest recommendation in whatever his new duties were to be. His *actual* testimony and written recommendation, which Smith would never see, was, in its entirety, "Send him to the colonies."

Smith recalled reporting to army headquarters for his assignment when his commission came through. The officer he met with, bored nearly to distraction by the unending stream of clerical minutiae of administrative duty, sat and listened to yet another newly minted young officer demand a position in some prestigious unit, and at some exotic locale. And every single one of them wanted to be a cavalry officer. There were only so many openings in the cavalry, while on the other hand openings for infantry officers appeared almost on a daily basis. Some things just never change. It seemed to the assignment officer that no one ever wanted to walk to war.

"No, you don't want the cavalry!" Smith remembers him insisting. "What's the first thing that's going to happen when you go up against those Prussian bastards?"

This question confused Smith. He was unaware that Britain was currently at war with Prussia. With great concern he asked, "Are we at war with Prussia?"

The interrupted assignment officer sensed immediately that this sales job might be easy. "Prussian bastards, French bastards, Spanish bastards; it doesn't matter. It's all the same. You're going to be mounted on that great white horse they always seem to give to the lieutenants. Fast as blazes, he will be, too. Your company will be lined up a mile from those Prussian . . . or, whatever, bastards. There they'll be." The assignment officer stretched his arms out in front of him and swept them left to right in a broad arc. "Thousands of them, armed to the teeth with cannons, and muskets, and lances, and so on. Can you see it?" Smith could; and he started blinking faster. "Then your Captain, positioned behind you, of course .... Hell, behind the whole lot of you . . . will give the order to charge." And then in a voice barely above a whisper, "And who has got to be out front there leading that charge?" He didn't wait for Smith to answer. "You!" he peeped. "Right out there in front; leading your horsemen forward, as they fire their weapons wildly behind you. Their bullets flying willy-nilly past you at those . . . whoever . . . in front. And there they'll sit; thousands of them pointing their weapons, as you approach; as you race across that open ground into their waiting lines. Riding on that big . . . fast . . . white horse." Smith suddenly realized he was sweating. "Why do you suppose they give those big, white, fast ones to the lieutenants?" Smith was shaking his head, acknowledging that he could not answer that question. The officer slid a paper across the desk for Smith to sign, mentioning that the Pennsylvania colony "had very few foreign bastards", and needed infantry officers. And two weeks later, while Colonel Highcross was already on his way to India, Lieutenant Smith was packing for his trip in the opposite direction to the New World.

Major Highcross stayed silent as he thought Lieutenant Smith would have more to say about his uncle, but he didn't. "Yes, I'm in command. Temporarily. Captain Wallingford is currently back east on the King's business. I'm in command until he returns." Lieutenant Smith hoped this would cover the Captain's absence; he did not want to explain any further. Changing the topic, he asked, "What is it that you require, Major?"

Momentarily unsettled by the abrupt shift, the Major hesitated, and then said, "I'll need an escort to my new post. I have been assigned to command at Ft Dubois, on the frontier. Here's a copy of those orders signed by General Tindale in Philadelphia. You can see that he requests your complete cooperation in helping me to reach my command."

Smith said nothing, but looked across the desk at him. Thinking to himself, "My God, first his despicable cousin gets sent to Calcutta; and now this twit is assigned to Dubious?"

"I'll, of course, need a guide. And an armed escort too. I have been told it is still hostile territory, despite our recent successes against the French. As many soldiers as you can spare."

Smith took it all in. And none of it sounded too good. He sat very still for a minute, and then began shaking his head. "Can't help you with a guide." Major Highcross raised his eyebrows, and slumped his shoulders in disappointment. Lieutenant Smith went on, "You see our two guides . . . the two guides we use . . . the only two reliable ones in the whole territory, Edgar and Horace…. they're both out on the trail right now. Can't even begin to guess when they'll be back."

That was true. Both men had left the settlement nearly a month ago without saying when they'd be back. The better of the two, Edgar Twibbleton, had eloped in the middle of the night with Rhoda Simpson. Most people at the settlement thought that that was quite romantic. Not so much for Horace Simpson, her husband. Returning from a hunting trip five days later and learning the news, he immediately went out after his wife. Some people thought that was romantic too.

That wasn't, at all, the news the major wanted to hear. "There aren't any others? No one else knows the way to Fort Dubois?"

That didn't sound right to the Major. "How about you? Or any of the men on the post? None of you can guide me to Fort Dubois?"

"This wasn't going to be easy," Smith thought to himself. Fort Dubois had originally been built by the French as an outpost for their larger fort, but when they abandoned Fort Duquesne in 1758 they left Fort Dubois too. That, however, was never confirmed. Captain Wallingford had been ordered to reconnoiter the fort, and report back. Preoccupied with some pressing commercial interests at that time he never went and looked. And sensing some financial gain could be had from keeping the threat alive at Fort Dubois, he sent back word that the French had left a small force, with allied Lenape and Shawnee Indians in the area to continue hostilities. The captain's estimates of the size of this force varied over time from 25 to 50. He actually had no idea. No one did. As the supreme authority in the area he restricted all activity westward to only a chosen few. (Lieutenant Smith was not among them.) He thought that a number in that range was large enough to be a concern to the British strategists back at the headquarters, but not large enough to warrant a preemptive strike. And, because Captain Wallingford was an earnest practitioner of 'padding the payroll', the commanders back in Philadelphia and New York thought that the force at Fort Royal was 23; 11 soldiers more than the actual 12. That was, they thought, an ample deterrent to any French offensive moves in the area.

The general in Philadelphia woke up one morning, and unaware of the actual numerical mismatch, wrote orders to Captain Wallingford to "take Fort Dubois, and remove the threat". The captain wanted very much to maintain the status quo and, more importantly, not go off and engage an enemy force of unknown size. He offered every conceivable objection he could imagine to change the general's mind. He even went so far as to start increasing his estimates of the opposing force. The general dismissed his objections by telling him to recruit local militia to augment his force, and remove 'those bastard Whitecoats".

Wallingford stalled as long as he could, but, at last was forced to commence the campaign. He took every available man he had at the fort, but Lieutenant Smith, whom he considered useless, and an elderly private named Tilden, who was incapable of walking more than a few hundred yards each day. Using the fort's "emergency fund" (he had pocketed the incremental recruiting funds the general had given him for the local militia) he was able to recruit 15 local militiamen. (The mission did offer some financial gain for them, and for a few of them it provided a temporary escape from the drudgery and duties of home life.) However, none of them, secretly, intended to remain in the vicinity when the shooting started.

When delay was no longer a viable option this meager force of Wallingford and 24 reluctant men marched off to assault Fort Dubois. According to the official "Battle Report" Captain Wallingford submitted later, they, at first, ambushed the larger French force outside the fort, and then fought a running battle over the surrounding terrain. Using cunning tactics they were able to slowly reduce the odds against them until the French were completely disheartened. The Captain's report went on, and surmised that at this point most of the remaining French soldiers deserted, and what few officers remained soon followed them. Captain Wallingford ended his report by saying that he had suffered numerous, but unspecified, casualties, and had left a small occupying force at the newly conquered Fort Dubois in case the general visited Fort Royal and found far fewer soldiers than the roster count indicated.

The true version varied somewhat from that report. At first, and not surprisingly, Captain Wallingford moved very cautiously toward his objective. Very, very cautiously! In just short of a month's time they had approached, and circled the suspected location of Fort Dubois several times, giving it a very wide berth (actually without ever seeing it). On day 29 the troop's cook advised the Captain that they either had to take the fort, or go home because they were just about out of food. In a rare display of personal bravery Wallingford crawled a mile through bush and bramble, taking several hours, to a point at the edge of the woods on a ridge overlooking the fort to spy on it.

It was abandoned. And from the looks of things it had been abandoned some time ago. When the troops were rallied and entered the fort they found that when the French had left they had travelled light, and had left quite a store of supplies. Not the least of which was a quantity of wine. For the next few days, while Wallingford inventoried the spoils of war, the men ate, drank, and slept. When the wine ran out they burned the fort to the ground, and went back to Fort Royal with a well-rehearsed tale in hand. (The 'spoils of war' were retailed by Captain Wallingford to settlers passing through Fort Royal over the next several months. He did quite well.)

Unfortunately this did not end matters because the general in Philadelphia sent word to the captain that Fort Dubois should be reinforced, and he would send reinforcements as soon as possible. Since receiving that message, Captain Wallingford had been juggling Commanding Generals in New York and Philadelphia trying to keep them as far from Fort Royal, and Fort Dubois as he could, in both body and spirit. He thought he was being quite successful at it too. But someone, somewhere in the Royal Army administrative branch read, or misread an instruction and blindly assigned a recently available Major Aaron Highcross to assume command at Fort Dubois in the Ohio Territory. The news was not passed along to Captain Wallingford.

"Well, Lieutenant Smith? Can't anyone here lead the expedition?" asked the major. The lieutenant couldn't very well lead it. He had no idea where the fort was. He'd never been there. And instructing one of the remaining soldiers still at Fort Royal, who had been there, wasn't really possible either. In all probability, Smith thought, they'd refuse to go. But he had to say something.

"With the Captain away ……. I can't leave." He said with absolute certainty. "And as for the men …. We are dangerously understaffed now due to the …… to the ….. to the PATROL!" the thought flashed through his head. "Yes, the patrol we already have out right now." Smiling now, pleased with his idea, he continued, "Yes, Sergeant Cumbers has most of our men out right now searching for hostiles." He nodded when he finished talking, as if approving his comments.

"What 'hostiles'?" the major asked.

Lieutenant Smith thought that over, and then answered, "Indians. Or Whitecoats. Or whoever out there is . . . well, hostile." Plain as day thought Smith. "This guy must be an idiot.," thought Smith.

"Good God, lieutenant, there must be someone! I can't very well wander off into the woods by myself."

"Why not?" thought Lieutenant Smith. "I do it every day."

The major asked if the merchants in the area ever sold their goods to Fort Dubois. Not waiting for an answer, he asked if the local farmers sold their crops to that fort. Still not waiting for an answer, he asked how these people got their goods to Fort Dubois. "Lieutenant! I demand you produce a guide to lead me to Fort Dubois. General Tindale's orders are quite clear." The major was not to be denied. He was going, and to put additional pressure on the lieutenant, he continued, "And lieutenant! Be advised. My safety on the journey will be your personal responsibility. Your failure to provide a suitable escort will be reported to General Tindale. I don't expect he will be too pleased should I fail to reach my post."

The lieutenant took in the warning with a straight face. His eyes were blinking furiously, but there wasn't a trace of a grin on his lips. In a rare bit of insight, for him, he sat thinking that the major was saying that if HE was killed, *the lieutenant would be in trouble*! He wondered if there was anyone in the Highcross family with an ounce of brains. It was difficult for him to not to smile. "Sir," he began to say, and then, out of the blue, it hit him. "Wait a minute….." he smiled slyly and rubbed his chin, "There is someone." It was diabolical. It was perfect. Doing it would, he thought, rid him of this pesky major. And he would be held blameless because the major insisted on leaving before qualified guides became available. Even Captain Wallingford would be proud of him. "There's a trapper," he said. "A real woodsman hereabouts who knows the frontier as well as I know …. ." No good example occurred to him so he switched gears, "Like you know London?" he guessed.

"I don't know London," corrected the major.

"Whatever," Smith went on, "Like you know Oxford. This man can lead you right up to the gates of Dubious."

Highcross was going to inform this Smith that he didn't know much about Oxford either, but when he heard "the gates of

Dubious" he was instantly distracted. "'Dubious'?" asked the puzzled major.

In his haste to hatch this devious plan as it unfolded in his brain, Lieutenant Smith had referred to the former French fort using the nickname the locals used. In the cities and towns along the eastern seaboard, and in military circles it may have been known as Fort Dubois., but in the Fort Royal area it was more commonly known as Fort Dubious; or simply "Dubious". Ever since the expedition by the Fort Royal garrison, the former French post was occasionally referred to; but never visited by anyone in the area. Its name has slowly morphed into "Dubious'.

Smith waved off the interruption, and raced on. "Now I want to warn you, this man is a real frontiersman. Not a gentleman, like yourself. A bit rough around the edges, you know."

"I don't care about his manners." The Major said, "All I'm concerned with is if he can guide me to Fort Dubois. What's his name?"

"This might be tricky," thought Smith. He put his hand over his mouth and mumbled something.

The Major didn't hear him clearly. He leaned toward the blinking officer and asked, "Falwyn? Did you say 'Falwyn'? F-Á-L-W-Y-N?'"

"I don't really know how he spells it," said Smith. "I doubt he does, either. He isn't exactly a man of letters. But that's close enough, Major" assured Smith.

"And he can guide me to Fort Dubois? He knows the way?"

"As well as anyone around here can." This was basically true. No one really knew where it was, so Falwyn was as likely to find it as anyone else would. And, Smith was thinking, when Falwyn takes this newly arrived pest off into the wilderness and very likely disappears forever; I can go back to doing what I like to do best, which is nothing.

"Where can I find him? This Mr. Falwyn," asked the Major.

"This time of day. . . " mused the Lieutenant, "I would say over by Ludlum's stable." At this time of day there was, in Smith's opinion, virtually no chance that Falwyn was already awake. "And oh," he added, "You don't have to call him *Mister*. Just plain …. *Falwyn*…. will be okay. That's all anyone ever calls him." The furiously blinking lieutenant was smirking, but the Major didn't notice.

The Major asked several more questions about making the trip, and Smith assured him that whatever he needed would be provided. After all, thought Smith, the sooner I get him on his way, the better.

The major followed Smith's directions to Ludlum's stables, and only got lost twice. A burly man in a blue cotton shirt and leather apron stood in front of the stable, and was leaning on a railing smoking a pipe. The major introduced himself, and asked him if he knew the whereabouts of a trapper named Falwyn. The man looked over the officer with careful consideration, identified himself as "Mr. Ludlum" and then asked, "Really? You're looking for Falwyn? What's he done now?" The officer explained he wanted to hire him, and repeated his question. This seemed to amuse Mr Ludlum, and he smiled. He gestured with his thumb to the stable door behind him and said that he could find Falwyn inside the stable. "Probably in one of the stalls in the back," he said, and then added, "An empty one, I hope."

The man watched the major as he carefully let himself into the stable. The outside light barely lit the interior through knotholes and cracks in the walls. The smell was atrocious. The combination of wet straw, urine, feces, and rotting feed nearly made the major's eyes water. And the major's eyes had trouble enough trying to adjust to the low light as the door slid closed behind him. The inside revealed the building to be perhaps 20 feet wide, and half again as deep. The front of the barn was an open space, and four stalls lined each side wall further back. There were horses occupying the two nearest stalls. There were no humans, Falwyn or otherwise, that he could see. "Falwyn, are you there?" There was no answer. The major repeated the question, louder. Again, there was no answer. He began moving up the row between the stalls. Looking carefully in the low light into each stall as he passed it, he saw nothing but soiled straw, dirt, a water bucket or two, and a canvass sack in the last stall. As he approached the back wall he noticed a door. He decided to step outside that door to see if

Falwyn was out there (and also to catch some fresh air; the air in this stable was putrid). He opened the door.

"JISSES! Close the door before ye blind me!" The startled major jumped, and hit his elbow on the door jam.

"OW! ….. Damn! ….. Who's there?" The major whirled around and attempted to draw his sword, but his elbow refused. "Who's there I said!" the Major looked into the darkness again, and could see no one. After another moment he got his sword out.

"Quit yer yellin'! Fer the love a god, I ain't deff." said the sack.

The major, now in repossession of most of his senses, peered into the stall at the talking sack. Still battling the smell, he looked down at it and it began to move. Unfolding itself, out came a leg; then another; an arm stretched toward the ceiling; then up came a face. "Are you Falwyn?"

"What?"

"Are you Falwyn?' the major repeated.

"Who wants to know?" answered the man on the floor.

While the body seemed to be quite small, almost that of a child, the face was definitely a man. The unkempt hair on his head was long and stringy, his beard and moustache were uneven. The cheeks were hollow, and the nose was long and hooked. His eyes were deep set, and half closed. A condition the major would find existed whether Falwyn was half asleep or wide awake. The major introduced himself, and repeated his question once more to the man on the floor.

"Yeah, that's me. Whaddya want?"

"I need a guide. And Lieutenant Smith (pronouncing it 'Smythe") said you were available for hire."

"What? He did?" Falwyn shook his head. "How much will ye be willin' to pay?"

Major Highcross thought it odd that Falwyn didn't even ask where they would be going, or how long it would take. "I'll make it worth your while, I assure you.' The major thought it best to check with Lieutenant Smith on the local rate before making a promise. "I'll pay for all the provisions and any other necessities as well." After a moment's hesitation, as Falwyn remained silent, the officer continued, "When do you think we can leave?"

Falwyn was awake enough to know that this man was talking, and talking to him, but what he was saying was totally lost. "I need a few minutes to gather myself," was his only thought. "Why don't we step outside, Sir?" he said after an awkward silent moment. Getting out from the stench of this barn seemed like a wonderful idea to the major; he whirled around and was out the door in a flash. It took Falwyn a few minutes to stand up, to step toward the door, and then to fight off the bright morning light outside and step outside through the door. Once outside he shielded his eyes and made his way to the bench against the outside wall, where he plopped down.

"Would ye do me a great favor, Sir?" Falwyn finally managed to say to the major standing in front of him.

Confused initially by the request, the major said he would try.

"Could ye fetch me a bucket of water?" He gestured out to the well in the yard. Surprised by the request, the major silently complied.

Walking from the well back to the seated Falwyn, the major looked him over carefully in the daylight. The major thought the man was barely over five feet tall, and couldn't weight 100 lbs. Falwyn wore mismatched boots on his feet. They were torn on top, and threadbare on the bottom. His pants were made of purple wool, and there was a hole on the left knee. His tunic was made of canvass, and by the looks of it to the major, he had sewn it himself. Boots, pants and shirt were filthy.

The major laid the bucket at Falwyn's feet, but said nothing. Falwyn sat motionless on the bench for a few moments. The major wondered whether he might have fallen back to sleep. But then, suddenly, Falwyn slid off the bench and landed on his knees. After another moment he pitched forward, and his face disappeared into the bucket with a splash.

The major had to jump back to avoid the splashing water. Falwyn remained on his hands and knees, his face still deep in the bucket. The major just watched. Seconds ticked by, and the major began to worry that the man might drown. An occasional bubble broke the surface of the bucket as more time went by, and the major tried to decide if pulling him out was going to be necessary. Finally, Falwyn jerked his head out of the bucket, spraying water all over, and then staggered back up onto the bench. The hair on the front of his head hung in ringlets around his dripping face. His eyes were closed, and his mouth gaped open. His breath came in gasps.

"Jisses, I needed that," he said after he caught his breath. He opened one eye, and turned slowly to look at the major. He looked him up and down, and then asked, "Who the hell are you?" The major, feeling slightly frustrated, re-introduced himself and repeated the brief conversation they had just had in the stable. Falwyn listened intently as if hearing for the first time. "Yer gonna pay me how much?" he asked again.

"How much would you charge" the major counted, "How much would it be to take me to Fort Dubois?"

Falwyn remained silent. Major Highcross thought he was calculating his fee. But Falwyn wasn't thinking about that at all. He was wondering two things. First he was wondering if this major meant Dubious when he said Fort Dubois. And secondly he wondered how hard this was going to be because he didn't know where Dubious was. After a few minutes of silence Falwyn thought he had best say something, so he looked at the major and said, "Depends."

The major was beginning to feel very uneasy, "On what?" There was a pause. The major then asked, "How long will it take us to get there? How many miles away is it?"

"That's hard to say," dodged Falwyn. He didn't know either answer. "Keep talking," he told himself, "There could be money in this." "Oh, we're goin' to be goin' deep inta hostile territory, Sir. I assure you of that. How long will it take?" Falwyn was trying to think fast. He wasn't good at that. How could he know? He didn't know where he was going. "I could give yer an exact answer, Sir. Oh sure. An exact answer if you could answer me how the weather's going to hold up. How many days of rain will there be? There ain't no roads out there yer know., no Sir." The major started to agree, and nodded. Falwyn saw an opening and ran for it. "And beasts, Sir. We'll no doubt run into some very dangerous animals out there. Bears and such." He nodded. The major just looked back. Falwyn had no intention of letting up now. "And hostiles! How many times are we going to hafta dig in and defend ourselves against those savage Shawnee . . . (he was, for a moment, at a loss for words) savages?" "Keep goin'. Keep goin'." he told himself, "Don't stop!" "And French Whitecoats? Some are still out there, yer know?" He winked. The major stood up straighter. "And highwaymen and bandits? Maybe even Jesuits?" The major's eyes widened. "No Sir, I don't wanna make a guess. I think it's fair to tell you it could take about a month." A 'month' was a very round number, and Falwyn thought that it would leave him plenty of wiggle room. He waited to see the major's reaction. He was ready to cut that estimate in half if it looked like the major might balk. The major arched his eyebrows and let out a very long breath. He hadn't planned on it taking that long, but how could he argue with the "guide"? Falwyn peeked up at his face, and saw that he had sold it.

The fee was brought up again, and Falwyn, now armed with a time frame, thought a moment longer. "Well, considerin' as how long it's gonna take," he said. "And rememberin' I've got to get back here all on my own .....Hmmm" He was silent for a moment. Falwyn wasn't calculating his fee based on 30 days. He couldn't multiply anything by 30. Multiplication wasn't in his skill set. Nor was addition or subtraction for that matter. "I'm thinkin' fi . . . TEN! Crowns would be fair."

"That seems a bit much," said the major, "I'll have to think about that before we shake on it." There were two things preventing him from agreeing right here. The first was that he thought he should check with Lieutenant Smith about what was the usual rate in this area for guides. The second reason he didn't shake on it was that Falwyn's hands were filthy; as was his entire body. The major had realized as they stood outside the rear of the stable it was Falwyn that smelled so badly. Major Highcross was sincerely hoping that perhaps later in the day Falwyn would clean up. And he thought that he would insist upon that before the two began their journey.

The conversation was interrupted when Mr. Ludlum came around the corner of the stable into the rear yard. "You're not going anywhere until you muck out those stalls. All of them! No argument, now. You said you'd do it yesterday. And that wood around the side; that has to be stacked too, before you go wandering off. I'm going to be watching you. You've received your wages already; now get to it. No nonsense, now." The tone of his voice left no doubt that he meant what he said. Falwyn nearly flinched at the sound of his voice. He turned and looked at Major Highcross. He looked defeated. They agreed to meet later, and went their separate ways.

Under the very close eye of Mr. Ludlum, Falwyn began a number of chores he had promised to do. The wages he had already received were paltry for the work he had promised, but at the time he had desperately needed the money to pay off a debt owed to a very angry man. His mind was not on his work, however. He was thinking that if this major paid him what he asked for this trip to Dubious, and if he found it, and if he got back to Royal, he could pay off all his debtors. The tavern keeper, the two soldiers, Mother Farrington, and Sho-Taka would all be paid off! He would even have some money left over for new clothes, or lodging, or more whiskey (the most likely candidate). He wasn't sure, of course, how much would be left over because he wasn't very good with numbers. "Anyways" he thought to himself, "It ain't likely I'll make it there and back, so I don't hafta worry about all that, no how."

The major wanted to talk with Lieutenant Smith again. This time the topic was about supplies he might need for this trip, and whatever else he might think to bring to his new command. He would also ask him about the fee Falwyn had requested for guiding him to Fort Dubois. He suspected it was excessive. He also suspected Lieutenant Smith would provide little help. He was starting to catch on.

The community surrounding Fort Royal had a population numbering perhaps 600. And in any community that small there was virtually no chance in keeping anything secret. Perhaps it had been Mr. Ludlum listening at the back door of the stable to the discussion between Falwyn and the major, or maybe it had been Private Purpley listening at the door in Fort Royal's headquarters to the conversation between the major and Lieutenant Smith. Of course it might just as easily been Lieutenant Smith mentioning it to everyone he met that day that let the secret out. But, no doubt, by midafternoon there weren't many people in the Fort Royal settlement who did not know that the newly arrived Major Highcross was enlisting Falwyn to lead him to Dubious. Every one of them thought that was funny.

Chapter 3 - Tyson Joins the Party

Young Tyson with the steely gray eyes,
In the ways of the frontier was wise,
He said without braggin',
"I've got this big wagon.
And you'll need it to get there. No lies!"

Things weren't going right for Major Highcross at Fort Royal. After spending the entire morning trying to locate the wandering Lieutenant Smith, he gave up. He began questioning the soldiers at the fort, and found that none of them admitted to knowing where Fort Dubois was. It seems that whenever Captain Wallingford ventured out to Dubious (as they all called it) he would travel alone. They seemed in agreement that their one trip out there nearly two years ago was a vague recollection now. They remembered that they had taken a very circuitous route then, and only Captain Wallingford had been familiar with the territory they covered. To a man they suggested that the major wait at Fort Royal until Captain Wallingford returned from back East; or at the very least until one of those local guides returned from that three-sided honeymoon. After talking with the soldiers the major pursued his quest with the townspeople. And it became apparent in no time at all that the civilians of the Fort Royal settlement agreed with the soldiers' right down the line. There was no doubt in anyone's mind that Falwyn was a poor third choice, at any price. And while they all doubted his ability to guide the major there, they were unable to suggest anyone else. No one he met could say with certainty that they themselves knew precisely where Dubious was. Estimates by soldiers and locals varied as to how far away Dubious was, and subsequently, what supplies were necessary for the trip. By midafternoon a melancholy Major Highcross sat on a bench, wondering why everything in this assignment had gone wrong. It should not have surprised him. Much of his entire life up to this point had been, well, a misadventure.

His grandfather, Lord Nunch, was a wealthy and powerful politician from the southwest corner of England. When he married in 1699, he had three children in rapid succession starting with a son in 1700, followed by two daughters, Louise and Sophia, in 1701 and 02. Lord Nunch had said then, and repeated it many times over the following years that 'three children, two of them daughters, are enough'. So in 1707, when Lady Nunch told him that she was, again, 'with child' Lord Nunch was not thrilled. No, his Lordship was not thrilled at all.

The oldest child, Oliver, upon reaching maturity, was granted a military commission after a horrendous academic career. And based on, in equal measure, his surname and blind luck, he slithered up the ranks. He wooed and married a third cousin shortly after his 25th birthday. His bride was promptly returned to her family as he took off for the continent on some British military expedition. His visits home ever since were invariably rare and short; hence there were no offspring.

His sister Louise married an extremely eligible widower several years her senior. He was a member of Parliament, an eminent physician, a successful novelist, and an owner of a vast estate just outside of London. While she spent most of her time at that estate, he lodged in London attending to affairs of state, his medical practice, as well as his many other hobbies and interests. It was whispered among their social circle that "his social *affaires* outnumbered his professional affairs by a wide margin". In order to cement her status as lady of the house she proceeded to have four children over the first six years of her marriage. None of them bore much resemblance to the doctor.

The second daughter, Sophia, married a lawyer who owned several businesses that involved banking, insurance, manufacturing, and trading. There were some who said the list should also include smuggling. In any case his bold initiative and total lack of scruples made him extremely wealthy before his 30th birthday. And as time went on he would only get richer. This union produced two children, despite an almost total lack of affection between the couple. But oddly enough it worked for both of them. He was consumed with making money, and she was consumed with spending it.

In spite of what Lord and Lady Nunch considered minor flaws in these marriages, they were very proud of their three eldest offspring and their spouses. And then there was Martin, their fourth. Martin Highcross grew up in almost total obscurity at the bustling ancestral family estate called Nunch Manor. He displayed neither unique talents nor abilities. While the other children seemed to thrive in their privileged upbringing, Martin had to struggle harder and longer just to get by. Although his father and siblings virtually ignored him, Lady Nunch's heart filled with love on those occasions when she thought of him. That just didn't occur too often.

When it came time for him to launch a career he sought out the advice of his family. His father didn't respond. His brother Oliver told him that, for him, military service was out of the question. In his words, "Martin, my boy, you just don't have what it takes." He did not explain what "it" was. Louise and Sophia referred him to their husbands, who in turn smirked and laughed and pooh-poohed any ideas Martin may have had about the law, public service, medicine, commerce, the arts, letters, etc., etc., etc. Convinced that they were right, he ultimately joined the clergy. After a period of study, and intense pressure by anonymous powerful interests, he was assigned to a parish in a small village near his parent's home. A year after his posting he met a plain looking, shy young lady from the village, and was married five months later. They were prepared to live happily ever after.

Aaron Highcross was born to the Reverend and Mrs. Highcross an appropriate ten months later. He was named Aaron by his father for two reasons. First, because 'Aaron' was a biblical name and that seemed appropriate to a man of the clergy. And secondly, and this was important too, because it started with the letter 'A'. When he explained this to his wife, still lying there in the birthing bed moments after delivery, and still very much in pain and exhaustion from her ordeal, he said, "Next will be Bartholomew, or Beulah! We can name the third Christian, perhaps? Maybe Caleb? Claudia, if the Lord blesses us with a girl. They're all in the bible. Then Daniel? What do you think of the twelfth? James or John? Joseph, maybe?" He remained silent for a moment, and then said hopefully, "Maybe God will bless us with triplets?" His wife just stared. He was beaming. After another moment's silence he clapped his hands together in joy and said with glee, "One down, twenty five to go." This grand plan of his (his, not hers) was never to be, however.

One night, when Aaron was still an infant, his father went on a mission of mercy to bring some provisions to a poor widow in their parish. The weather that evening was foul, but Martin felt it was his duty to bring the old woman the basket of much needed food. As he trudged along that deserted road through the cold wind and torrential rain, he had an experience similar to that of St. Paul's conversion as told in the Bible. Both experienced "a light from the heaven [that] flashed down upon him". In St. Paul's case it was called Divine Enlightenment. Not so much in the case of Martin Highcross. He was hit by lightning.

The widow Highcross and her young son were granted a modest annuity . . . a very modest annuity by Lord Nunch, and went on to live in a small cottage in that same village. Their involvement with the in-laws decreased as the years went by. The invitations to Nunch Manor, while never warm, became more infrequent. As the seventh grandchild in the family, he was the youngest by six years. He was never close to his cousins, and was as alienated from them as his late father had been from his siblings. On those rare visits to the manor with his cousins, when he wasn't being ignored by them, he was being tormented. But mother and son were quietly pleased with the increasing familial distance, and spent the ensuing years getting by on their small income. And as time went by, the widow Highcross was able to develop additional income by becoming quite adept as a cook; often watched and aided by her ever present son. Over the years her continued progress as a cook resulted in ever increasing income for the widow and her son. And over those same years young Aaron Highcross grew into a man.

When Aaron had finished his adolescence and education, and started to look about for a career, like his father, he was at a bit of a loss. His four male cousins were gravitating into the careers of their fathers. Aaron, though a god-fearing man, had no interest in becoming a man of the cloth. His uncles, who had ushered their own offspring onto the career paths they could open, showed no inclination for doing the same for their nephew. Perhaps that was just as well, as Aaron showed neither interest nor talent in business, arts, or sciences. His only real talent was what he had learned at his mother's knee – cooking. But he never considered that a viable option. He attempted to learn some different crafts, but met with no success. Most recently he had attempted to work a small farm, but found he couldn't grow weeds! Once again back home with Mother, he was at wit's end.

In 1757, while serving with the English Army in India, his Uncle Oliver died. This unfortunate development for Oliver was a godsend for Aaron. The family, due to the rank and prestige of Lord Nunch, was entitled to a commissioned officer's slot in one of the Royal regiments. His cousins had solid careers already in place and felt no desire to trade them for one which included living in a tent and facing hostile fire in the current Seven Years War. The opening fell to Aaron.

It took virtually no time for the officer charged with assigning the newly minted Captain Highcross to a regiment to see that Aaron had no abilities in the military arts either. But sending him back home was not an option; and neither was posting him somewhere where he might be killed, which, he assumed, would displease the influential Lord Nunch back home. In a stroke of luck for all concerned, Aaron found himself assigned to the Commissary of the General Staff of the British Army.

Once more in the familiar surroundings of a kitchen, far away from the action, he oversaw the veteran cooks who prepared the daily meals for the vast array of high ranking officers. Their diligence and expertise required very little input from him. His free time, and ready access to unlimited supplies, allowed him the means to explore any dietary avenue he chose to pursue, as the army meandered around the European continent.

But, like most ideal situations, it ultimately came to a crashing halt. Newly posted to the General Staff was an artillery officer named Major Graham. It was immediately clear to everyone that he had substantial talents in his field. But, unfortunately for those around him, he didn't possess a single other saving grace. He was crude and foul, and in no time at all he had antagonized everyone he outranked, including the cooks. After a few weeks of his abusive behavior toward them they began 'tinkering' with the ingredients of the meals that they had prepared for him. He didn't notice. So they began increasing the dosage of the disgusting supplements they were inserting into his food. Their mischief was finally uncovered, and the miscreants were immediately reassigned to the frontlines. Captain Highcross, after an inquiry, was held blameless, but sent packing anyway. And he was sent as far away from those headquarters as they could manage. He was off to the hinterlands of the New World Colonies, with a promotion to major as a consolation.

The journey taking him to his new post was another example of what seemed to be his lifelong string of misfortune. The voyage began as Highcross sailed from the coast of France back to England. A violent storm caught the small boat soon after leaving port and tossed it around unmercifully for two days. When the storm broke, and the ship found itself only two miles from shore, they made straight for the nearest harbor. Unfortunately, when they landed they discovered they were back in France. His second attempt to return to England involved another storm tossed trip taking three days. A very long and uncomfortable carriage ride led him back to London, where he remained awaiting the arrival of his official orders to proceed to Pennsylvania.

After waiting for weeks for those orders to arrive and nearly out of patience, a drunken courier delivered them late one night to the squalid inn where the major was lodging. (He had gotten very bad advice about where to stay.) Earlier that day that same courier had been instructed to tell the major he was to report to the captain of the frigate Revenge, docked on the Thames waterfront near the London Bridge by Tuesday, two days hence. Somewhere between his eighth and ninth noggin of gin on his way to the major's lodgings that courier turned 'Tuesday' into 'today', eliminated the designation "London" from the bridge location, and had mutated the name of the vessel into Avenge. Painfully aware that he had no time to spare for questioning and/or thrashing the drunken courier for his jumbled message, Major Highcross raced to the waterfront where his transport was undoubtedly making final preparations to leave. Encumbered by an abundance of trunks and sacks of personal belongings and a dearth of time the trip there was frantic.

"Waterfront' is a relative word. It can refer to a pier or two, or it can mean something somewhat larger; i.e. a very long stretch of real estate. And that is especially true in a large city with a river running through it. Major Highcross covered a great deal of ground in the next several hours. Racing along the shore of the River Thames he went from dock to dock, lugging his enormous load of baggage, trying to find the ship that would take him across the Atlantic to his new post in the New World.

Approaching another ship, he called out for the twentieth time, "Ahoy there! What ship is this and where are you bound?"

The man left in charge (it was a newly minted young midshipman who pulled the duty, while the captain and master and lieutenants were out on this last night in port with their wives . . .or whatever!) on deck turned and looked at the struggling and frantic major. Shouting out in his squeaky 16 year old voice, "Who is it that's asking?"

"I am Major Aaron Highcross and I have orders to proceed across the ocean to my new post. I am looking for my ship. What ship is this?"

"The *Prince of Orange* is her name. Is this the vessel you seek, Major?"

Highcross, unsure whether he had heard the slobbering courier correctly, repeated what the midshipman said several times to himself. "*Prince of Orange* . . . Orange . . . OR - ENGE . . . Enge???" Could this be it? It might be? "Where are you bound for?" he asked the midshipman.

"Port Royal," was the squeaky reply.

It surprised the major when he thought the lad said Fort Royal. Although he wasn't absolutely certain, he didn't think Fort Royal was on the coast. "Fort Royal, you say? Are you certain, young man?" He had assumed that his transport ship would take him to Philadelphia, and from there he would proceed overland to his post. "But on the other hand," he thought, "these naval people know this business best, so perhaps I shouldn't question it?" He was unsure.

The midshipman felt put out by the "young man" remark. He was a newly appointed midshipman in His Majesty's Royal Navy, and no British soldier – officer or not – could deny him the respect his rank demanded. He shouted down in the huskiest voice he could conjure up, "We sail – with or without you – on the midnight tide. Are you coming aboard or not?"

With only minimal help from a deck hand Major Aaron Highcross and all his belongings boarded the Prince of Orange and were assigned a miniscule cabin in the bow. His bunk ran the length of the cabin and wasn't long enough to allow him to lie down without bending his knees. He had to move his belongings whenever he wanted to enter or exit the cabin.

While awaiting in London for his orders to arrive Highcross learned that the voyage to the New World could take anywhere between several weeks to several months depending on where in the New World you were going, it depended on the wind and weather they encountered at sea. While destinations to the south would normally be smoother and involve balmier weather, they were more distant than the ports in the north. Crossing the Atlantic Ocean to the northern ports was more direct, but in turn it was more likely to encounter inclement weather, especially during the winter months. He was embarking in March, and was hoping spring would come early this year. Highcross dreaded the thought of more stormy seas, but welcomed the fact it would be a shorter voyage. Based on the young major's recent experiences trying to cross the channel, he was ardently hoping that the captain would sail as far south as practical. The two week layover on solid ground in London had allowed his *mal-de-mer* to subside and he had once more resumed eating without repercussions.

After boarding and securing his belongings the exhausted Major Highcross stretched out on his bunk. "Stretched out" is a figure of speech. It was hard and short, but his mad dash to find his ship had worn him out, and he soon fell fast asleep. When he awoke in the morning it was a beautiful sunny, but windy day. The ship had already passed out from the River Thames into the rolling English Channel. He was again out on the high seas, and was seasick within the hour.

Over the next three days he went on deck only to get fresh air and regurgitate. His introduction to the ship's captain was brief, and consisted of "Hello", "I'm Major Aaron Highcross", "Glad to meet you too", and "You'll have to excuse me!" as he darted off to the rail.

On the third day out at sea the weather turned nasty, and the ship's captain was forced to steer into the wind for safety's sake. He changed course with every wind shift. Two days after the first gust of wind had hit their sails the storm grew in intensity. The sea began tossing the ship and men around like cheerleader pompoms as the storm raged on for the next five days. At the end of that time the men and ship were worn to a frazzle, and barely able to function. The rain stopped in the late afternoon and the wind calmed down by dinner time. That was irrelevant to Major Highcross; he had begun "fasting" since the first gale.

The lull in stormy weather allowed the major to spend some time on deck, and not surprisingly he spent most of that time near the rail. It was here, while he gasped in fresh air between bouts of abdominal spasms that he engaged in an idle conversation with a nearby sympathetic sailor.

"Yes Sir, once we git a little further south a here the weather should ease up a bit, and you'll be feelin' better, Sir. And it'll be smooth sailin' from then on."

"We'll be sailing farther south?"

"Well Sir, I 'spect we'll be goin' due south for a spell; to get us outta this nasty nor'easter weather. Ship and crew could use some calmer weather until we can all git back ship shape."

Highcross questioned the sailor about them going so far off course to the south. His knowledge of world geography was not extensive, but he knew Philadelphia was more west of Falmouth, their point of departure from England, than south.

The sailor, who was busy securing ropes to the sails above, didn't answer for a minute. "It won't really be so far off course as you think. We got to go a long way south afore we see green water."

"What's 'green water'?" Highcross asked.

"The water down in the Caribbean. Ain't you ever seen it? Beautiful, I tell you. Beautiful."

Highcross stared at him. Racing through his mind was the limited knowledge he had of world geography, and the Caribbean Sea wasn't near Philadelphia; he was pretty sure. He was half way through his question when the location of the Caribbean Sea popped into his head. "Why are we going . . . Good God! Why are we going to the Caribbean Sea?"

The sailor raised his eyebrows and looked at the Major, "That's where Jamaica is."

Five stuttered questions and five astounding answers later Highcross was roaring up to the captain's cabin for confirmation. "Major," the captain finally said, "Port Royal is in Jamaica. And Jamaica is about . . . well, it's got to be a good 2,000 miles south of Philadelphia. Probably more. And I can't tell you where your ***F***ort Royal is. But we're bound for ***P***ort Royal. And that's in Jamaica. And Jamaica's in the Caribbean."

The captain listened carefully and sympathetically to the major's dilemma, but he had his own problems. His ship had been battered badly. He had serious concerns about its continued sea worthiness. Until he was sure of his ship's condition, and able to fix his position at sea he was unable to focus on the major's problem. He didn't even mention that he thought they were in for another storm. "I can let you off the first time we spot landfall, but until then I'm afraid you'll be stuck with us."

The realization of his situation, and his total inability to change it were the only things that allowed him to forget his seasickness. That all changed as the clouds began rolling in later that night. In the brief time the captain of the ship had clear skies above him he fixed his position. There wasn't any good news to share with passengers and crew. Before midnight the *Prince of Orange* - etal - were being tossed around again faster and more furiously than their entreaties to God for mercy.

For the next several weeks it never got better, at least not for long. The ship, and its unfortunate passengers, took a terrible beating. Unceasingly cloudy skies hampered navigation until one morning when the ship's company woke up to sunny skies; and absolutely no wind at all. They floated in place for the next four days. The captain and crew tried to make the required repairs to the ship in order that she become more seaworthy. It was no secret that captain and crew were wondering if the ship would stay afloat. In his heart of hearts Major Highcross didn't care if the boat made land or sank. He just wanted to get off the damn thing.

At the first sign of a breeze the Captain steered west, trying to reach dry land at the earliest possible moment. The bilge was filled with water. Despite the titanic efforts of the crew the ship was taking on more water than they were throwing over the side. The main mast had a very suspicious crack in it. In order to make the boat lighter the Captain ordered everything non-essential to be thrown over the side. Highcross had to sit on his belongings to avoid losing them.

Highcross lost track of time in the days that followed. Calm seas allowed him to eat, but he knew that those calm seas also prolonged his voyage. Any kind of wind allowed the ship to pick up speed, but eliminated food intake for the Major.

After an unknown number of days of alternating slow going and high winds, with its resultant malicious nausea for Highcross, a lookout finally spotted land. The battered ship, with its equally battered passengers, sailed right for it. Highcross raced down to his cabin and began putting his things in order; he was getting off this ship.

The captain sailed as close as he dared, and then dispatched a small boat to discover where they were. Highcross first asked the captain if he could be in that boat with his belongings. He didn't care where they were; he just wanted to get off. The captain refused, saying that the small craft had only enough room for the lieutenant and four rowers.

"I'll row," offered Highcross.

"No."

"I'll leave my things on board. Just me! I'll go."

"No."

The boat moved off toward shore (without Highcross), which was a rocky shore line that offered no apparent place to dock for either large or small craft. The rocks rose five to ten feet above the water line, with a plain above. On that plain the ship's company could see a man tending to a flock of sheep. He wore a rough linen green shirt with black linsey-woolsey pants. He had tan leggings and a brown waistcoat, but wore no hat. The shepherd's name was Stephen Brown, and he had been born in Belfast, Ireland, but raised in London. By birth he was poor, charming and good-looking, a combination that led invariably to mischievous behavior. And he never, never once, gave a straight answer to anyone. He had earned the wrath of neighbors and the law by that behavior well before his sixteenth birthday, and had signed on as an indentured servant to escape their looming retribution. His master was Daniel Mitchell who owned a large plantation. Mr. Mitchell had learned early on that Stephen wasn't one to be ordered around. But if he was *asked nicely* to do something he was a lamb. This would have been valuable information to the ship's officers of the *Prince of Orange.*

He watched them as the ship drew near, and then as it lowered the small boat. He came to the edge of the rise, and waited as the small boat came toward him.

"Where are we?" asked the lieutenant

The shepherd looked out at the naval officer for a moment, and then said, "Oh, I'd say . . . in about three feet of water."

The lieutenant shook his head, "No, no, my good man, Where are we? Where is this?" he gestured with his hand.

"Are ye lost?"

The lieutenant was starting to lose a little patience, "What colony is this?" His small grin was now gone.

The man turned to a nearby lamb and whispered, "Gertie, I was right. They're lost." He turned back toward the boat, "Murrell's Inlet."

That did not answer the question the lieutenant asked, at least not to his liking. "Where is this Murrell's Inlet? What colony is this?"

Again the shepherd turned to the nearby lamb, "Really lost," he nodded. And, once again looking back at the lieutenant he said, "You are off the shore of the South Carolina colony." He then turned his head sideways and asked, "Yer not from around here, are ye?"

"Where is this inlet? We have been battered by storms and need a safe harbor. The ship is badly damaged and I don't think we will be seaworthy unless we do immediate repairs." The lieutenant thought adding a bit of drama to his inquiry would speed things up.

The man grimaced slightly, thinking it over, and then decided that he thought that maybe trying to do repairs in the harbor wasn't a good idea. "That inlet is a pretty busy place. They use it every day. I don't think the Proprietors (a name given to the town leaders) would like it much if you sunk in the inlet, and clogged it up for a spell."

The lieutenant had heard enough. "We are a ship in the service of King George! We are a ship of his Royal Navy. I demand you stop all this foolish nonsense immediately, and go get us help."

"And who might that be?"

"Who might who be?"

"This 'help' you want me to go get."

"What are you talking about?" The lieutenant was thinking about getting out of his boat, crawling up the embankment, and thrashing this young shepherd severely. But, in truth, that would have been a mistake, and would have actually resulted in the lieutenant winding up in three feet of water.

The lieutenant calmed down and, as pleasantly as he was able, asked, "Where's Charleston?"

Stephen Brown pointed to his right, smiled and said, "Fifty miles, or so. Right on the coast."

The lieutenant reported back to the captain when back onboard, and explained, "There's a fever in that village. The man said it was best we don't go ashore but go directly to Charleston; only a short sail down the coast."

When the battered *Prince of Orange* finally anchored in Charleston harbor, the passengers – led by Major Highcross – left the ship as if it was on fire. Those passengers – again led by Major Highcross - raced into town as if the streets there were made of gold (perhaps that's how that rumor started?), looking for food. Racing away from the ship Highcross swore two things. He would eat the first chicken, pig, or both, he saw; and he would never – NEVER – go to sea again!

After consuming a prodigious amount of food that startled the innkeeper and several other diners, Major Highcross assessed his situation. He was far behind schedule for assuming his duties at Fort Dubois. He only vaguely knew where South Carolina was, but was unsure in what direction, or how far away, Pennsylvania was. He would have to retrieve his baggage from the ship tomorrow, and that he intended to do without the necessity of putting his foot back on 'that damn vessel'. That, he thought, could all be taken care of tomorrow. For now he decided he would have another meal!

With some local assistance he was soon on his way to Philadelphia (after having to wait for two days for a five minute courtesy meeting with the local military commander in Charleston). Despite it all his innate optimism finally resurfaced and allowed him to smile as the carriage carrying him and his baggage north struggled over mud clogged roads, marshes, treacherous ferries on swollen rivers, and never ending delays of one kind or another. He was nearly there.

Now, seven days later, he sat under the oak tree in the Fort Royal settlement enduring another delay. But he knew he was nearly there. He was close to his first real independent command. He had some doubts about his ability to handle that command, but he had no doubts he would try his best. In the middle of this interior debate, he noticed a man approaching. He was younger than the major, probably in his early twenties. He was shorter than the major, and wore civilian clothes. He wore brown linen pants and a dark brown shirt, and high deerskin boots. He carried a flintlock rifle in his hand, and a large knife hung from a strap at his side. He had a vest made of leather, and a broad brimmed hat. The major didn't think he had met him before, because he was sure he would have remembered this stranger's bright gray-blue eyes. It was the first thing someone would notice about this man.

"Major Highcross? Are you Major Highcross?" the man asked.

"At your service, Sir. How can I help you?" The stranger looked like a woodsman to the major, and he had the sudden idea that perhaps he was one of the missing guides he had inquired about.

"My name is Tyson, and I want to speak to you about the trip you're planning on taking to Dubious."

The Major didn't remember the exact names of the guides Lieutenant Smith had mentioned, but he knew that 'Tyson' wasn't one of them. He silently cautioned himself about revealing his traveling plans to a total stranger. There were many stories about highwaymen who took advantage of people once they were out on the road alone. "My plans aren't made yet." He thought that was a good way to dodge the question. "Why do you ask?"

"I want to go along with you."

"What business do you have at Dubious?" asked the Major, using the name "Dubious" for the first, but not last, time.

Tyson explained to the Major that he was heading toward Dubious, but would continue past it. He said he planned to travel further on to Kan-tucky, which was another 100 miles to the southwest. Tyson had been purchasing some supplies for his trip, and waiting for some party to come through Fort Royal heading southwest. He had obtained the necessary items he wanted, but there weren't any groups going in his direction. It seemed most pilgrims were heading northwest to the vicinity, and protection, of Fort Pitt. He said that having the major and his accompanying soldiers, for at least part of the ride, would be more agreeable and safer than going it alone. The major remained suspicious of the stranger, and decided not to tell him at this time that there were no other soldiers going. Instead he began warning Tyson of the hazards they would likely face. He mentioned some of the hostiles that they might encounter in the frontier. He mentioned the dangers of wild animals and adverse weather.

"I've spent a lot of time in the frontier with those animals and the weather. I know how to handle them. And as far as Indians and bandits ….' His voice trailed off for a moment, but then continued, "I can take care of myself." He said it with absolute certainty. He said it. He believed it.

"The guide you've hired doesn't come too highly recommended, in case you're interested," said Tyson, changing the subject. The major almost didn't pay attention to what he was saying. He was staring at Tyson's face; it didn't change expression. "I don't know him myself. I only arrived here a week ago. But I haven't talked to anyone here who has anything good to say about him."

The major shook his head to break the trance he had on Tyson's eyes, and then said, "Lieutenant Smith says Falwyn knows the way to Dubious. And I can't find anyone else who does! I think I'm stuck with him if I want to go anytime soon."

Tyson couldn't disagree with that for he too had been told of the sudden departure of both the settlement's reputable guides. "I was about to head off by myself when I heard about your plans. I wasn't lookin' to go to Dubious, but I was planning to go in that direction. I figure I can get you close, and then he can take you the rest of the way." The Major started thinking that proposition over when Tyson added, "Besides, I have a wagon." The Major returned a puzzled look. "A wagon, major. From what I hear you ain't exactly travellin' light. You're going to need something besides a little old pack horse to tote all that stuff you got."

It was true. The major had brought along everything in the world he owned. Cautioned before he left England that the Colonies offered no creature comforts of any kind, he had left nothing behind. That wasn't the only reason. After his arrival in France his mother wrote him that she had taken up with a widower, and his five children. They had moved *en masse* into his boyhood cottage home, and space there was now at a premium. In the two trunks and large wooden crate he had brought with him were other uniforms, a ceremonial sword, civilian clothes, spare shoes and gloves, books, a favorite set of prints by the famous English artist William Hogarth, two pistols, various personal items, as well as two small pieces of furniture from his mother – a lap desk and foot stool. He was talked out of bringing a small stove.

The major changed the subject. "That gun you have there; that's what they call a 'Pennsylvania Long Rifle', isn't it?"

"Some do."

"Are you proficient with it?"

"I hit what I aim at."

The major thought having a marksman along for the ride might be beneficial, because he himself was a terrible shot with a musket. He had been issued one in Philadelphia, but in times of trouble it was an afterthought. With his pistols he was slightly better. The major consoled himself with the fact that he thought he was an excellent swordsman. "I, myself, am partial to the sword for personal protection," he boasted. "Nothing like a sword when you're up against it, I say." He paused only a moment before continuing, "Yes indeed, when you are confronted with three, or four, brigands there's no time to be reloading, I say."

"I suppose if you let 'three or four' –what did you call them? Brigands? If you let them get up close to you then I reckon that a sword might come in handy. But this here weapon," He lifted his rifle up, "It'll do just fine keeping those 'brigands' out a ways …… with their heads down."

Tyson suddenly reached into his shirt pocket and produced a piece of paper. He handed it to the major. The sudden movement startled the major, but after a moment's delay, he took and read it. It was a letter of introduction signed by General Tindale in Philadelphia. It stated that Tyson was from a fine Virginia family, was of high moral character, and should be accorded all due care and consideration by all loyal subjects of King George, etc, etc. Highcross knew it was authentic because he had one just like it in his pocket that he had received from the same General Tindale just last week. He read the letter through, and began thinking that perhaps letting the young woodsman come along would be a good idea. He could aid Falwyn in guiding them toward Dubious; he seemed to be a knowledgeable woodsman; he would be added defense in case of trouble; his character was attested to by General Tindale; and he had that *wagon!*

Their conversation lasted another hour. Tyson agreed to pay part of whatever fee they would pay Falwyn for guiding them as far as Dubious, although neither one was confident he would earn it. They talked about supplies, and the major asked Tyson many questions about living and traveling in the frontier. They agreed to meet for dinner later, and also to tell Falwyn that they planned to begin their journey as soon as they could obtain the supplies they needed. And also tell him he needed a bath, and to change clothes.

Chapter 4 - The Expedition Grows

Persistent as tide
Focused as a lightning strike
As certain as spring

Mr. Philyaw, the innkeeper, stood behind his bar, between his kitchen and dining room, and smiled. His inn and his dining room were full. And despite how busy he was he had told his wife she wasn't needed to help out and therefore wasn't on the premises (and hadn't been all day). The young lady he had hired was a hard worker, a good cook, and very pretty. It was the best of all worlds, and he was delighted.

When he saw Falwyn walk through the door, his mood darkened ever so slightly, and he moved to intercept Falwyn immediately. "Oh no, yer don't!" he growled as he grabbed him by the shirt. "You'll not come in here and spoil everyone's dinner." Taking the much smaller Falwyn by the shoulder, he turned him around and started him right back out the door.

"Whaddya doin'?" the manhandled Falwyn yelped, "I'm here to have dinner with the major, if ya please!" Philyaw stopped and glanced back across the room to where the major was sitting. The major nodded. If Philyaw's sour disposition had grown a bit worse when Falwyn tried to enter it became considerably worse when he realized now that Falwyn was going to stay.

Falwyn approached the table where the major sat on one side and Tyson on the other. He paused for a moment to decide on which side of the table he would sit. Both the major and Tyson held their breath. (Always a good idea when Falwyn was nearby.) Slightly more intimidated by the major, Falwyn sat down on the empty chair next to Tyson. Tyson got up and moved around to the one next to the major. There was a embarrassing pause, of which Falwyn was oblivious.

Major Highcross looked across at Falwyn and asked, "We've been waiting for you. Where have you been?"

"My boot broke." Falwyn said. Both men opposite him raised their eyebrows and leaned closer. This was never a good idea where Falwyn was concerned. They quickly leaned back.

"What did you say?" one of them said.

"My boot broke. Bottom fell off. Have to get Charlie .... Er, that's Mr. Ludlum to you ....have to get him to nail it back on before we leave for Dubious. I can't be leadin' yer through that wilderness with my foot hangin' out of my boot." After a moment he added, "I hope he can. The damn thing is pretty worn out now." Falwyn leaned in, and said, "So's yer gonna have to give me my pay first. Charlie ain't gonna trust me fer no more money."

The major recalled seeing Falwyn for the first time that morning and remembered the sorry condition of his entire wardrobe. Avoiding the issue of payment up front the major said, "We'll see that Mr. Ludlum fixes your boot."

Their conversation was interrupted by Philyaw as he brought a pot and some plates over to the table. Falwyn looked at the two men across from him, and was told they had already ordered the dinner. The major said he'd pay the bill. Falwyn immediately ordered some whiskey.

By the time they had emptied the pot of the meat and vegetable stew Falwyn had had three small glasses of whiskey and very little of the stew. The two other men drank water. Their conversation over dinner had included the preparations they needed to make before leaving on their journey. Supplies, routes, and expectations were discussed. Falwyn added little, and agreed to everything. Even when his requested fee was halved he quickly agreed, as long as it was paid up front. The major immediately informed him that half would be paid before they left and the other half when they arrived at Dubious.

"Let's drink on it," was all Falwyn said. Relenting, the major bought Falwyn another whiskey and a brandy for himself. Tyson ordered a cup of tea.

A few minutes later, Tyson was explaining the size of the wagon he had, and how handy it would be to them all. This wagon held his store of equipment and all the possessions he intended to bring to his new homestead on the frontier. Besides his horse, which pulled it, and a cow tied to the back, he also intended to buy some chickens before they left. Despite his extended list of cargo he told them that there would be room for their supplies and necessities too.

A woman walked across the room and stopped at their table. She had been noticed by Tyson earlier as she wandered past their table several times. She was young and had long and unruly light brown hair. It was closer to red than blonde Tyson judged.. Her eyes were green, and she had a small mouth. He thought she was thin, but it was difficult to tell because she wore an oversized white blouse and a billowing gray skirt held in place by a thick black belt He was sure she was not one of that large party of travelers that sat at the long table across the room. He had supposed that she was working at the inn in some capacity, as he had not seen her sit down at any table in the room.

"How'd you like the dinner?' she said.

The three men looked at one another, and then, finally, the major said, "It was quite good."

"I made it." she said.

"I liked it." added Falwyn.

"And the biscuits, too. Baked them up myself." She paused for moment to see if they'd say anything. They didn't, so she went on, "I can cook just about anything. Any game. Fish. Can clean 'em up, and cook them. Cakes and pies too." There was another pause. "Can make a full dinner out of a squirrel and two ears of corn!" she smiled.

Her comments about cooking did not register at all with Tyson. She was even prettier up close he thought, but he remained silent. Falwyn just stared. She reminded him of a servant girl named

Violet he knew when he, himself, was just a child. He hadn't seen her very often since she arrived here in Fort Royal because he wasn't allowed in Philyaw's very often, and her work schedule hadn't allowed her much free time outside of the restaurant either.

Her remark about "cakes and pies" had suddenly reminded the major of his mother's vocation. An awkward silence followed as the major's mind wandered back home.

Tyson politely decided to end that awkward silence and said, "That's nice."

The major's attention returned but the young lady spoke first. "Heard you're heading out for Dubious in the morning." Suddenly her smile was gone, she was all business now. "If it's all the same to you, I'll go along with you."

"I beg your pardon. You'll do no such thing!" Major Highcross straightened up in his chair. Falwyn and Tyson remained silent. "Why?" the major then said.

"I have business there."

"I'm the commanding officer," he said; and those words, said out loud, brought him to a momentary halt. He collected himself, and went on, "Well, I am going to be the commanding officer when I get there. What business do you have there?"

"My father is there. He's a soldier there."

"What's his name?"

There was a hesitation before she answered. Tyson noticed it, but the other two did not. "His name is Clark." This was tricky she thought because the major probably had a list of the soldiers at Dubious, and there probably wasn't any "Clark" on that list. And knowing her father as she did, she couldn't even begin to guess what name he was using now. She leaned over and placed both her hands on the table, and continued in a softer voice, "But to tell the truth, Sir, he might be under another name. He's a rascal, that father of mine." She thought she had better make a stronger case for going, so she added, "My mother's terrible sick in Philadelphia, and I thought I better go fetch him back while there's still time."

Philyaw came up behind her and swatted her bottom. "Come on, Shea, get a move on. There are dishes to be collected. Those very good people in the corner need you to bring 'em their food. "

She was standing bolt upright before he finished talking. She whirled around at him, and Tyson could see the anger flash in her eyes. But she took a half step back and said, "I think you and me need to have a little talk." Her hand was at her hip. There was a moment of silence and staring, and then they both walked off to the kitchen.

When they arrived inside the small kitchen she turned on him immediately. "If you touch me again, I'll kill you on the spot." The words were barely out of her mouth when he suddenly noticed the large knife in her right hand. "Don't you doubt it for a minute." she warned. His eyes went from her face to the knife and back again. The thought of arguing with her was gone in a flash. She held it at her side, and said, "I told you when I got here I would be leaving with the first group going to Dubious. And that's where they're goin'. I'll take my wages now, and be off with them in the mornin'."

He had no intention of crossing her, but he didn't want to lose her. Since he had hired her, shortly after her arrival a few weeks ago, she had proven to be very helpful in both the kitchen and waiting tables. She was also working very cheap. Best of all, with her working here he didn't need his wife, or her attitude, hanging around the inn all day. Replacing the attractive Shea was the last thing he wanted to do. He started off with, "I hate to lose you." She remained on guard three feet away from him. He went on to say that he could raise her pay; shorten her hours; never touch her again. There were a few things he would do, and nothing he wouldn't say, to keep her from leaving. He warned her of the dangers of such a trip. He suggested that her companions just might not be the gentlemen they pretended to be. "He might not even be an officer in the King's Army at all. How do yer know? And that Tyson fella! Who is he? Just some fella come out of the woods for all yer know. And Falwyn! FALWYN! Fer Chrissakes. Two hours with him and yer'll be lousy with fleas."

She had no intention of arguing with him; and the knife remained at her side. "I'll take my pay now. All of it." She said flatly. He told her that she shouldn't be in any rush. "Groups headed out toward Dubious all the time," he lied. He tried to persuade her to finish out another week. "No." He tried again to get her to finish out the day. "No." He asked that she, at least, clean up the kitchen before leaving. "No." He tried to shortchange her by saying that she didn't finish the day. "Pay me, now. Put it on the table in front of you, and move away." Her voice was as soft and unimposing as her exposed knife was hard and threatening. He entertained the thought, briefly, of getting close enough to grab her. But he quickly, and correctly, assessed she wasn't to be trifled with, and realized that any miscalculation on his part might very well be fatal. He tried one last time to shortchange her, and failed. She collected the coins off the table after having him back away, and left the kitchen; never once taking her eyes off him.

She returned to the dining room with the knife out of sight, and walked directly back to the major's table. She leaned both her fists on the table next to the major and said, "I'll be leaving with you tomorrow. What time are we going?"

The major had no intention of allowing her to join the expedition. "We're not leaving tomorrow. We will be setting out two days hence, and you'll not be joining us." Then in an effort to placate her somewhat, he added, "When I assume command at Dubious I will send your father back as soon as conditions permit." Believing that that had settled the matter, he nodded.

"I'm going with you." she said.

The major exhaled deeply and shook his head. Tyson remained motionless, but Falwyn thought her persistence, and what she proposed, was funny and sat back and smiled. The Major again began to explain to her that she could not join them, "Missus ......?"

"Shea," she said.

"Missus Shea..."

"Just Shea, thank you, major."

"Very well then, er .... Shea, this is not going to be a Sunday stroll, I assure you. I don't know what you think this trip will be like, but let me advise you that it will be perilous."

"I'm no stranger to the frontier, Sir. I know how difficult these journeys can be."

"Missus Shea, please," the major replied...

"It's Shea."

"Yes, of course. Sorry. Shea, I really advise you to reconsider. Our guide here," he gestured toward Falwyn, "He has told us that we might very well face grave danger every step of the way. I cannot even guarantee with certainty my own safety; much less assure you of your own."

Shea glanced briefly at Falwyn, and then turned again to Highcross. "You do not have to guarantee my safety. I can take care of myself. Thank you."

Tyson remained silent while the major tried not to smirk. Falwyn's smile grew wider. He was enjoying this. The major went on, "Please Missus Shea.... I'm sorry, Shea, please understand that the country we are heading to is hard and unforgiving. There will be little in the way of refuge along the trail. There are bandits and highwaymen of every sort lurking behind every tree and bush. There are hostile savages looking to prey on weary travelers."

Without warning Falwyn sitting just to her left, suddenly grabbed the woman by the wrist, and said, "And what'll ya do if one of thems jumps out and grabs hol' of ya?" He was grinning while holding tightly onto to her. His actions startled the major, but the woman didn't seem to react at all.

Tyson, momentarily startled by Falwyn, slowly shifted his gaze up to the woman's face. A moment went by as he looked to see if she showed any shock or fear. He saw neither. But then, with her free right hand, she apparently brushed the folds of the skirt at her side, and then brought her hand forward. But as that hand reappeared, it now held a knife with a large blade, which was instantly pressing on Falwyn's wrist.

Falwyn froze with his mouth wide open as he felt the sharpness of the large blade pressing against his flesh, his smile was gone. Neither the major nor Tyson said a word. Shea broke the silence, speaking quietly and slow she said to Falwyn, "Remove your hand from my wrist . . . or I'll remove it from yours."

Falwyn was unable to say a word as his eyes went back and forth from her face to the blade held against his wrist. The major, with his eyes bulging, stared at the blade creasing the skin on Falwyn's arm. Tyson spoke, as quietly and slowly as Shea had just a moment ago, to Falwyn, "I would release her, if I were you." And then he added, "Very, very slowly."

One by one, Falwyn uncurled his dirty little fingers from around her wrist. When he was done and his fingers were held spread out above her hand she lifted the knife ever so slightly away from his skin. He placed both hands in his lap, and exhaled. Tyson glanced around the room and saw that the flurry of action at their table had caught everyone's attention. There wasn't a sound in the room. "Why don't you sit down, and we can discuss this?"

She glanced back at Tyson and the major; then again at Falwyn. "You aren't going to do anything stupid again, are you?" He was speechless, and just shook his head.

She sat down at the table in the only unoccupied chair; the one next to Falwyn. Scrunching her nose, she leaned away, but turned toward him. "You will take a bath before we leave, I hope." He gave her a weak, noncommittal smile populated sparsely by yellow teeth. She turned back to the two men across the table, and declared that Falwyn would bathe and change clothes before they left. She left no room for debate. Both men silently agreed that that was a good idea, but neither man agreed that she was going to join their party.

The major picked up the conversation. "No, I can't accept the responsibility of bringing you along."

"I won't be your responsibility. I'll be my own." She insisted right back.

"I can send your father back when I get there. You needn't make the trip at all."

She thought that over for two seconds and immediately came to the conclusion that her father couldn't be trusted to come back on his own. She felt he would just as likely head off again. "No, I want to see him, and I promised my mother when I left that I would personally bring him back to her. I don't know how much time she has left." The major thought he wasn't making any headway with her, so he appealed to Tyson to reason with her.

"Ma'am," he started.

"Call me Shea"

"Okay. Shea, I see that you think you'll be okay out there. But it'll take more than just a big knife to protect yourself. Me and the major, and Falwyn too, may not to be able to protect you if we come across some war parties. And there are gangs of very bad people out there. Whole families of them; who don't care a hoot about civilized behavior. We're going to be pretty busy just taking care of our own skin to be watchin' out for you."

"I can help you watch out for that skin of yours."

Tyson shook his head. She didn't seem to understand the danger they might face. "If these kinds of people get close enough for your knife to be any use, we are going to be in a lot of trouble. There won't be but four of us; and you can bet that anybody that figures to take us on will have a lot more than four on their side. No, Ma'am, if they get that close . . . ." He didn't finish the thought. "Knives," he turned to the major, "and even swords won't do much good once the shooting starts. Or even when arrows start flying around." He felt he was making sense. "We'll have to shoot our way clear when it comes to that." He finished with, "That knife of yours may be good for skinnin' squirrels; or scaring off *grabbers*," he smiled, "but out where we're going we are going to have to be able to shoot." It occurred to Tyson at this moment that he hoped Falwyn was good with a gun because the major had admitted he was only fair.

"I can shoot better than you," she said.

Now it was Tyson's turn to sit back and smile, and the major raised an eyebrow in disbelief. He wasn't sure if the assertion, or the arrogance of it, amused him more. Falwyn had become a true believer in Shea, and just rubbed his wrist. Tyson, in all modesty, knew he was a very good shot. But he was also a gentleman, and did not want to insult the lady. Maintaining his smile, he softly said, "I doubt that."

"I can out shoot you," she said flatly.

Falwyn leaned forward, and asked in a hushed voice, "You callin' him out?" He turned quickly toward Tyson and with wide eyes and a gaping grin declared, "She's callin' you out!" Shea smiled as Tyson tried to figure out what she was up to. In the true male chauvinism of the times, he didn't think for a minute that this woman, or any woman, was a better marksman than he was.

He remembered being warned when he left home to be on guard against tricksters and swindlers he would meet with on his journey from home. He was told that cheaters would be smooth talkers and fancy dressers, but he should never let his guard down no matter how sweet and innocent strangers appeared to be. Or, he thought to himself, how pretty they may be. In his mind's eye Shea wasn't 'sweet and innocent'. Not the way she flashed that knife around, but how was it possible that she could out shoot him? He wasn't sure, but he wasn't going to get tricked into bringing her along either. He was about to say he would not shoot against her, when the major spoke up.

"Fine!" said the major. "We'll have a contest tomorrow, and if you prove yourself a marksman, you can come along."

"Wait a minute!" was all Tyson could say. Falwyn was beaming. He had been her adversary a short time ago, but now had a greater respect for her ferocity than either of his friends. He wanted her on his side.

The major was smiling too. He winked at Tyson, and said, "Why not? If she's as good with the gun as you are, she'll be welcome. Can't have too many marksmen along now, can we?" The major would later tell Tyson that he didn't think for a minute that she could match up with him, so when Tyson bested her at shooting the issue would be decided. She'd be left behind.

With that issue resolved, they discussed a planned delivery from a local farm tomorrow, as well as a few odds and ends to add to their supply wagon. They would take care of that; have their shooting match in the afternoon; and leave at dawn the following day. When they left the inn an hour later, Shea went back to her rented room by herself. She refused the offered escort of the three men to reassert her independence. The major and Tyson went back to their rooms too, after agreeing to meet up at dawn the next day.

Falwyn, after getting a small advance of his pay, wandered off into the darkness to find the nearest alehouse. He hadn't gone a hundred feet when he was suddenly grabbed by the collar from behind, and dragged into a dark alley. He hadn't heard a sound before he was manhandled with ease to the ground. Pinned in the dirt by a pair of knees, and with a hand covering his mouth and nose, he knew exactly who it was.

"Going somewhere?" the assailant whispered.

Chapter 5 - And Grows…And Grows

We all really have to wonder why
This multi-lingual talented guy
Would pack up with no hesitation,
Then head off with no destination.
Searching for someone? Some place? Something?
Hoping some way he'll snatch the gold ring?
What is he seeking? I have no clue.
Hope he finds it, I hope they all do!

The following morning's sun hadn't peeked above the horizon yet, but the early dawn light showed activity in the stable by Mother Farrington's. Tyson was getting his horse ready for a planned ride out into the countryside. It would be the last ride the horse would provide for him for the next few weeks. The horse would be pulling the supply wagon for the trip to Kan-tucky. Tyson's cow had been milked, and would now be led to a field where it would spend the day. Tomorrow it would be tied to the rear of the wagon for the long walk southwest. Tyson was glad that the final leg of his journey was so near at hand. He talked to his horse as he saddled him, telling him about the plans made last night.

The major too was up this early, and was finishing breakfast. His plans included taking his horse for a ride also; for the same reason. The major's horse would join Tyson's in pulling the wagon. His overburdened pack mule, no longer needed, had been sold to a local merchant. Things were starting to finally come together for the long delayed posting of Major Aaron Highcross. He was in a very good mood.

Shea was not in a good mood. She sat in the kitchen of the boarding house where she stayed, stirring her tea. She had been awake all night thinking about the shootout, and trying to figure out some way she could succeed. But these thoughts were often sidetracked by the image of the young woodsman she was up against. She had instantly liked his quiet manor. She didn't think she knew many men like that. As often as his image intruded on her planning, she would dismiss him and return to her problem at hand. By dawn she was no closer to solving her problem than she was when she started. How could she renege on her agreement to a shooting match deciding her inclusion on their trip to Dubious? How could she change the rules, or even the contest itself into something she could win? She had been bluffing about her ability with a gun. She had been desperate to go along, and had seized on the idea of a shootout when it popped into her head. She now regretted it, and tried to think of a better way. It wasn't that she had never fired a gun before, she had. She had learned to shoot while a youth in New Jersey, before she had moved on to Philadelphia two years ago. She had hunted small game, and was occasionally successful. She had once shot and killed a deer. But she suspected that the young frontiersman, Tyson, was a far more experienced marksman than she was. She had to come up with some way to win the shootout, and get to join the expedition.

Falwyn was not in a very good mood either, and he had several very good reasons why. He was awake, and it was far too early to be awake he thought. He didn't normally arise until well after sunup. He also felt quite well and that, contrary to what most people would think, annoyed him. It reminded him that his encounter last night with the assailant was the reason why he had no hangover this morning. He had been forced to turn over nine of the ten shilling advance he had gotten from the major. The shilling the assailant left to him was hardly enough for the quantity of liquor he had planned to buy with the advance. And he knew that his pay for the entire trip was now in serious jeopardy. Sho-Taka had somehow learned of every detail of his dealings with the major and Tyson.

Sho-Taka was an Indian but, unlike many Indians, he kept his black hair cut short. He had a rectangular face, more tall than wide. His small black eyes were set close together, and the eyebrows above them were short and diagonal. His hooked nose was long and narrow and bracketed by flat cheeks. The grim set of his mouth kept his lips thin. Although the moccasins made of deerskin that he wore reflected his Indian heritage, the rest of his attire was more common in Philadelphia. A brown woolen sleeveless waistcoat covered his white shirt and tan breeches. On his head he wore a hat with a 5 inch brim that always seemed to keep his face shaded.

He had come to Fort Royal several years ago, and had always been very vague about his background. He was quiet and kept mostly to himself, and made his living doing odd jobs with a seemingly inexhaustible pool of talents. He was a large man and muscular, and capable of hard labor. He was able to work with animals on one hand and, on occasion, he helped neighborhood children learn how to read and write. He knew about farming, and about carpentry. He had helped the people of the settlement cure leather, and he was able to distill whiskey. It was, in fact, his distilling ability that had led to his association with Falwyn.

A few months after arriving at Fort Royal Philyaw had hired Sho-Taka to help him clear some tree stumps from a field he owned. Although basically a man of few words, Sho-Taka revealed, in the course of their efforts, that he knew how to distill whiskey. Philyaw sensing a cheaper source of supply than he currently had, offered Sho-Taka a deal for two barrels. In no time at all Sho-Taka had acquired the necessary equipment and ingredients and delivered his product. Philyaw deemed it acceptable ("good", in fact), and struck a longer term deal, with the stipulation that the arrangement be kept secret. Philyaw knew he had an acceptable supply at a low cost, and this was not something he wished to share with anyone.

Occasionally Sho-Taka would set up his still in a hidden glade on Philyaw's property, and cook up several gallons. He kept his set-up and technique to himself; having no doubt that if Philyaw learned how to do it himself he most certainly would. The arrangement worked pretty well for the next two years.

How Falwyn learned of the arrangement, including Sho-Taka's skill, no one ever knew. But once he found out about it, he ceaselessly pestered Sho-Taka to brew a few extra bottles every time he made a batch for Philyaw. Insisting they were good friends, and that Philyaw wouldn't miss it and never know, he badgered Sho-Taka without let up. Sho-Taka realized that Falwyn's awareness of the deal meant his secret agreement with Philyaw was in jeopardy. Falwyn's legion of past indiscretions was legendary. In what was a monumental mistake in judgment on Sho-Taka's part, he sold Falwyn two bottles from a recent batch . . . on credit. Two days later, Falwyn was back for more. Avoiding Falwyn whenever he could, he was able to delay the inevitable for a few weeks. Then two more bottles – on credit – bought Sho-Taka another month.

After a few repetitions of this dance Sho-Taka came to the conclusion that a deal with Falwyn was going to have to be struck if the situation was going to remain under control. He knew only too well that Philyaw would be furious if their deal was revealed. He also knew that Captain Wallingford, at the fort, would 'tax' both the maker and the buyer, as soon as he learned about it. He didn't want that any more than Philyaw would. His solution was to allocate a small portion of each batch to Falwyn. It was going to have to be a 'small' portion for two reasons. First, a small portion would have an insignificant cost, and two, a large portion would certainly result in the spectacle of Falwyn stumbling all over the settlement for days on end, and that would not go unnoticed. It seemed like a sensible solution.

Not to Falwyn. "Small! How small?'

"Well, I can let you have pint every time I make a batch."

"A PINT!"

"That's a *free* pint, I might add."

"I want a quart. And I'll pay fer it. It's not like I'm askin' fer yer charity."

"I haven't seen any of your money yet. Take the pint, and we'll forget about the bottles you owe me for already." Sho-Taka really had no hope of ever seeing that money anyway.

"Damn yer, yer blasted savage!! Stop yer cryin' like a baby about a few shillings, fer the love o' God? I'll pay yer. I'll pay yer."

"It's not 'a few shillings', Falwyn. It's more than £3, isn't it? Or is it more?"

"WHAT! THREE POUNDS? Where in hell did yer come up to that figger? It ain't no three pounds." After a moment's hesitation, he quietly asked, "Is it?"

That amount was more than Falwyn had had in his possession since......since......since Falwyn didn't know when! Heated negotiations began between the two. Sho-Taka raised or lowered the allocation and/or price while Falwyn simply disagreed with everything. He wasn't very good at negotiating because he didn't realize what his only true bargaining chip was. He could reveal Sho-Taka's skill with the still. And if Captain Wallingford learned about that nobody would benefit. Except the Captain!

Sho-Taka steered the debate around until finally a tentative agreement was reached. It was loosely structured that Sho-Taka would provide Falwyn with five jars of whiskey a month, and Falwyn would help Sho-Taka, without pay, with any job Sho-Taka undertook. If their secret got out, Sho-Taka told him, not another drop would be forthcoming. This cold hard fact was accepted by Falwyn, and sent a chill down his spine. He vowed to abide by the covenants of this agreement with a fervor not seen since the Christians were ushered into the Coliseum.

Sho-Taka was shocked, as was everyone else in the settlement, when he learned that Falwyn was going to guide the British officer and the stranger from Virginia to Dubious. It was a double shock that he was actually going to be paid to do it. And, although the quoted amount varied by who was telling the story, it would be more money than Falwyn had earned in many months. Falwyn owed many people in the area money, and before they descended on him Sho-Taka wanted his share. This had prompted that surprise meeting in the alley the previous night.

Sho-Taka rose at daylight, as he did every morning, and prepared to shadow Falwyn until he was paid his fee. Thinking that the small advance Falwyn had received last night was only the first installment, Sho-Taka wasn't going to let him out of his sight. But he underestimated the major and Tyson. They too had a less than a high opinion of their guide's integrity, and had no intention of paying him anymore until he had guided them to their destination.

After looking over his shoulder all morning and seeing Sho-Taka standing there, Falwyn asked him "Why?" The Indian's explained his motive.

"Well the jokes on you," Falwyn laughed, "They ain't gonna pay me no more till we get to Dubious!" He shook his head at the displeased Indian, and said, "Yer gonna have to wait till I git back."

It didn't take Sho-Taka more than two seconds to dismiss that possibility. If he let Falwyn out of his sight it would be likely that he would never see the money Falwyn owed him. The thought of traipsing after Falwyn into the frontier in search of Dubious wasn't all that appealing either. Sho-Taka didn't know where it was; he had never been there. And he had the sad suspicion that Falwyn didn't know either. "How are you going to lead this expedition to Dubious? You don't know where it is."

"I do too," said the nodding Falwyn.

"How? You've never been there."

"Captain Wallingford told me."

Sho-Taka didn't believe him for a minute, but he couldn't take the risk of Falwyn being paid when Sho-Taka wasn't standing next to him. If he wanted his money he would have to be there. He thought about the problem for a minute and came to the only acceptable solution. He had to go along. "We have to talk," Sho-Taka said, grabbing Falwyn by the arm.

There was a field just south of the settlement that belonged to Amos Fitch, and because he was unable to grow anything on it, it was always barren. They had decided last night that this was the place where they would hold their shooting contest. Just after lunch the principals began to congregate at the scene. When Falwyn arrived, with Sho-Taka, he found that Shea was already there. Dressed in black leather boots, her ominous (to Falwyn)billowy gray skirt, white linen shirt and broad brimmed hat, she was sitting on a tree stump, and as far as Falwyn could see, all she had with her were a few pieces of paper, but no musket. "Didn't yer bring a musket? Or are yer gonna quit?" he asked.

She glanced up at him, half smiled, and simply shook her head no. She turned to Sho-Taka, whom she knew, and asked if she could speak to him privately.

After stepping away from the puzzled Falwyn, she turned to him once again, and said, "I hope I can trust you to keep this conversation private. I need some help." Sho-Taka shrugged. She knew she was taking a chance, but there wasn't much of a choice. "You're his partner, right?"

"His partner?" Sho-Taka shook his head no. He felt very uncomfortable being linked to Falwyn. "No, we sometimes work together. But no, he and I are definitely not partners. What kind of help do you need?"

"I need him to miss the target. Do you think I can bribe him?"

A surprised Sho-Taka asked, "He's shooting?"

Of course Sho-Taka knew nothing of what Shea had planned. "I'm going to shoot against all three of them." she answered. "They just don't know it yet." Then she asked again, "Can I bribe him to miss? Should I use money or whiskey?"

"Let me do you a favor." Sho-Taka said with a hint of a smile. "Save your money. He's the worst shot I have ever seen. He couldn't hit the outhouse wall if he was shooting from the inside." He stood silent for a minute, then added, "If you can shoot at all…..at all" he repeated, "All you have to do is come close. He won't."

"Thanks," she said. "I owe you."

"I won't forget," he said. They both returned to the stump.

"You don't have your musket?" asked Tyson when they returned.

Actually she didn't own one, but that was a topic for another time. "I thought we'd all use the same musket; just to keep it fair," she replied. She was starting to feel, for the first time since she 'hatched' it this morning, her plan just might work. She only had to beat one of them.

He began to nod in agreement to let her use his musket when suddenly it dawned on him what she had just said. "All," he asked? "Who's 'ALL'," he wondered. "It's me against you."

"No it isn't. It's me against you.' There was a moment's delay. "And me against the major. And me against Falwyn." All three men began to speak at once. Shea didn't listen to any of them. When they began to run out of breath, she threw up her hand to silence them, and said, "Last night, I said I could outshoot you. Didn't I?" After a moment's reflection, all three nodded yes. "Wasn't I talking to all three of you?"

Tyson disagreed. "You were talking to me."

"Perhaps? Just perhaps, I was looking at only you when I said it, but I was definitely talking to all three of you at the time." Now she thought she'd give them the clincher. "You aren't afraid to shoot against me, are you? Major? Falwyn?"

The men said nothing, and shuffled their feet. Tyson was confident in his ability to shoot. And he was using his own weapon, which gave him even more confidence. Besides, he thought, if she can out shoot me she would be a welcome addition to the group.

The major was not so confident. He tried to remember the last time he had fired a musket. It did not come easily to mind. He was better with a sword. But that would be ridiculous. Dueling with a woman! God! What if he lost? Fortunately, he only had one sword, so that was out of the question. It suddenly occurred to him that he was better with a pistol than with a musket. After all, he was an officer. But his pistols were packed away in his baggage back in Tyson's wagon. He hadn't thought he would need them until they left tomorrow. Asking to delay the shootout until he could to go back and get them would be embarrassing. No, he reasoned, he would have to proceed with the contest on her terms.

Falwyn was considering a number of scenarios. He could shoot. He could hit the target dead center and everyone would pat him on the back, maybe even buy him a drink. Maybe he would just hit the target somewhere, and the attention would move on to one of the others who shot better, or worse. Or, as he glumly came to realize, what the likely scenario was, he would miss the target entirely. This he realized would open him up to ridicule and perhaps even dismissal from the expedition. The loss of face he could handle, but the loss of the pay from dismissal was unacceptable. Perhaps he didn't have to shoot? But how? The first possibility that occurred to him was for him to simply start running. But where could he go? He had no money. Then he correctly remembered that there were very few people he could out run. He rationalized that if he were injured he would be excused from shooting. A cinder in his eye? A pebble in his shoe? If he tripped over something, fell, and broke his arm? He sidled up next to Sho-Taka, and asked, "Whatta my gonna do? I ain't too good at this."

Sho-Taka whispered back, "Doesn't matter. You're the guide. They have to take you whether you can shoot, or not."

The crowd of onlookers continued to grow. Amos Fitch and some other people from the settlement, including some children, who had learned about the contest, began to crowd around the contestants. For the sleepy community this was a major event. Three soldiers from the fort also wandered up. They certainly had the free time available, and besides, this might easily turn into a wagering opportunity. That was always a come-on for the soldiers at the fort. Philyaw showed up because any excuse to leave his tavern was welcome. Now that Shea had left, his wife was back at work there. And being in such close quarters with her made him, and her, irritable.

The crowd continued growing, reaching nearly 50, as they crowded around trying to listen to the apparent disagreement the contestants were having.

Suddenly Shea began talking loudly. "Okay folks, move back. We have some shooting to do." She turned to the three men, and said, "I'll shoot first. Ladies before gentlemen." She was talking fast and loud. No one was going to interrupt. "Then Falwyn, there, will fire away. Third shooter will be Mr. Tyson. And finally, Major Highcross will have his chance." This order was not randomly selected by Shea. She had her reasons. According to her thinking the first shooter has the least pressure. There was no one to beat. And Falwyn, if he was as bad as Sho-Taka said he was, would not beat her shot – or not *badly* beat her shot. Tyson she suspected was a good shot. If he beat her, so what! And if he didn't, she was assured of going. And finally, there was the major. She had a plan for him alone.

The people moved around a bit, formed into a semi-circle around the tree stump. Several of the men there began bickering about the terms of proposed wagers. Shea handed Tyson a piece of paper about a foot square, and told him to affix it to a fence post roughly

25 yards away. In the middle of the paper someone had used a piece of charcoal to make a large letter “V”. Tyson, not used to taking abrupt orders, hesitated a moment, and then did as she said. Two soldiers began debating whether Tyson or the major would be the better shot. Neither thought that the ‘girl’, nor Falwyn, would hit the target. A soldier named Selkirk, considered by everyone who knew him as too crafty, too shifty, and too dishonest to be trusted, could not get anyone to bet with him. He wanted to bet on the lady.

Once the paper had been placed on the post Tyson returned, and the crowd grew silent. Shea took the musket from Tyson after he had loaded it. “You want to take a practice shot?” he asked.

“If I don’t get one, no one does.” She didn’t want any one of them feeling any more comfortable than she was. The other shooters muttered agreement. She knelt behind the tree stump and laid the barrel of the musket across it. Tyson bent over, and whispered, “Just to be fair. This piece tends to be a little partial to the right. You might want to favor the sight a little left of center.” He could afford to be magnanimous, he was sure he could out shoot her. He stepped back away.

Shea looked down the barrel of the gun, and sighted on the paper with the “V” down range. She tried to breathe evenly. “Stay calm” she told herself. She tried to remind herself of all the things she had been taught about shooting years ago back in New Jersey. A few seconds passed, and she reached up and cocked the hammer. “Calm” she said. “Inhale” she added. “Let a little out”

BANG!

The musket kicked back, and almost knocked her over. She hadn’t remembered the recoil of the musket being that forceful. The noise and smoke were more than she had expected too. She collected herself; took a deep breath and blew it out. Suddenly people were talking all around her. She stood up, and looked down at the fence post. She spotted it, and saw no mark on it.

Words began to register to her. She heard some voices she knew, as well as one or two others.

"Nice shot!"

"Missed!"

"No, she got it"

"Where?"

"Lucky shot"

"She missed, I think?"

"No, she just nicked it."

She turned to those around her. The major was staring down at the target with a puzzled look on his face. Sho-Taka was pointing at it, and Falwyn was squinting so hard she thought his eyes were closed.

Tyson walked quickly past her and was the first to reach the fence post. When the rest of them joined him down at the target he had already pulled it from the fence post. "She hit it top right. Just barely, but got it." He turned back toward her and said loudly, "Told you it favored the right," he said, smiling at her. She looked toward the target, and couldn't really see at this distance. But if Tyson said she hit it that was good enough for her.

A few minutes later, Shea was still exhilarated. But she knew she wasn't assured of accompanying them yet. Down at the fence post, people were hanging around the target; staring at it from all angles, trying to see where the ball had torn through the paper. A small semi-circle of paper was missing from the top edge of the target.

Back at the stump, Falwyn was getting ready to take his shot. After fidgeting around for a few minutes, he knelt down behind it, and put the musket barrel across it, and placed the stock firmly in his right shoulder. Everyone got quiet. He sighted down range, then, after a long pause, he relaxed. He scratched his right leg. He wet his finger to check the wind. He got into position again. Everyone got silent. Seconds passed. He stood up. "Can't get comfortable," he explained. Once more he knelt down on his right knee. A moment later, he got up and then knelt down on his left knee. That position was obviously uncomfortable, so he changed back again. "Winds movin' the damn target," he complained. Several people shot glances down at the post, and saw the target dead still. "Maybe we better wait till this wind dies down," he suggested.

"Shoot the damn thing, willya?" someone said.

"Quit all the jabberin' fer Jissus sakes! I'm tryin' to concentrate here," Falwyn yelled. If he thought he could wait out the crowd he was wrong. He knelt there in silence, staring down the barrel to the target on the post. And he knelt there. And knelt there. And the crowd didn't move, or make a noise. Falwyn put the musket down again, and somebody groaned. "My eyes are going blurry on me. I can't shoot straight if my eyes are blurry," he explained.

"You can't shoot straight, anyways. If'n your eyes are blurry, or not," a soldier said.

"If you shoot one of my cows, Falwyn, I'm gonna skin you alive," Amos Fitch said.

Waving his arms in two nearly opposite directions, Falwyn shot back, "How ken I shoot one of your damn cows when they are way over there, and I'm aimin' this way?"

Before Fitch could respond, a soldier yelled, "He got no worries about things you aim at. They're safe. He got plenty to worry about things you ain't aiming at!" People started laughing.

"Okay, okay. Let's get back to the shooting." The major shouted, and raised his arms trying to restore order. People started to quiet down, and Tyson stood next to Falwyn, offering words of encouragement. He reminded him that the musket would fire a little to the right; he told him to breathe easy; and he gave him one, or two other tidbits of advice. And lastly, he told him to just go ahead and fire without hesitating.

Anticipating that the recoil of the musket would be painful, Falwyn flinched when he jerked the trigger. He also shut his eyes. Neither of those two things contribute to good marksmanship. The only thing that all the observers could agree on was that the shot did not hit the target, or the ground in front of it. There wasn't any mark or hole on the target, and there was no telltale puff of dirt on impact off the ground; there definitely wasn't any sound of ricochet. One person said he thought the ball went high and to the right toward the river; four others said that it went high and to the left into the trees. No one was really sure.

Tyson's turn to shoot turned out to be the highlight of the match, not that anyone was really surprised. He was, by appearance, a frontiersman and his shot showed he was, indeed, a marksman. Familiar with musket's tendencies he compensated correctly, and sent his ball down range without fanfare. The paper target rippled on the post, and then fluttered to the ground. One or two at first started for the fence post to get an up close view of the paper, and then everyone else scurried after them. The target was picked up and passed around the admiring crowd. There was a hole near the top right inside the "V". It wasn't dead center, but it was close. Everyone who looked at it had a comment, and Tyson secretly enjoyed every one of them. He turned slightly to see where Shea was, anticipating what she would say, but she wasn't in the crowd. She and the major were alone back by the stump.

Up at the stump Shea had her back to the crowd at the fence post, the major faced her. She held a new target in her left hand at her shoulder. It was identical to the one that the first three had shot at; with a slight variation. The paper was still about a foot square. And it still had the letter "V" in charcoal at its center. But perhaps the letter was just a bit narrower, and there were two small, blackened circles on either side of the "V", which were barely visible. Shea held the paper in front of the major, and said, "This will be your target. It's almost the same as the other one we used. But not exactly." She smiled sweetly at the officer, and undid the top button of her shirt. "You see how much it looks like my shirt?" He was puzzled by what she said. "There are *some* differences, as you can plainly see." She undid the next lower button. The major's mouth opened a tiny bit, and his eyebrows rose. "Of course, you should ignore those smudges on the sides. Forget they're even there," she said in a very low voice, as she undid the next button down. The major glanced quickly back at her face, but then lowered his eyes once more. After she undid the fourth button down, she placed two fingers inside her shirt, and then spread them. She exposed a great deal more cleavage then the major had ever seen. "You are looking at the target, aren't you?'

The Major Aaron Highcross responded with a very breathy, "Huh?"

"When you're sighting down at the target, just try to remember what this looks like." She wiggled the paper in her hand, and try to forget about these smudges."

The crowd was now returning to the stump, and Shea could hear them. A voice called out to them, reminding them that it was the major's turn to shoot. Someone else asked if he was ready. Tyson wondered what they were talking about; so did Private Selkirk. The calls finally drew the major's attention, and he looked away to the crowd. Shea buttoned up quickly before turning around to them. She walked over to Falwyn, and told him to place this new target on the post. He didn't understand why, but he had resolved last night never to disagree with her again.

The major was babbling something about being a better shot with his pistols . . . and perhaps he should go and get them . . . and it wouldn't take very long. But before he could arrange his thoughts, Tyson's musket had been reloaded and placed in his hands. The crowd wanted no delay, "Just shoot" several people said. A moment later Falwyn had returned to the stump and the new target lay flat against the post. Only Tyson and Selkirk, in the crowd, sensed something was amiss. Tyson looked down at the target, and wondered why a new one was used. So did Selkirk, but he couldn't see any difference. Tyson peered down at the new target 25 yards away and just wasn't sure. Something wasn't right.

The major, still objecting weakly to using a musket, was finally convinced to make his shot. Without kneeling down, or using the stump to steady his aim, he raised the weapon to his shoulder. Everyone fell silent, and then Shea, standing right at his side whispered, "Remember the target ….. forget the smudges." She then added a very quiet kissing sound. She considered inching nearer and blowing in his ear, but he was too tall.

Perhaps one or two people in the crowd heard what she said. There wasn't anyone who heard the kiss, except the major. He attempted to inhale, but failed. He stared down at the target, but immediately found that distracting. He blinked a few times to try to clear his vision. He sighted again, and with an acuity he didn't know he had he clearly saw the two smudges on the target. He tried to breathe, but only swallowed. He attempted again to focus on the space inside the "V". He didn't see it. He saw a breast bone. A beautiful, soft, pink breastbone between two rounded . . . .

BANG!

Tyson, Selkirk, and just about everyone else saw the leaves fly off the low branches of the tree behind and to the left of the target. Almost everyone smiled at the apparent ineptitude of the major. Falwyn smiled, because now he wasn't the only one to miss the target. Shea smiled triumphantly, and Sho-Taka smiled sadly. Selkirk noticed their smiles and wondered what he had missed. The major turned and glared at Shea. "You cheated," he said.

"No," she answered back, "I won."

The crowd had mostly dispersed a few minutes later after they were assured there would be no more shooting. Tyson and the major were preparing to mount their horses when Shea, Falwyn and Sho-Taka approached. "It's settled then. I'm coming, right," Shea said.

Tyson waited a moment, but then saw that the major was not going to answer. He was still upset about his poor showing Tyson thought. "Sure," he said, "you can join us. But you'll have to carry your fair share of the work," he said. "If you hold up your end of the bargain, we'll be glad to have you along. Four is better than three," he said.

"Four **is** better than three," Shea agreed.

"Yeah, but five is even better," Falwyn jumped in. "I'm gonna bring Sho-Taka. He's my assistant. My assistant guide," he added. The major and Tyson exchanged glances. Before they could say anything Falwyn continued, "And he won't cost yer a farthing. His pay will come outta my pay." Falwyn grinned, and then added, "For you, major, he's free! Yer can't argue with that."

"What do we need him for?" the major wanted to know. He was suspicious. He had seen Sho-Taka around, but had never spoken to him. He continued to speak directly to Falwyn, "Does he speak English?"

"As well as you, Sir," the Indian said in a clear voice. And then, "Perhaps better?" Tyson sat atop his horse, and just watched quietly.

"And get this, major," Falwyn said, and then turned to Sho-Taka, "You speak a buncha languages, doncha?" Turning back to the major Falwyn, "Who knows who we'll run into out there? That just might come in handy out there in wilderness, right?"

"You speak *another* language?" asked the major skeptically.

"Five other languages actually," responded the tall Indian. "Besides the King's English."

"Six languages!" Shea interrupted. "Major, we have to bring him along. Having this man along makes all the sense in the world. At no cost!" She knew she owed him a favor. They exchanged looks, and he nodded 'thanks'.

The major turned to Tyson who just shrugged. Turning back to Falwyn he asked, "You know this man? You'll vouch for his integrity?"

The question was nearly painful to Sho-Taka. Having to have Falwyn vouch for his integrity was the equivalent of asking him to comment on Isaac Newton's Principia Mathematica. It was debatable upon which topic he knew less.

Falwyn's answer covered it nicely, in his mind, "Oh, he's the best, Sir."

Trying to recapture some dignity as the expedition's leader, the major asked, "Can you defend yourself." It was a dumb thing to ask in light of his own demonstrated shortcomings with a weapon just a few minutes ago.

Diplomatically Sho-Taka answered, "Like you, major, I am not the marksman Mr. Tyson here appears to be, but I assure you, I can handle myself in any tight spots in which we find ourselves. And you will, no doubt, should one of those occasions arise, be glad I am one of the party." The major, eager to get off the topic of marksmanship, granted, or rather "grunted" his permission for Sho-Taka to join the expedition.

Now they were five. As they began to move back in the direction of the settlement, following the crowd, they talked with each other about schedules, and cargo, and final assignments. The sixth person tagging along, very unobtrusively behind them, was Private Selkirk. He too had an assignment scheduled for this afternoon. He owed Mrs. Devonshire a full report.

Chapter 6 - Wallingford's Grand Tour

There once was a fellow from Royal
Who despite the trouble and toil
Found it very tough
To get rich enough
And would wind up a Wackentute foil

A few weeks earlier, on Thursday April 21st, Captain Wallingford was in his office at the fort finishing up some paper work before his planned trip to New York and Philadelphia the next day. He hadn't been back there since February, and was looking forward to the ladies and libations these towns had in abundance. And, truthfully, he felt that fulfilling the military aspects of these visits were a very small price to pay for these excursions. As he created some small fictitious military encounters with some local rogue Indians for his reports, he was distracted by some minor commotion coming from the adjoining settlement. Fort Royal and its environs was his domain and if something was going on he wanted to know what it was. All military matters, civil administration, and most commercial activity fell under his purview. He was not open for debate on these topics.

He was out the door and headed in that direction in a matter of seconds. Although there were several hundred yards separating his office in the fort from the settlement he could see that something was indeed afoot.

When he arrived in town he immediately saw the crowd in front of Mother Farrington's boarding house. This was the place where most pilgrims lodged when stopping over at Fort Royal before proceeding west. Apparently a group of settlers had just arrived, and the hustle and bustle of the crowd in front of the boarding house clearly centered on the figure in blue. The blonde blue eyed lady, clad in blue silk, was the center of attention. His instincts had been right, she was well worth the interruption.

Captain Wallingford was dazzled by her the instant he laid eyes on her. Most men were. But for Wallingford, it was more than just the physical attraction. There was so much more to this woman than her beauty. He knew that - again - the instant he laid eyes on her.

Like most men at Fort Royal (and everywhere else) the arrival of a beautiful woman on the scene was always welcome. The new barmaid down at Philyaw's had also been a welcome addition to the Fort Royal area, and Captain Wallingford had been meaning to welcome her personally since she arrived. But one thing or another had delayed his plans regarding her since her arrival. Now his designs on that barmaid were going to have to be delayed again, as this new arrival had leapt to the top of his list. The barmaid wasn't going anywhere, and could wait. He made these decisions in a heartbeat as he looked this new beauty over from the edge of the circle surrounding her.

Her head, and hair, were covered by a Bregere type hat. She was tall and thin. Her face was populated by two very bright blue eyes, a small mouth filled with white teeth, and a perfect little nose. There was only a touch of makeup on her cheeks and lips. Her skin was flawless. Although she was well past 30, some would have guessed she was closer to 20. She spoke lowly and slowly, and with a faint trace of a French accent.

The Captain plunged into the crowd, and inserted himself right in front of her. "Captain Wallingford, at your service," he said interrupting two other men.

She smiled, demurely of course, "I am Mrs. Delilah Devonshire; of the Boston Devonshires."

She offered her hand, and he kissed it. Beneath a grin that promised everything he thought to himself, "No, you're not!" He began escorting her away from Farrington's. "You don't want to stay there." He assured her, "The Bardleys' place would be so much more comfortable." They walked arm in arm the short distance to the home of Josiah Bardley. As they walked she explained to the captain that she had been travelling with that group of settlers all the way from New York. (This wasn't exactly true.) She told him she planned to continue farther west as soon as arrangements could be made. She was not specific as to how much farther west, nor what those arrangements were. Something wasn't right here, and he thought he knew exactly what it was. He cautiously expressed polite skepticism about her ability to undergo such an arduous journey, but she laughed it off.

He stopped in front of an enormous house, a mansion really. Far larger than any other home in the area, it was the residence of the Bardley family, the closest thing this region had to royalty. After knocking on the front door, they were admitted and led to a parlor inside.

Moments later Mrs. Bardley made her entrance, and Captain Wallingford made the introductions. The blonde stranger added, "Of the Boston Devonshires" to Wallingford's introduction. Idle chit-chat followed while servants prepared tea. Mrs. Bardley explained away her husband's absence, and inquired about Mrs. Devonshire's journey so far, and Mrs. Devonshire complimented her on the surprising elegance of this home, 'despite being so far into this wilderness'. In reality Mrs. Bardley didn't care a fig about the Mademoiselle's journey, nor did the Mademoiselle think the furnishings were anything but primitive. They both smiled a lot.

After the tea was served, Captain Wallingford stated that Mrs. Devonshire would be staying there for the next few days. And he insisted she would require the master suite.

"Beg pardon?" was all Mrs. Bardley was able to say.

"I'll see to it that her luggage is brought over directly."

"I'm sorry, captain, but Mr. Bardley and I use the master suite," she said flatly.

Captain Wallingford looked at her for a long moment, and then said, "Not while she's here. The fort, of course, is out of the question, and Farrington's is not quite the accommodations that this lady is used to. I assure you that Mr. Bardley will insist on being the perfect host, and allow Mrs. Devonshire to enjoy the comfort of your home . . . and also the adjoining sitting room." While she sat there, too stunned to reply, he added, "I am *certain*." Mrs. Bardley stopped and started to say something several times, but finally said nothing. Certain the issue was decided the captain went on, "Now why don't you send one of your people down to Farrington's to fetch her baggage. And while they do that you can prepare Mrs. Devonshire's room. She and I will bide our time here."

Totally flummoxed by the captain's seemingly outrageous demands, Mrs. Bardley suddenly rose to follow his instructions. In her absence the captain and Mrs. Devonshire chatted about her journey so far. She told him her trip from New York had been quite enjoyable, and she looked forward to the next part. He asked her questions about New York, their route from there, and where her destination might be. Some of her answers were lies, he knew. He wondered if she thought he was being taken in. Some of her answers were very vague. On this point he had no doubt.

The abrupt arrival of Mr. Bardley was heard by everyone in the house. He bellowed and slammed doors all the way from the street to the inside of the house. He had somehow been advised what Wallingford was doing, and didn't sound as if he approved one little bit. Wallingford was off his chair and into the entry foyer in an instant to intercept the homeowner.

"What in the name of......" he started to yell as Wallingford appeared out of his sitting room.

The captain had him by the shoulders in a flash, and twirled him around toward the door on the opposite side of the house. "Sssssshhhh!" he commanded.

"Who is that woman?" the short portly Mr. Bardley began to ask.

These two men were business partners, not friends. And while the Captain was the senior partner, both men were ingenious in creating deals that would result in their making money. Fort Royal was being overly allocated, due to the exaggerated troop roster, in supplies and rations. The "extras" were passed off to Bardley. And Bardley was adroit at moving merchandise. As shopkeeper and trader, he was as shrewd as anyone in the colonies. And in this vicinity he had a total monopoly on many of the products. The captain, as military commander of the area, used his position and its influence to make sure that Bardley had little competition. He also imposed a 'Royal Tax' on everything else anyone tried to sell. It was quite a profitable arrangement for them both.

It took the captain ten minutes to fully explain, and convince, Mr. Bardley that there was a reason .... a *very good* reason .... to allow Mrs. Devonshire stay at the Bardleys'. He told Bardley that he thought she was actually Delphine "Dellie" d'Argent, a wanted fugitive with a large reward on her head. He did not want to go into details with Bardley because he wasn't absolutely certain yet. But if he was right they would reap quite a large reward for her capture. All Bardley had to do, Wallingford told him, was keep her keep her here until he got back.

"What is she wanted for? What did she do?" Bardley wanted to know. "Why such a big reward? After all, Wallingford, if she's going to stay in my house I ought to know."

Wallingford didn't try to sugarcoat it for his junior partner, "The poster sent out on her says she's wanted for murder, treason, robbery, arson, smuggling, etc, etc, etc."

"Murder? I don't want her in my house!" Josiah stammered.

"Relax, I've read she deplores violence. She much prefers poisoning her victims," the Captain explained.

"Oh, that's a relief! Now I only have to keep my door locked," said the unrelieved Mr. Bardley.

Remembering what he had read on the poster, Wallingford said, "Don't bother. I'm told she can pick any lock they make."

Under normal circumstances the Bardleys would not even begin to think of renting space in their home to anybody, and certainly not to this 'French tart', as Josiah Bardley put it. But the Captain advised him they could split a great deal of money if she was who he thought she was. But it would require keeping a very close eye on the lady. He explained he would have to go back to New York (he left out "Philadelphia, too") to confirm who she was. That would take about a week he told Bardley (that was a conservative estimate, for he never hurried while enjoying the fruits of the big city), and in that time she had to be watched very, very carefully. "Keep her happy," the captain told Bardley. "Keep an eye on her at all times. Keep her content," he said, "But above all, keep her here!"

"I can't do that. I can't be watching her night and day. I've got a business to run."

The captain thought that over for a minute, and then said, "Okay, but she stays here at your house. I don't want her slipping off somewhere."

"Keep her at the fort. In irons!" said the exasperated Bardley.

"No," said the captain who was deep in thought. "I want to keep her in the dark. I don't want her to catch on that we're on to her." He remained silent for a moment, and then went on, "No, she's to be kept here until I'm sure. Until I get back."

"Where is she going to go?" Bardley wanted to know.

"Never mind. That one is as slippery, as sly, and as dangerous as a snake." The Captain again went quiet as he thought this problem through. He finally began poking Bardley in the chest, and declared, "She will board here with you, and she is NOT to leave the house unless she is escorted. And I'll have the soldiers .... No! Not the soldiers. I don't want them poking their noses into this. They'll be telling Selkirk all about it, and in no time at all he'll figure out what the game is. No! I'll have Smith escort her every time she leaves this house." He was nodding in agreement with himself that this was just a perfect way to handle the situation. Smith was, at least, an officer. She couldn't object to that. And Smith could be kept in the dark about the situation, and not likely ask any questions. His instructions would be simple enough that even Smith would understand them. "Escort her around the settlement every time she steps out of the house, until I return." He went on as if talking to himself, "Keep her within the confines of the settlement; never travel out into the countryside. And never . . . NEVER . . . is she to be allowed to mount a horse."

Looking at Bardley again, he added, "She's going to pay you rent while she stays here! I got her to agree to pay you a half a crown for every night she's here." (She would have agreed to any amount, because she had no intention of paying it.) "Meanwhile I'll head for New York. Do what needs being done. And I'll be back in a week's time." He thought over what he had just said, and added, "Maybe a little longer, but if she is who I think she is we are going to make a lot of money. And if she isn't? Well then we will not be out a farthing. You'll have her rent money in your pocket, and she'll be none the wiser. And she – whoever she is – will be free to go off to wherever she wants. Everyone comes out ahead." The men negotiated for a few more minutes over how they would share the fruits of their scheme if this woman turned out to be the infamous Dellie d'Argent, and then returned, with broad smiling faces, to the sitting room to rejoin the beautiful lady sitting there.

Late this afternoon the captain advised the pilgrims she had been travelling with that Mrs. Devonshire would be staying here at Fort Royal when they left in the morning. He assigned Private Selkirk to make sure they left early, and quietly. Bardley was assigned to make sure the lady slept late. That evening Mr. Bardley tried to come up with some plausible reason to give Mrs. Bardley for the necessity of having this houseguest. The truth, of course, wouldn't do. Captain Wallingford was making final plans for his trip back east.

Once the pilgrims had left the next morning the lady would be stranded at Fort Royal. If she realized that he was on to her she would look to leave. But where could she go? At night she would be safely ensconced in the Bardley home.

"She's not to be allowed out of the house when it's dark. Never out between sunset and dawn, do you understand? I want her where you can see her." Wallingford spelled it out for Bardley.

"How can I do that?" asked Bardley with a pained face. "What if she wants to go out for a stroll? I can't stop her, for God sakes!"

As if this answered his question, or any other questions Bardley might have, the Captain whispered, "I don't care. Just do it!"

And by day Lieutenant Smith would be stationed at the front door, ready to escort her whenever and wherever she chose to go; as long as it was within the confines of the Fort Royal settlement, and on foot. He called Lieutenant Smith into his office and gave him explicit instructions. And he repeated them twice. "Sun up to sun down," he said three times. Despite a vague, nagging feeling that he was making a colossal mistake, the trip east was essential, and he had to go.

After he had given his instructions the captain went back to his to-do list for his trip back east, and financial matters topped the list. He would, of course, stop first at his favorite roadhouse in New Jersey on the first leg of his trip. The roadhouse was run by a beautiful redheaded widow with a set of two dazzling skills. One was cooking; the other was not.

Then it was on to New York where first he would visit the Chief Magistrate's Office in an attempt to determine who exactly this Mrs. Devonshire was. If she was who he thought she was; who he *hoped* she was, his agenda back east might have to be abbreviated. Her capture brought with it a substantial reward, and the sooner he retrieved her and turned her in the better. Subsequent stops at that favorite New Jersey roadhouse may have to be postponed to some other time. That was truly a shame, he told himself, but "business comes first".

There was also a substantial profit to be made by purchasing and shipping back to the waiting markets of the western interior a number of items that were only available at the large Atlantic seaports. He had a growing and waiting market that was willing to pay handsomely for certain items, and he intended to satisfy them. Additionally Bardley and Philyaw had given him a list of requested items that he would obtain and ship back to them – plus commission.

Of a secondary nature was the meeting with his two respective commanding officers, and the reports he had to produce for them. More important to him were the requisitions he had to submit for approval to those generals in order to receive those abundant supplies that were subsequently retailed by the enterprising Mr. Bardley. Subsequent trips to both quartermasters to submit those requisitions and arrange shipment to Fort Royal would follow, but that should take no more than one, or two, hours of his time. Then, if time permitted while in New York, he would squeeze in a social call to the home of his uncle and aunt. And of course, there was always time for a few rounds of "'socializing" to be done in both New York and Philadelphia. And last, but certainly not least, he had the young Miss Audrey Tindale, daughter of the Commanding General in Philadelphia, in his crosshairs.

The general's young daughter was, most certainly, on that to-do list. Miss Tindale was young, rich, and pretty. And despite the fact she had been born and raised in England, and had only recently come from there to Philadelphia, she spoke with a faint French accent. It was explained away by her friends that her private tutors had all been French. Ahem.

Accent or not she had caused quite a stir in Philadelphia, and suiters of all stripes were storming the city in an effort to court her. She had been in the city since last July, and as of yet no winner had won the prize. There wasn't even an apparent frontrunner. British Officers in Philadelphia, due to their proximity, had the inside track but that did not dissuade single (and some married) officers from the entire northeast from jumping into the fray. Captain Phillip Wallingford was nobody's fool, and was fully aware of the dogfight that was going on. He had met her on a few occasions during his routine visits to Philadelphia, and like everyone else, had been smitten. He understood that while business or duty required his presence back at Fort Royal (or New York) the chase was on in Philadelphia, and due to his absence he was falling further behind. He knew he had a lot of ground to make up, and was very anxious to get started.

General Augustus Fothingill was commanding officer of all His Majesty's armed forces from New York north to the newly acquired far reaches of Canada. This was an enormous task, both in area and men under his command. It was one of the most prestigious commands in the British Army. His rank and responsibility gave him enormous power, perks and pressure. There were very few senior officers in the British Army that didn't want his job. There were many officers serving under him that would have traded their soul to sit in his seat. And there wasn't a single soldier in the entire command that didn't think he was an incompetent fool. His resume contained, at least for his King, one extremely positive attribute. He was the father of a particularly ravishing young lady that the 22 year old bachelor King of England – George III – was currently pursuing. And having 'the old man an ocean away' seemed like a very good strategy.

Like every other man in the command, Captain Wallingford thought very little of his commanding officer. He loved going to New York, but detested the time he would have to spend in the presence of this officer. Careful preparations were absolutely necessary for these meetings.

On the bright side these mandatory appearances before the general at headquarters were usually brief. Somewhere in the back of the general's mind he knew he was in over his head. In a valiant, yet idiotic, attempt to avoid being duped by anyone in his command, he ordered that all officers must report directly to him. There was no chain of command. At headquarters officers were shuffled in and out of his presence at a dizzying speed. Upon assuming command seven months ago the general conducted these audiences eight hours a day, five days a week. His refusal to delegate any authority resulted in backlogs. He extended the working hours. The backlogs expanded. He added Saturdays to the work week. It didn't alleviate the problem. Lines formed outside the office. There was no respite. Not surprisingly they wore the old man out in a very short time. Officers rushed into the office when their turn came. They blurted out incoherent verbal reports, and dropped papers on the poor man's desk. A properly bribed aide-de-camp would thrust his finger down to a place on the page, and whisper, "Sign here'.

Captain Wallingford, not surprisingly, had learned how the game worked early on, and was able take great advantage of the system. Requisitions with the Commanding General's approving signature on them were the equivalent of having the keys to the Bank of England's vault.

There were, unfortunately, three drawbacks to the protocol. The captain, like just about everyone else, had to spend hours in the waiting room before gaining admission to General Fothingill's office. It was especially galling to him because he knew what fun awaited him when this dreadful business was concluded. The second was that nosey officers were always prowling about that waiting room trying to poke into his affairs; asking impertinent questions, or insinuating themselves into private conversations. He thought they were spies. But he didn't know (or care) for whom. The last drawback was the most infrequent, but definitely the worst of the lot. The General, on rare occasions, would halt in mid-signature, look up and ask a question. Sometimes he would ask two. And on extremely rare occasions he would ask the officer to sit down and join him for tea. Wallingford had heard about this happening, he shivered whenever he thought of it.

As he began his trip east he found himself thinking more and more about Mrs. Devonshire, and the large reward she represented. And the more he thought about that money the more uneasy he felt with the custodians he had left in charge. Bardley was his partner, and somewhat shrewd, but he was also a bit weak. Wallingford had to admit that all too often he had to tell Bardley what to do, and when to do it. And as for Lieutenant Smith; that was a lost cause. Wallingford argued with himself that using Smith instead of Selkirk was the right thing to do. If he had given the job to Selkirk it was entirely possible that that "snake" would ferret out who she was, and turn her in for the reward himself. He didn't think Lieutenant Smith could figure out who she was; he didn't think Lieutenant Smith capable of figuring out which gender she was. "All those two idiots have to do is hold onto her while I'm gone." That sounded simple enough. "Where can she go by herself?" He was sure she did not possess the skills to be traveling out into the wilderness by herself. "I'll be back there in no time at all." He was sure of all these things. Why was he so uneasy?

He decided to cut corners on his to-do list. He would ride his horse a bit harder than usual to cut his travel time shorter; maybe even limit the roadhouse stopovers he had planned for each leg of his journey.

Once he arrived in New York (a two hour ride from the roadhouse) bright and early he would go to the magistrate's office first, and nail down the particulars of Mrs. Devonshire. From there he would get the HQ visit over; he fervently hoped that the waiting time in the General's office would be less than the normal six to eight hours. After getting in and out with the reports submitted and the requisitions signed, he would submit them to Supply for shipment back to Fort Royal later. Then he would be off to order some things for Bardley, Philyaw and himself at one of the large trading houses on lower Broadway. Then, and only then, he would spend one day and night enjoying the city. He would even skip the usual visit to his uncle, a commander in the Royal Navy, who was stationed here in New York. This was not much of a sacrifice because he did not like his uncle very much. He was coarse in his personal habits and foulmouthed. The real reason he had always made that visit in the past was that his uncle's current wife (his third) was very attractive, extremely friendly, and a decidedly warmhearted aunt to her nephew. Decidedly.

His plan now had him spending three days, at the most, in New York socializing, and then proceeding to Philadelphia the next day. He was even open to the possibility of shortening his stay here in New York to perhaps only two days. He was flexible.

Then he would go to Philadelphia (skipping the roadhouse?) and report in to General Tindale immediately upon his arrival. He had planned to spend no more than five days there. He felt he owed it to himself to make a full frontal assault on the lovely Miss Audrey Tindale, and that would take more than just one, or two days. But plans don't always work out the way they should; even very simple ones.

He did indeed ride his horse harder than ever before on his trip to New York. He had started, as planned, on Friday the 22nd, and made it to that favorite roadhouse of his in New Jersey by the evening of the 23d. But there his schedule went all to hell. He got a late start on the 24th due to a very late night the evening before. That late start on Sunday and the aftereffects of that Saturday evening caused him to arrive in New York in no condition to do much of anything; he slept the day away.

His first stop on this Monday morning was the Chief Magistrate's Office on lower Broadway. The streets were full of pushcarts, merchants, shoppers, wagons, buggies, and generally people in a hurry. He found the office and went inside. While the Chief Magistrate was "out on official business", the second in charge, Colonel Worth, was only too glad to help when Wallingford indicated he was here about "Dellie d'Argent". Captain Wallingford did not want to raise false hopes for the Colonel, but felt he may have located the culprit and needed more information to be certain. Over the next hour an active exchange of information was passed back and forth between them. He left the office with all the information they could provide, and a high degree of certainty that he had indeed captured the infamous Mad Madam of Montreal. The reward for which turned out to be higher than he had thought. The colonel offered several times to provide additional troops to aide him in bringing her to justice in New York. He declined their offer. Her capture would be electrifying, and he did not want to share the spotlight (or reward) with anyone else. After all, how difficult would it be bringing a woman in manacles back to New York? And if worse comes to worst, the warrant did say, "*dead* or alive". What could possibly go wrong?

When he arrived at the headquarters of General Fothingill just before 11AM the anteroom was nearly empty. He was surprised and thrilled. He was, until, an aide there told him that General Fothingill was at his regular Monday morning meeting, would not see anyone until this afternoon. And the aide went on to say that the commander had a very full agenda for the afternoon. Wallingford's name would go on the waiting list, but it was a very long list.

"Can't I squeeze in there somewhere? I only need a minute or two for him to sign some papers." Wallingford was looking for any opening, and he had come prepared. A small bottle of very good brandy was passed from Captain Wallingford to the aide. The gesture was appreciated but there was little the man could do. By way of gratitude the aide provided several tidbits of personal information about the general to Wallingford.

But there were only so many hours in the afternoon and many other officers trying to get in to see General Fothingill; all of whom preceded Wallingford on the appointments list (and some of whom had also thought to bring brandy!). The captain decided to remain in that anteroom, and pray for a miracle.

It was all to no avail. At 2:15, people began getting admitted into the General's office. At 6 PM the aides to the general began filtering out of his office and closing shutters and windows. As candles were extinguished the other officers in the room were bid "Good night" (and told to leave). The office was closing for the night. Wallingford protested to no avail. "Come back in the morning' was the only response to his pleas. The only positives gained in that idle afternoon in the anteroom were the collection of some personal tidbits concerning General Fothingill, provided by a less-than-helpful aide.

He returned to headquarters the following morning, but the wait grinded on for another three hours before he was finally summoned into the office of General Fothingill. Upon entering the spacious office Captain Wallingford saw the commander seated behind his desk. It was an enormous desk, and it was covered with scattered stacks of paper, with a few candles and empty plates here and there. There were two or three pieces of paper lying on the floor nearby. An aide hovered at the general's side, while three others were busy at a side table, apparently searching for something. The commander himself roared, "Sergeant!!! Sergeant FORBISHER! Where in blazes are you?"

A small side door opened, and a man, apparently Sergeant Forbisher, walked in. The general yelled at him for a minute about some misplaced report, and then, as quickly as he had called him, he dismissed him. Aides wandered in and out of the inner sanctum of the commander. The general suddenly looked up as if to ponder some thought, and noticed the Wallingford standing there. "Who the hell are you?" he asked

Before Wallingford could say a word the aide to the general's right said, "Captain Wallingford, Sir. From Fort Royal."

The general turned to the aide, and asked in a whisper too loud, "Where the hell is Fort Royal?"

"Out on the western frontier, Sir. In Pennsylvania."

The old general turned once again to Wallingford, "What do you want?"

The captain began his spiel, "Just to give you my regular report, Sir. And pick up some supplies for the men, Sir." He offered the general a sheath of paper.

The general took the papers, and began reading them. Captain Wallingford gazed nonchalantly around the room. The aides around the room went about their business. The aide at the desk began reading over the general's shoulder. The gift by Wallingford to the aide of a very nice bottle of brandy was supposed to have induced that aide to point to the dotted line at the bottom of the page, and mutter to the general, "Sign there, Sir." Wallingford waited to hear that, but instead only heard the general turning papers and muttering to himself. In the past the general had always flipped through the papers, became bored, and signed where instructed by the aide, and then dismissed the captain. This usually took less than five minutes. This was definitely taking longer. He was curious what the general was doing, but he dared not look at him. Eye contact could be fatal to his plan of swift departure.

"Why do you need a cannon?" The question, innocent enough, devastated the captain. He felt the air noiselessly seep out of his body. How did the old man see that on his requisition slip? Looking down at his shoes, his mind began to race. It was only one of 33 items on the list. He had strategically placed it toward the bottom of the list, thinking the general's eyes would glaze over by item 15. On a list containing fuses and flints, pots and tent poles, iron nails and shovels, the old man had spotted "Cannon, Six Pounder, one"! "Son of a bitch" the captain breathed and looked up. A huge smile was now on his face.

"What's that, Sir?"

The general did not like having to repeat himself to junior officers.

"Why do you need a cannon? They don't grow on trees, you know," the general said. "We don't have them lying around here all over the place."

The general was going to continue but Wallingford interrupted. His smile disappeared, and he put on his most earnest face. "I wouldn't want to trouble you, Sir, with my little problems. Why they would seem almost trivial to a combat veteran like yourself." He waited a moment, and then added, "But ours was lost in battle, Sir. We need another."

The general, who was sitting bolt upright, hands on hips at first, slowly placed his arms on his desk and leaned forward, "Battle?" he repeated. His facial demeanor went from severe disapproval to concerned curiosity. The word 'battle' stirred his very soul. He hadn't arrived in North America until the local hostilities with the French were practically over, and he had missed the combat on the continent because he had been assigned elsewhere. The aides around the room turned in unison toward Captain Wallingford. "What battle?" Fothingill asked in a hushed voice. "Are those French bastards still out there causing trouble? Or is it the savages?"

Wallingford sensed he may be on to something, moved on, cautiously. "Worse than the French, Sir. And, no, not the Indians either. Still worse than those savages; it was the McGintys." Wallingford let a moment pass to let the information sink in.

Yesterday, while waiting in the outer office the captain had engaged in a lengthy conversation with an aide to the general. He was a junior officer who had served with Fothingill for a time in his former post in Ireland. The aide relayed that the general had spent the previous eight years as commander of a small detachment in southeastern Ireland. The Seven Years War was passing him by there, and he deeply resented it. He hated his post. The Irish he lorded over hated him. And he returned that sentiment. The time he spent there started out badly, and deteriorated from there. The more he tried to establish order, the more the locals rebelled. The ensuing clashes resulted in ever increasing hostility between the two parties. He was barely able to control the situation, and was constantly asking the War Minister in London for increased men and munitions, or another posting in the 'actual war'. The War Minister quickly became angry at the pestering commander in Ireland while he attempted to deal with much larger concerns he had with the French. He advised General Fothingill, in no uncertain terms, that he would remain in Ireland 'until the French swim in the Thames'. The general furiously accepted his fate, and blamed the Irish.

"Yes Sir, the McGintys! A family of scurrilous thieves and murderers that were terrorizing our poor local settlers south of Fort Royal."

Wallingford watched as the general processed this bit of information. The general's face now went from concern to a scowl. A seething anger could be seen just below the surface. Then in a moment, he bellowed out, "SERGEANT FORBISHER! FORBISHER!" The small sergeant entered as he had before, and looked meekly at his commander. "Bring us some tea, sergeant." He turned to the captain, "You'll join me for cup of tea, won't you, captain? Of course you will. And tell me all about these McGintys." He almost spit the word "McGinty" out. He turned again to Forbisher and said, "And bring us some of those spice cakes you have out there. Those little brown ones with the sugar on top. You know what I mean, don't you?" The sergeant nodded glumly and retreated once more through the door.

It took an hour and a half for the general and the captain to take turns in telling their stories. First, Captain Wallingford told his tale of how the cannon had been lost. He told about how this McGinty family ("More gang than family, really") had moved into the area only last January. From where, he didn't know. "But I suspect, Sir, they're from the bowels of Ireland." Since their arrival they had been robbing the outlying farms, and waylaying travelers throughout the territory. They had, Wallingford said, injured many of their victims, and on one occasion had killed a man. They would commit their crimes and then disappear into the woods. The captain told how he tried to protect the innocent people under his care, but the cowardly McGintys always seemed to slip away before he and his soldiers could come to the rescue. Wallingford could see by this time that General Fothingill was enthralled, but some of the aides seemed to be smirking. "Don't overplay it," he warned himself.

"Then Divine Providence interceded. An Indian . . . a *friendly* Indian came across their trail and tracked them. And then he came back to the fort to tell us what he'd done. Thank God I've have been able to reach some of these poor innocents, and turn them to our way of thinking." He paused, allowing that thought to simmer for a moment, and then continued, "Well, he told us that the McGintys were holed up in a box canyon; in a place the Indians called . . . ." He hesitated. If you are playing with the truth, the fewer facts used the better. "It's an Indian name that is very hard to say in English," he explained. "He also told us that they had built themselves a veritable fortress as their hideout. Natural granite walls on three sides, and in front they had built a timber wall. They probably thought their fortress was impenetrable." The general was now hanging on every word. "But I mustered the troops; and I *limbered* our cannon (he hoped that that was the right verb?), and went off to confront them." No one said anything, but a few people in the room mouthed the word "limbered'. The captain went on to tell the story of how he stealthily advanced his troops to surround and trap all the McGintys inside their hideaway, and then announced his presence and demanded their surrender. The McGintys, of course, refused and the battle began. "It became a furious fight with our fire pouring in, and theirs coming right back out. Truth be told, our musket balls had little effect on their front wall, and they initially had the upper hand. But I had anticipated that, and that is why I had brought along our cannon." The general nodded slightly in approval. "We soon began by firing our beloved cannon at their walled front."

"'Beloved'?" the general interjected.

"Why, yes Sir, I'm almost embarrassed to tell you this but we called her 'Sweet Lizzie'; after the youngest sister of one of our soldiers. That cannon was like a little sister to us all. " In what was certainly no coincidence the general called his own daughter, across the sea in England, 'Lizzie'.

(In reality the soldiers usually called the cannon, "the cannon". Well, perhaps Private Purpley and a few others occasionally used a nickname for it. They sometimes called it "Old Eunice", after a barmaid that once worked at Philyaw's., because they thought they both had a similar sized mouth.)

"We all loved that gun," Wallingford continued. "She fired straight and true every time, and never let us down. It got us out of many tight spots in our recent struggles against the French and hostile Indians. There's many a man at Fort Royal that owes his life to that dear cannon. But alas, what's done is done." He let a moment go by in silence. "C'est la guerre," he then added. Captain Wallingford considered wiping his eye, but thought better of it. The aide at the general's side rolled his eyes.

"What happened to it?"

"After we had battered their wall with shot after shot from Sweet Lizzie, it came crashing down. We held our fire, and inched closer to give them one last chance to surrender." There wasn't a sound in the general's office. "But only one of those fiendish McGintys was still breathing, Sir. And it was the worst of the lot, their leader, Mickey McGinty. He must have known a hangman's noose awaited him (after a fair trial, of course)."

"Of course," muttered the general.

"So, in desperation, he raced out of the flaming wreckage that was their fort, and fired one more shot, as he, himself, was cut down by a fusillade from our ranks." Wallingford glanced quickly around the room and saw all of them staring right back. "Fortunately he didn't hit any of us." Now the captain went on slowly, "But his errant shot somehow managed to hit the keg of powder lying beneath the under carriage of Sweet Lizzie!" It was even quieter now than it had been a moment ago.

One of the aides said to no one, "Must have played havoc with her trunnions."

The word "trunnions' caught the captain off-guard because for a moment he wasn't exactly sure what it meant. It sounded vaguely obscene to him and he turned to look at the aide. The man's face offered no hint as to what he meant. Wallingford searched another moment for a clue for the aide's meaning, but then returned his gaze to the general.

Finally breaking the silence, the general asked, "What? What happened to her? What happened to Sweet Lizzie?"

The captain raised his eyebrows for a second, and then let them fall, while letting out a sigh. "Had that keg been empty, instead of full…" his voice trailed off. He shook his head. There were no words.

"Boom'" someone in the room whispered.

"What happened to that McGinty fellow? The one who destroyed Sweet Lizzie?" finally asked another straight faced aide.

"Tell me you hanged the scoundrel," snarled the general.

The captain felt compelled to answer the general even though he had already told him he had been shot by the soldiers. "He was already dead, Sir. I didn't think it necessary."

The room remained silent for an uncomfortable period of time. Captain Wallingford thought the longer the better. Finally the general spoke, "And that's why you are requisitioning a new cannon? To replace Sweet Lizzie."

"*Replace* her, Sir? No, we could never replace her. No two cannons could replace her, but we can't let sentiment prevent us from adequately serving those settlers who look to us for protection. And, to do that, we need a new cannon."

The general's story ran longer than Captain Wallingford's, a great deal longer. He told of how he had been unjustly kept at 'that dirty little outpost' in Ireland for nearly ten years. ("You know they don't really have a dry season at all there! They have a wet and cold season, and that's followed by a wetter and colder season. And MUD! You've never been anyplace that had more mud than that damn place.") He complained about the place for twenty minutes, then about the people for forty more. ("Hard headed? They can't be reasoned with! And ungrateful? I can tell you . . . .")

It was nearly 2 PM when Captain Wallingford was finally able to make his way out of headquarters. Courting the danger of insulting the general, he used every excuse he could think of for not agreeing to dine with him that night. Promising that he would return soon he squirmed his way out the door, with his signed requisitions in hand, and ran. He was behind schedule, and the ladies of New York waited.

His first stop was at the Royal Quartermasters warehouse to drop off his requisitions. The building was across the street from the huge military dock on Manhattan's lower east side waterfront. Tons of cargo shipped from England and from other points all over the globe came off ships docking at that harbor, and were carted into that warehouse; then dispersed all over the northern colonies. The officer in charge of this massive operation had two conspicuous traits. He was extremely lazy, and a remarkably astute judge of men. He saw early on that his subordinate, Sergeant Brightman, was perfectly capable of running the entire unit without oversight or interference. The arrangement had worked perfectly well for over a year. The officer, Colonel Henry, hadn't been inside the building in three weeks. He had no intention of being there in the next three weeks either. If Brightman needed him, he would send a message. He rarely did.

Sergeant Brightman took full advantage of his delegated authority, and ran the operation as smoothly as a baby's behind. He was diligent, hardworking and extremely honest. Captain Wallingford, early on sensing the awesome potential of 'cooperation' between the two, had approached him with a subtle hint of a bribe. Sergeant Brightman's shock at the suggestion removed any doubt in Wallingford's mind that an 'understanding' would ever be reached. From that point on Wallingford knew that although Brightman would never be an asset in his various schemes, nor would he be a detriment either. He could depend on Brightman getting him his supplies on time, and in good condition; as long as he had the *signed requisition.* And today he had the signed requisition.

"Good afternoon, Brightman! How's His Majesty's Navy treating you?" he said as he walked through the door. The quartermaster was always complaining about how slow the Royal Navy was in resupplying him from England.

Looking up, somewhat surprised, Brightman said, "Well hello there, Captain Wallingford. How are the savages out west treating you? How's the war going?" The questions required no response Wallingford knew; they were totally rhetorical.

Putting the requisition down on the sergeant's desk, he smiled, "Here you are, sergeant. Thank you. If you'll be so kind as to gather these items up, I would be grateful. Here's the list; a bit longer than usual, but we've been busy lately, and we're running short of some essentials."

Brightman checked immediately for the approving signature. If that wasn't there, there was no need to go any further. But once found, and looked at it for authenticity, he then began scanning the list. "Hmmm ...... Yes ..... Yes ...... hmmm .... Don't think we have that many on hand. I'll have to check. .... Yes ....What ho! What's this? A cannon?" He looked up at Wallingford, and back down again to re-check the authenticity of the approving signature. "Well" he said to himself, "If the old man says so ...." Wallingford did not want to go through the story again, that wasn't necessary. Sergeant Brightman did his job mechanically. If the list was signed he tried to fill it. He would not for a minute question whether the items on it were appropriate. Not for a minute did he believe that he should. "A cannon, eh? Let me think for a minute." Brightman stared up at the high ceiling, and then turned toward the rear of the warehouse. "You know, Captain, we have a very nice swivel gun back there somewhere, I bet that...." He was very adroit at rotating his stock, and moving excess inventory.

The captain interrupted him, "Wait a minute! A 'swivel gun'?" A swivel gun was a small version of cannon that usually fired grapeshot. It measured less than three feet in length, weighed about 50 lbs, and had a bore of 1 ¼ inches. Its value lay in its portability. It could be carried from spot to spot, and anchored to anything heavy. Captain Wallingford knew full well what it was, but it wasn't what he wanted. "No, no, no! I don't want any little swivel gun. We need regulation cannon. A full sized six pounder; if you please."

"Hey captain, let me tell you that a swivel gun can be mighty handy if used correctly. It fires and reloads faster than a big clumsy six pounder. It can be moved from here to there in no time flat. It needs fewer men to handle her, so you have more men to use elsewhere......"

"Hold on, sergeant, hold on! Forget the swivel gun. I want my six pounder. Nothing less."

Sergeant Brightman came right back at the captain, "You're lookin' for firepower, captain? You want some real bang, Sir? I've got a cannon for yer, all right! I've got an 18 pounder fresh out of the foundry. Came in here not two weeks ago; off of a ship-of-the-line that didn't have room for it. Needed some minor retooling, Sir, that's all. But they were in an awful hurry. Couldn't wait for the work to be done before they needed to shove off. Left it here." And then with a sheepish grin he confided, "I can let you have it. Do a little work on the bore and you'll have yourself one hell of a cannon." Nodding knowingly at Wallingford Brightman went on, "That there's a piece of artillery that the natives will stand up and take notice of. Somethin' your troop will take pride in!"

Wallingford thought of what he could do with an 18 pounder! And it was an appealing thought. He tried to remember what the range was for a cannon that size. He probably had learned that back in his younger days while in training to be an officer, but the answer eluded him now.

He started to daydream. Something that potent could probably knock down all four walls of Fort Royal with just two shots! He thought about how powerful that cannon was, and therefore how powerful he would be as its commander. That had to be worth a lot of money. That was a lot of firepower. He wondered how much he could get for an 18 pounder. But then reality started to rear its head. It must weight a ton he thought. And that was another answer from his training days that eluded him now. The powder and balls necessary for it would also be enormously heavy. How would he ever maneuver it around? And finally, he would never be able to easily explain its disappearance to his superiors when it was gone. And to clinch the debate in his head, he realized that before he would be able to retail it, it would have to be test fired to prove its worth. And based on its need for "retooling", he had no intention of being near it when that test firing occurred. Who'd load it and fire it? Obviously he could always assign Smith as Fort Royal's Artillery Officer. He could be the one standing next to it when it was tested. He could order Privates Thompson, Tilden, and Purpley to do the loading. They're all stupid enough, and expendable. But if the 'minor retooling' hadn't been done correctly, or if those three idiots didn't load it correctly, that test could result in a misfire that would leave Fort Royal as a large hole in the ground.

Looking once more into Sergeant Brightman's eyes, he reluctantly said, "No! I don't want an 18 pounder. We need a six pounder, thank you." And then he added, "I'll take that swivel gun, if you want to get rid of it."

When his business was concluded with Quartermaster Brightman, the captain headed off for lower Broadway and the several trading houses that he needed to visit. Their proximity to each other, combined with his specific list of items to be purchased, allowed him to finish this task in record time.

It was not quite 6 PM as he made his way back toward the boarding house that served as his New York base. He considered taking a hot bath before changing into his freshly laundered uniform that awaited him in his room. He could take his bath; then dinner, and perhaps a drink or two, before proceeding to one of his favorite haunts on Pearl Street. It was an establishment that offered three of his favorite New York treats: drunken gamblers, fine wine, and female companionship.

He entered the boardinghouse and made for the staircase with long strides. But before he disappeared up those stairs, the barman called his name. "Capt'n Wallingford, Sir. This here come fer you while you wuz out and about." The man was waving a note.

Altering his route, he veered toward the bar. Taking the scented envelope he examined it, and then said to the barman. "An ale, if you will." He then returned his attention to the note. It was sealed with red wax, and bore the initial "W". His first thought was his uncle, and that was not a pleasant thought. But then the fact that it was scented led him to quickly concur that it was from his aunt. He opened it, and read

Dear, Dear Phillip

Your wicked Uncle Rodney has gone off on one of his tiresome official voyages, and left me all alone. I am so very bored, and

lonely. But I am thrilled to learn that you have just arrived in our fair city, and I do hope you will race to my rescue. Please come tonight, after 10PM

Your loving, and soon to be grateful,
Aunt Marta

As he was reading the note the ale appeared at his elbow. He raised it to his lips and concluded that, although a bit behind schedule, it was all going so very well.

Large portions of the next 17 hours he spent with his aunt were lost in the haze of a drunken stupor and naps. During that time he never left the bedroom, and the servants were never admitted. And although Aunt Marta was a few years older than the captain, she was every bit as spry and energetic. And not the least of her favorable traits was her largesse with her husband's wine cellar.

When news of her husband's premature return to port reached the house at midafternoon on the 27th, the aunt and nephew bid each other a very, very fond farewell and parted.

The somewhat worn out captain returned to his boarding house with every intention of making an appearance that evening on Pearl Street. And, to his credit, he made a gallant attempt to repeat the previous day's activities. But the cold reality of physical exhaustion set in by 9 PM, and he was back in his own bed asleep by 10.

By noon the next day Captain Wallingford was on his way to Philadelphia. He had bid farewell to no one upon departure, and had instructed his landlord to tell any inquirers, should there be any, that he had left before sunrise.

Ever cautious about being spied upon, he made his way due west leaving New York, as if heading for Fort Royal. Once well out of sight and convinced he was not being followed, he turned left and went south toward Philadelphia, to tend to more *official business* there. If he was in no particular hurry, the 90 mile trip would take the better part of two days. The journey would be shorter if he pressed his horse. It would be longer if the captain opted to take a night's detour to that roadhouse in New Jersey near the Delaware River. But considering his rather lengthy recent escapade with Aunt Marta, and the fact he was behind schedule, he thought it best to skip the roadhouse on this leg of the journey. He was quite proud of his decision. As he rode slowly southwest the debate renewed itself with vigor in his mind.

"Haste makes waste" he told himself. "Act in haste; repent at leisure" he remembered hearing somewhere. There must have been a dozen common sense quotes he could recall that counseled that it was always wise to proceed with caution. And he couldn't recall – he didn't try too hard - even one that recommended hurrying. His course from New York to Philadelphia was primarily southwest. Late that afternoon the course was altered to a more westerly direction. The roadhouse won.

From the time Wallingford arrived at the roadhouse on Friday until he left on Monday he was in a state of total relaxation. Oh yes, there was fun and frolic. There was good food and good drink. And there was plenty of all. He even picnicked on Saturday afternoon! The next day, Sunday May 1, dawned like every spring day ought to dawn. Beautiful sunshine and a cool, but not chilly, breeze greeted the captain when he awoke. The recollection of the previous evening's activities, and the beautiful day, made him smile. Today was the Sabbath, and the captain even thought about attending services somewhere. After dismissing that thought very quickly, he did decide to observe the day by not travelling. He guessed that that might be a Christian thing to do. Although a bit behind schedule, his plans were going very well. The New York stop had been a complete success; the roadhouse hospitality had been everything he had expected; the weather was beautiful. Things just couldn't be any better; why didn't he just relax and enjoy his good fortune? He would stay over one more night. Life was good.

Captain Wallingford arose on Monday morning well rested; then dressed and ate at leisure. He was on his horse heading south to Philadelphia before noon. Initially he hadn't planned on hurrying, but thought better of it after a while. After all, the less time spent on the road meant the more time he would have to enjoy in Philadelphia.

(Little did he know that over a hundred miles to the west, Major Aaron Highcross, after a disappointing conversation with Lieutenant Smith, was damning his own continuing bad luck.)

Wallingford had planned to report in to General Sir Godfrey Tindale upon his arrival in Philadelphia. With the dust of the trail, and a slightly disheveled look from the journey still on him, he thought it made a good impression on the pompous old man. He would show up at headquarters, and then begging forgiveness for his appearance, ask if the general would grant him a few minutes the following day to make his official report. The general always seemed to be pleased with this approach.

When Wallingford arrived in the late afternoon on Monday in Philadelphia, he learned that General Tindale was away on a 'short military expedition'. This could mean anything from him making a legitimate incursion (accompanied by a hundred soldiers) into Indian Territory to pursue (no more than five) hostiles; or he wanted to spend a few days off in a cabin somewhere with his mistress. In any case it meant that no official business would be conducted at headquarters until he returned. It was explained to the captain 'that the general would likely be back in three, or four, days". He would have preferred business before pleasure, and this unexpected delay in his schedule was mildly disturbing, but he rationalized that he had planned to spend five days here anyway.

The next three days were hectic for Captain Wallingford. He went from tea parties to soirees; from a wild turkey hunt to a leisurely horseback ride in the country. He was hosted and joined by fellow officers and business associates. But the lovely young Miss Tindale remained elusive.

He heard from other officers about her. She had done this, or had been there, but try as he might their paths did not cross. And despite his considerable efforts, he could not arrange a rendezvous.

He did see her in passing one afternoon, but it was only a fleeting glance. Told she was going to a tea party at the home of some officer, he raced to the house. And to his delight he arrived just at the same moment she did. The fact he had not been invited to attend was irrelevant in his mind. He was going in, and he was going to sit next to her if he had to draw his sword and carve his way there.

But, alas, he was blocked at the door by the hostess, who was as adamant as he was. In no uncertain terms she told him it was 'Ladies only' and he was not getting into the house. If there were any positives to be taken from the entire episode, it was that he did receive a very sweet smile from her as she passed him on her way into the house. It wasn't much, but it was something.

She was everything he remembered her being. He remembered the few times he had spent in her company on the previous visit to Philadelphia. Her manners and dress were immaculate. She had been smart, witty and, he thought, cautiously flirtatious. And he never forgot for a minute how wealthy she was.

Not surprisingly, when the general arrived back at his home on late Thursday afternoon, Captain Wallingford arrived shortly thereafter. (He had bribed a stable hand at the residence to advise him whenever the general returned.) Insisting to staff that he 'must see the General immediately' he bluffed his way into the house. Both the household and military staff were shuffling in and out of the parlor when he entered. His arrival into the parlor interrupted the family gathering. He stood at attention, as one by one, the occupants noticed his presence. Already barking orders at everyone, General Tindale was startled when he noticed the captain standing at attention over by the window. Lady Tindale was mystified at his sudden appearance. Miss Tindale simply looked at him with a beatific smile.

"Captain . . ." the general's voice trailed off; and then was back as boisterous as ever, "Captain Wallingford isn't it?"

"Yes, sir," came the hesitant reply.

"Good to see you, man. How are you? What are you doing here? How are things out at Fort Royal? A bit more lively now, I'll wager, with the new man about," he nodded knowingly.

Captain Wallingford didn't understand, so he smiled and nodded right back.

"We, of course, have to talk!" the general declared, but waving a hand said, "But not now. I haven't had a decent hot meal since I left. I am starved to the point of distraction!" He started giving orders again to the staff that dinner was to be served immediately. There was no invitation to the captain to join them. "Come see me on the morrow. Bright and early! We have a lot to talk about, do we not?" With that he wrapped an arm around his daughter and wife and whisked them out of the room.

Captain Wallingford was left standing alone in the parlor. Although disappointed at not being invited to join them, the captain remained optimistic. This minor setback would be more than made up for when he had his private tete-a-tete with the general tomorrow.

Once out of the house and on his way back to his quarters he began rehearsing tomorrow's presentation in his mind. He would start with some short tales of recent derring-do with some hostile Indians. He would invent some new adversaries. He thought it best not to repeat the McGinty Brothers story, as keeping the two commands separate in all things seemed the safest way to manage it. He would follow that with some written reports he had already prepared. And end it as he always did with some supply requisitions. He was quite confident that it would all go smoothly. He thought the only difficult task before him now was how would he obtain an invitation to dine with the general (and his daughter!) tomorrow night?

The missed opportunity of dining with the young Miss Tindale tonight meant that he would have to prolong his stay in Philadelphia. His meeting with the general tomorrow might run long, and could also result in a follow up meeting next week. The supply requisitions would have to be submitted, acquired and their transportation to Fort Royal arranged. That could delay his return to Fort Royal until Tuesday at the earliest. But he could put this delay to good use he reasoned. It would allow him the entire weekend to continue his pursuit of Miss Tindale; although now under the close watchful eye of her father.

However, there was one nagging thought he had concerning the delay. He was anxious to return to Fort Royal, and to, once more, have his prize prisoner under his personal control. Handing Mrs. Devonshire, aka the notorious Dellie d'Argent, over to the authorities in New York would not only be most rewarding financially, but elevate his stature to the highest ranks among all the British officers in the colonies. If he could establish his presence in the eyes of Miss Tindale this weekend, his delivery of the French harlot to the authorities next week would propel him into the forefront of the horde of eligible bachelors pursuing her. Although the additional delay in returning to Fort Royal bothered him, he dismissed it. After all, what could possibly go wrong with all those people back at Fort Royal watching over one little French tart? He barely thought of it over the next six hours while he enjoyed a night out on the town.

Despite suffering a tempestuous (well earned) hangover, Captain Wallingford arrived at the general's office early the next morning. But it was to no avail. He sat in the outer office for several hours as the general called in other officers before him. Antagonism and antagonistic stomach contents alternately welled up in his throat as he languished in the outer office awaiting his turn. The general's adjutant, a Lieutenant Crosly, seemed to take pleasure in the frustration the captain displayed each time he was skipped over. Captain Wallingford noticed and fantasized about various scenarios he would like to use to kill the smirking lieutenant. The tormented captain was finally called.

When he entered the office, General Tindale did not rise to greet him, but merely waved a hand at him, and then gestured toward a chair facing his desk. Captain Wallingford sat down and said nothing as the general continued reading some documents in front of him. Wallingford reminded himself to be on the alert for any opportunity to steer the conversation into a dinner invitation.

As his mind wandered and his eyes scanned the room, General Tindale suddenly barked, "Well captain, let's hear what you have to say."

Wallingford began his well-rehearsed report. "Although the situation at Fort Royal is currently stable, we remain alert to various dangers posed by several hostile groups known to be in the nearby frontier. Whitecoats have been supposedly seen in the area, but I view those reports with some skepticism. We will, however, remain vigilant just in case. Small rogue Indian groups continue to harass homesteads along the outer frontier, but so far they have been more of a bother than a serious threat."

This report was nearly identical to every other report he had delivered since assuming command at Fort Royal. It always included both French and Indian hostility, however vague. It painted the fort as the first line of defense for these western settlements. The general seemed to take the reports at face value, and the captain saw no reason to alter them. With the sole exception of the general's order to 'take Fort Dubois" a year ago he had, for all intents and purposes, ignored the fort and its soldiers. That was fine with Captain Wallingford.

The captain had just begun to report on the recent appearance of a band of outlaws in the area when Audrey Tindale burst into the room. Ignoring the general's clerk and with only a perfunctory bow of her head to the captain, she went immediately to the front of her father's desk – her back to Wallingford - and began complaining, "Father! Have you told him? You'll let me go, won't you Father dear?" Jumping from anger to tears and back again, she went on about – as far as Wallingford could make out – her necessity of travelling to some locale that her mother had apparently vetoed.

Her father attempted to soothe her, but she wouldn't hear him out. Every time she ran out of breath, he would begin to assure her that he would discuss it with her mother; but she never let him finish. He finally got the upper hand when he motioned toward the captain, now standing, behind her, and said, "Audrey dear, you know Captain Wallingford."

She turned toward him and smiled. It made the captain's knees weak. At this proximity she was breathtaking. He hesitated for a moment, collected his breath, and softly said, "Of course, Miss Tindale, how nice to see you again." He had the floor; he wasn't going to surrender it. "I don't wish to intrude, but I'm sure whatever it is that distresses you so, your father will surely make it right." His smile did not have the effect on her that her's had on him.

She bowed slightly to the captain, and turned back to her father. "Of course, Father, I saw him come in." Her smile was gone, and replaced by a scowl.

He spoke before she could, "We'll talk later, my dear, Let me finish talking with the captain." She began to say something, but he beat her to the punch. "Now, now, my dear. I promise I will talk to Mother, and we'll get this all straightened out. You're not to worry." He waited a moment, and then added, "I promise." She stood there looking at him, but not moving. "I assure you that I will talk to Mother. But right now, I have to talk to Captain Wallingford. You go off now, and leave us to get on with our business."

"Thank you, Daddy," she whispered, and after tipping her head once more to the captain she left the room. Both men, for different reasons, watched her leave.

When she was gone the general plopped down in his chair, and let out a long stream of air. Wallingford then also sat down. After a moment the general sat up in his chair, "Where were we? What other business do you have?"

Wallingford saw an opportunity. It was a longshot, but the prize was worth it. "Sir, I don't mean to intrude but, if your daughter needs an escort somewhere into the frontier I would be honored to accompany her." He wished silently that he had known about this disagreement between father and daughter beforehand, and that he had had some time to prepare the wording of his offer so it was more eloquent.

The general glared at him for a moment, and then barked, "No! She's not going anywhere! With you or anyone else!" There was an awkward pause. "What else have you got? I haven't got all day!"

The suddenness of the answer and follow-up question caught Wallingford off guard. He fumbled the papers in his hand, and mumbled something, and then tossed the requisitions onto the general's desk. "I . . . . rather *we* need some re-supplies at the fort, Sir." He began to list some of the items on the pages, but the general was signing them before he finished the thought. Pleasantly surprised at this turn of events, Wallingford shut up.

After signing (without reading) the three pages of requisitions, the general was on his feet. He excused himself as he made his way to the garden door. Almost apologetically he said to the wide-eyed captain, "Sorry I have to rush off, something just came up." He turned to go, but once more addressed the captain, "Come to dinner tonight. Seven sharp." And a moment later was out the door and gone.

Wallingford rose and moved around the desk to collect his requisitions. The general's aide, Lieutenant Crosly, came over to the desk too, and started to tidy up the cluttered desktop. "What just happened," Wallingford couldn't help but ask?

Crosly explained that the preceding scenario was not uncommon in the Tindale household. Miss Tindale was a somewhat willful young lady, he said. She and her mother were frequently at odds over one thing or another. And after each disagreement the daughter would appeal to her father, who always sided with her, and he would overrule the mother. The mother, in turn, upon learning of his decision would storm after her husband, and bellow her disapproval. His hasty departure a few moments ago was his attempt to avoid her wrath.

Wallingford couldn't help but smile. The meeting had been very short. Far shorter than any he could remember. The requisitions were not only signed, but hadn't even been scrutinized! And the topper was he had the invitation to dinner. He thought this couldn't have gone any better. Unknown to him, his opinion was a bit premature.

He brought the supply requests to the Philadelphia quartermaster, and arranged to have them packed off to Fort Royal the following Tuesday. That was more time than the quartermaster needed, but Wallingford wanted a reason to stay in Philadelphia a few more days.

With that done he returned to his quarters. He left his horse at the local stable to be groomed. He had something to eat, and then sent his uniform out to be freshly laundered. His boots were delivered to a shop where there would be polished to a high gleam. He wanted to look his very best tonight. He arranged to have a hot bath ready for him at precisely 5:30 that afternoon. Then he retired to his room for a much needed nap. He had great expectations for what this night may hold in store.

At ten minutes before seven a very polished Captain Phillip Wallingford turned the corner from Front Street onto Walnut. Two blocks in front of him lay the well-lit home of General Tindale. It represented everything Captain Wallingford wanted in life. It was the quarters of the Commanding General. It was large and expensive. It had immaculate, tasteful and expensive furnishings. And, of course, it housed Miss Audrey Tindale.

As he drew nearer he noticed two officers standing at the front door. In a moment the front door opened and they went in. He hoped that whatever their official business was that it would not delay his dinner with the Tindales.

As he neared the entrance to the house he saw three other officers approaching the house from the stable area on the far side. He began to wonder what was going on. Had something occurred that required a sudden meeting of senior staff? He watched as they approached the house. They seemed in no hurry; one even let out a laugh. Wallingford slowed his horse, and allowed them to enter the house before he went up the drive to the stables. He noticed that there were more than 15 horses in the cramped stable.

The walk from the stable to the home's front door, and the wait to be admitted took a few minutes. It allowed him to imagine several scenarios which would explain the appearance of the five officers entering the house. An emergency somewhere in, or around, the Philadelphia area; a staff meeting with the general's adjutant and junior commanders; final preparations for a military mission heading out early tomorrow morning; these and a few others occurred to Wallingford and were quickly dismissed. He hoped that whatever the cause that they did not interfere with his plans for the evening. He even optimistically considered the possibility that perhaps the general might be drawn into this staff meeting, which would result in Wallingford being left alone with the mother and daughter. That, he thought, would be too good to be true.

He was admitted to the house and led into the study where he was stunned to see 12 other officers, and no women, standing around sipping sherry. He swallowed hard and took a deep breath. What the hell is this?

A few of the officers glanced in his direction, and one or two smiled. Wallingford tried very hard to smile back. He gazed around the room trying to recognize anyone he knew. He knew, or could name, perhaps half of them. Lieutenant Crosly, the adjutant, was there. Two captains he knew from previous trips to Philadelphia, Winfield and Belford, smiled and waved. A Major Fitzwalter, an artillery officer who had passed through Fort Royal on his way to Fort Pitt some months ago, just stared at him for a moment, and then looked away. Wallingford remembered that he had gotten him drunk one night during his stopover at Fort Royal, and thoroughly fleeced him while playing whist. There was a Colonel Kenilworth talking with two officers who might be Captains Garwood and McLayne. But Wallingford wasn't sure.

Lieutenant Crosly came over and re-introduced himself. "And you're Captain . . . ," he hesitated for a moment and then said, "Captain Waddington at Fort Royal?"

"Wallingford," the captain corrected.

Lieutenant Crosly suddenly had him by the arm and walked him around the room. "A Captain Wallinfred, in command out at Fort Royal in the far reaches of our western frontier," he said to each officer as he introduced Wallingford. They, in turn, introduced themselves. Wallingford didn't bother to correct Crosly, or remember their names.

After the room-wide tour Wallingford took Crosly off to the side. Exasperated, he said, "What's this all about? I thought I was having a private dinner with the Tindales!"

Crosly smiled, "Oh no, my boy. This will be all officers tonight. No wives . . . no girlfriends . . . no daughters, my friend. The General likes to have his various subordinates over regularly so he can get to know them. And they can get to know him," he paused for a minute, "And they can get to kiss his arse too." Wallingford looked stone-faced back at the smiling Crosly.

An enlisted man stepped into the room unnoticed and sharply called out, "ATTENTION!"

All the men in the room snapped to attention as the general walked in. "Stand easy, men, stand easy," General Tindale said with a laugh. "How are you all? Good to see you. Glad all you gentlemen were able to join us tonight."

"Like we had a choice," several of the officers thought.

"Damn all these officers. Damn this party. And damn General Tindale to the lowest tiers of hell." thought the smiling Captain Wallingford.

At the call for dinner there was a mad dash for the seats next to the General. Wallingford, unaccustomed to the protocols of these soirees, was left in the dust. He sat at the far end of the long dining table unable to hear most of the conversation at the general's end, and uninterested in that small part he could hear. He sat between Captain McLayne and some officer whose mouth was never empty, and therefore Wallingford never got his name. McLayne on the other hand ate very little, and so was able to constantly lean close to Wallingford and breathe into his face. Wallingford tried to remember anything – anything at all – in his entire life that smelled as bad as McLayne's breath. As his mind raced from one despicable possibility to another, he decided the only way to shut McLayne up was to out talk him. He began to pepper him with questions, never allowing him time to answer. McLayne, it turned out, had been stationed in Philadelphia for a long time. He knew a great deal about the city and its environs. Wallingford cut his answers short. He also knew a great deal about the commanding general. Again, Wallingford cut those answers short. But he also knew quite a bit about the General's daughter, and here Wallingford allowed McLayne to say his piece.

Several hours later the group had migrated out into the garden at the rear of the house to enjoy some of the general's port. Wallingford followed McLayne out there, and continued to question him. McLayne, who was more interested in drinking the port than discussing Audrey Tindale any further, had joined a trio of other officers comparing notes on London. Wallingford was standing next to, but not listening to one officer blabber on about some exploit he had had this past winter in London. There was nothing in the tale Wallingford cared one iota about.

Suddenly there was a hand on Wallingford's shoulder. The blabbering officer shut up. Wallingford half turned, "Wallingford! So glad you came." It was the general. Wallingford tried to smile, but just couldn't pull it off. The general went on in almost a whisper, but everyone there heard him, "You and I have some matters to discuss about Major Highcross, don't we? How's he getting on?" After only a momentary pause the general, not waiting for an answer went on. "NO! Not here," he looked around at the other listeners, "I want your candid evaluation of him, and I don't want every person in Philadelphia to know it before Audrey does."

The mention of her name stunned Wallingford. "Audrey" and "Highcross" in the same sentence made no sense to him. Confused, shaken, and wide-eyed he turned to the general and was only able to say, "Excuse me!"

The general, ignoring his response, pulled him away from the group, and whispered in his ear, "Tomorrow morning at seven . . . . at my stables." A moment later he was off and calling out loudly to another officer ten feet away.

Wallingford had lived most of his adult life priding himself on knowing more about what was going on than anyone else in the room. Equally critical to him, in those rare occasions when someone knew more than he did, was to not let them realize it. He had work to do. Who the hell was this Highcross? And why would Audrey want to know Wallingford's evaluation of him? Why would *anyone* want his evaluation? He told himself that he better find out.

He stood off to the side of the garden eyeing the entire group. He would have to sit one of them down and find out all about this Highcross. The party would break up soon; he had to act fast. One by one he scanned the garden. The officer would have to have a position where he was familiar with the officers in Philadelphia. Senior officers couldn't be badgered and wouldn't do. Sober officers wouldn't do. Some of the Captains and lieutenants present had been shy in partaking of the general's alcohol, and had stayed sober. They were eliminated. Clever officers wouldn't do. Lieutenant Crosly was out, and the two newly arrived lieutenants from Boston were too new to know anything. That left only one candidate. Wallingford grabbed McLayne (who was somehow involved with billeting officers in Philadelphia) by the sleeve and said, "Let's go get something really good to drink. I'm buying."

Twenty minutes later Wallingford and McLayne – who had nearly fallen off his horse twice – arrived at a tavern well off the beaten track. McLayne, who had eaten little at tonight's dinner, but had not been shy with the pre-dinner sherry, the wine with dinner, and the post-dinner port, was drunk before he walked in the door. By the time they were ensconced in a booth in a dark corner McLayne was teetering between intoxication and oblivion. Wallingford poured three noggins of rum into McLayne and then began the interrogation.

"Tell me what you know about Highcross," he asked McLayne out of the blue. He had no time to waste.

"Who?"

"Highcross, damnit!" What was he? A major? Yes! "Major Highcross."

"Oh, him!" slurred McLayne. "He's gone!" McLayne smiled, "He's off to the west." He burped, and then added, "Heading out to Fort Royal, I think."

"To Fort Royal? To do what?"

McLayne made a face and said, "I don' feel so good."

The questioning by Wallingford came too fast for McLayne, he tried to keep up but it was a lost cause. There were questions about what mission Highcross had. He didn't know. What was his connection to Audrey Tindale?

"Who?" he asked. Wallingford had to ask that question three times before it registered in McLayne's mind. With the biggest sloppy grin McLayne could muster he answered, "I *think* she loves him."

"What? She loves who? Highcross?" The answers Wallingford was getting weren't answering the questions he asked. McLayne, by this time was having trouble staying upright. He held his rum in his right hand and the table with his left. One more drink and that one hand wouldn't be enough.

Another ten minutes of badgering by Wallingford produced no further information. All he knew was that Highcross was a major, and was in transit through Philadelphia to his new post. But which fort that was to be was still up in the air. McLayne changed his answer every time Wallingford asked him. The answers were Royal, Pitt, Venango, or "that other one". He knew nothing of Highcross personally. Attempts by Wallingford to get McLayne to elaborate were fruitless. To his dismay it was clear to Wallingford that it was pointless to go on. Wallingford went to the bar and ordered two more noggins of rum for the table, and then told the barman he was going outside to relieve himself. Once outside he mounted his horse and left. He left the two noggins, the barman, the bar bill and the unconscious McLayne to work it all out.

This night had fallen far short of his expectations. Tomorrow morning . . . early tomorrow morning . . . he was to meet with the general on a topic he knew nothing about. Who was this Highcross? Where was he going? Why did Tindale want to talk to me about him? And before he went to sleep that night he wondered again about what McLayne had said about Audrey Tindale being in love with this Highcross fellow. "By God, I'll put an end to that!" he vowed.

Chapter 7 – The Expedition's Final Preparations

You cannot fool a fooler,
'Specially the female kind.
They're simply far more clever,
And possess a sharper mind.

You set the stage – plot laid out,
And your plan is well designed.
You place the bait – you spring the trap,
But find you've been left behind.

When the shooting match on Amos Fitch's field had concluded each of the five pilgrims still had final preparations to make for their trip. They each made their way back to the settlement, as Private Selkirk watched them from the rear. He was watching everything they did. He was being paid to do so.

Very few of the things that occurred around Mrs. Devonshire escaped her notice. When she had been sequestered into the Bardley residence upon her arrival her suspicions were immediately aroused. And those suspicions rose higher when she was advised at breakfast the following morning that her recent travelling companions had already departed the settlement without her. She immediately realized she was, in effect, stranded. She was also told that Captain Wallingford had departed the settlement, and had gone back east to tend to some official business. She idly asked what that business was. She wanted to gauge their reaction. The Bardleys, talking over each other, said they had absolutely no idea. Mr. Bardley also told her that a Lieutenant Smith would be her escort "*every time* you leave this house". He said the area was fraught with danger, and it was Captain Wallingford's strict orders that she not ever go out alone. "Ever!" he repeated. She responded that she wasn't afraid, and did not want to be a bother to anyone. And most assuredly did not want to be a burden to the officer, who probably had many more important duties to attend to than watching over her. Again, she was looking for the reaction. Mr. Bardley raised his voice and nearly stood up. "Mrs. Devonshire, I must insist! Under no circumstances are you to leave this house alone." The lady smiled demurely, nodded her assent, and thought to herself that this appeared to be very much like she was under arrest. From that moment on she began making plans.

In the days that followed Mrs. Devonshire was unfailingly escorted by the physically, and socially, awkward Lieutenant Smith whenever she left the Bardley home. He must have slept on the front porch, because he was invariably there whenever she went out the front door. The Bardleys would race to the front window to check on his presence whenever she would mention that she was going to go outside. Captain Wallingford had warned Josiah Bardley that his share of the reward would depend on it; and Josiah, in turn, had informed his wife and house servants that if they didn't also watch her that the consequences would be very severe. He did not, however, explain why.

The captain had been very explicit in his instructions to Lieutenant Smith. He was, first and foremost, to be her constant companion whenever she left the Bardley house. "Morning, noon, or night! Don't allow the local riff-raff to bother her." the captain had said. He was thinking of Selkirk. "Mr. Bardley will see to her meals. Keep her out of Philyaw's. As a matter of fact keep everyone away from her. I don't want anyone bothering her. Do you understand?" That was all; it was clear and concise. The captain thought that even Lieutenant Smith would be able to handle that kind of instruction.

Lieutenant Smith had been at this post for over 12 years. His first commanding officer had been Captain Weeber, a kindly old officer who accepted Lieutenant Smith for what he was; and recognized immediately what he was not. Captain Weeber required little assistance from the junior officer in running this small detachment, and left him to his own devices. Lieutenant Smith had always assumed when he was an enlisted man that officers didn't really do anything, so, upon becoming a lieutenant, this ample free time was not the least bit surprising. Free from any official duties he wandered alone around the Fort Royal area learning (mostly through trial and error – a lot of error) everything he could about this forested wilderness.

After Captain Weeber left to return to England, and Captain Wallingford replaced him, the lieutenant's "duties" changed very little. Even when Captain Wallingford left on trips back to New York (or Philadelphia – Smith could never get that straight) every few months, this never posed a problem because Sergeant Kennedy was there. Sergeant Kennedy was an experienced non-commissioned officer who ran the troops and official business of the post in the name of Lieutenant Smith. Each time, before leaving, the captain would sit the lieutenant down, and tell him, "Although you are the commanding officer, Sergeant Kennedy will be in charge. You don't have to do anything, or say anything. Sergeant Kennedy will. Do you understand?"

This formality took place prior to every trip back east the captain took. When Sergeant Kennedy retired to his farm, nothing changed except the identity of the man in charge. Captain Wallingford instructed Smith that Private Selkirk was the 'temporary sergeant in charge' whenever he was away. The change didn't seem to affect Lieutenant Smith's life one iota. He continued his daily wanderings around the forests and meadows of the Fort Royal area without interruption.

The escorting duties of Mrs. Devonshire were the first responsibilities he had been assigned in a very long time. He had almost forgotten what it was like to be an officer. The night he had been instructed by the captain what his duties were to be he raced back to his quarters to clean his boots and uniform. He didn't wear them regularly on his jaunts into the countryside. His sword, not having seen the light of day for many months, had become stuck in its scabbard, and took quite an effort by him to get it to come out.

Over the next few days some people at the settlement, seeing him in uniform for the first time, didn't recognize him. He was as proud as a peacock walking around, in uniform, with the lovely Mrs. Devonshire at his side.

This escorting was not even a mild hindrance to the lady. It was, in fact, beneficial. She wandered around the settlement every day asking Lieutenant Smith questions about everybody and everything. The second day he was escorting her she asked him where the captain was.

"He went to New York (I think) to get us some supplies."

"Why New York?' She wasn't sure why, but that seemed odd to her. "Why not Philadelphia? It's closer."

"I don't know. We get stuff from both places sometimes. I can never figure it out." He remained quiet for a minute, trying to figure it out. "Maybe New York has cannons, and Philadelphia don't."

"That's what he's getting? Cannons?"

"Not cannons. Just one. One cannon. To replace the one we lost."

She had been only paying slight attention to him until he said that. "You lost a cannon? How does one *lose* a cannon?"

"I didn't lose it! I wasn't even there." He tried to explain. "The captain lost it."

She really didn't know the captain very well, having only been with him that one day when she arrived, but he didn't seem like the kind of man who would be that careless. "How, in the name of God, did he lose it? It is not the sort of the thing one misplaces!"

"Oh he didn't lose it like that. It blew up. At least I think that's what happened. He never wanted to talk about it. I think he felt really bad. We all did. Told me never to talk about it. No one was allowed to talk about it." Lieutenant Smith then proceeded to tell Mrs. Devonshire everything he knew about their old cannon. For nearly an hour he regaled her with stories he had heard about the prowess of their now departed piece of artillery. She was only half listening when he said, "Some of the guys said they could fire that six pounder time, and time, and time again …. As fast as you could load her …. 20 times …. She'd get hotter than a stove in January . .

. and all you had to do was sponge her down and she'd be ready to go."

The lady murmured to no one in particular, "I knew an old whore in Paris like that."

The combination of her soft voice and not hearing exactly what she said derailed the lieutenant's train of thought. He went off on another topic. Lieutenant Smith knew all about everybody and everything at Fort Royal. He had been here a long time. And he wasn't the least bit reluctant about sharing it with the newcomer. He thought he was being helpful, and following the captain's orders exactly. This was the most fun he had had since being assigned here. It just might be the most fun he could remember ever having! But, at the end, it went terribly wrong for him.

He had wanted to go see the shooting match that everyone in town was talking about. But the mademoiselle did not want to go, and stayed inside the Bardley home at the scheduled time. He didn't dare leave his post outside. So he sat forlornly on the front steps as people from the settlement wandered by on their way up to Fitch's field to witness the contest. A little while later he heard shots fired that told him the contest had begun. Now he waited impatiently by the street for the people to return and tell him what went on. He craned his neck to see any signs of them. He wanted to race up the street, but dared not to leave his post.

An hour or so later, when people finally began streaming back into town he questioned every one of them. Who won? Who lost? How many shots? Where did the winning shot hit? How close? Any miss? He was unable to get his fill of the results. Some people ignored him. Some others stopped and talked with the animated lieutenant

At the end of the procession he saw Private Selkirk walking alone. And as he approached Smith he, unlike all the other people in the procession, turned into the walkway leading up to the Bardley front door. He nodded toward the lieutenant as he walked past him, went up the steps to the door and knocked. A moment later he was granted admission into the house and disappeared.

Mrs. Devonshire had been at the front window shortly after the shots were heard. She waited for Selkirk to knock before opening the door. She led him up to her sitting room, and closed the door behind them. Mrs. Bardley did not like the thought that 'the French tart' was entertaining men in the house. She would not have permitted it if she had her way, but the mademoiselle had rudely shut the door in her face when this same man had visited yesterday. He was one of the soldiers at the fort, and Mrs. Bardley had every intention of bringing this up with Captain Wallingford when he returned. This man and woman would answer to the captain for their rudeness. Who, she was sure, would see it her way.

Inside the sitting room Mrs. Devonshire sat primly in the chair in the corner, her ankles crossed; her hands were folded in her lap, holding a small knitted bag. On the table next to her were a half-filled decanter and a small glass filled with an amber liquid. She took a sip and nearly shuddered at the taste. It was almost undrinkable. She thought to herself that she would be willing to slit the throats of ten kittens for a decent bottle of genuine French wine. "Gonna offer me a bit of that fine brandy, Miss?" asked Selkirk. He was guessing what it was.

She looked at him oddly and simply said, "No."

Selkirk shuffled his feet as he stood just inside the doorway. "Mind if I take a seat then, mademoiselle? Been on my feet all day,"

"Yes, I do. Stay where you are. What happened at the match?"

Selkirk, slightly peeved at not being allowed to drink or sit, remained quiet for a moment. He just looked blankly at her face. "She was a pretty one all right," he thought. But this thought disappeared quickly as he began to notice her piercing eyes. Those eyes, and now the expressionless face, started to give him a very uneasy feeling. He looked away from her and gazed around the room. "So this here is your – what they call – your boood-wah?" He looked back at her and smiled.

She didn't flinch. She looked straight back at him and barely moving her thin lips hissed, "I am not English. I do not sleep on a chair. Or the floor. I am French. I sleep in a bed. Do you see a bed? This is not, as you say, my boood-wah. " She let the harshness of her words sink in for a moment, and then repeated, "What happened at the shooting contest?"

"First, let's get the payment out of the way. I think you said you'd give me a gold coin. Let's see it."

"There was no mention of a gold coin. I said if you tell me what I want to know there may be half a crown – a silver coin – in it for you. And that's more than you see in a month, I would wager." Again there was no smile. She continued, "But if you going to be obstinate, I suppose I could ask one of the 30, or 40 other people who were there these same questions, and give them the coin. And you can get nothing! Decide quickly, I have things to do."

"Let's see your money first. I don't think I trust you either."

She moved her hands and opened the small bag in her lap. She put her right hand into the bag, and felt around for the coin in the bottom. In the bag also was what is called a "Queen Anne gun", or a pocket pistol. She was not someone who took unnecessary chances. She found the coin and took it out to show Selkirk. He looked at the coin, and then back at her face. He never noticed that she had now placed her other hand in the bag.

In his mind he thought that he could take the coin away from her without too much trouble, but she would likely scream her head off. There were probably other people in the house who would hear her, and possibly interfere, including that damn old Mrs. Bardley. He decided that he would tell her what went on and then take his money and go.

Their conversation didn't last very long. He gave a fairly complete recap of what had occurred, and she asked several questions about it. She also wanted his impressions of the people who competed. What kind of people were they? She seemed to be most interested in the major. She also asked one question about Kelly's Crossing. When all was said and done, she tossed him the coin, and told him, "Get out." He didn't say "Thank you", and left. He passed Lieutenant Smith, without a comment, in the front yard when he left.

He sat in Philyaw's drinking whiskey for the rest of the afternoon getting progressively drunker. If he had wondered for even a minute that afternoon why she had wanted him to spy for her, he wouldn't remember the next day.

The night of the shooting match Tyson and the major had dinner at Philyaw's. They had spent the last three hours packing, and re-packing, Tyson's wagon. The major thought they were finished several times when Tyson would say he wasn't satisfied with how it was balanced. And they did it all over again when Sho-Taka and Shea appeared with their baggage. Sho-Taka had far more than then they expected him to bring for such a trip. Sho-Taka's included two large barrels apparently filled, because they were heavy. He also had a trunk and several boxes. He avoided answering questions about what they held. If there hadn't been plenty of room in the large wagon it might have been an issue. Shea's baggage included only two bags. One was large, and the other small. By their heft Tyson thought that they contained mostly clothes.

The two men relaxed after their dinner, sitting on the wagon. They planned to spend the night at the wagon that was going to be their home for the near future. It was filled with all their earthly possessions, and needed to be guarded, and that would also allow them an early getaway in the morning. They were leaving at first light, and had strongly advised their companions not to be late. With or without Shea and Sho-Taka they were leaving before the roosters crowed in the morning. Tyson and the major stared up at the early stars and were both glad knowing that tomorrow they would start on the final leg of their journey. Both had begun their trips from different points, and at different times. And in varying degrees both had been hard and long. But both men were confident that they would find, at the end of the road that it had been well worth the hardships they had endured. They both breathed deeply, and relaxed in the cool night air.

The same could not be said for their traveling companions. Those three, each in their own way, were stressed. Right after the shooting match had ended, Falwyn disappeared. He had been advised that Ludlum was looking for him, and that might mean several different things. Falwyn didn't think any of the possibilities would be pleasant. He was right.

Ludlum had inexplicably advanced some salary to Falwyn in anticipation that he would do some menial tasks around the stable. Now Ludlum had learned that Falwyn was preparing to leave for an undetermined period of time, and those tasks had not even been started. By Ludlum's reckoning Falwyn had all afternoon and evening to finish mucking out the stables, and cleaning up the neglected corrals. This did not sound unreasonable to Ludlum.

Falwyn, on the other hand, saw it differently. He was going off in the morning into the wilderness. There he would face unknown danger from the perils of traveling in unexplored territory, from nature, from fierce animals, from uncounted hostile Indians. And even he didn't know how long it would take. This trip to Dubious may take a week . . . or a month . . . or, whatever? Who knows when I will once again return to the safety and warmth of my home and hearth? (Not for an instant did Falwyn realize that the 'hearth' he was referring to was a stall in Ludlum's stable.) Besides, he reasoned, I've got other more important things to do with my time right now. "I have to get over to the fort right now, and talk to someone there who might be able to give me some very important information." He was about to guide his four companions on a 200(?) mile trip into the wilderness. "Hell, it could be 300 miles!" he whispered. He would be the one to lead them. They would be entrusting him with their lives as they headed off to Dubious. And he had no idea where it was.

Sho-Taka knew all too well that a conversation with Philyaw would not be pleasant. He had every intention of avoiding it. It certainly hadn't been him who let it be known he was leaving with the major's party. The minute Philyaw found out he was furious. "Where in hell am I goin' to git my whiskey"? Philyaw didn't wait for an answer. "With you off wanderin' around those godforsaken woods behind .... OF ALL PEOPLE ...." He shouted, "FALWYN!"

He paused a minute to catch his breath, "Ya gotta better chance of findin' King George out there with that twit leadin' the way!" Philyaw shook his head in disgust.

"I brewed you a batch a week ago. It's not like I am leaving you without any."

Philyaw wasn't listening to him. "You could be out there for six months with that little shit guidin' yer around. Hell, you might never get back at all!" This was a real possibility in Philyaw's eyes.

Sho-Taka knew, of course, that Philyaw's concern had nothing to do with his well-being, but rather that he was important to Philyaw for one reason and one reason only. "Where in hell am I goin' to get my whiskey?"

"If I don't come back, you can always go back to getting your supply from Moore's Station, like before."

"Have ya lost yer senses? Drink that piss? And he charges me twice what you do. And it's piss! Did I tell yer that?" He was distraught.

This week had started out so well for Philyaw he had almost smiled. The new barmaid, Shea, was pretty to look at, and was cheap to pay. His wife was staying home while Shea was around from sunup to closing time. Sho-Taka had delivered another batch of whiskey to him that his customers liked so much he was able to raise the price again. And Captain Wallingford was still oblivious that the majority of the whiskey Philyaw sold was supplied by Sho-Taka, and not the "watered down piss" he got from Moore's Station, and Wallingford taxed. And this same Captain Wallingford, currently in Philadelphia, was ordering a supply of brandy and wine for him. And, even after Wallingford's commission, he ought to make a very handsome profit on that when it arrived. Things were really going good for him. And then this major showed up and said he was heading out to Dubious. Philyaw couldn't have cared less about that. And it also didn't bother him very much when he learned that he was taking that Virginian and Falwyn too. But then Shea quits! And to top it all, Sho-Taka decides to go too. "This week has turned into pure hell fer me," he moaned to Sho-Taka. Sho-Taka almost felt sorry for him.

The source of Shea's stress wasn't coming from somebody else. It was coming from inside. This trip to see her father was something she had promised herself to do. Her mother had tried to convince her it was a fool's errand. Shea had left New Jersey two months ago, and it had been a tearful departure. She wondered now if that had been a mistake. She sat now wondering if she would ever see her mother again. She knew it wasn't likely if things worked out as she planned.

Mrs. Delilah Devonshire was also very busy. After Selkirk had left, she spent the next two hours in her room. She told the Bardleys she had napped. But Mrs. Bardley knew that wasn't true. She had put her ear to the door and heard her moving around in her room the entire time. Then Mrs. Devonshire had told them that she was going out for some air. They, of course, raced to the front window to make certain that Lieutenant Smith was there for escort duty. They watched as the lieutenant and Devonshire walked off in the afternoon light. When she returned several hours later she told them that she had probably overdone it. After she ate a light supper, she told them that she was dreadfully tired and was going to go to bed early. Before going up she asked if they'd excuse her if she slept late in the morning. She asked that she not be disturbed until 'at the earliest, lunchtime'! The Bardleys said that they understood, and wished her a restful night. Before disappearing up the stairs she simply said, "Au revoir."

Chapter 8 - The (Bumpy) Road Begins

A journey of one thousand miles;
It begins with just one step.
And though that makes it sound shorter,
Man! That is a real long schlep!
But don't let all this deter you,
Cause fortune favors the bold.
(But taking risky trips like this,
It's unlikely you'll get old.)

In what was considered by one and all as a good omen the expedition of the five pilgrims started before dawn. Highcross and Tyson had been up and puttering around the wagon when Shea arrived. She hadn't slept very well, and finally gave up trying. She got up, dressed and ate some leftover porridge with tea, and headed off to where the wagon was.

It took Sho-Taka only a short time to figure out where Falwyn would have spent the night. It couldn't be far from Philyaw's, where he had consumed far more alcohol than he could handle, and therefore would be incapable of going very far. And despite being totally inebriated, he would choose a spot that was covered. He preferred his sleep uninterrupted by weather or humans. A lean-to shed at the rear of Ludlum's was perfect. Falwyn, using foresight that was somewhat rare for him, had put his bag of belongings in the lean-to earlier in the evening. It was next to him when Sho-Taka found him. Giving a nearby parading rooster a wide berth, Sho-Taka collected the barely conscious Falwyn and proceeded to the rendezvous.

Opening the gate the procession advanced out into the street. Major Aaron Highcross walked in the front. He was dressed in full uniform. His brilliant red coat was outlined by snow white sashes and pants. His boots were a contrasting black, as was his hat. One of his prized pistols was proudly displayed in his belt, and his highly polished sword hung at his side. He would have greatly preferred riding his horse, but Tyson had insisted that the mount was needed to help pull the wagon. With every ounce of dignity he possessed he walked, or rather marched, out with all the military bearing he could muster. Bolt upright, and alternating his glance from left to right and back again, he moved on with perfect military precision. It was if he were leading a coronation parade. And because it was so early there wasn't a single soul on either sidewalk to see.

Behind him shuffled Falwyn, still half asleep. He had lobbied the others to allow him to ride in the wagon, where he intended to instantly fall asleep. He request was vetoed because there was room for only two riders on the wagon. Tyson would drive it, and the lady, Shea, would be allowed to ride. Besides no one wanted to sit close to Falwyn who had not bathed nor changed clothes.

Sho-Taka walked alongside (up wind from) Falwyn, and he was smiling. He was glad to be leaving Fort Royal. It had never held any special hold on him. To him it was just another unwanted European incursion on what he felt was rightfully Indian homeland. Besides Falwyn's grumbling there wasn't any talking.

The wagon was last in line. It was pulled by the two horses owned by Tyson and the major. A cow was tethered to the rear. A crate, with a wire mesh top, contained a few chickens and a rooster and sat on top of all the earthly possessions of both Tyson and Major Highcross, as well as the baggage of Sho-Taka, Shea and Falwyn. Besides the heavy footsteps of the horses and the cow, the chickens made the only noises. Neither Tyson nor Shea knew how to start the conversation.

The group went through the town before almost anyone was up. They went south along the road by the river nearly a mile before arriving at Kelly's Crossing. A ferry there would take them across the Susquehanna River, and there they would begin the journey southwest toward Dubious, and further on, Kan-tucky.

The sun was barely above the horizon when they approached the riverbank at Kelly's. The ferry was tied fast to a tree at water's edge. Gideon Kelly sat on a tree stump a few feet away.

"Mornin," he said when they stopped in front of him. The travelers returned the greeting. With no more conversation they began to board the ferry that would take them across. The horses required some encouragement to get on the slightly unstable ferry, and the wagon needed some pushing to raise the wheels up on to it; but it was all done in a short time. The wagon was fastened to the side rails to prevent it from shifting on the trip across the water, and the horses were held at their bridle to keep them from being skittish.

Kelly went about his business of getting them across the river without saying very much. He was preoccupied with watching how the ferry managed the current, and how hard he had to work pulling the craft across the moving water by a rope. Without being asked Tyson started helping him with the rope. Not too much later the major and Sho-Taka also pitched in. It wasn't so much they wanted to ease his burden, but the sooner they reached the far shore, and got back on solid ground, the better.

The gesture was appreciated by the boatman and may have contributed to his offering a word of advice. "You folks heading out into some wild country," he said. "You best be on your guard."

Highcross responded, "We'll keep on the lookout for trouble. Thank you."

"Brought someone over last night. Woke me up in the middle of the night. Paid me extra! Said he had to cross over right away, couldn't wait." He didn't mention that he charged the single, impatient rider as much to cross over as he charged their group. "Gonna be a little out in front of you. You just might wanna be on the lookout. Highwaymen like to fall on unsuspecting folks, you know."

"You brought someone over? Last night?" asked the major. "Where did they say they were going?"

"What did they look like?"

"Not 'they'. Just one! Never got a good look at him, though. He was wearing a cloak, and a hat pulled down over his face. Kinda on the small side; but that don't mean he can't be trouble." He continued to struggle with pulling the rope.

"One person," smiled the major. "I think we five can handle that sort of thing."

"Pays to be careful. All the same," said Kelly.

"Where did he say he was heading," Sho-Taka asked.

"Didn't say,' answered the ferryman. "Matter a fact, 'bout the only thing he said besides 'I gotta go right now', was 'How much?'." He paused for a minute, resting his arms, then added, "Gotta watch those quiet ones, ya know."

Little else was said as the ferry reached the far shore. It was unloaded quickly as the party of five thanked Kelly, and received his "good luck" in return. They resumed their trip southwest and as quiet as the trip had started, their conversation soon perked up about that pilgrim out in front of them. Each one of them speculated as to whom it might be, and what motivated the stranger to travel alone. There were plenty of suggestions about how best to deal with any confrontations, should it come to that.

Tyson suggested that Falwyn travel out in front of the group by a half mile, or so, to scout out the terrain. "What? By myself?" asked the wide-eyed unbelieving Falwyn.

"I'll go with you," said Sho-Taka.

Tyson noticed right away that Sho-Taka carried no firearm.. "You better take a weapon," he suggested.

Falwyn didn't like the sound of that. "Why? You think there's somebody out there?"

"We know there's somebody out in front of us. I just think Sho-Taka ought to be careful," Tyson explained.

"Falwyn is armed. I should be all right." Sho-Taka answered. Falwyn carried a musket that appeared to be in very poor condition. There were rust spots in several places on it. Tyson took one look at it and doubted it would fire. Sho-Taka seemed to be quite unconcerned with having his safety guaranteed by Falwyn's weapon. The others all had their doubts, but said nothing.

After a few more minutes of coaxing and insistence by the others Falwyn, with Sho-Taka by his side, moved off in front to lead the way. The 'half mile' suggestion was dismissed by Falwyn right away. His caution prompted him to take small and infrequent steps which resulted in him never being more than 100 yards in front of the slow moving wagon.

Several nerve wracking (for Falwyn) hours later they decided to stop for lunch. As they gathered around the wagon and began eating the small bits of chicken and deer jerky they had brought, Falwyn started wondering out loud about whose turn it would be to be out front when they resumed their journey. It seems he failed to realize that as the guide he was expected to lead the way . . . out front . . . all the time. He disagreed, and felt it was unfair that this burden fell solely on him. Despite the concerted efforts of his four fellow travelers he could not make the connection between being the guide and leading.

When they moved out again, Falwyn and Sho-Taka once more led the way. The major walked between them and the wagon, with Tyson and Shea riding in it. It was a beautiful spring day as the group moved through the countryside. Falwyn was cautious and fearful of any motion or sound he detected. Sho-Taka walked beside him enjoying the view and the weather. Fifty paces behind them the major was so caught up in the beauty around him he was oblivious to everything else. Meanwhile Shea and Tyson began a conversation filled with fits and starts. There were abbreviated references to their past and their families. Tyson seemed more willing to discuss his reason for taking this trip than Shea was. He was excited about establishing his own homestead in the far frontier. His sense of enthusiasm and purpose was not lost on Shea. She wished she had it.

An hour later, during one of the many periods of silence, Tyson suddenly pulled back the reins of the horses and stopped them. With his hand he motioned Shea to be silent. He stared out to the front of him, concentrating very hard. Then he suddenly looked off to the right. She alternated looking at him, then off to the right. She didn't see anything of note.

"What," she whispered?

"Quiet!"

She continued looking to the right, and then back at him. He finally shook his head and turned his eyes back to the trail. He snapped the reins once more to get the horses moving again, and said, "There was something moving out there. Probably a deer."

The conversation between Shea and Tyson petered out as Shea began to notice that he seemed preoccupied with the little noises that came from out of the woods around him. He tried to make sense of every one of them. He turned his head from side to side as the noises came out from the dense foliage on either side of the path they travelled. Not as experienced as he was, she thought the sounds were indistinguishable. He began turning around and looking behind them every few minutes. She began to get nervous, but said nothing.

"You can handle the reins, can't you?" he asked after twenty minutes of silence. She nodded she could. "After we pass that bend up ahead on the right, I am going to jump off. Take the reins, and keep the horses moving. Not any faster . . . not any slower. Just keep going. Don't turn around and look for me. Don't wait for me, I'll catch up."

After passing that bend Tyson handed the reins to Shea and reached down to pick up his rifle. She took the reins, and shook them twice on the horses' rumps. Without a word Tyson leapt down off the wagon and moved into the bushes off to the side. She didn't turn her head, but watched him from the corner of her eye until he was out of her sight. She listened for him, but heard only the clicks, and taps, and knocks, and occasional bird trilling that she had been hearing all morning.

He moved off into the thick woods to the side of the trail. He began calculating what he may be up against. A large number would have made more noise; he thought their stalkers numbered maybe two, or three at most. Although he conceded that experienced woodsmen or Indians could be quiet, the woods were too thick to move through silently. Whoever was behind him was most likely taking the quieter route, and that meant they were following them on the trail. He moved slowly through the woods himself to a concealed spot that offered him a good view of the trail, as well as the woods around him.

He thought about how he would confront them when the time arrived. He thought it best to allow them to go on by, and then come up at them from their rear. He wondered if he should have included the rest of party in his ambush. He thought that if the stalkers had seen him drop off the wagon they would be circling him now. While he remained motionless in a thicket, his eyes raced back and forth over the surrounding terrain. The small forest noises continued at irregular intervals. He didn't think he would have to wait too long before his suspicions would be confirmed.

He heard them yelling his name long before he saw them. When he first heard it he thought it was the stalkers doing the yelling. That confused him. Then he realized that the calls came from in front, not behind. The major came stomping up the path from where the wagon had just recently disappeared.

"TYSON!" shouted the major.

"HEY, TYSON, WHERE IN HELL ARE YA?" called Falwyn as he followed the major up the trail.

With his ambush plan of the stalkers now wrecked, he showed himself to his friends. A few minutes later he finished explaining what he had heard and had attempted to do. The others doubted him at first, but then as belief crept in, so did fear.

There wasn't much conversation the rest of the day. Each pilgrim tried very hard to listen for any sounds of the stalkers. And, not surprisingly, each heard very suspicious sounds all afternoon. It only got worse as they made camp for the night, and it grew darker. Little was said as they ate dinner, and made plans for them to take turns remaining awake during the night on guard duty.

Falwyn asked Tyson, while looking all around, "How many do you think there are out there?"

"One, maybe two," Tyson said.

"Only one? One against five shouldn't worry us so much," said Shea.

"One or two," corrected Tyson. "And there may be more on the way."

Falwyn was still turning his head left and right, scanning the surrounding woods. "Why do ya think there's only two?"

"If there were more, they'd be making more noise."

"When do you think they'll attack?" the Major asked.

"I expect they are waiting to meet up with more of their gang. Even up the odds a little. And maybe they want us to get a little further away from the Fort Royal settlement, or have us move a little further on to a place that makes a better ambush site for them." He shrugged and added, "Who knows?"

"So you don't think that they'll attack tonight? Tomorrow then? Tomorrow night?" The major was now scanning the woods that surrounded them, as was Falwyn.

Before Tyson could answer Falwyn suggested, "Maybe we oughta turn back. They won't expect that." Turning back would not only relieve the prospect of them being ambushed, but would also relieve him of the responsibility of leading them on, blindly, to Dubious.

Sho-Taka and Shea, who so far had said nothing, were thinking that the suggestion might have some merit. But then the major blurted out, "No! We can't turn around and go back. I'm pressing on. You're all welcome to join me." Tyson and Shea quickly decided that that was what they wanted to do too. Sho-Taka made his decision to continue on only a moment later. Falwyn had no choice but to join them. It was not what he wanted to do. Several times before they bedded down for sleep Falwyn warned that they would regret not turning back. No one agreed with him, out loud. And no one slept very well that night, either.

The following morning – daybreak – couldn't have come too early for the five of them. The onset of daylight was greeted like it was Christmas morn. They busied themselves with little chores, which granted them a welcome respite from the fitful sleep of last night. Breakfast was over quickly, and they were soon on their way. It occurred to them one by one that their haste in pushing on did not mean leaving their troubles behind. No, they imagined that their troubles were probably trailing along right behind them.

The possibility of an ambush was real to all of them. While some considered it a somewhat remote possibility, others thought it only moments away. Whichever way they felt it caused them all to alter the way they proceeded. First of all, they stayed closer to the wagon as they walked. A very reluctant and hesitant Falwyn led but only by a few feet in front of the horses. Sho-Taka, Tyson, and the major took turns walking alongside of him. Everyone carried their loaded gun with them at all times. Conversation between them was sporadic and brief. They remained alert to the sounds around them. Whenever any one of them gave a start, especially Tyson, they all froze.

Back in the wagon Shea handled the reins, and remained alert to the surroundings too. When the major joined her in the wagon he tried to make conversation, but she remained preoccupied with the woods around them. It was a harrowing morning.

The afternoon was only slightly better. The constant state of anxiety and nervousness caused by the claustrophobic forest weighted heavily on each one of them, and was only alleviated by occasional bursts through open country. A squeak developed in one of the wagon wheels and it created far more jagged nerves than its volume warranted.

Selection of a campsite for the night required a great deal more consideration by them all than it had the day before. The first, suggested by Tyson, was dismissed out of hand. They continued moving on, suggesting and dismissing one site after another.

"Too open."

"Too confined."

"We should be closer to the water."

"We should have some cover closer to us."

"That little ravine is too close. Someone could sneak along in there, and be on us before we knew it."

It seemed everyone was fast becoming an expert in the art of defensive tactics. After the sixth or seventh veto, the major raised his voice, "I'm in command here. This is my party. I'll decide." He shot several glances over at Tyson while he spoke. "Tyson, you've told me you've made several expeditions with the militia before; I'd be interested in knowing what you think of . . . of that spot there?" He pointed off to a small pond in front of them.

"Well," said Tyson, "That's a pretty good one there, major. But if I can, I suggest we head on over to the other side of the pond, where there's a clearing. It's wide open. It makes no sense us trying to hide ourselves. If there's someone following us they know where we are. So if we set up on the other side, we'll have the water protecting our back, and a clearing out in front." That made a lot of sense to Highcross, and he nodded.

It apparently made sense to the others too, because they all quickly approved. Tyson led the horses into the open field so they could graze. He was uncomfortable out in the clearing, and kept moving around. As the horses grazed he continually tried to keep them between him and the nearest woods. As Sho-Taka and Falwyn gathered up some wood for the fire, they did not venture too far into the woods; they also kept the campsite and each other in view. The major unloaded some essentials from the wagon, and again tried to engage Shea in conversation. For the most part, Shea ignored him. Besides, she had her hands full preparing the meal, and like the others, she was also concerned with the possible threat of the stalkers.

"It was a spice of some kind. I don't remember what it was, but she used to put it on beef when she roasted it – not that we had beef that often when I was a child – but Good God! It was delicious," the major rambled. "God bless her, she could cook."

Shea suddenly realized the major was still talking, and still talking about food. He had been since they stopped for the night. She turned toward him and asked, "Who?"

The major was startled by the question because he didn't think she was actually listening to him. "My mother! God bless her."

"She put spice on roasted beef?"

Again surprised by the question, the major paused before answering, "She put spice on everything!" He thought over his answer, and then corrected himself, "Well, she *flavored* everything. She had a way in the kitchen. She could make a piece of wood taste like a cherry tart." He smiled broadly.

"She liked to cook?"

Inspired by a seemingly earnest question the major took off, "Oh, very much so! Why she would spend the entire day in her kitchen making up things for the entire village. And they would come around and buy up everything she had." He nodded in agreement with himself. "Kept the wolf from the door with her cooking, she did. We weren't living like the lord of the manor, mind you. But we had a roof over our heads, and food in the larder. Thank God for that, what with my father gone to his final reward when I was just a babe, and all. No, her talents in the kitchen kept us from the poor house."

The exuberance of the major surprised Shea. She hadn't seen this side of him before. Her occasional past experiences with British officers had not left many pleasant memories. Her initial reaction when seeing a man in uniform was to go the other way. She painted them all with a broad brush. Her most recent encounter with the military was with Captain Wallingford at Fort Royal, and she had heard that it was wise for young ladies to give him a very wide berth. Major Highcross had seemed more reserved than arrogant since she had made his acquaintance, and his interest in cooking was, to her, totally out of character for a male, especially a military officer. "Was he just trying to make conversation," she thought. She was about to ask about the 'spice' used on the beef, when the major tripped over an exposed root, and fell. He and the pot he was carrying made a loud noise when they hit the ground. Everyone came running.

The false alarm of the major's fall, the tasty dinner of carrots, sweet potatoes and venison, and the surprise cup of hard cider provided by Sho-Taka combined to allow them all to relax. And because no one had thought they had heard anything suspicious in several hours, they began to unwind. They sat around the fire enjoying their dinner and the fading daylight. The conversation was dominated by the major, who again discussed his mother's cooking ability. He spoke knowingly and Shea was fascinated by it. She asked question after question about technique, ingredients, and varieties. And to everyone's surprise the major was able to answer them all. He had apparently learned quite a bit at his mother's knee.

During the course of the conversation Shea casually advised them that their supply of meat was starting to run low, and they would have to do some hunting soon. They agreed that they had seen some deer and wild turkeys along the way. Falwyn said he had seen many rabbits; Tyson mentioned he had seen some bear tracks. They weren't fresh, he said, but there were surely bears around. In fact they agreed there was probably plenty of game around them, and no one thought it would be too difficult to shoot something the next day.

"We'll have to go in two's," the major said.

Tyson misunderstood what the major meant, "If we have to, okay, but off in different directions. If we all cluster together we'll make too much noise." Then it suddenly occurred to him that the major had meant 'in pairs'. "Why do we have to 'go in two's?"

"There's more than game out in those woods," the major whispered.

Shea stirred the fire, and then threw on another piece of wood. "Let's cook up the rest of this meat here, and get a good night's sleep. We have a lot to do tomorrow."

They awoke in the morning as they did the day before, at the first hint of sunlight. And again, it had been a night of easily interrupted, light sleep. The breakfast conversation was sparse, and it seemed everyone was grumpy. Once they were on their way, Shea again brought up the need for fresh game. This led to more conversation.

"Why don't I just go off by myself," offered Tyson, "That way you four can stay together and protect the wagon and things."

"Oh, I don't know about that," the major said, shaking his head.

"Just you, by yourself?" asked Shea. Sho-Taka and Falwyn remained quiet. Tyson looked around at the group and got the impression no one agreed with that idea.

"We need to get some meat. I don't see any other way. It ain't going to come dancing into our camp."

"You and Falwyn should go out together. Maybe Sho-Taka too," the major said. "There may very well be stalkers out there, you know." There were some objections, of course, but no one really had a better idea.

"I can go off by myself, and that will make less noise. Better chance to find something, and get a shot off," he said. "And as long as I move off to our front there's less chance I'll run into trouble if someone's following us." That logic didn't seem to change anyone's mind. He grabbed his weapon and powder, and started to leave before there was any more discussion.

"Wait." Sho-Taka said. He was looking at the forest that surrounded them, and thinking fast. He remained quiet for a moment then turned to Tyson. "We don't know who's out there or how many there are. We shouldn't split up until we do." Tyson started to disagree but Sho-Taka spoke up, "Going out alone makes no sense. And splitting us into two groups doesn't either. "Again he was silent for a moment before adding, "They're probably watching us. They'll know if you go off alone. Or even if two of us go out together. If there are two of them, or worse even more, I think they'll attack whichever they think is weaker." He looked around at the four others for any disagreement; he didn't see any.

"All together or split up? I don't know which is worse," Tyson thought. He had said he had wanted to go out alone to hunt. What he hadn't told them was that he intended to circle back behind them and track the stalkers. Letting these stalkers pick the time and the place for the attack just went against every instinct he had. He was determined to find them, and turn the tables on them.

"We'll stay together," Tyson said breaking the silence. He relented, knowing it would serve no point in arguing. They were uncomfortable letting him go off by himself, but he was more uncomfortable being stalked. He would find a way.

The major tried to make the best of the situation, "But let's try to keep quiet, and hope we see some game near the trail." They moved off, clustered together. Conversation was sparse as each one focused on the woods around them.

Sho-Taka walked along beside Falwyn, in front of the wagon as it rolled through the forest. Neither man said a word. Sho-Taka, using an old hunting technique, walked along staring straight ahead; his eyes fixed on a point 50 yards ahead. Without staring he kept his eyes steady, and depended on his peripheral vision to detect any motion around them. Falwyn, on the other hand, twisted his head around every few seconds; his eyes darting in all directions. He was sure, on several occasions, that he heard someone talk. Or he heard a horse step or whinny. He stopped short once after hearing what he thought was a weapon cocking. More and more, as the morning wore on, Sho-Taka, annoyed by Falwyn's useless gyrations, increased the distance between himself and the guide.

The major had wanted to walk along beside his two companions, as opposed to riding in the wagon but Tyson had taken him aside and asked him to ride along next to Shea. And he had to agree that he thought honestly that it wouldn't be the gentlemanly thing to do to leave her alone in the wagon. The panting horses, the uneven trail, and a squeaky wheel prevented him from hearing any suspicious sounds from the forest around them. He tried several times to initiate a conversation with Shea, but each time he spoke he seemed to catch her daydreaming. She would appear startled, and then respond with a short answer. He finally gave up.

Shea couldn't separate the noises made by them from whatever noises came from the woods either. She was thinking about Tyson, who had stationed himself behind the wagon. He was alone, which is what he wanted. There would be no distracting conversation, and that would allow him to concentrate on any noise coming from behind them.

In the wagon Shea turned around several times to reassure herself he was still there. And he was each time she looked. There he was, twenty-five paces behind them, his head turning right and left, and on occasion back to the rear. She had to admire his willingness to go alone. She could identify with someone taking on a necessary and dangerous task. It was just that she did not know many men who would do it.

The morning went by slowly. The tension seemed to be growing more intense as conversation ceased. The pilgrims strained their eyes as they peered into the dense foliage on both sides of the trail. Steps were getting shorter and slower. It was approaching noon when a brief flash of activity off to the right of the trail caught Sho-Taka's eye. He stopped walking, and slowly turned his head in that direction. His eyes widened. He raised his arm indicating the wagon should stop. Shea pulled in the reins instantly.

Falwyn, who was inching along and peering into the woods on the left, didn't notice what Sho-Taka did. He started to take another step, but Sho-Taka, wanting him to remain still, snatched him by the back of his collar.

"JASSUS CHRIST!" Falwyn screamed.

With bulging eyes and gaping mouth, a quivering Falwyn backed away, on very shaky legs, from Sho-Taka. He took a deep breath before saying with a high pitched voice, "Whaddya do that! Are you crazy? I almost peed my pants!"

Sho-Taka was talking over him, "There, you idiot! Right there!" He was gesturing toward the right of the trail. Falwyn never looked in that direction. He never took his eyes off Sho-Taka.

"Gawd Almighty, I gotta sit down."

Sho-Taka grabbed Falwyn's musket away from him, whirled around and aimed at the clump of trees thirty yards away. But he didn't shoot. The wild turkey, there a moment ago, was gone.

Sho-Taka turned back to Falwyn, "Why did you scream? There was a fat tom turkey just sitting there. You scared it off! What's the matter with you?"

"What's the matter with me?" Falwyn was having trouble speaking and trying to inhale simultaneously. He stood, bent at the waist with his hands on his knees, "How can you just go and grab somebody who ain't expectin' to be grabbed? And . . . ahhhh, Jassus! Lord have mercy! I gotta rest a minute. I don't think I can walk."

Sho-Taka explained the commotion to the major, Shea and Tyson. Tyson said, "I think you were lucky that turkey disappeared before you could get a shot off."

The major thought that odd, and asked, "Why?" Sho-Taka also thought that was curious.

"You grabbed Falwyn's musket? You were going to shoot with that?" Sho-Taka nodded. "Have you looked at it? It's got rust all over it, and I'm pretty sure that barrel's bent. I don't think you want to be anywhere near that thing when it's fired." He added, "It's a lot more dangerous to whoever is behind it than in front of it."

They took Falwyn's temporary weakness as an opportunity for a lunch break. They ate some raw carrots and deer jerky. It wasn't too tasty, but it was something. They refilled their water cask from a stream nearby, but Falwyn wanted none of it. He asked Sho-Taka several times for some of the hard cider he had. He explained he needed it to settle his nerves. Sho-Taka refused each time, and Falwyn cringed each time he got that answer. The others began seeing some humor in Falwyn's frightening episode, but felt a little bit guilty about enjoying his discomfort. They couldn't refuse him when he begged to be allowed to ride in the wagon that afternoon.

As they moved off for the afternoon Falwyn slept contentedly in the rear of the wagon, and Sho-Taka held the reins. The major insisted on talking up the post in the rear, as Shea and Tyson led the way. Not long after they started they came to a large stretch of open country and the feeling of claustrophobia and lurking danger slowly slipped away.

Shea had been trying to have a conversation with Tyson as they walked through the open country, but wasn't having much success. The open ground between them and the distant tree line on both sides and to their front allowed him to feel far safer than during this morning's walk. She had learned somewhere in her youth that the best way to loosen a man's tongue was whiskey. And the second best way was to ask him about himself. She didn't have any whiskey, so she started by asking Tyson about Kan-tucky.

She asked him anything that came into her mind. His responses were quick, but brief. She wished he would elaborate because she found herself liking the tone of his voice.

"Why are you going all the way out to Kan-tucky?"

"I own land there."

"Why did you buy land out there? Why didn't you want to stay in Virginia?" She knew too many men that needed to get away from home.

"Didn't buy it. I inherited it."

"Your folks rich?"

No matter how many questions she asked, and he answered, she had another one right behind it. He told her that he was a farmer, and had a gift for growing things. His stepfather had left him a plot of land, and he intended to farm it. Five more questions ferreted out that the land was virgin forest, and Tyson figured it would take years to for him to turn it into the farm he wanted, but he was okay with that. She asked questions about his stepfather and brothers, but he just waved them off. When he stopped answering questions and still did not ask any of his own, she finally gave up. He just wasn't much of a talker. She was okay with that.

After crossing the open country for most of the afternoon they approached the wooded border on the western side. Tyson stopped and scanned it as they drew near. The major and Sho-Taka approached and asked what he was looking for.

"Don't know. Just looking," he said.

"You think the stalkers are in there? Waiting to ambush us?" asked Shea. The major scanned the woods back and forth. Sho-Taka looked at Tyson, and then back at the woods.

After a moment Tyson said, "No." He was silent for a moment, and then added, "I think they stayed in the woods for cover. I kept looking back behind us and they never showed. I think they had to circle around the open . . . stay in the woods; to the north I figure . . . it looks like there's better cover over there. Pick up our trail once we get back into the forest."

Once more, the real possibility of stalkers returned and swept away the lightness they had enjoyed in their afternoon in the sun. As they scouted around for a place to spend the night they became more aware of the noises and movements around them. Darting eyes and heightened senses brought a gloom to the campsite.

The spot selected was at the edge of the woods. A small stream ran along the border of the trees and some seemingly out-of-place boulders provided some partial cover from prying eyes in the woods. The usual preparations for making camp were made without much conversation.

Dinner was prepared and devoured quickly because there wasn't much to prepare. The conversation at dinner revolved around food. The food supply was precariously low. There was only enough left for breakfast in the morning.

"We should have brought more supplies," the major said.

"We should have . . . but our guide was vague about how long it would take us to reach Dubious," muttered Sho-Taka glaring at Falwyn.

Everyone looked at the guide but he didn't notice. He was gnawing on some jerky. The silence finally struck him, and he looked up. "What?" he asked. He looked around.

The silence lasted until Falwyn decided to ignore them and go back to his jerky. The major spoke up, "These woods look promising. I'm sure we'll find some game in here."

Tyson did not know why the major thought these woods "looked promising", but wasn't going to argue. Sho-Taka glanced around and suggested, "We should head off tomorrow morning to hunt . . . *early* tomorrow morning . . . and see if we can get something. The earlier the better."

"Why?" asked Shea.

"If the stalkers don't come at us tonight, then I don't think they'll come at us early in the morning. And while they hold off, that'll give us time to split up a little and get some game. The sooner we can get something, and get back together the better." Without voicing it both Shea and Tyson agreed with that logic. Falwyn continued to gnaw. Sho-Taka began to explain what he thought would be the best way to go about splitting up.

The major held up his hand, "I don't disagree . . . but!" They all turned to him. "I don't know if any of you think this way, but this might not even be real. We don't know if it is; yet we seem to be making more and more of our decisions based on what might not be real! There are five of us. And, Tyson seems to think, based on the noise, that there are only two, maybe even only one of them. IF there are any at all! Five against two, at most! Let's go about our business, and let them worry about us. If they add to their numbers . . . well then, if we heard two we'll surely hear four, or five. Then we can take more defensive maneuvers." The major looked around at the faces. He zeroed in on Tyson. "Let me ask you, sir. What's your best judgement? How many stalkers do you think are we up against?"

Not for a second did he doubt that he heard something. Tyson tried to remember the circumstances of that first sound. Based on his hunting experiences; based on his numerous trips into the woods since he was little; based on what he had been taught by his family and farmhands he judged that he had heard one rider, or two very cautious ones.

"Can't be sure until you put eyes on 'em, but I think there's one. I wouldn't swear to it. Outside chance of two," he shrugged. He then decided to add, "Heck, I could be wrong. Could have been a clumsy bear or some deer mating out of season," he smiled weakly. "Like I said, can't be sure until you see 'em with your own eyes."

No one spoke at first, but after a minute Sho-Taka said, "I think we will be okay if it's only one. But if it's two?" he shook his head. Well, then they have the upper hand," he finished the thought.

"Why?" asked Shea. "Why do you say that?"

"One can't take us on. But two? I can see it. Because, if I was them, I would pick a spot where we could get a close up shot and get two of us before we knew what was happening. And you know who those two are going to be?" No one spoke, so Sho-Taka went on, "They'll shoot the major and Tyson. They're the ones carrying the firearms. That'll leave Shea, Falwyn and me." He let that settle in for a moment.

"I got a musket too, ya know," objected Falwyn.

Sho-Taka ignored him, "I don't want to be one of the two shot dead, but I don't want to be one of the three left alive to the mercy of these villains either. It won't be pretty."

A glum major said softly, "It seems we are at their mercy."

Falwyn spoke up, and asked, "Why don't we head back to Fort Royal?"

"The major's right," Tyson said, "We are at their mercy."

"Why don't we go back to the fort?" Falwyn asked again.

"But we can turn the table on them," said Tyson. A disappointed Falwyn made a sour face. The others looked at Tyson. In a lowered voice, he said, "They think that when they're good and ready they will take us by surprise. What they don't know is that we know they're out there. Why don't we surprise them?" All eyes were on him. "Tonight, when it gets dark, we'll bed down and let our campfire burn down to just a glow. Then, when it's nice and dark, we'll head out after them!" The response was eight eyebrows rising. "Quietly and slowly, the four of us will move out into the woods and find *them*!" He smiled, and then added, "Probably sleeping."

"We don't know where there are. How in hell we gonna find them in the dark?" Falwyn had instantly decided he wanted no part in this.

"With us stomping around blindly in the woods, I don't think we'll surprise them," surmised the major.

"Why only four?" Shea wanted to know.

"Night maneuvers are very difficult under the best of circumstances, Tyson. I doubt we have the training to accomplish what you have in mind," said the major. The debate continued on as daylight faded, and bedding was spread out.

"You're right," said Tyson answering Sho-Taka, "I can't be exactly sure where they are. Or rather where they'll be tonight, but if I was in their shoes, planning on doing what they're going to do, I know where I'd be."

"Where is that?" Sho-Taka asked.

"Yes, where is that?" added the major.

"They've got to be downwind. Whenever you track something . . . anything . . . you have to stay downwind. That way you can keep track of it, and it doesn't know you're there." Tyson gestured off to his right. "Wind is coming out of the south, so they have to be north." The others resisted the impulse to look off that way. "I s'pose that when we made camp, they moved around us that way, and made their own camp. And it's probably less than a quarter of a mile away."

"That's pretty close, Tyson."

He was now speaking in a lower voice, and the others leaned in closer to hear him. "Well, they want to be close enough to hear us and smell ….." he paused a moment trying to use words which wouldn't be too insulting to Falwyn, "at least, the horses." He let that sink in for a moment. "They might be watching us right now. They'll want to watch us to make sure that we settle down for the night. Be close enough to see us, and hear us, and maybe even smell us too. They'll watch us settle down, and then move off a little bit and settle down themselves. Might even light a fire for themselves to cook up their dinner. They'll set it up so it can't be seen from this direction, I figure. Shield it somehow. And then tomorrow morning, they'll want to hear us as we get up and fuss around a bit." He looked up into the now dark night sky, "We only got a half-moon tonight. That means it won't be too dark, and it won't be too light. That'll be good for us."

He told them his plan, and then had to tell them again. They had so many questions, and objections. He told them that when their campfire was nearly out they would sneak off into the woods. One at a time, and it had to be done without any noise. In the fading light he pointed out a boulder at the edge of their campsite (downwind) that would serve as the rendezvous point for the four man party that was going to go out. Shea objected to not being included. Tyson explained to her that someone had to stay behind to guard their wagon and livestock. Falwyn offered to stay behind with her. When that suggestion was disregarded, he offered to switch with her. He was, again, ignored.

After the plan was repeated a third time, and all questions and objections were dealt with, the party meandered about for a few minutes, then shuffled off to their blankets. Shea climbed up into the bed of the wagon, and tossed her blanket over herself. Her eyes peeked out just above the side of the wagon. Two of the men chose spots to sleep that were obscured by a fallen tree. The other two men spread their blankets near the base of the wagon. A smart observer would have noticed that the men did not remove their boots when bedding down. That same observer probably would have wondered why they did not add wood to the fire to ward off any animals, as they went to sleep. As the fire slowly died out it became very dark.

They waited for the signal. After what seemed like half the night, Tyson clucked his tongue. He had already slipped away from his resting place and was kneeling beside the big rock. The click he made carried throughout the campsite. One by one the other three men joined Tyson. He looked at each man as he motioned for them to be silent.

"Where's your gun," he whispered to Sho-Taka?

"Don't need one," he answered, "I have this." He raised his left hand holding a knife with an eight inch blade.

Although Tyson thought the knife was impressive, he wasn't sure Sho-Taka understood what he was up against. "They're going to have guns," he said by way of argument. Sho-Taka waved him off. Tyson looked at the other two. Falwyn was shaking, and moon eyed. The major was wide eyed too, but seemed ready for the quest. He held a long sword in his right hand and a musket in his left. He had two pistols tucked into his belt. "Why don't you let Sho-Taka have that extra pistol, major?"

The look on the major's face said very plainly that he did not want to give away any of his weapons. Tyson got the impression the major would have been very glad to carry even more weapons if he possessed any.

"They're my pistols, Tyson; they've been in my family for years. I brought them," the major said as if arguing the point.

"No, major, I know that. It's just that Sho-Taka here ain't got a firearm. And you got three. Can't you spare one? How about letting him use your musket?"

"Let him use your sword, major," Falwyn suggested.

"I should say not! A British officer does not go into battle without his sword. I need my sword."

Tyson put a soft hand on the major's arm, "Major? You've got four weapons, and only two hands. Surely you can spare one?"

An awkward silence followed with the major shifting his glare from one to another of his companions. His mind raced as he tried to decide what he was going to do. Give up a weapon, or no? Which one? He finally realized he had to do something so he reluctantly thrust his musket toward Sho-Taka and quickly withdrew one of his pistols from his belt. Sho-Taka took the weapon and shrugged. The major examined the pistol for a moment, and cocked it.

Tyson heard that, and again motioned for silence. He leaned over to the major and whispered, "We are going to be going through some tight spots, major. I think maybe you better keep that thing uncocked. You wouldn't want it going off before you need it." He thought this made perfect sense.

The major stared at him as if he was insane, "I want to be ready in an instant, Tyson. A second late is certain death!" Tyson had his doubts, but Falwyn, listening, was convinced. He pulled back the hammer of his musket too.

The plan had been that Tyson would lead the three others in single file into the darkened woods. They would move behind him as he, 'slowly and quietly', moved in the wind's direction. He felt confident that there were stalkers out there. And that they would be in this direction, and not too far away. He also thought that these stalkers could be taken by surprise. But success depended not only on Tyson's instincts being right, but on all of them all being quiet. He wasn't sure they would be able to do that. He second guessed himself, and thought perhaps he should have made this sortie alone. It was too late for that now. He looked at his companions again, moved his finger to his lips to reiterate the need for silence, and started off.

He moved slowly at first, more concerned about the nervous companions with loaded weapons behind him than with whatever lay ahead. His steps were small and slow. He hoped the three behind him followed his track exactly. He peered into the darkness ahead and saw very little. Moving along in a low crouch, he moved his hand along the ground in front of him to avoid snapping branches or twigs. To his relief his night vision improved gradually as time passed despite the darkness. To his dismay he heard one of his companions trip, stumble, clear a throat, and catch on a branch, or whatever, every few minutes.

He used the wind as a compass in the dark. Wetting a finger and holding it up in the breeze every few steps he tried to stay on the path which he thought would lead downwind to the stalkers. He had told them to stay low, to stay in single file, and to stay close to the man in front. Every time he stopped the men behind him would invariably bump into one another. It seemed that he must have turned around and gave a whispered 'sssshhh' to his compatriots every ten steps.

Thirty minutes into their patrol Falwyn, who was lined up right behind Tyson, reached up and grabbed the leader's shirt. Tyson stopped, as had Falwyn. Sho-Taka, the third in line, had enough night vision to see Falwyn grab Tyson, and instantly turned back to the major and throw up his hand to halt him. The major froze. Tyson, in slow motion, turned around to face Falwyn. His eyes shifted right and left, expecting to see something amiss. He saw only the darkness of the woods, and then redirected his eyes at Falwyn. Falwyn's face was twisted in pain. Tyson mouthed "What?" to him. Falwyn leaned closer to Tyson's face, "I gotta piss." Tyson's reaction was initially revulsion at Falwyn's breath. He leaned back away from him and blinked several times to recover. Realizing that the stalkers might very well be only a few feet away he knew that the any noise at all might prove fatal. He turned back to Falwyn, and with his free hand covering Falwyn's mouth, he leaned in to within two inches of his face, and whispered "Can't you hold it?"

"I can't!' came the reply.

Tyson again leaned in close to Falwyn and whispered ever so gently, "Hold it! And stop talking! Don't make any noise!" That wasn't the answer Falwyn wanted, and he wrinkled his nose. In the darkness Tyson made eye contact with the men behind him, and waved them on to follow him again.

They went on in the dark for another ten minutes. Their steps were getting slower and shorter as they moved forward. Barely inching along Tyson felt that they must be very close to the stalkers, if there were any? Self-doubt was beginning to creep in. This had to be the right direction. Had they passed by them in the dark? Perhaps he should have had the four of them fan out to cover a wider swath? But he hadn't seen a sign of any kind. He hadn't detected the smell of a campfire or horses. And he hadn't heard any noise either. It was probable the stalkers had horses, and they too had been stone silent. Horses were by nature a bit skittish, and it would be unusual for a horse not to stir a little bit if they heard anything at all stirring in the woods around them. He recalled being told that some Indians had the ability to keep a horse absolutely still and quiet, no matter what was going on around them. Were they being stalked by Indians? And if the stalkers were sleeping, why weren't they making a sound? No snoring? Not even heavy breathing? The questions began coming faster and faster at him in his head when he heard simultaneous gasps behind him, and was grabbed again.

He turned around and saw a horrified look on the major's face as he was looking, and pointing, off to the right. Falwyn too, was looking that way, his eyes bulging out of his head. Sho-Taka simply looked puzzled. Tyson turned and looked off to the right, but saw nothing. Ten feet away to the right there was a break in the trees. Beyond that was a clearing, perhaps 50 feet wide by 100 feet long. The dim moonlight was, of course, brighter out there than in the woods. "What," he asked them?

"I saw something move out there," the major whispered, a bit too loudly.

"Me too," Falwyn said. Sho-Taka eyebrows were raised, but he said nothing.

"What was it?" Tyson whispered, reminding them with his hands to be quiet. No one offered him an answer, so he whispered, "What did you see major?"

In a hoarse whisper that was, again, a little too loud the major said, "I'm not sure. But something moved. Over there. Near the other side." Sho-Taka looked in that direction, while Falwyn just stared wide-eyed. Tyson looked out at the clearing, but saw nothing but the waist high grass that covered it.

"Go flush it out, major. I'll cover you. But be careful," Tyson said softly without taking his eyes off the clearing. The major slowly turned his face toward Tyson with a look of complete disbelief. Tyson, who had by now shouldered his rifle and was pointing it out into the clearing, didn't notice. After a moment of staring, the major turned to Falwyn, who ignored him. The major finally turned to Sho-Taka who was right beside him, and looked at him shaking his head.

Sho-Taka mouthed "Good luck, ' to the major.

The reluctant major rose to his feet, and began moving cautiously toward the open space beyond the tree line. As Major Highcross took his third step, only one step from the edge of the clearing, in the absolute silent wood, Sho-Taka, on one knee behind him, cocked his borrowed musket. It was a very loud click.

The major, who was entirely focused on what was in front of him, was caught him off-guard by the sound coming from close behind him. He froze in place, and then a few seconds later began quivering. His eyes bulged and despite a wide open mouth he was unable to either inhale or exhale for a moment. Struggling to stop the quivering and regain composure, he turned around to face Sho-Taka, who was behind him pointing his musket in the major's general direction. The major's head was tilted to the side, and his face was contorted. His upper lip was curled and his eyes were bulging very, very wide. He suddenly tucked his sword under left arm and with quick, short waves of his right hand motioned Sho-Taka to move to the right. Sho-Taka complied.

After some moments of more glaring, the major re-gripped his sword and turned once again toward the open field. His progress started out slowly and regressed, especially as he emerged from the woods into the open. Moving into the thick, high grass his head swiveled far faster than he walked. Holding his sword in his right hand and a pistol in his left, he was bent over at the waist as he went. His chest was barely above the top of the grass, as he moved deeper into the field. His three companions, still in the darkened woods, were hardly breathing as they watched him in the somewhat brighter field of grass. Each step the major took advanced him barely six inches further. His head erect and his arms extended to his sides, he looked like an eagle soaring over the top of a forest; but much slower. It now occurred to Tyson that at this rate they might be here until morning. He was going to say something when Major Aaron Highcross screamed.

It was a piercing scream that frightened every living thing in the vicinity. Falwyn, Sho-Taka, and Tyson flinched and stared in horror as the major pirouetted in place, as he waved his arms in wide circles, and then came to a halt with his arms extended downward into the tall grass.

"DON'TYOUMOVEORSOHELPMEGODI"LL . . ." at this point the major ran out of breath. When he took a moment to inhale he continued, "Don't you move, you filthy bastard!" His alarmed companions (all three had shouldered their weapons) looked out at him, and then all around to see if there were other dangers lurking.

"If you move I will shoot you dead," asserted the major in a very loud voice.

Sho-Taka began to rise, but Tyson stopped him. "Don't move. They may be more of them out there." After scanning around again, he whispered, "Keep your eyes open."

The major had stepped on something lying obscured in the tall grass, and instantly concluded he had stepped on a stalker! He – after a moment of sheer terror – had stuck the muzzle of his pistol into it. Losing his balance he nearly fell. He regained his balance, and tried to take a moment to regain his composure. But his captive was apparently trying to wiggle free. "Stop moving," he ordered, "Or I'll fire!"

For a moment then, everything settled down. The major assessed his situation quickly; it wasn't good. He himself was in a very awkward position. When he had first tripped over his captive in the dark he had lost his balance. In the resultant fandango to regain his balance he had wound up standing on his captive with his left foot; his left hand held the pistol that stretched down behind and under his left knee. Its barrel was hard against his left foot, but the muzzle was firmly pressed into the reclining captive. It was too dark to see clearly, but the major was acutely aware that that captive underneath him might very well be armed to the teeth. And although it was dark, the major was fully exposed in the open, and as such was a very inviting target. He also didn't have any faith in the marksmanship of two of his companions still in the woods. He was in a very bad place should a gun fight erupt. As he began to twist around toward his friends to say something, his captive moved too.

"Stop moving or I'll shoot!" he growled, jabbing the muzzle of his pistol down harder.

"Shoot the sonuvabitch, major," Falwyn yelled.

"Shut up!" snapped Tyson. "Suppose there's more of them out there? Don't want 'em to know where we are."

The major considered shooting his prisoner, but judged it morally wrong. "I am now placing the tip of my saber against you," he told the reclined captive. And he did so. "If you so much as flinch I will push this blade through you, and pin you to the earth for all eternity. I am an officer in the service of King George of England. Do you understand?" He thought he sounded very authoritative. There was no answer. "**Do you understand**?" he repeated angrily. Again he waited for a reply, but there wasn't any. "Don't move, I warn you." Lifting the gun muzzle from the captive, while pressing with the sword he began to rise from his bent over position. He felt the movement first under his left foot as the captive began to roll away. "DON'T …" he started to say as he began to lose his balance. He had no choice.

BANG!

The nearness of the noise, the flash, and the smoke from the discharge completely disoriented the major. That disorientation was the reason it took him several moments to realize he was shot. And that realization needed a few moments of its own to be fully understood by him. He turned back toward the woods, perhaps searching for some sense of fellowship with his friends still hidden in the trees, but he never made it. He lost consciousness.

The initial reaction to the gun shot by his three friends behind him in the woods differed greatly. Sho-Taka leapt to his feet instantly while holding the musket uselessly in his left hand. His right hand however, he held high behind him with his knife's blade between his fingertips. And while Tyson barely flinched, Falwyn jumped to his feet. The three men watched as the smoke began to clear, and the major started to turn toward them. Their initial reaction of surprise turned to shock when he keeled over.

It took several moments for the three men in the woods to regain their composure. Sho-Taka was the first to move. "Cover me," he said to Tyson, and handed him his musket. Then he started walking to where the major had gone down. Tyson also moved, but only to the edge of the woods. He knelt behind a small tree, with his musket at his shoulder.

Sho-Taka took little time moving out the 25 feet into the clearing and finding the prone major. He squatted down beside him and tried to assess the situation. In the darkness he could make out the major's saber, still standing upright near the major's feet. The smoking pistol was in the major's hand. He looked carefully at the major's prostrate body for any signs of blood or wounds. As he did the major seemed to start regaining consciousness.

"Is it bad?" he asked in a feeble voice.

"I don't think so," Sho-Taka answered saying one word at a time.

"Is the bastard dead?"

Sho-Taka peeked over to his left, and then back at the major, "As dead as last Christmas's goose."

The major grinned briefly, and then grit his teeth again. "I'm afraid he got a bit of me too," he said. "I think he got me in the leg." He paused, and then sputtered, "Tell me, Sho-Taka," he looked at his friend in earnest, "I can't look. Is it bad? Will I lose the leg?"

Again Sho-Taka measured his response, "I don't think so."' He said again. Then in a more upbeat tone he said, "Why don't you just try to relax, and we'll get you back to camp. Then we can take a good look at it."

"Can I be moved? You think it's wise?" He started to pant, then catching his breath he blurted out, "Holy Mother of God, I don't want to lose my leg!"

Sho-Taka thought of several things to say, but they were all unkind. He patted the officer on the shoulder, and whispered, "Can't leave you here all night, can we? Why don't you just relax, and let us get you back to camp. Everything's going to work out just fine."

Sho-Taka stood up, put his knife back into its sheath, and waved Tyson and Falwyn to come over. When they did they saw him smiling. So the major couldn't hear him, he said, "I don't think we got any stalkers nearby. And if there are, they are awfully sound sleepers." He gave them a quick rundown on the major. He had apparently, in the darkness, stepped on a log. Thinking it was a man, he had jabbed it with both his pistol and sword. It began to roll as he jostled it; he lost his balance and tried to shoot it. "His sword is still stuck in it; but he shot his own foot." Both Tyson and Falwyn looked down at the major, and then back at Sho-Taka. "It doesn't look like it's too bad. His boot's got a hole in both top and bottom now. Won't be able to tell how bad it is until we get the boot off. Let's get him up on his feet, and get him back to camp. We can help him along, but I don't think he needs to be carried. He can use Falwyn's musket as a crutch if he needs it. "

"Why mine?" Falwyn asked immediately.

"Because he's going to lean on it pretty hard, and he just might bend it; leaning on it and all. And yours don't fire anyway; so what's to lose?"

"Who says it don't fire?" Falwyn wanted to know.

Tyson, who agreed with Sho-Taka on this point, didn't think this was the time or the place to argue about it, so he said to Falwyn, "Go ahead. Just point it out there somewhere and pull the trigger. But, first let us step away a bit, so when you do fire that rusted piece of shit . . . and it blows up in your face . . . we don't get hit with any of the pieces."

It took the three men some time to convince the major he was fit to travel. The distance back to the camp was less than a quarter mile, yet it took almost as long to get back as it did in going out. The major used Falwyn's musket as a crutch; with the stock under his arm and the muzzle on the ground. This kept Falwyn muttering the entire time, "Sweet Jisses, yer gettin' dirt in the barrel. It won't ever be good to fire agin!" There was very little conversation, especially after the one between Tyson and Falwyn.

"By the by, Falwyn, didn't you say when we were crawling around out there, you had to relieve yourself; and I told you to hold off. And you said you couldn't! Well! What do you say now? With all the excitement, you were able to hold off after all. Do you need to stop now?"

"Nah," he muttered, "I already done it."

Tyson was surprised by that answer. "When? In all that excitement? When did you pee?"

"When the major shot his foot."

It wasn't very difficult for the men to find their campsite. The flames from the campfire were visible almost from the time they turned around and started back. It was a concern to them that Shea had apparently thrown more wood onto the dying fire after they had left. They wondered out loud why she had done that. Was it a signal? Had the stalkers doubled back behind them while they were out?

As they approached they became very cautious. Peering through the woods they saw Shea sitting at the campfire, and across from her sat a stranger. Hunched over in a dark cloak the stranger's face was obscured. Was this the stalker? Was this the person who crossed over the river at Kelly's crossing before them? They halted, watched, and wondered what was going on?

Shea, without looking out at them, called out, "Are you going to stand out there all night? Come in and warm up around the fire. And meet our 'stalker'." The men walked (the major hobbled) in. They first spent a few minutes tendering to the wounded major's foot.

"What happened? I heard the shot," Shea asked? She had to ask twice because the men were all staring at the new arrival. Tyson recapped the events. Sho-Taka added some color. The major just moaned a few times, and Falwyn only stared the newcomer in the green cloak.

Tyson then squatted down in front of the major and told him he had to take a look at the wound. The thought of this did not appeal to the major. He strenuously objected. "That ball went through your boot. I expect you got hit in the foot. You're probably bleeding in there. We got to take it off."

"Ya gonna cut off his foot?" Falwyn leaned in and asked. Tyson gave a disbelieving look over his shoulder at Falwyn. When he turned back to the major, he saw the major staring at him in wide-eyed shock. Before Tyson could reassure him, Falwyn said, "Can I have the boot major? Hell, yere gonna be walkin' all funny anyway . . . can I have 'em bofe?"

"We are not cutting anybody's foot off!" Tyson said flatly. He turned to Falwyn, and said, "Shut up." Once more he said to the major, "We are going to take your boot off to dress the wound. That's all." It took a few more minutes to convince the major this was necessary. And it took more than a few minutes to gingerly remove the boot, because the major moaned louder with every inch it descended.

The group examined the foot once it was clear of the boot. The major opted not to look.

"Damn, lookee that. It's just gone! Damnedest thing I ever saw," Falwyn whispered.

"What?" asked the major; still preferring not to look himself.

Other comments passed around.

"It didn't bleed much."

"Didn't even scratch the little boys on either side!"

"Helluva shot!"

"I've seen a lot worse."

"We'll wrap it up tight, and major, you can ride the wagon for the next few days. You're going to be fine."

"Better shake out the boot. That little fella has got to be in there somewhere."

It took only a short time to bind up the major's foot and a little longer to assure him he would probably never miss the middle toe on his left foot.

Once that was settled they found their places around the fire facing the new arrival. Tyson was first to speak, "Mrs. Devonshire! What are you doing out here all by yourself?"

She smiled at the amazed quartet. "How do you do, Mr. Tyson."

"Just 'Tyson', Ma'am."

She turned toward the prostrate officer, "Major Highcross? I hope this injury isn't serious." He waved her off, but said nothing. She looked at Falwyn, "And you are the guide, Falwyn." Once more turning slightly, she said, "And you, of course, must be Sho-Taka."

Each man muttered some form of greeting. And each man was somewhat unnerved by her dazzling smile. Shea broke the spell, "Tyson? You were right, and you were wrong." He turned to her. "You were right. We did have someone stalking us. And you were hearing noises made by that someone. But it wasn't a highwayman, or a gang of bandits. It was her, Mrs. Devonshire."

The questions that followed came from all directions. Mrs. Devonshire decided to explain her attempt to follow them. She told them that she had been following them since they had crossed the Susquehanna at Kelly's Crossing. And she had had practically nothing to eat since she left. The aroma from Shea's cooking was driving her to distraction. When she heard the major's shot in the woods it frightened her. She decided that it wasn't safe to be on her own anymore so she decided to show herself. That's what she told them.

She did not tell them that she wanted to put some distance between herself and the fort before making her appearance. She did not want to be turned back. She told them she left because she was a virtual prisoner there. That was true. She was running away; trying to go west. Again, that was true. *(Southwest,* actually, but that was close enough.*)* She was attempting to escape from a cruel and abusive husband. ("Who beat me every time he drinks; and that is quite often!") She went on to say that after she had convinced him that she was leaving him, he told the authorities that she was a spy for the French and a traitor to the English Crown during the recent hostilities. They believed him, and now they were after her. There was some truth in what she said because, in fact, the English authorities very much wanted to get their hands on her (the most recent addition to that list was a certain Captain Phillip Wallingford of Fort Royal). But in regard to the 'traitor', or the 'cruel and abusive husband' part, she was playing fast and loose with the truth. There were, indeed, a great many serious charges pending against her by the British, but spying wasn't one of them. Because she spoke with a slight French accent, she assured them that it wasn't very difficult to portray her as a spy. Once more, that much might very well be true. She explained she had been born in France, but had moved to England as a young girl; and then onto the colonies later on. This was two thirds true; the 'born in France' and 'moving to the colonies' parts. She had never, in her life, set foot in England.

By this time the group was starting to feel a little sorry for her. And that included the major too, despite the fact he realized he was duty bound to turn her in to the authorities back east; but his foot hurt like hell, so he decided to postpone that for now.

The conversation went on around the camp fire. The original five asking Mrs. Devonshire questions about her recent, and not so recent, background. She, in turn, tried to steer the conversation to their respective backgrounds. She didn't want to appear secretive, but being perfectly frank with them – and 'them' being English – seemed to her unlikely to aide her cause. She explained her questions away with, "After all, I do need to know who I'll be travelling with. N'est-ce pas?"

In time they all agreed that she would join them, at least as far as Dubious. The major asserted that his duty required that he contact his superiors back east as to her whereabouts. Mrs. Devonshire thought that the further away from the authorities back east she travelled the better off she'd be. Besides, escaping from the grip of this major when the time came wouldn't be any more difficult than the escape from that hideous Captain Wallingford had been. Falwyn was totally taken by her good looks, and wanted her around as long as it was possible. Shea didn't see how her presence would matter one way or the other, while escorting her back to Fort Royal would again delay her trip to Dubious. Tyson and Sho-Taka both agreed with Falwyn that she was pretty, they also agreed with Shea that bringing her along was a better choice than bringing her back.

Mrs. Devonshire was relieved when Shea changed the topic from backgrounds to 'stalkers'. When asked by Sho-Taka, she said that while she was following them she had neither seen, nor heard, any other people. Shea asked Tyson, "Do you think you heard more than just Mrs. Devonshire? Do you think there are others on our trail too?"

Tyson shook his head, "I don't know. It might have been only her I heard. We'll find out tomorrow when we get back on the trail."

Sho-Taka agreed, and added, "If they are there, they'll likely trail us from further off. Might be harder to hear any noise they might make."

"They'll still be able to track us, even if we make no noise," Shea said.

"You mean the tracks our wagon makes?" Tyson started to explain that there wasn't any way to avoid that.

"I bet they can smell Falwyn from a mile away." Everyone turned and looked at him. She spoke again, "Didn't we agree on this back at Philyaw's?" She turned toward Falwyn, "You have to clean those clothes. Matter of fact, you have to take a bath in the next river we reach."

Before he could stop himself Tyson added, "It wouldn't kill you if you washed out your mouth with some salt water either."

"What in hell you talkin' about? I washed." Falwyn answered back.

"When?" four of them said together. Falwyn didn't answer.

Tyson waited a moment then said, "You have to get rid of those pants. They really smell."

"And the shirt too; while you're at it," someone added.

His clothes, it was decided (by a vote of 5 to 1), would be burned; there had to be an extra set of clothes in all the baggage the group had. "I ain't gonna wear nobody else's clothes." he protested. Shea thought that, as long as they were at it, his shoes should be tossed away too. Falwyn was horrified. Sho-Taka said he could make him a pair of moccasins, but it would take him some time. Tyson thought that as long as the major was going to be riding in the wagon for the next few days, Falwyn could borrow his boots until the moccasins were ready. Only a few minutes ago Falwyn had been eyeing these same boots, but now he protested, "They're too big." Shea told him that her brother used to stuff their dad's shoes with rags when they got handed down. She made that up, but it seemed to placate Falwyn.

The major started to object about Falwyn wearing his boots, "Now wait a minute! I don't think it would be proper for me to arrive at my post half dressed." He was not enthusiastic about the prospect of Falwyn wearing anything of his, and was preparing to offer a litany of reasons why it was not going to happen.

Mrs. Devonshire chimed in, "Before you go putting all those new clothes on him, I would recommend he bathe first." Everyone but Falwyn agreed that that was a very good idea. Falwyn looked on in stunned silence. Sho-Taka told them that there was a small pool fed by a creek just a hundred yards away. He had seen it when they had made camp that night. Falwyn objected. "I ain't goin' to drown myself is some damn crik."

"The water is only up to your knees. You won't drown."

"I won't do it. Ya can't make me."

"You'll do it," Sho-Taka assured him. "You are going to clean up in that creek tomorrow morning. You aren't going to drown; I'll go there with you just to make sure." Falwyn hadn't bargained for this. "You might get a little chilled up in that water," Sho-Taka went on, "But I can get you warmed up – when you're *finished* – with a little home brew I have."

Falwyn's eyes lit up, "I can?" Sho-Taka smiled, and to Falwyn the deal looked suddenly brighter.

The following morning started for Shea as it had since as far back as she could remember. At the first hint of dawn she awoke. She began to move about, and that noise, although faint, aroused the others one by one.

Mrs. Devonshire was up next and helping Shea where she could. Tyson and Sho-Taka were up as well and without speaking, they both prepared mentally for the difficult task that lay ahead. Falwyn remained wrapped up in his blanket, but was awake. Only the major remained asleep, and snored gently.

Shea began cooking some cornmeal with the last bits of deer meat in a pan. She said to Tyson that they were now out of meat. Mrs. Devonshire offered to share with the group some tea she had with her. Major Highcross somehow heard her in his sleep and awoke abruptly. He complained about his wound, as he looked around the campsite to see who was listening.

"Come on, Falwyn. Time for us to head on down to the creek," Tyson said, looking down at the still snuggled guide. Sho-Taka stood right behind him. Everyone looked at Falwyn, but said nothing.

"What are yer saying?" Falwyn asked, squinting up at Tyson.

"We're going to get you cleaned up. Remember?"

"Nah," Falwyn answered. "I changed my mind about that."

"We haven't," Sho-Taka said.

The disagreement lasted another ten minutes, until it became clear to Falwyn that he was going to go with them to clean up in the creek whether he liked it, or not. He thought briefly about trying to run away, but realized there wasn't anyone there, except the major with his wounded foot, that he could outrun. They suggested that if they had to, they would throw him into the water and let him drown if he continued to argue. He believed them.

In the interest of modesty the two women in the party remained in camp, as did the hobbling major. When Sho-Taka and Tyson walked Falwyn to the water's edge they halted him, and told him to strip.

"Why?" he wanted to know. "You mean you want me to git nekked?" He looked at them in disbelief. "And then get into the water? I'll freeze to death!" They explained to him the need for disrobing in order to get completely clean.

"Take off your clothes, or I'll cut them off," Sho-Taka calmly informed him. His large hunting knife was in his hand. Falwyn couldn't believe what he was being told. He started to argue again, and Sho-Taka stepped toward him and raised his knife.

"OKAY! Okay! Okay," he said. He began to slowly remove his shirt.

Sho-Taka stood impatiently behind him. "Take off your boots," he said.

"Nah, I'm gonna leave 'em on. Don't wanna cut my feet on the rocks in the water."

"Then how are you going to take your pants off?"

"Oh no," Falwyn said, waving his hand back and forth. "I ain't getting nekked in front of nobody."

"I'll cut 'em off you if you don't take them off **now**!"

Falwyn stared at Sho-Taka to see how serious he was. He didn't like what he saw.

In the next twenty minutes the argument went on non-stop. Tyson or Sho-Taka barked instructions, and Falwyn objected to each one. Being overruled, he attempted to offer more acceptable alternatives. They wouldn't listen to him. He ignored physical threats, and delayed complying at every turn. When he had finally stripped off all his clothes, and had been herded to the water's edge by his two companions, they backed him into the creek. After being forced to wade into the water up to his thighs, and howling like he was stabbed, he refused to totally immerse himself. Losing patience, Sho-Taka removed his own moccasins and waded into the water with him and grabbed him by the shoulders. Falwyn knew what was coming but wasn't quick enough, nor strong enough, to prevent it. He was only able to shriek briefly before the large Indian lifted him off his feet and dropped him sideways into the creek. Perhaps the people back at camp heard the splash, but everyone within two miles heard Falwyn when he resurfaced.

"AAAAAAAAACK!' he gasped, spitting water from his mouth. "God in –GAAACK - heaven," he gasped as he tried to regain his balance while backing away from Sho-Taka. "Save me from this savage!" he pleaded. Water poured down from his soaking head over his face as he tried to wipe his eyes. He instantly realized that while wiping his face he might need his hands to ward off Sho-

Taka again. He seemed unable to decide whether to use his hands for wiping or defense. In the midst of his confusion he stumbled on some rock under the surface and fell over again into the water. As he resurfaced one more time, he was disoriented and gasping for breath. He whirled left and right trying to locate Sho-Taka. "DON"T TOUCH ME, DAMNIT!" he screeched. "Don't touch me," he said again as he tried to catch his breath. Holding his hands out in front of him to ward off whatever might come at him, he got his bearings. "Don't …" he began to say, but didn't finish. He stepped backwards away from Sho-Taka, holding his hands out in front of him while carefully trying to stay upright. "Don't come near me." He looked off at Tyson, seeking some sympathy. Tyson tossed him a bar of soap.

There was no escape. Sho-Taka stood four feet away in the creek to his left, and Tyson stood on the bank to his right. He accepted his cruel fate and began the painful process. After ten minutes of soaping up and rinsing off he was given his reprieve.

"You better get out of the water before you freeze to death," Sho-Taka said unexpectedly. Falwyn watched him carefully, but didn't move. "Go ahead, before you catch your death of cold."

"Come on. Get in this blanket," added Tyson from the bank. Falwyn looked at him, and saw him holding up a large brown blanket. Shivering, frightened, and exhausted by the ordeal Falwyn began to make his way over to Tyson. From the corner of his eye he saw Sho-Taka move too. It caught him by surprise and caused him to jump away. He unfortunately stepped on something very slippery underneath the water and, again, flopped into the water. This final dunking washed away whatever soap and resolve he had left on him or in him and he meekly allowed himself to be lifted from the water onto the shore and wrapped in the brown blanket.

When the two others started to head back to camp, Falwyn asked for his clothes. "No," Tyson answered, "Keep the blanket on until you're dry. We'll get you some new clothes when we get back to camp." They informed him that getting clean would be pointless if he put his dirty clothes back on. Falwyn didn't like the sound of that at all, but he didn't have an ounce of fight left in him.

By the time the three men returned to camp (Tyson and Sho-Taka in front, and the blanket clad, head dripping guide 10 steps behind) Falwyn had stopped muttering to himself and was grumbling out loud to no one in particular. Clutching the blanket around him tightly, he plopped down on a log and said, "Nearly drowned me." The major and Mrs. Devonshire watched them as they came back into camp, focusing on Falwyn, but said nothing. Shea fixed a sympathetic smile on her face and brought him a bowl of warm cornmeal and bits of bacon. Falwyn took it from her and said, "They cudda killed me. Held me under the damn water so I'd catch the chills, they did."

"You'll feel better when you've eaten," Shea assured him. "Get some nice fresh clothes on you, and you'll feel even better. You'll see."

"Chokin' me! That's what he done. The murderin' savage. Picked me up and threw into the river. Cudda drowned if I hadn't fought him off." He turned to Tyson. "And you! You was no help! You wudda let him kill me for all you cared. You wuz in on it!"

Sho-Taka took exception to "murdering savage" and cautioned Falwyn about calling him names. Tyson shook his head, but said nothing, and smiled.

The party busied themselves with collecting some replacement clothes for the irate guide. After some short discussion, and grudging donations, Falwyn donned a pair of knee breeches that the major was willing to part with. The length was nearly perfect, while the waist was too large. That problem was solved by a piece of rope. Shea parted with a red cotton shirt that was too big for her anyway. It was too big for Falwyn too, but he accepted it. He didn't mention it but he was secretly pleased with how nice it felt. Sho-Taka promised again that he would begin making a pair of moccasins for him, and until he was finished Falwyn could use the Major's boots. The Major wouldn't have need of them for the next few days as he would be riding in the wagon while his foot healed. Neither man was comfortable with this arrangement. Falwyn was not convinced that stuffing rags into the boots would make them fit any better. ("And that little toe might still be in there," he whispered to Tyson holding up the boot with the hole in it.) The major was very uncomfortable about having Falwyn wear any of his clothing.

Falwyn continued complaining about how he had been 'attacked' that morning. The others ignored him and went on with their breakfast. The conversation was lighter, and there were more smiles going around. Even Major Highcross, despite his wound, seemed in good spirits. The arrival of Mrs. Devonshire on the scene had apparently explained away the noise, and threat, of stalkers.

It wasn't long before Shea reminded them all about the meat shortage. And Tyson, who had been studying the clouds, said he thought they might be in for some wet weather soon. The major even suggested that with tomorrow being the Sabbath, it might be a good idea for them to go hunting today, and use tomorrow as a day of rest. The horses could certainly use it. It was agreed all around that a getting some fresh game should be the day's priority. With a full larder and a day of rest in store, added onto a bathed Falwyn, a recovering major and the disappearance of a stalker threat, things were looking up for them all. If only their guide knew where they were going.

Because the fear of "stalkers" had faded to almost nothing since the appearance of Mrs. Devonshire, it was decided that Tyson and Sho-Taka would go out hunting separately. That would double the chances of obtaining fresh game. Tyson would hunt to the north of the west bound trail and Sho-Taka to the south. Still cautious, and with warnings of "Be careful" and "Don't wander too far off", those two made their way into the forest, as the other four made ready to pack up camp and start again travelling southwest.

It did not start out without disagreement however. The addition of Mrs. Devonshire's horse to the party allowed some relief to the original two pulling the wagon. Major Highcross removed his own horse from the harness, with Shea's help, and replaced it with Mrs. Devonshire's mount. It was understood that the major couldn't walk so his options were to ride a horse or in the wagon. He silently made his decision by saddling his own horse, and gingerly mounting it. With him riding it left driving the wagon to Shea, and she climbed up into the driver's seat. Mrs. Devonshire, glad to not have to ride a horse anymore, climbed up into the remaining seat next to her. As Falwyn took stock of the scene around him he realized he was going to be walking. And walking alone!

"WALK BY MESSELF?"

He looked from person to person, expecting somehow that one of them would explain this gross injustice to him. He wasn't riding. (He didn't want to ride the horse. He never liked horses.) And there was no room on the seat of the wagon. Oh, he could probably squeeze in with Devonshire (not an unpleasant thought to him) and Shea, but when he started to suggest it Shea said firmly, "NO!"

"No," the major quickly concurred, "You walk out in front there to lead us. That's your job. You show us the way."

"I gotta walk? By mesself? In front?" He was stunned.

"You're the guide! You must be in front." The major explained. "I'll position myself in the rear."

"Why can't I ride in the wagon?"

"The wagon's heavy enough. Tyson said only two people." Shea ruled it out. "Besides, you have to lead. You know the way we have to go."

He stood looking down the trail he was supposed to take, and then back at his companions. There had never been a better time for him to fess up than now. He thought with Sho-Taka out in the woods hunting (and Tyson too), and only the major here to hear him admit his fraud, this was the time to own up to the fact he didn't know where he was going. And neither of the women would be too harsh with him, he guessed. He stood there, arguing with himself, about whether to come clean. He looked at the three faces looking back at him. "What?" he said, and then turned and started trudging down the trail gripping his rusty musket. He didn't take quick steps, or long ones. He was more wary and alert than ever before, and would remain so for the rest of this morning which was, so far, shaping up as one of the worst mornings of his life.

Several hours later, Shea was the first to see Tyson when he reappeared from the woods just behind them. That wasn't a surprise. Although she was hardly aware of it, she had been glancing around for his reappearance every few minutes since he had left this morning.

Mrs. Devonshire had noticed it. She sat next to Shea and had tried making conversation as they inched along behind the wary Falwyn. She had thought that Shea's constant checking of the surrounding wood was concern for their safety, but soon realized that Shea only looked to the right, the north side of the trail. She became certain that Shea was looking for Tyson.

The emerging Tyson was a sight to see. His hat was gone. His hair was dripping wet and plastered to his head. His clothes were wet and stuck to his body. He held his rifle with the muzzle down and the stock above his right shoulder. Draped across his left shoulder was a dead deer. If it had any life left in it, it could have easily shook itself off the hunter's sagging shoulder. Tyson had only a bit more fight left in him than the deer did.

"Whoa," said Shea pulling in the reins and stopping the wagon.

Mrs. Devonshire heard Shea and turned quickly back toward her. Her hand plunged into her small bag, and clutched her gun. Falwyn heard Shea and turned around.

Major Highcross was falling asleep in the saddle and only became aware of the halt when his horse stopped walking behind the wagon. Opening his eyes he looked at Shea and then followed her gaze back to Tyson. "My God, man! Whatever happened to you?"

Tyson, who had had a very tough morning, let the heavy carcass slide from his shoulder to the ground. He was only too glad to be rid of his burden. Without saying a word he reached into the wagon and removed a strip of cloth, and then looked around for a place to sit down. He spied a fallen tree trunk a few feet away and plopped down on it. He began wiping his rifle with the cloth. "I ain't had a very blessed day, so I'd be obliged if you'd all just go about your business . . . and let me go about mine."

As if he hadn't heard a word Tyson said Falwyn laughed, "Gawddamn! Yer look like you been swimmin'!" The major opened his mouth several times to ask a question, but didn't. Mrs. Devonshire had spent lifetime learning when to keep her mouth shut, and remained silent.

Shea allowed her concern to override her better judgement and said, "You better get out of those wet things. The breeze is picking up, and you'll not do yourself any good sitting around in those wet clothes."

That annoyed him, but he knew she was right. He muttered to no one in particular that he had to get his rifle dried off first and continued wiping it. The others talked among themselves until he was finished. They talked about the approaching weather; they talked about finding shelter for the night and the impending storm; and they wondered where Sho-Taka was and how he was doing. Tyson listened in.

"There's a small gully back that way," Tyson gestured, "There's some rocks that should be a good place for us to make camp." He had seen them as he caught up to the wagon. In fact he had seen a good deal of territory this morning. He normally enjoyed hunting, but today it had been one trial after another. He had no desire to share today's experiences with his companions. "I think we should be able to find something in among them that we can use."

Over the next half hour Tyson got on dry clothes and led them back along the trail to a narrow path leading off to the north. The wagon inched along it twenty yards before it opened up in a small glade. There were large outcroppings of rocks on three sides with deep overhangs which would provide some shelter from the rain and wind.

Mrs. Devonshire wondered out loud about the whereabouts of Sho-Taka, and would he be able to find them. Tyson explained that he would make his way back to the trail, and simply follow the wagon tracks. "I wouldn't worry too much about him. He can't be too far off," he said, "If he can't find the trail, he'll hear us, or smell the smoke from our fire."

"He might not be as close as you think. We heard your shots when you were hunting, but there have been no sounds of shooting from his direction since he left," said Mrs. Devonshire.

Tyson noticed that she had said "shots". He wondered if they had heard how many shots he had taken. "If no one mentions it then neither will I," he thought. "He might be off in deep woods," said Tyson. "The noise won't carry if you're in thick woods. Or, maybe in a gully somewhere? Behind some rocks?" These were all plausible he thought, and no one raised an objection. "I don't think we ought to worry. He can take care of himself."

Falwyn, who knew Sho-Taka better than any of the others, nodded his agreement, "He sure can take care of himself. Knows more damn things about more damn things than anyone I ever knowed."

"Really?" whispered Mrs. Devonshire.

They all began immediately with the various jobs of setting up their camp. Water and firewood needed to be collected. Falwyn tended to the horses. Tyson, at first, emptied his powder horn to dry it. He also hung up his clothes, boots, belt and knapsack to get them dry. Then he turned to the task of butchering the deer. Major Highcross watched intently as Tyson harvested the meat (and other bits and pieces) the deer provided. The major hovered over Tyson asking many questions. Several times Tyson handed the knife to the major and let him try his hand. At first the major was tentative about the process, but soon was going at it with enthusiasm.

"Oh, I haven't done much hunting, but I certainly know how to prepare it," he answered when Tyson complimented him on cutting up the deer's carcass.

Mrs. Devonshire and Shea, although busy themselves, couldn't help but notice how intrigued the major was with the process. Shea also wondered why Tyson hadn't butchered the deer when, and where, he had shot it. It would have made its transport back to the wagon far easier; but she didn't ask.

Falwyn wasn't as reticent. Curiosity was getting the best of him and he wanted to know how Tyson and all his things had gotten so wet. And why did Tyson say his "day wasn't so blessed." He stared at Tyson, but Tyson ignored him.

Conversation around the camp touched on different topics, but it never strayed far from wondering where Sho-Taka was. Shea got Tyson's baking pot from the wagon. She knew she had the rest of the day, and all of tomorrow to make some biscuits and bread. Tyson continued working on the deer carcass. Falwyn looked longingly at Sho-Taka's baggage, which he imagined held quantities of his friend's home brew. It was only a short time before he fell asleep. The Major took the time to walk around a bit to test his wounded foot. Conversation petered out as the group thought more about their missing friend.

It was growing late, and the light was fading. "The breeze is picking up, and those clouds are closing in," said Shea breaking a long silence. Major Highcross and Mrs. Devonshire followed her eyes up to the dark sky.

"Rain's comin'. That's for sure," said Tyson without looking up. "Those thunderheads look awfully big up there." He had been watching them.

"Where is he?" Mrs. Devonshire asked out loud what everyone else was thinking. "Should we go out looking for him? He may be in trouble."

Falwyn was awake, and said, "He ought to be back by now."

They all thought the same, and the question was directed at Tyson. He continued working on the skin of the deer. One by one each of the others turned toward Tyson.

"Whaddya think, Tyson? Should we go out lookin'?" asked Falwyn.

"We ought to do something," the major said.

Tyson didn't say anything as he continued to stretch the deerskin onto a wooden frame he had made with branches. It took him a minute to attach the last edge. "If he needed our help I suppose he would have signaled, somehow. Fired off a shot, or two." He looked at their faces, "If he can't get a shot off, for one reason or another, then I don't think we can help him anyway." He didn't want to go into the possibilities.

The major wasn't as reluctant. "What if the poor man is lying helpless somewhere? We can't just sit here and not go to his aid. If he's taken a fall . . . . or been attacked by a bear? Or worse! What if savages have fallen on him? If he's wounded? And been taken prisoner! God knows what they'll do to him!"

The remarks about "falling" and the "bear" hit home with Tyson, but he didn't let on. He looked around at the faces. "We can't all go wanderin' around in the dark . . . in the rain looking for him. He could be anywhere. If he was hurt, or needed our help he would have fired his gun. Only reason he wouldn't would be because he's laying low for some reason." It sounded plausible to them. "If we go marching around the woods making all kinds of noise . . . yellin' out his name . . . we could just be walking into the same mess he's trying to avoid." No one argued with him. "I'm thinking by tomorrow mornin' it's gonna be raining here. I'm guessing it will be coming down pretty hard. If he ain't back by then, me and Falwyn will go out and try to pick up his trail."

Falwyn sat up straight at the mention of his name. "What?" he asked.

Tyson continued, "Nasty weather will probably keep every living thing out there under cover for a spell. Give us a chance to take a good look around without causing too much commotion. Probably give him a chance to slip away if he's cornered." Again he scanned the faces of the others, and then decided to add, "He's probably on his way back right now. Probably carrying a big old boar he got! Hey, we're all going to be eating roast pork tonight . . . thanks to Sho-Taka. You all wait and see."

Nobody was satisfied, but they all believed that Tyson probably knew best. Almost with a sense of guilt Shea began preparing dinner even though Sho-Taka was still missing. Tyson occupied himself by cleaning his rifle again, and checking his powder horn for dampness. He also had some odd pieces of the deer that needed cleaning and sharpening. Very little was wasted from the carcass.

Mrs. Devonshire asked Falwyn questions about Sho-Taka's background. Falwyn didn't know very much about that, but amazed them with tales of the many talents he had seen Sho-Taka display. In Falwyn's estimation Sho-Taka's greatest gift was ability to distill liquor. But he could also read and write, Falwyn said. He'd seen him tan hides and butcher cows. He was handy as a blacksmith and as a carpenter too. Could do just about everything Falwyn assured them. Mrs. Devonshire was impressed; Major Highcross was amazed.

The aroma of the baking bread and roasting venison soon was having a soothing effect on them all. Their concern for Sho-Taka had not diminished, but it didn't have their full attention anymore. Darkness fell, and a soft rain followed soon thereafter.

He walked into camp without making a single noise. One minute they were all sitting around quietly enjoying their roasted venison, and the next they were on their feet talking over one another. He came into camp carrying two rabbits and a wild turkey. One of the rabbits was huge. They all agreed it was the largest one any of them had ever seen. Between the size of the rabbit, the abundance of meat for them all, and especially the return of their friend, it took them some time to calm down. He was bombarded with questions. He was also ravenously hungry, and the others now had renewed appetites. They all ate their fill.

By the time their meal was finished and they began settling down it was raining harder. They had arranged their bedrolls under the large overhang so they would stay dry. The wagon and extra firewood were also under cover. Tyson went back to work on the buckskin. Shea packed away the extra venison while Highcross peppered her with questions about how she prepared the venison and preserved the rest. He also complimented her on the biscuits she baked. Mrs. Devonshire joined Sho-Taka as he skinned and butchered the rabbits. She made herself useful by plucking the turkey as they talked. He told her to save the feathers, as he had use for them.

"Are you going to make a pillow?" she joked.

He shook his head and continued working on the rabbits. He was very careful skinning them, and then carefully laid the skins on a flat rock. He harvested the meat by cutting it up and tossing the pieces into a pot. "We can cook this up tonight, and eat it over the next few days."

Tyson and Falwyn, sitting nearby, glanced at the pile of rabbit meat as it began filling the pot. "That's the biggest rabbit I ever saw," Falwyn said, not for the first time. Tyson silently agreed.

Sho-Taka peeked over at Mrs. Devonshire as she was plucking the feathers. "It looks like you've done that before," he said by way of a compliment.

"I've plucked many a chicken in my time," she assured him. She didn't smile as she said it. Perhaps it was the tone of her voice;

perhaps not, but Sho-Taka, Tyson and Shea all had the very same thought. *That could have two meanings!* Mrs. Devonshire noticed the awkward silence, so she went on, "When I was a little girl I never wanted to kill the chicken for dinner, but my mother wanted me to learn. She would take me with her out to the . . . to the . . . how do you say? . . . Oh yes, the henhouse . . . take me with her to the henhouse. She'd say she was going to have a little *tete-a-tete* with the chicken. I came to know what she meant." She had everyone's attention. "She would say it was a '*tete-a-tete*'. *No, not a conversation, 'a tete-a-tete'!".* She would grab that chicken by its *head* . . . then swing it over her *head!*" She swung her arm around her head. "*Tete-a-tete,* you see?" She laughed, "Then I would have to pluck out the feathers. She taught me well." With her very pleasant smile she looked around the circle at them all. They could not resist smiling back.

The conversation meandered around several topics including Sho-Taka's delayed return, the weather, tomorrow's day of rest, etc. Falwyn suddenly spoke up, "Why were so wet when you came back today, Tyson?"

Tyson's foul mood when he returned today had been forgotten by the group, and Sho-Taka had not returned until later, so the question seemed innocent enough. They all turned toward Tyson. Sho-Taka wondered out loud, "I thought you got back earlier; before it started to rain?"

"He did," answered Falwyn. He turned to Tyson, "You were back before it rained. What got you all wet," he repeated?

When he had returned, and for several hours after, Tyson was in no mood to recount his hunting exploits. But as the day wore on, and Sho-Taka safely back among them, he was in a better frame of mind. "I didn't have much luck out there today, and, I guess, I didn't feel much like talking when I got back."

"But you did get the deer," Shea offered.

"But how did you get so wet," the major persisted.

After a moment's silence he said, in a low voice, "I fell crossing a stream." Instantly he regretted saying "stream", he should have said "river". It sounded better. Embarrassed by it, he was not going to tell them the whole story.

He had started out that morning trying to find some game. He had come across some squirrels and rabbits, but had passed them by as a matter of pride because he was looking for something more substantial. As the morning wore on he began to question his choice because he could not find deer tracks anywhere. He didn't find any bear or boar tacks either. As a single hunter he would have to be more careful with them because they were larger, as well as more fierce and dangerous than deer. But as time went by he was starting to become more desperate.

These woods, he assured himself, were teeming with game, but he could find none of it! Where was it? The more he looked, the less he saw. And the less he saw the more frustrated he became. He would NOT go back empty handed.

At one point he fired a hurried shot at a pheasant, but he missed and the bird vanished. He wandered farther afield as the day wore on; fully aware that the farther he went meant the farther he would have to travel to return. It was going to be a long day.

Just when the idea of bagging a few smaller animals started to gain some appeal in his mind he spotted large buck. His first reaction was to race after it, but his experience as a hunter reminded him that any unnecessary noise would spook the animal into racing off into the wilderness. He forced himself to remain motionless. The buck was too far off to risk a shot. Taking a deep breath he started to stalk it to close the distance.

He moved with silent and cautious steps. Several times his prey would interrupt his grazing, raise his head to look around, and wander off a few feet. Each time it did Tyson would hold his breath. After a few times Tyson noticed that every time the deer moved, it moved away from him. He cursed his luck that it never moved closer! Several times as he moved closer he was forced to take indirect routes in order to remain concealed. After what seemed like an eternity of stalking Tyson came to an open area. To cross it would mean revealing his presence. The distance was still farther than he would have preferred, but the buck was within his range. It was now, or never.

Slowly he shouldered his weapon, and sighted. Very slowly he cocked the hammer of his rifle.

CLICK

The sound was louder than he thought it would be. The buck raised its head, and took a step. Tyson held his breath. The buck took another step, stopped and then looked in Tyson's direction. Tyson watched, praying the animal would stand still a moment longer. Hunter and hunted were motionless.

BANG!

It did not end well for either party. Tyson did not make the perfect shot. The deer was hit, but not dead. The ball hit the deer a few inches above where Tyson had aimed. It staggered; regained its footing, and then ran off into the woods. Tyson cursed; reloaded his rifle, and began his pursuit. The race was on.

The pursuit lasted longer than Tyson had ever thought possible. Back and forth the bleeding animal and the tracking Tyson zigzagged around the forest starting and stopping many times. The buck, fatally wounded, futilely struggled to escape the huntsman. Tyson followed the blood trail as best he could. Although Tyson could take no pride in his hunting skills this day, it was a better day for him than it was for the deer. It finally succumbed to its wound and died. It took Tyson another fifteen minutes to find the carcass. The slightly errant shot and the long chase were behind him. But the harvesting of the meat and the long trek back to his companions with it still lay ahead.

He had not even begun to work on the carcass when he heard a grunt in the woods. He had been so focused on the cut he was about to make that it startled him. And what was worse, he was unsure of its direction. But he was sure what had made the sound; it was a bear. The deer had been bleeding as it ran around the woods, and the scent of it had had a chance to drift far and wide. Tyson thought that the bear was now circling around trying to zero in on it. The deer had chosen a wide cluster of bushes as its final resting place, and Tyson had had no clear field of vision around him and the carcass. After all he had gone through to get this deer he had no intention of abandoning it to the scavenging bear. But this was no place to begin skinning it and harvesting the meat. He had no choice; he was going to have to carry it to a safer place where he could defend himself while he butchered the carcass. He would have to move quickly. He looked around, trying to get his bearings, while listening for any sounds of the prowling bear. With great effort he hoisted the deer up onto his shoulder and began moving toward what he thought was south. The deer was very heavy, and he struggled underneath it. Adding to his burden was that every sound he heard he interpreted as the bear coming up behind him.

Fifteen minutes of carrying the heavy deer over rough and uneven terrain had taken a terrible toll on the hunter. He was almost glad when he was halted by a wide stream. He hadn't crossed it earlier, and he began to wonder if he was going the wrong way. When he heard another sound, he began again to worry more about the bear than his direction. He knew he needed to find a place where the woods weren't so thick; where he could defend himself and his kill.

Perhaps under less stressful conditions he would have prudently chosen to cross the stream at a narrower place. Or rather than carry the carcass across on his shoulder, he would have taken the time to build a makeshift litter to put the deer carcass on, and then drag it across. If he had taken the time to consider his options there might have been a better outcome, but he didn't. Three steps into the thigh high water he stepped on a mossy rock beneath the surface and fell. Completely under!

Splashing and thrashing in the water he fought to regain his footing. He held tightly onto the deer and his rifle. When he was once again upright and *fairly* sure he had slipped, and not been attacked by a bear midstream, he stomped across the stream to the opposite bank. He had to look twice to make sure he had not, in his confusion, returned to the same side he had left.

On solid ground, he stood still for a moment and took stock. He was now soaking wet. His hat was gone and his gun and powder were wet. His rifle was useless. His only defense now against the stalking bear was his knife. And he knew that a knife was not a very good option against a bear. But now he was mad. Damn mad! His choices now were to stay here, or move on. Easy choice. He wasn't going to wait for the bear. He could leave the carcass for the bear, and make his getaway unburdened. Or he could keep his prize, and make his way back to camp with his pride intact. Again, that was now an easy choice. Soaking wet, alert to every sound, and struggling under the weight of the deer, he began his long trek back to the trail where he would pick up the track of his companions and rejoin them. And, he told himself, if that damn bear shows his face I'll kill him.

It would be a long time before Tyson would admit to anyone how wet and tired he was making his way back to the trail that day. He would always remember how unsure he was of his direction, and the exhilaration he felt when he first saw Shea on the wagon through the trees.

"You fell in a stream," Sho-Taka asked? "A stream?"

"Before or after you shot the deer?" the major wanted to know. Tyson wondered what difference that made.

Tyson wanted the conversation to go in another direction, so he ignored the question and asked Sho-Taka one instead. "What are you making?"

The question worked, and everyone turned toward Sho-Taka. He was working on the skin of the large rabbit. He had already scraped the skin of the smaller rabbit clean and had stretched it a wooden frame.

The conversations continued on about how best to dry animal skins and turn them into something useful. Occasionally the major asked a question about the process, but for the most part the others just listened. Shea busied herself with putting pieces of the venison and rabbit on sticks, and place them over the fire to slow roast them. Mrs. Devonshire was still not finished plucking the turkey. Falwyn seemed mesmerized by the rabbit skin Sho-Taka was working on.

As Sho-Taka answered a question by the major, Falwyn interrupted, "Where's the other rabbit skin?"

Sho-Taka, who knew him best, just ignored him. But the major turned to him, "I beg your pardon?"

Falwyn was looking at Sho-Taka, "Can I look at the other skin? The one you already done. Where is it?"

"I put it on a frame. It's by the wagon wheel," he gestured behind him. "Drying out." He thought for a moment, "Leave it alone. It's got to dry out."

Falwyn shifted his position so he was able to see around behind Sho-Taka, where he spied the frame with the skin next to the wagon wheel. "I ain't gonna touch it," he said defensively. He continued to look at it while the others returned to their conversation. A few minutes later, Falwyn interrupted them again, "Where'd you shoot it?"

The question, like most irrelevant questions, halted the general conversation. They all turned to him, but only briefly. Sho-Taka gave Falwyn an annoyed sneer and went back to his explanation of drying hides.

Falwyn repeated his question.

Sho-Taka turned slowly toward Falwyn and stared at him in silence. Knowing him as he did, he thought any answer would suffice so he gestured in a southerly direction and said, "About a mile off that way." And, although he really didn't care he asked, "Why?"

Falwyn shook his head, "No, I don't mean where; I mean *where?"* His hands fluttered in front of his chest. "There ain't no hole."

No one quite understood what he meant. They all looked back and forth at Sho-Taka and Falwyn, and then at each other. It struck Shea first. She was looking at Falwyn when it dawned on her. "Hole? You mean bullet hole?"

They all began to maneuver around to look at the rabbit skin stretched on the frame. And, each in turn, then glanced at the skin in Sho-Taka's hands.

Falwyn and Sho-Taka were looking at each other. "There ain't no hole in either one," Falwyn tried to explain. "I didn't even hear no shots. Not one," he said as if apologizing.

"Nor I," added the major three seconds later.

Everyone was now looking at Sho-Taka. "I didn't shoot them. I didn't use a gun." Then as if explaining he added, "Makes too much noise."

The listeners took some time to process that information, and it was Falwyn who asked the obvious question. "Whaddya use? How'd you kill 'em? You trap 'em?" Falwyn scrunched up his face because he knew that last question made no sense. One would need traps, and a lot of time, to trap three animals. Sho-Taka didn't have either.

In a flat voice Sho-Taka answered, "I used a rock."

Again it took them a minute to process what they thought they had just heard.

"A rock?" Tyson mouthed. Shea knitted her eyebrows and tilted her head. Mrs. Devonshire looked around at the others to gauge their reaction.

The major, trying to picture it, simply said, "Oh!"

Falwyn asked, "You dropped a rock on them? What? What were you up on? You climb up a tree?" He leaned in toward Sho-Taka, and looked very confused. "How'd ya get them to walk underneath ya? And how'd you climb up a tree carryin' a big rock?" Falwyn was having a very hard time understanding this.

So were all the others. They each tried to picture him climbing up a tree with a large rock cradled in one arm. And Falwyn was right! How did he know the rabbits would pass underneath him? How did he lure them there?

Finally Sho-Taka spoke. "I don't climb any trees, and I don't use a big rock. I use a small rock. A stone, really. A round stone."

Everyone spoke now. "A stone?" "A round stone?" "How?" These were only three of the many questions flung at Sho-Taka. He raised his hands in an effort to quiet them all down.

Only the major ignored him, "Am I to understand that you killed these rabbits, and that turkey, by pelting them with stones?"

Before he could answer, Tyson asked, "You mean you got all three without firing a shot?" He was impressed. "How do you do it?"

"With rocks? I never knew anyone who could throw rocks or anything else - 'cept maybe knives - that straight. Damn!!" Falwyn looked stunned, like he had been hit with a stone.

Sho-Taka shrugged off the compliment, and explained, "You need a rock that's round. The rounder the better! Those go straightest. And about the size of a crab apple is best. Chestnut size is too small; can't grip them. And if it's too big . . . well, you just don't want one that's too big. So you just find yourself a good stone, or two; then get in a good spot where the game will come by. Or you can spot something and then sneak up on it."

Falwyn said softly, "You can do that all right. You can sneak up on anyone." It wasn't a compliment.

Sho-Taka just shook his head and continued, "Nothing too big, remember, nothing like a bear . . . or even a deer. Small game; just keep quiet and let it come by. Then you hit it. If you hit it solid, you may kill it, but if not you will at least stun it so you can run up on it and . . . ." His voice trailed off and he looked over at Mrs. Devonshire as he waved his arm around his head. She smiled and nodded that she understood. The others did too. "Either way, you have your dinner," he said, "Without making much noise."

Their individual reactions varied. Tyson thought it was a pretty good idea under certain circumstances. Shea remembered once a neighbor had shot a rabbit with a musket too large for the job, and it was a very messy affair. Falwyn thought that Sho-Taka was the sneakiest, slyest, slickest person he ever knew, and nothing he could do would ever surprise him on that score. Mrs. Devonshire thought it was brilliant. The major's opinion differed.

"That's barbaric," he said.

The comment surprised them all, but it annoyed Sho-Taka. "We needed to eat, didn't we," he asked the major.

"You stoned the poor beasts? My God, Sho-Taka, I'm appalled by that."

"Not so *appalled* that you didn't eat your share of them tonight, major" He answered back. He resented what the major was saying.

Tyson jumped in, "I think we owe Sho-Taka our thanks, major. That rabbit tasted pretty good."

"It was good," Shea agreed.

"Oh, don't misunderstand me. I couldn't agree more that the rabbit was delicious." He was aware that he had offended the Indian, and that really wasn't his intention. And he didn't want to offend the cook either, so he added, "And it was prepared wonderfully. My compliments, Miss." He nodded his head to Shea. "But," he just didn't know when to shut up, "pummeling the poor creatures with rocks until they're dead is . . . My God, is uncivilized. Your hit it with a rock!" he repeated.

"So, Tyson hit his with a rifle shot." Sho-Taka saw no difference.

"The major was searching for the right word. "It's cruel." He paused, "It's savage."

That word struck a nerve with Sho-Taka. He had a long unpleasant history with it.

The major, in his mind, could separate the man and the action, and did not mean to insult Sho-Taka. He wanted to explain what he meant. "Oh no, my good friend, I appreciate that you and Tyson were willing to go out and hunt and obtain our daily bread. That task, although necessary for us all, was without doubt dangerous. And I doubly appreciate it that because of my wound I was unable to do my fair share and assist you in any way. I am in your debt." He waited for Sho-Taka to acknowledge the gratitude in some way. He didn't. A more prudent man would have remained quiet, but the major went on. "What I am referring to is the significant difference between Tyson's deer and your rabbits. And," gesturing toward the bird still in Mrs. Devonshire's lap, "Of course, the turkey too."

Devonshire, Shea and Tyson could see the ire the major was raising, but the major, and Falwyn, were oblivious to it.

Sho-Taka asked, "We both kill an animal. We butcher it, and then we eat it. What's different?"

"Tyson,"" the major began to explain, "Went out into the woods. He found tracks. He followed them to his prey. He stalked it. He used all his hunting skills to draw closer, and then, when close enough, "He stopped, and everyone leaned in closer to hear. "Slowly, silently, he raised his weapon . . . and then he fired. And with that shot made a deadly, clean kill."

Correcting the major's version, and giving an accurate account of how his hunt today went, thought Tyson, would do no one any good. He said nothing but thought back to the many times hunting when his shot wasn't "deadly" or "clean". He recalled once shooting a pheasant in the head (he had aimed at the body) with a large caliber weapon, and the shot exploded it. It went like that sometimes.

"I expect he would have shot a rabbit if he had come across one first. Or a turkey, maybe too, if that had strolled on by," Sho-Taka insisted. Tyson said nothing. Unlike the major he knew when to keep quiet. "I don't suppose he was being any too particular."

"That's not my point, Sho-Taka. You went out and lurked behind some tree. You ambushed some poor beast . . . by your own admission, usually one of Almighty God's smaller creatures . . . walking along a quiet forest trail. You sprung out at it, and stoned it. Like poor St Stephen in the Bible! And if that didn't do the deed, you pounced on the poor injured thing and delivered your coup de grace by wringing its neck. That, I must say, is *entirely different!*"

There was complete silence for a few seconds, and then Falwyn whispered, "Not to the rabbit."

Chapter 9 - Wallingford's Eureka!

He's who? He's what? He's going where?
Good God! You must be kidding.
He outranks me? He'll be in charge?
And I must do his bidding?
Oh no, my friend, this must not be,
This change cannot be allowed.
I'll sort this out. I'll have my way.
And emerge, at last, unbowed.

Captain Wallingford arrived for his appointment with General Tindale a few minutes before 7AM. General Tindale did not. Wallingford paced the stable area wondering if he should knock on the door. The plus would be if Audrey Tindale answered the door. But as Wallingford thought about it, that possibility seemed very unlikely. The more likely outcome would be that a servant would answer the door, as Audrey was likely still sleeping at this ungodly early hour, and the general would be annoyed at the captain's attempt to hurry him. "No, bad idea," he thought to himself.

He continued to fidget around the side yard, and began again to admire the house. It was one of the largest in Philadelphia. He began trying to estimate what it was worth. The general came from a wealthy family, and Wallingford wondered what the general's estate would be worth to his heirs. He had only one child, Audrey. Whoever married her would wind up a very rich man. He let his mind wander over the inside of the opulent house as he remembered it from several visits in the past, including last night. A portrait of Lady Tindale was hanging on the wall in the parlor. The captain had seen it and thought it was hideous. He wondered if

Audrey Tindale would look like her mother in the years to come. He prayed not.

When General Tindale finally appeared a half hour later, he approached Wallingford with a sour look on his face. "Have you had breakfast, captain," he asked?

He hadn't, and was surprised by the general's impending invitation. "No Sir, I have not," he smiled.

"You should have, it's a long time till lunch." He mounted his horse, and started off. Wallingford gritted his teeth, mounted and caught up.

They rode down Front Street at a leisurely pace as the general made disparaging remarks about the people and places they passed. For forty five minutes the general did not see a single person, or location, that he could say anything nice about. Captain Wallingford said only "Yes, Sir" and "No, Sir" as the case required the entire time.

Suddenly the commander turned to him and asked, "Well captain? Let's hear what you've got to say."

"About what, Sir?"

"Highcross, of course! What do you make of him?"

"Careful," he warned himself, "This major could be anyone." "Well, Sir," Wallingford began, "I don't really know very much about him. I don't know anything at all about his background. Or his family" he added quickly.

Staring straight ahead, the general said, "I'm told he comes from money. Gobs of it." Wallingford instantly hated him. "Family ties to Lord Nunch, so they say. Relatives in government service. House of Lords, I think. Maybe Commons, I'm not sure." They rode a few steps in silence. "He said nothing to you?"

"Why would he speak to me?" Wallingford wondered. "Who the hell is this guy?" was the question he kept asking himself. Wallingford was getting the impression that the general thought he should know the man; that they had spoken to each other. "Let's dispel that goddamn notion right away!" he told himself. Knowing that no conversation is easier to lie about than an actual one, Wallingford answered, "No, Sir! Not a single word."

"You know my daughter seems quite smitten with the man."

This caught Wallingford completely off-guard. And after processing that bit of information for a moment Wallingford *really* hated him. All he was able to say was, "Highcross?"

The General ignored the question, and went on, "I'll be damned if I can understand why. He seemed to be a blithering idiot who stammered and stumbled without stop when we met in my office. Okay, I can expect a bit of nerves at a first meeting, but Good God, he never calmed down." Wallingford didn't know what to say. The general wasn't looking for agreement. "I cannot understand what my dear Audrey finds so appealing in that young man! God knows what goes on in young peoples' heads these days! All she talks about . . . day and night . . . Major Highcross this, and Major Highcross that!" He paused again before blurting out, "And he's to be entrusted with command at Fort Dubois?"

Captain Wallingford nearly fell off his horse. After a moment to steady himself, he was only able to say, "Who?"

The general turned to him in a flash. He had a very angry look on his face. "Highcross, damnit! Who the blazes do you think we're talking about." Then he turned away, and almost as if he was talking to someone else, the general said, "You know, captain, I was hoping to convince Major Highcross to wait here for his troop before proceeding west."

Wallingford's brain was swimming, so that barely registered. "Yes, that would have been better." replied the captain, who was only able to prevent himself from falling off his horse by a firm grasp of the saddle's pommel.

"But he was quite anxious to get to his post, it being his first . . . after all the delays he has already encountered. I'm sure he told you all about them. I almost felt sorry for the man."

"Certainly understandable, under the circumstances," answered the dazed Captain Wallingford.

"Remember my first posting. Back in '33. Couldn't wait to have a go at it. Arrogant and impudent as can be! Thought I knew it all."

The general paused a moment before continuing, "Suppose we are all that way, eh, Wallingford?"

The mention of his name brought the captain's attention back to what the general was saying. "How's that, Sir?" answered the captain with raised eyebrows.

Annoyed at having to repeat himself again, the general barked, "Highcross, of course! Hope his enthusiasm doesn't get him in a pinch out there at Dubois. Told him several times he best tread carefully." The general nodded in agreement with himself, then added, "At least until he gets his feet solidly on the ground out there. Can't be too careful, you know."

"No, of course not," Wallingford agreed, but then suddenly asked, "Wait! What did you say about Dubois?" Captain Wallingford was confused, and he did not like being confused.

The general, taken aback at the captain's annoyed tone of voice, shot right back, "Major Highcross damnit! The new commander at Dubois. What is wrong with you this morning?"

"The new commander at Dubi…., er, Fort Dubois?" he corrected himself. The very pained expression on the general's face warned Wallingford to be careful. "My apologies, Sir, but I am a little confused right now. Who is this Major? And what is this you say about command at Fort Dubois?"

"Major Highcross. Major …." He hesitated a moment, then went on, "Major Aaron Highcross. Who in God's name do you think we've been talking about?" The general looked at the captain, and could see the confusion on his face. "Major Aaron Highcross! Surely he reported in to you at Fort Royal? He left here 10 days ago."

"No, Sir" answered the captain in a very low voice. The ground beneath him was shaking and falling away. Despite how unsteady he felt, his mind was racing.

"And you didn't meet him on the road? On your way here?" the general asked. The general now seemed more puzzled than annoyed. "I had Sergeant Poole take him as far as Moore's Station, and make sure he took the western road. He refused an escort. Said he'd be fine." Tindale shook his head, "He couldn't have gotten lost. It's as straight as an arrow, and clearly marked." There was a pause, then shaking his head he said to himself, "And this is the man Audrey is enamored with? Good God!"

Captain Wallingford wasn't thinking about a 'lost' officer. He was asking himself, "Who the hell is Highcross?" Collecting himself he said, out loud, "Er, Sir. Who is this Major Highcross?"

It was now obvious to General Tindale that Captain Wallingford had missed connections with Major Highcross, and was unaware of his mission. He briefed him quickly. "Major Highcross has been sent out here to take command of Fort Dubois. Headquarters will be sending orders soon about an additional detachment of troops to be assigned to him." The general did some quick math and went on, "They should send 25, or so, additional troops. And, I suppose an officer and sergeant too. That, with *your 25 soldiers*, should give him a command of more than 50."

"The reference to Wallingford's "25 soldiers" made the captain shiver.

"He's to clean out the territory out there. Rid it of all the scum that's been causing all the trouble for you. Was supposed to report in to you at Royal, and then proceed to Fort Dubois and assume command." Almost as an afterthought the General went on to say, "He, of course, will assume overall command of all His Majesty's forces at Fort Royal and Dubois. You'll report to him, and provide any assistance he may require." Tindale looked curiously at the Captain Wallingford, and asked quietly, "And you say he never reported in to you at Fort Royal?"

"Breathe . . . Focus . . . Breathe . . . Focus," Wallingford keep repeating to himself. After a moment he had gotten himself under control. Although there were so many questions swirling around his head he couldn't count them, he was able to ask, "And when did he leave here, Sir?" The commander told him he had left Philadelphia ten days ago, and then asked again about the captain not meeting him on the road. "No, Sir," he answered, and then by way of explanation, "I travelled a rather circuitous route to here from Fort Royal, Sir. I wanted to look in at some settlements along the way."

The general wondered out loud if he should mount a search party for the missing officer. "Oh no, Sir. That . . . that won't be necessary." Wallingford said with absolute certainty. He did not want any troops from Philadelphia wandering around his backyard at Fort Royal. He realized that as this major had been traveling west toward Royal, he had been traveling south from New York, Not east from Royal as the general thought. That's why they hadn't met. He's probably already at Fort Royal; the captain was thinking, and if he really isn't lost he's probably already dealing with Lieutenant Smith. This isn't good he thought to himself. "I've got to get back there," he whispered to himself.

"We've got to go find him if he's lost, you know. He doesn't know the territory, and we can't have him wandering around the countryside with all the danger that's lurking there. Rampaging Indians, and what not," said a very concerned General Tindale.

Captain Wallingford knew better. There were very few Indians out there between Philadelphia and Fort Royal. And none of them that were there had "rampaged' in a very long time. He also knew that with the arrival of this new 'commander of Fort Dubois' his idyll at Fort Royal was in serious jeopardy. "I'll do it.' He said suddenly. "I'll find him. I know that territory better than anyone. And I'll use a small party from Fort Royal to assist me. A large military force moving around will only frighten the savages, and cause heightened tensions between them and the settlers in the area. We don't want that, do we Sir? Leave it to me. A week's time is all I'll need" He started to turn his horse around, but reconsidered. "Better say two weeks, Sir, just to be on the safe side."

Yes, he thought, two weeks should give him enough time to organize a plan to deal with this interloper while Tindale sat here on his hands. Captain Phillip Wallingford had always considered the possibility that his enterprises at Fort Royal could come to an abrupt end. But he was not ready to concede that this was it.

"I'll report back, Sir, in two weeks' time. Wait for my report, Sir."

The general didn't even get to say a word before Wallingford spurred his horse and was off. At first General Tindale was stunned by the abrupt departure of the captain, but then he was filled with admiration for the resolute officer as he dashed off to rescue the wandering major. Watching Wallingford race off he mused, "I should have asked him to stay for dinner."

As Captain Wallingford raced back to his quarters, he began ticking off some steps that needed to be taken immediately. Certainly he thought that his occasional sojourns to Philadelphia were likely to be finished. That would mean that all the things he had in Philadelphia that he couldn't take back with him to Fort Royal (and for the sake of speed he would have to travel light) he would have to sell or pawn. These included several personal items, some military regalia, and his government issued horse. He would, in turn, steal another one for the trip back. He returned to his lodgings, changed into civilian clothes, collected his items for sale, and then headed out to complete his tasks.

When he returned to his room 90 minutes later he bounded up the stairs to collect the few possessions he still had. Throwing them into a sack he left his room forever. He didn't take one last look around, he was in a hurry.

Reaching the first floor he was surprised to see the seriously hungover Captain McLayne, with a face and a uniform looking very much the worse for wear, standing midway between the stairs and the front door. His hands on his hips, he glared through frighteningly blood-shot eyes at the surprised Captain Wallingford.

"You, Sir, are a contemptible scoundrel!" snarled the hatless captain. "You deserted me last night to the mercy of that thieving barman! You're without honor and a disgrace to . . . . "

He didn't get to finish what he wanted to say because Phillip Wallingford was in a hurry and never broke stride. Two steps away from irate McLayne Wallingford grabbed a bottle off the table he was passing and brought it down on McLayne's head.

Captain McLayne had not anticipated that, and as a result took the brunt of the assault without any defensive maneuvers. Not surprisingly, he was unconscious before he hit the floor.

Phillip Wallingford stepped over the prostrate McLayne, leaving everyone in the tavern in stunned silence, and went out the door, got on his newly acquired (stolen) horse, and was racing west moments later. He was leaving Philadelphia for perhaps the last time. He didn't say good-bye to anyone.

As he rode away moments later, his mind was analyzing his predicament. As he considered the various scenarios that his future might present, he regretted only two things. He would probably never get a second chance at Miss Audrey Tindale, and because he was in such a hurry to get back to Fort Royal, he would have to skip the usual detour to the roadhouse near the Delaware River.

The frenetic ride west to Fort Royal was done at a relentless pace. It was approximately 125 miles distant, and the captain allowed himself only the shortest breaks for rest and water. There would be no time for sleep on this trip. The captain drove himself on without mercy. Of course, as hard as it was on him it was even harder for his horse. The horse, after all was doing all the running and carrying! The captain had only to hold on, spur his mount, and plot strategy.

His first, and most important, objective was to prevent this Major Highcross from reaching Dubious. This was about self-preservation. That had to be done first. After that, his second objective was all about money. He had to get Devonshire back to the authorities in New York and get that reward.

First things first! What to do with Highcross? The strategy would depend on several factors that were not yet certain. Where was Highcross? Wallingford assumed he was sitting on his hands at Fort Royal. Who was with him? General Tindale said he had gone to Fort Royal alone. He had no troops with him. Had any been sent down from Fort Pitt? If he had no accompanying troops (and the troops at Fort Royal didn't count!) he would be easier to handle. Ah, but what to do with him? He can't be allowed to reach Dubious. Delay him at Fort Royal? But for how long? And what if he insists on returning to Philadelphia and reporting the nonexistence of Dubious to General Tindale?

Wallingford found himself repeatedly asking the question, "How can I get rid of this meddlesome major?" He asked himself that question many times, and the macabre answer was always the same.

Obtaining the reward for turning in Devonshire should follow quickly behind the elimination of Highcross. Wallingford could not guess how much time he had if something - anything – went wrong.

After twenty hours of almost non-stop riding the road weary three year old colt staggered into the Fort Royal settlement on Sunday morning May 8th. Dirty, sweaty, thirsty and tired were only the first four of the many complaints the captain had.

Riding his leg weary mount through town, heading for the fort, the captain spotted Private Selkirk walking along the street. Wallingford spurred the poor animal once more and cut off the unaware soldier mid-stride. Selkirk, lost in thought, nearly walked into the sagging horse before he stopped.

Squinting up through blood shot eyes at the rider; Selkirk took a moment to recognize his disheveled commanding officer. "Oh, it's you captain. When did you get . . . ?"

"Where is he?" interrupted the officer.

"Who's that, Captain? Who are you looking for?"

Captain Wallingford didn't know if Selkirk was being dumb or coy. He didn't care. He took a deep breath, and tried to conjure up bit of patience. Selkirk probably wouldn't have asked that question if he knew how dangerously low Captain Phillip Wallingford was on compassionate understanding at the present moment. "Where is Highcross?" asked Wallingford.

Noting the tone of voice Wallingford used Selkirk correctly gauged the Captain's state of mind as he leaned over him from atop his horse. Don't push it he told himself. "The Major? Oh, the Major left a few days ago. He's on his way out to Dubious. I mean Fort Dubois."

The Captain shook his head. It wasn't the expected answer, and not the one he really wanted. "How many troops has he got with him?"

Now Selkirk shook his head. "None! Didn't bring any with him, and didn't take any of ours when he left."

"Any of *mine*," Wallingford quickly corrected. He thought for a moment, and then asked, "He's alone? He's out there by himself? How's he going to find Dubious?"

"He got himself a guide," Selkirk smiled.

"Simpson? Twibbleton is back?"

"No Sir. Them boys are still both out chasing each other around, I guess. This here Major got himself another guide."

Captain Wallingford was glad it was not either of those two. They were both surly, tough men, and he would prefer not dealing with them at all. But whoever was with this Major Highcross would have to be dealt with. "Who's out there with him? Who's his guide?""

Selkirk smiled, "Falwyn."

"Falwyn?" Wallingford whispered. Selkirk nodded, and the Captain said "Falwyn!" louder. It was a half laugh. That was definitely better than Simpson or Twibbleton. The Captain gazed off toward the woods. He asked Selkirk when they had left, and was told it was four days ago. Had it rained here since they left? No, he was told. This was welcome news. Falwyn was probably wandering around, hopelessly lost, and their tracks would be easy to follow. Wallingford scanned the sky and saw the heavy clouds off to the west, and wondered how long the rain would hold off. His mind shifted back to Falwyn as the guide, and after thinking about it for a moment the obvious question was, "How is he guiding Highcross? He doesn't know where Dubious is. He's never been there."

Selkirk just shrugged, "Maybe one of the other folks know? There's five of them out there . . . maybe six in the party?"

Wallingford turned back to the private below him. "Five? Six? Who else is out there? Who else besides Highcross and Falwyn?"

'Well," Selkirk began, "Sho-Taka is with them. He went."

"The Indian? Sho-Taka? Why did he go? What's he doing with them?"

Selkirk shrugged again. He really didn't know. He moved on because he wanted to see the captain's reaction when he told him the last name. "And that settler from Virginia went too. He got here after you had gone east. Pretty sure his name is Tyson. Least that's what he said his name was."

Wallingford asked a few questions about this stranger "Tyson". He learned that Tyson was looking to farm some property out in Kan-tucky. They were heading in the right direction and so he joined them. It seemed innocent enough.

"Who else?"

"Shea. That redhead from Philyaw's. She went along with 'em too." The Captain said nothing. It took a moment for him to place her; she wasn't a 'redhead'." But when he did remember who she was his first reaction was a tinge of regret that that young lady had left. As a general rule of thumb he never liked it when any young woman left the settlement. He recalled she had once asked him several questions about Dubious and the soldiers who were stationed there. He had, of course, been evasive. He wondered about that for a moment, but then dismissed it.

"That's five. You said 'maybe six'. Who else went?"

Now Selkirk came to the person he had been saving for last. He couldn't wait to see the captain's reaction when he said the name. 'We ain't sure," he said offhandedly, "but the lady disappeared the same time they left, so she might be with them."

"Who? What lady?"

"Mrs. Devonshire." He waited just a moment, and then added, "She's gone."

It was more than Selkirk had anticipated. The captain was still thinking of the departure of Shea when Selkirk added Devonshire to the list. Selkirk hid a smile as the captain's eyes suddenly fixed on his face, while he mouthed the name 'Devonshire'.

"What did you say?"

Selkirk repeated the name.

"She left?" he asked softly. "She's gone? She's not here?" he asked. He gazed up into the sky. "And that goddamn fool let her go," he said in a somewhat louder voice to no one in particular. He began shaking his head in disbelief. Selkirk tried hiding a smile. Suddenly the captain's demeanor changed in a flash, with a voice quaking with fury, he glared down at Selkirk, "I'll kill him. I'll have him facing a firing squad in the morning." His face had turned crimson red. "Go get Smith. Go get him RIGHT NOW! And bring him to Bardley's. I don't care if you have to tie him up and throw him over a horse."

"I don't know where Lieutenant Smith is." was all Selkirk could say.

The Captain was fed up with Selkirk. He was at his wit's end! "I DID NOT ASK YOU WHERE HE IS!!! I said 'GO GET HIM!'. I do not care *WHERE* he is! Go get him and bring him here or you'll be joining him in front of that firing squad in the morning. Go get those motherless bastards in the barracks out of their beds to help you! No one sleeps or eats until you find him. I want him here within the hour or you'll all be on your merry way to the killing fields of France on the next boat." This was a threat he had sometimes used in the past, but this time Selkirk thought he meant it. He was stunned. And, to the captain's dismay, he remained motionless. "GO, GOD DAMNIT, GO!!!!"

Selkirk hustled off toward the fort, not daring to turn around to see if the captain was watching him. He had never seen Wallingford so angry, and was, at least a little bit, intimidated. Selkirk had been sure that Devonshire's departure would bother the captain; but he still wasn't sure why. He had suspected something was going on the minute he found out (by idly questioning Lieutenant Smith) that Lieutenant Smith had been assigned to 'accompany' her at all times during the captain's absence. The suspicious Private Selkirk wondered why such a task had not been assigned to the soldiers. Why Smith? His manners weren't any better than the rest of the soldiers, and a fence post was a better conversationalist. He still did not know who this mysterious woman was, but the captain's reaction to her departure far exceeded Selkirk's expectation. His mind was racing (not as fast as his feet) as he went off to the fort to wake the rest of the troop, Behind him Captain Wallingford had yanked the reins and spurred his poor exhausted horse in the other direction down the street toward Josiah Bardley's house. And when Josiah Bardley heard the racket coming down the street, and suspected it might be Wallingford, he winced.

Selkirk had a bit of luck and found Lieutenant Smith the first place he looked; in his quarters. When Selkirk knocked on the fastened tent flap the lieutenant jumped to his feet. And although the lieutenant always seemed a bit jittery to Selkirk, he now appeared beside himself. He told the nervous lieutenant that Captain Wallingford was back, and he wanted to see him immediately at Josiah Bardley's house. Lieutenant Smith had dreaded this since he had found out Mrs. Devonshire had slipped out of the Bardley residence sometime before dawn last Wednesday morning. When Lieutenant Smith seemed to hesitate a moment Selkirk said to him, "I don't think you oughta keep him waiting, Lieutenant. He don't seem to be in a very good state o' mind right now."

"He's not happy?"

"I'd say he is peeved, lieutenant."

"Did he mention me by name?"

"It weren't me he threatened to shoot, lieutenant. "

Selkirk took the officer by the arm, and gently walked him from the fort to the Bardley house. The walk of several hundred yards to Bardley's took longer than it should have because the lieutenant took very short, slow steps. Several times Selkirk heard the lieutenant mutter, "Oh my …. Oh my!"

As they got within fifty yards of the house they could hear the captain yelling. When they arrived on the porch they could then hear Josiah Bardley's faint responses. It was not a pleasant conversation. It was actually too one-sided to be even called a conversation. Captain Wallingford screamed and hollered at his cowering junior partner. Questions fired too rapidly to leave any room for answers kept Josiah Bardley stammering.

"HOW COULD YOU LET HER GO?"

"Well, I didn't …."

"WHEN DID YOU REALIZE SHE WAS GONE?"

"It was …. "

"DO YOU KNOW WHERE SHE'S GONE?"

"I think she …."

"YOU THINK! WHY DIDN"'T YOU GO AFTER HER?"

"I'm not a …."

"WERE YOU AFRAID OF HER?"

"Of course n...."

"ARE YOU A DAMN COWARD?"

"I say!"

"DO YOU HAVE ANY IDEA WHAT HER ARSE IS WORTH?"

Wallingford had no intention of telling Bardley the true answer to that last question. In their initial conversation the he had estimated that the reward for her may be as much as £1000 He had originally promised Bardley 250 for his help in 'housing the French bitch' while in Fort Royal while Wallingford went east to confirm who she was. In New York, at the magistrate's office, he had learned a great deal about Mrs. Devonshire including, to his delight, that his original estimate of the reward was far too low. Now, to Wallingford's disgust, Bardley had let this bonanza slip through his fingers. All was not lost, he thought. We can still retrieve the wench, and cash her in for the money. But it seemed perfectly justifiable to Wallingford that in light of Bardley's bungling, his share of the prize should remain at the original lower figure. "Perhaps even cut it a bit?"

Selkirk didn't bother to knock on the front door; he just let himself and the lieutenant into the house. He gently pushed the Smith in through the doorway into the parlor where Wallingford and Bardley were. The lieutenant took a few short steps into the room as Selkirk, determined to watch this play out, slid into the room behind him and moved away to the side.

Noticing their presence the captain turned toward his lieutenant and snarled, "Oh, here's my other genius!" The lieutenant smiled weakly. After a moment's glare the Captain, trying to control himself, whispered, "Where is she?"

Mistaking a muscle spasm of the captain's for a gesture toward Bardley, Smith became confused. Had he meant Mrs. Bardley? "Who," he asked?

The captain threw his hands in the air, "Christ Almighty! Who the hell are we talkin' about? DEVONSHIRE!!! Where's Devonshire, you damn fool!"

"She's gone," the lieutenant offered, but he doubted that was the answer the captain wanted.

"I know she's gone. Gone where? You were supposed to be watching her."

"I did, Sir, when she was here. Every day she was here I was with her." By way of explanation he went on, "Every time she stepped out the front door, I was there. Day or night, Sir." He gestured toward Bardley, "You can ask him, Sir, I was there every time. I slept under the porch, Sir."

"Well then! Where is she? She's not in this house. So where is she? Is she out on the porch?"

The lieutenant didn't think his answer would sit so well with the captain, but he gave it anyway, "I think . . . er . . . *we think*," he gestured toward Bardley, "We think she snuck off, Sir."

"Oh, you do? The both of you think that, do you?" He turned and shot a quick venomous glance at Bardley. Turning back to the lieutenant, he asked calmly, "Where do *you two* suppose she snuck off to?" He began looking back and forth at the two of them.

Smith and Bardley remained quiet because neither wanted to be the captain's focus of attention. The silence became unbearable for the frightened lieutenant and he said, "I think she went off with them folks headed for Dubious. They were the only ones who left the fort lately. And she probably stole a horse, too. We ain't sure, though." He hoped that this answer would be viewed by the captain as being helpful. He sincerely hoped so.

The captain turned and looked at the smirking Selkirk leaning against the wall. "I told you to watch the pilgrims who came and went while I was gone. So tell me; did she leave with them people?"

Acutely, and very uncomfortably, aware that he was now in the captain's crosshairs, he stood straight up and spoke quickly, "Captain, I was there when they headed out last Wednesday mornin'; and she wasn't with them." Just to make it clear he said it again, "When they left here it was only the four men and Shea. And two horses; and those horses belonged to that Major Highcross and Tyson."

The captain, pointing at Selkirk, turned again toward Bardley and Smith and yelled at them, "He was watching them when they left, and she wasn't there! Why do you two morons think she's with them?"

Bardley had no opinion, about anything. He said nothing. Smith finally offered, "She can't have gone off alone. I don't think she'd fare too good out there all by herself."

More to himself than anyone else, Wallingford said, "Oh, is that what you think?' He shook his head in disgust. "You'd be amazed at what that … that …," he was at a temporary loss for words. Finally he said, "THAT woman can do!"

At his recent visit to the Magistrate's office in New York Captain Wallingford had been told all about 'that woman'. He had gone in and told the Colonel in charge that he thought he had recognized the woman on the poster that the Magistrate had circulated to all commands north and west of New York. She was, 'at this very minute', being detained by his command at Fort Royal. He had seen the poster, and shortly thereafter she appeared at his settlement. He proudly told them he had immediately placed her in custody. "I hope you have her under 24 hour guard, and not left on her own for a minute," the colonel said. "She is as devious as any criminal in the colonies." He went on, "Her real name is Dellie d'Argent. She has various aliases. Dina D'Arnay. Desiree Dubonne. God knows what else!"

"You can add Delilah Devonshire to that list," the Captain told him.

"She is a prostitute and a madam," the colonel went on. "A woman without morals and a seducer of married men! A number of whom who have gone missing! She is a swindler and a thief. A horse thief and a sneak thief. A burglar! She will steal anything not locked down. As a matter of fact, nothing is safe from her, even when under lock and key! She is not only a master pickpocket, but can pick any lock she comes across." The colonel had many stories about how she had cheated and stole large quantities of money and goods from merchants and British soldiers throughout New England and Canada. She once had cheated an entire regiment of British soldiers out of their month's pay in a gambling scam. She had avoided capture in Montreal after its fall to the British, and was on the run somewhere in the colonies. The reward for her capture was 5000 British Pounds!

Captain Phillip Wallingford had a lot to think about. He started to put the facts together. The major was out there with a long head start. That was not a big problem because the weather hadn't washed away the trail they had taken and the captain felt he could track them easily. After all, how far could that idiot Falwyn have taken them? Once overtaken, he would let that fellow Tyson continue on. And perhaps if he was lucky, Tyson would take Sho-Taka with him; maybe even take Shea too. In any case Captain Wallingford would then insist that the remaining individuals return with him to Fort Royal. They would never arrive. That alternative, although unpleasant, was necessary. The major was NOT going to reach Dubious, under any circumstances. And if that meant that the others had to be eliminated before returning to Fort Royal that would be okay too. This brought a small smile to the captain's face. Bardley and Smith both saw it, and breathed a little easier. However they remained silent, not wanting to interrupt any thoughts which were apparently making the captain less angry.

The captain thought about Devonshire (or d'Argent, or D'Arnay, or whatever her name was!). What to do with her? The major, of course, came first, but what to do with Devonshire? First he had to determine if she was with them. If she wasn't, he would deal with the major (etal) first; then go off after her. How far could the wench have gone on alone? She couldn't, he decided. She had to be with someone who had some frontier skills. Either with them or not, she must be heading in the same direction. Back north, or east, was out of the question. That's where she was running from! West was Fort Pitt, and that was a large British fort overflowing with soldiers. She wouldn't be going near there. To the south were Philadelphia and Baltimore. No, further south only meant a greater English presence. It had to be southwest. If she was with them, he thought, the situation became a little more complicated, but still something he could handle.

Coming out of his reverie, the captain asked Selkirk again if he was sure she hadn't left with them. Selkirk repeated that he was at the corral when they pulled out of Ludlum's, and there was no sign of her. He added that there weren't any other westward, or eastward, bound parties since then. Wallingford turned to Smith, "And you were with her every second she was here? She didn't talk to the Major? Or anybody else?"

The Lieutenant hesitated a minute before giving an answer he wasn't sure the captain would like. "Well Sir, she did kinda talk to a few people, including that major. Sometimes we met up with some people as we walked around." The lieutenant paused, trying to gauge if he was getting himself in more trouble. "I couldn't tell her to just shut up, could I?"

"What did they talk about? Did you hear what they said?"

"Oh yes, Sir. I was standin' right there, just like you told me. I was with her every second. I slept under the porch. Every time she stepped out the front door; there I was. Every time! Morning, noon, and night, Sir. Never left her alone with anyone for a minute, captain. Heard every word."

The captain questioned him about what was said, not only with the major, but with everyone else she spoke to while at Fort Royal. For all of Lieutenant Smith's shortcomings he proved remarkably adept at repeating conversations verbatim back to the captain. He told Wallingford that the major had told her about his upcoming trip but, and Lieutenant Smith was very certain about this, they never discussed her joining up with them.

Selkirk continued listening to the conversation, trying to be as unobtrusive as possible. He thought it best not to offer the information about his little errand for the lady. How he had been walking past the house when she signaled him from the parlor window. In a hushed voice she instructed him to attend the 'shooting contest' that was scheduled to take place at noon that day, and then report back. He did, and although that meeting wasn't all he hoped it would be, he was compensated as promised. After all, the only things he told her about were the match results and some tidbits about the people involved. No, he decided, that little tete-a-tete would remain his and Devonshire's secret.

The captain continued grilling Smith about conversations. "And she was never alone with any one of them people that left? Even for a minute?"

"No Sir! I was with her every second she was about socializing. No one had any private dealings with the lady at all. Not them people who left, or anyone else." Smith was starting to feel better.

"Did she ask anyone about Dubious?"

"No Sir! Not a soul. Except the major. He told her he was going to Dubious, but she didn't even ask him when. Or how he was gonna get there. He talked about it, but she didn't ask no questions."

"She ever ask anyone about the territory between here and Fort Pitt? Or about any territory west of here?"

"Nope, not a single time, Sir."

The longer the interrogation went on with Smith the better Wallingford felt. And the better he felt, the better Smith felt. And Bardley remained as quiet as a tomb on the end of the settee where he sat. And finally, after a few more questions, the Captain asked again, "And at no time did she ever have a conversation with anyone, in the fort or the settlement, that you weren't there right next to her, and heard every word? She never spoke to anyone – outside the house – when you weren't right there beside her, right?"

"Yes Sir!"

The captain shifted his position slowly to face Bardley, and arched an eyebrow at him.

Bardley, anticipating the question, straightened up and declared, "Never, for one minute, did anyone, except me, in this house converse with that woman!" His voice left no doubt." I was very explicit with the servants, that there was to be no contact, other than necessary household instructions, with Mrs. Devonshire. They were to be polite, but nothing else. I checked with each and every one of them daily."

"And your wife?"

"She wouldn't speak to that French harlot if her hair were on fire!"

"And you?"

"I was civil to her, but not very accommodating. Our conversations concerned the weather, and that was all."

Once more Wallingford sat back and sorted through the information. She might have some wilderness skills, he thought, but not enough to go it alone, without supplies, into the Ohio Valley. No, she had to be with the major's party. They were her only hope. It occurred to him that perhaps she had met up with one of them before arriving at Fort Royal, and they had agreed to rendezvous at Fort Royal. It didn't matter. She had to be with the major's party. There was no one else.

The captain began to rise and offhandedly he asked, Smith, "So you heard her every word she said while she was here? She was never alone."

It was out of his mouth before he realized that perhaps he should have simply said 'Yes'. "I left her alone once, but there was nobody there."

A silence came over the room. Bardley froze in place, and his eyes slid toward the captain. Selkirk did the same. The captain, very slowly retook his seat. "You left her alone? Why?"

All eyes in the room now focused on Smith. "She felt . . . She thought she might faint, Sir. I went to fetch some water for her, Sir."

"You went to fetch some water for her? Because she felt faint?" Something was wrong here; Captain Wallingford could sense it.

"She needed a drink of cool water, Sir. So I got some water from the river. The water in our well is too warm, she said. So I got her some water from the river," he repeated. "The water from the river is cooler. She wanted a sip of cool water 'cause she thought she was going to faint, Sir."

"'The water in *our* well is too warm?'" Wallingford repeated, "What well? Where were you?" He still spoke quietly, but there was now an edge to his voice.

"The well in the fort, Sir. I was showing her around the fort. And we had been walking all over; the stables; the powder house; the barracks (none of the soldiers were there, Sir, I checked before we went in) and then she said she felt like she was going to faint, and I had to go get some cool water for her to feel better. So we got out of the sun, and I grabbed a bucket and went and got the water while she waited. And she told me to walk, not run, so I wouldn't spill any."

"While she waited? Out of the sun? In the fort?" he asked, his voice was now a level louder, but hard and flat. Smith nodded. "Where was she 'out of the sun', lieutenant?"

"In the office," Smith answered. He knew he was on very thin ice, but he didn't know why. "But she was alone, Sir." Shaking his head he went on slowly, "There weren't nobody in there for her to be talkin' to. Not a soul." Smith could feel the air leaving his lungs. He thought in a minute or two he was going to have trouble breathing.

Wallingford's voice was now definitely louder; and meaner! "In the office? You left her alone in the fort office, while you *walked* to the river and back with a bucket of water?"

Lieutenant Smith tried to clarify what he just said, "No Sir. I *ran* to the river, but I walked back 'cause I didn't wanna spill none."

"You left her in the office? You mean the office right next to my quarters?" hissed the captain. He wasn't waiting for answers again. Then he repeated it loud enough for everyone in the house to hear it. "RIGHT NEXT TO MY FOKKIN QUARTERS!" He was now standing.

"Your door was locked, like always, Sir. I looked. Padlock was clamped shut. I am sure of that, Captain." Smith was becoming frightened.

"OH? IT WAS PADLOCKED? YOU'RE SURE? WHILE YOU *WALKED . . . .*"

The captain seemed to have lost his breath. He turned around and stared at the far wall for a moment, and then turned back to Smith, stumbling. He reached for him, but the lieutenant stepped back out of reach. Bardley froze. Selkirk would have slipped out the door, but was afraid he'd call attention to himself if he moved.

The quivering captain was failing badly at regaining his composure. He shook as he pointed at Smith, "If anything ……. ANYTHING!!! ….is missing from my quarters …." He didn't finish the thought. He turned and lurched for the door. Selkirk moved the chair he was behind so it was between the departing captain and himself. Bardley was so frightened he thought that the knot in his stomach might be his testicles. Smith was transfixed by the fury on Captain Wallingford's face.

Before dashing out Wallingford whirled around once again, and pointed a crooked finger at Smith, "So help me God . . . if one shilling . . . if one …. AAAAHHHH! ….." and he was gone.

The three remaining men in the room, as well as everyone in the house, heard the Captain Phillip Wallingford race out the door and storm across the front porch. Not bothering with the steps, he leapt off the porch, and landed on the lawn. His sense of balance only carried him as far as the small picket fence surrounding the house and his attempt to hurdle it was nowhere near adequate. He knocked down an eight foot span of it when he crashed into it. It didn't faze him a bit as he was back on his feet in a flash. He didn't bother finding and mounting his horse, he thought it would only slow him down. He raced down the street, screaming intermittently, "*I'm* gonna kill him ….. I'm *gonna* kill him ….. Oh, I'm gonna **kill him**!" Very few people in the Fort Royal settlement didn't hear him.

It took Captain Phillip Wallingford less time to reach the fort on foot than if he had been riding on Mercury's back. A Private Finlay happened to be on duty at the gate that morning, and saw the captain's manic approach. His first thought was that the officer was being chased by hostile Indians. He raised his Brown Betty flintlock to his shoulder, and called out "Close the gate!"

This was precisely the correct course of action under the circumstances as he saw them. Reviewing the situation later Selkirk would point out two minor flaws in his performance. One was that he was the only one (as was always the case) on guard duty at the gate at that time. Ergo, if anyone were to 'Close the gate!' it would have to be, by process of elimination, him. And the second point being that raising his weapon to his shoulder was somewhat pointless, because it wasn't loaded. (Ever since Private Bloodworth celebrated Christmas Day last year by drinking his breakfast (rum) and *accidently* firing his weapon – three times – the captain had ordered that the main gate guard could not load his weapon until he was fired upon.)

This all became moot as Finlay watched the approach of the frantic captain, and finally noticed that no one was chasing him.

Continuing to hold the flintlock up to his right shoulder with his left hand, he smartly saluted the captain with his right as the officer drew near. Military protocol and courtesy were not very high priorities to Captain Wallingford at this moment, and he ran past Finlay without returning the salute.

After the captain departed the Bardley house (and they were sure of that before they dared move) the three men left in the parlor made their way – one by one – to the front porch. Looking off to the fort in the distance, they saw him disappear through the front gate.

Keeping his gaze on the fort Selkirk asked Smith, "How long did you leave her in there?"

Smith didn't know, he didn't have a watch. He had never had owned a watch, but he guessed it might have been 10 minutes. "Maybe twenty," he allowed. "It's a long way to the river and back. Carrying a full bucket; trying not to spill any." The three men continued to look down toward the fort.

"If she picked that lock; if she got into his room . . . if she took anything . . . he's going to be . . ." Bardley whispered. He didn't finish the thought. Smith looked at him as he said it.

"Maybe you ought to think about staying out of sight for a few days," offered Selkirk. Smith was now looking at him.

"Is there someplace you can stay for a few days?" asked Bardley. He was careful not to offer his own house as a possibility.

Smith wondered out loud, "Wouldn't that be desertion?" Selkirk thought to himself that Wallingford was probably going to shoot him anyway, so why not? When neither of the other two men didn't answer him, Smith returned his gaze toward the fort. "I done exactly as he asked, ya know," Smith said to no one. "All he said was stay with her when she goes out and talks to folks. I done that." There was a pause, then he said, "Why's he so mad? She can't get in his room with that giant lock he got on that door." He said it as if there wasn't a kernel of doubt in his mind. "What's she gonna steal, anyways." They all stared down at the fort for any signs of Wallingford.

In the headquarters office a Private Thompson sat behind the desk trying to take a nap. In an effort to remain undisturbed he had placed a piece of wood in the window jam to prevent it from opening, and he had propped a bench up behind the door to prevent that from opening too. It had recently become common sport amongst the troop to sneak up on Thompson as he dozed somewhere, and place a spider, or a snake, or anything of that ilk down his open shirt. Small burning wicks, or fuses, in his shoe were acceptable substitutes. Despite his unusual size and strength, he was the butt of most practical jokes; his gullibility knew no limits. However, his patience did. He had recently decided that the fun at his expense must come to a stop. But he wasn't thinking about these things now; he had drifted off into a deep sleep as he sat at the desk. He never heard the heavy footsteps coming toward the front door.

Without breaking stride as he whizzed past Finlay, Captain Wallingford crossed from the gate to the HQ building at full speed and launched himself at the door of the office.

Even from that distance each of the three men on Bardley's porch clearly heard the crash from the fort. The sudden sound made each of them jump. "What was THAT?" asked Selkirk.

'That' was the infuriated captain hitting the door with his shoulder, expecting it fly open. To his credit, although not a big man, he did make it give way despite the wedged bench. The bench itself broke into three pieces. A small part of one of the legs flew off to the side, as the rest of the leg skidded across the floor. The three remaining legs, with seat attached, soared across the room, clipped the top edge of the desk and hit Thompson flat on the top of his reclined head. His body position and weight allowed him to bear the brunt of the collision with the projectile hardwood without giving an inch. It did, however, render him unconscious.

"He didn't have a pistol with him, did he," Bardley asked? He hadn't noticed; he wondered if any one of the others had.

"No, but he must have one, maybe two, in his room? Don't he, lieutenant?" asked Selkirk.

Smith's mind was racing to remember if he had ever seen the inside of the captain's room. The lieutenant looked at Selkirk, "I think he got that big silver sword he sometimes wears, in there."

"That damn thing could cut a man's head off, I bet," Selkirk said without thinking.

Bardley assessed that information, and thought that getting Smith off his front porch should be a priority. He began edging back toward his front door. They became quiet as they listened for any sounds coming from the fort.

Back down at the fort Finlay, who had by now lowered his unloaded weapon, watched as the captain tore through the door of the HQ with a tremendous crash. He heard a commotion from inside as the captain, totally unaware (or rather *unconcerned)* with the man at the desk with the trickle of blood on the top of his head, began tearing at his clothes trying to find his key for the padlock on the door to his room. After a very frustrating three seconds he remembered that he kept the key to the padlock on a chain around his neck. Yanking it toward the lock; painfully jerking his neck, he inserted it and twisted. A small measure of reassurance came over him as the lock snapped open. The anxiety he felt at this minute made him nauseous. Taking a deep breath, he unfastened the padlock and pushed open the door.

It took a full minute for Captain Wallingford's eyes to become accustomed to the darkness in his room; and to completely survey the room from the doorway. It looked all right to his eye. Feeling a small bit of relief, he turned around to get a candle off the desk of the soldier, who was now sliding slowly toward the floor. Lighting the candle he moved back toward his windowless room, and slowly went inside. He heard the soldier in the outer room fall heavily the last six inches to the floor. He didn't turn around.

Cautiously he went around the room; touching nothing. Carefully examining everything he saw, he looked for anything out of order among his things. His heartrate and breathing slowed down. The room looked like it hadn't been touched in weeks. He even noticed the dust that had collected on his nightstand was undisturbed. His anger was starting to slip away.

He moved over to the large wardrobe he had in the corner. Its front legs rested on a 3'X5'carpet he had bought in Philadelphia at a shop recommended by General Tindale himself. Its border was a royal blue, and the center was a reproduction of some painting by Hogarth. He didn't remember its title. He tilted the heavy piece of furniture onto its back legs so it rested in the corner against the wall, its front legs six inches off the ground. He carefully got to his knees and rolled the carpet over to the right. He examined the flooring underneath. Everything looked as it should. He couldn't see a scuff mark, or scratch of any kind. He chided himself about the possibility that he had overreacted. He pulled a small knife from his waistcoat pocket and placed it between two of the boards of wood well under the askew wardrobe. With a gentle twist he popped up a large panel of the flooring. It had been almost invisible before his twist. He moved the piece of flooring carefully to the side, and looked down into the now gaping 2'x2' hole. There, exactly as it should be, sat a shiny black box nearly filling the hole it occupied. He exhaled a long slow breath, and he couldn't help but smile. The numerous frustrations, anxieties and disappointments heaped on him since Friday night's soiree were starting to evaporate.

In that box was his personal fortune. It contained all the money he had obtained *one way or another,* since his arrival at Fort Royal. The fruits of his creative payrolls, profits from the sales of redirected royal supplies to the public market, accumulated 'royal commissions', even the proceeds from the sale of the old cannon had been put into this box. He had occasionally even acquired a precious stone or two, as well as a nice tidy amount of gold, both raw and finished. And soon to be added, he thought, was the reward for that d'Argent bitch which, he assured himself, he would re-capture shortly.

He sat back on his heels and admonished himself for becoming so overwrought. He even felt a small twinge of guilt over the abuse he had heaped on Bardley. He decided that he would not reduce the share of the reward he was going to give him. Hell, he thought cavalierly to himself, he might even give Smith a crown, or two. He reached into the hole and lifted the box out.

It was too light.

Something was wrong.

He snatched open the box and stared into the almost empty interior. At the bottom of the box was a piece of paper, and scribbled on that paper was,

Vive la France

D

It was more of a howl than a scream. A long mournful cry into the night that a soul might make as it fell into the eternal fires of damnation. At the fort's front gate Finlay heard it as clearly as if he were in the room with Wallingford. He trembled. People throughout the settlement heard it just as clearly, and looked off fearfully in its direction. Horses at Ludlum's stirred nervously, and kicked at their stall doors. Mother Farrington clutched her breast and muttered 'Mother of God". Thompson, lying still on the office floor, never heard a thing.

The three men standing on Bardley's porch heard it and looked at one another, and then back down to the fort less than a half mile away. Selkirk was the first to speak, "I think she picked the lock."

"I think she picked the lock, and stole something," added Bardley, his voice wavering.

"You better go," said Selkirk to Smith.

"Where?" asked the moon-eyed lieutenant.

Bardley looked at him with compassionate eyes and said, "I think 'where' doesn't matter. I think 'any place else' would be a safer place than here when he comes back."

"You think he's coming back," asked the wishful thinking Smith.

Selkirk took hold of Smith's arm to get his attention, "You better go, lieutenant. You better go now."

Like his commanding officer only a few minutes ago, Lieutenant Smith did not use the steps leaving the porch. He vaulted, with surprising agility, the railing and began running very fast toward the woods on the far side of the Bardley residence.

The advice had been timely, because not two minutes later Captain Philip Wallingford came roaring out of the fort's gate at a full run. If it had occurred to Finlay to salute, he had disregarded it in a flash. He congratulated himself on his choice of simply stepping out of the captain's way as he flew by.

The captain headed straight up the road for the Bardley house. He held a pistol in his left hand and that large silver sword in his right. He was waving both in the air. His manic state of mind and maximum physical effort for speed did not blend well. As he came up the street he stumbled several times, once even falling hard to the ground. That only added to his foul demeanor.

The two men on the porch braced themselves as the captain came near. He came to a halt one step inside the Bardley fence. His face was smeared with dirt and sweat. His hair stuck out in many places and his shirt was open and torn. The pistol was cocked and the sword looked huge. He stared up at the two, his eyes were wild. With a low, coarse, guttural voice he spit at them, "Where is he?"

If he had been able, Bardley would have told Wallingford where Smith had gone. But at this moment fear had taken complete control of Josiah Bardley and he was physically unable to speak. He was, in fact, unable to do anything. Every fiber in his body was solely focused on him trying not to soil his pants. Selkirk was less frightened than Bardley, because he had already made a plan. He had decided that if the captain tried to come up the stairs he would push Bardley at him, and escape over the railing.

When the captain asked his question Selkirk nearly made a frightful error. His kneejerk response was going to be "Where is who?" But Selkirk correctly assessed the captain's state of mind, and instantly realized that that was how severed heads sometimes wind up rolling around in the dirt. "You mean Lieutenant Smith, don't you, captain?" The captain didn't dignify that question with a response, he just stared at Selkirk. "He left just after you did, captain. I thought he followed you down to the fort." Selkirk had his arm raised, pointing in the fort's direction.

The captain looked at him; then at Bardley, and then back at Selkirk, "If ya lying to me, I'll have you shot before sunset." He thought about that for a second, and then added, "By God Almighty, I'll do it myself." He turned and took a half step back toward Bardley's gate, but halted again. He swung around and pointed the sword at Selkirk and Bardley. He stood there a minute, looking left and right, wondering what he should do. The effects of the past few days, and especially the last few minutes, now took hold of the captain. The physical exhaustion; the emotional letdown; the financial catastrophe finally took their toll on the man. He dropped both hands to his side and began trudging down the road toward the fort, dragging the tip of the sword in the dirt.

Private Finlay saw him as he returned down the street to the fort. He eyed him carefully as he again approached the gate. This time the captain's demeanor was far more sedate. His last approach and departure had been fearsome and crazed. This time he walked slowly, and gazed only at the ground. Finlay was determined not to be taken by surprise, and cautioned himself to be alert. Being uncertain whether to salute or flee as the captain approached, he did neither. He just stood and watched, frozen with fear, as Wallingford trod past him, oblivious to his presence.

Captain Phillip Wallingford walked through the still open door into the HQ office, past the still prone Private Thompson, and into his private quarters. He bolted the door shut behind him, and sat on his bed. It had been a very, very long day, and it wasn't 10 AM yet. The last 24 hours had been full of unpleasant surprises, unexpected loses, physical exhaustion, and cold reality. He needed to sort things out. He needed some sleep. He had a lot of thinking to do.

Bardley didn't wait for the captain to go very far before hustling into his house and locking the door behind him. Selkirk, not invited to join Bardley within the safety of the house, sat down on the front steps and watched the captain return to the fort. He sat there, undisturbed, for a long time trying to figure out what was going on. Who was this Devonshire, and why was the captain so upset that she was gone? Selkirk recalled that the captain had screamed at Bardley about what her 'arse was worth'.

Maybe she was the wife or daughter of some rich man in New York or Philadelphia? A runaway? Maybe there was a large reward for her capture and return? He was fairly sure she hadn't left with the others because he had watched them go and didn't see her. But she couldn't be travelling alone; so she had to be with them! Who else was there? And what was the captain going to do about this major heading for Dubious? There was no Dubious! Selkirk had been one of the soldiers on that last mission when the troop had gone there, found it deserted, and burnt it to the ground.

Selkirk came to the conclusion that the captain would have to go after that major first. He couldn't let that officer see what was left of Dubious. A plan was forming in his head. With the captain out chasing after that major, that would give him the head start to go out on his own to find that Devonshire dame! He would bring some of the troop to help him cover more ground. He would figure out a way to cheat them out of any reward later. Yes, while Wallingford chased around after that Major Highcross he would go get the French tart and the reward. After all, the captain hadn't given any orders to remain at the fort. He thought about these things for an hour, before knocking on Bardley's door.

"It's me, Selkirk," he yelled through the still locked front door to Bardley. "What do I want? I wanna ask you somethin' about that French dame. She owes me some money," he made that up on the spot. Bardley had no intention of opening the door to anyone. And he did not see any reason on earth to engage in a conversation with Private Selkirk concerning the missing Mrs. Devonshire.

"Get the hell off my porch, and go away," Bardley screamed in answer. Selkirk turned and strolled back toward the fort. In all that time since the captain had trudged back to the fort he had heard no commotion or noise coming from it. He decided it was safe to return.

"Where's the captain?" Selkirk asked Finlay as he approached the gate. The sentry told him he had gone into the HQ. And replying to another Selkirk question he said that hadn't been a sound since. Selkirk cautiously approached the still open front door of the office, and peeked in. Thompson was on his hands and knees beside the desk. Selkirk moved cautiously into the office, and helped Thompson into a chair. Keeping an eye on the closed door to Wallingford's quarters, he whispered to Thompson, "Did the captain hit ya?"

"Captain Wallingford?" Thompson was confused. "I dunno. Somebody did, that's fer sure." The private felt around the top of his head gingerly. His head ached, and he was sure he was bleeding up there somewhere. "This really hurts. You guys gotta cut this shit out. I ain't foolin'."

Selkirk looked around the room. The bench pieces caught his eye. He assumed that Thompson had been hit by the bench. How? He did not know. "C'mon, let's get out of here." Thompson didn't argue, and with Selkirk's assistance they made their way back to the barracks.

Late that afternoon Captain Phillip Wallingford awoke from his long nap. Once awake he went over his plans once again for the dilemmas that he faced. He would head out after that major early the next morning. He had to be stopped. After that he would find that Mrs. Devonshire and what she had stolen. And then, at his leisure, would take care of that moronic Lieutenant Smith.

Right now he needed to prepare for his foray into the frontier. He needed to get his supplies and horses ready; eat a good meal; and give specific instructions to several people about what he wanted them to do while he was away.

He prepared supplies and equipment for his trip, and laid out his uniform for the morning, but dressed in civilian clothes for this evening's chores. When he walked into the barracks he found the troops all huddled around Selkirk. The room went instantly quiet when he walked in. He could sense that they were up to no good (in his opinion they never were), but he was impatient with his own problems, and immediately took the floor. He sent Selkirk out right away; telling him to go wait for him at Josiah Bardley's house. And while he was waiting there he had better make sure Bardley was home. Selkirk reluctantly left. Once he was gone, the captain looked around the room, trying to determine which of them was the most likely to follow simple orders.

He didn't think very highly of any of them, but the job he had in mind was so simple anyone would do. "Rawley," he pointed at the short, portly private standing directly in front of him, "Can you light a fire? And keep it going?"

"Yes, Sir," he grinned.

"A signal fire, Rawley. Not a cooking fire. And you may need to keep it lit for two, maybe three, days. Can you do that?"

"Yes, Sir!"

"You know throwing leaves on it, or even some wet wood, will make plenty of smoke, correct. A good signal fire needs plenty of smoke. You can do that, right Rawley?" Rawley nodded eagerly back at him. "You know that high ridge just north of Kelly's Crossing?" Again, Rawley nodded. "Okay, when Selkirk tells you, I want you to go up on top of that ridge and start that signal fire. Wait until he tells you. Plenty of wood. Plenty of smoke. All day long. Every day until I come and tell you to stop. Until I tell you. Me. Got it? Only me; until I come and tell you to stop." Rawley was nodding fast now. "For the next few days I want you," and he looked around at the other troops and pointed to three more of them, "And you three too, I want you to go help him stack some wood up there so they'll be plenty for the signal fire." And, now again, he looked right at Rawley, "Don't light it until Selkirk tells you to. Do you understand?" He was assured by Private Rawley that he understood perfectly. Captain Wallingford wasn't so sure.

As the captain made his way down to Josiah Bardley's house he noticed the heavy rain clouds in the west were fast approaching. "Damn!" When he arrived at the front of Bardley's house he found Selkirk on the front porch.

"He's home, but he won't open the door," Selkirk explained.

"JOSIAH! OPEN THE DAMN DOOR!" roared Wallingford, banging on the door.

He must have been standing right behind the door because the lock clicked and the door opened instantly. Bardley and Selkirk followed Captain Wallingford into the parlor.

Before they got settled into chairs Mrs. Bardley appeared in the doorway. She had every intention of giving Captain Wallingford a piece of her mind concerning the lascivious behavior of the tenant he had forced upon them, as well as her abrupt departure without paying the promised rent. Since Devonshire's departure Mrs. Bardley had zestfully prepared and rehearsed this presentation in anticipation of Wallingford's earliest return to their house. She took a deep breath as she stood in the doorway, but before she could utter a word Captain Wallingford slammed the door closed. Wallingford turned to Bardley, and said, "Open a damn window in here. Let some air in." Bardley jumped around like a rabbit in a room full of hunters following orders.

Once they were settled Captain Wallingford began to give both men very specific instructions. And then he repeated them! He then questioned them about these instructions. There would be no mistakes this time. Everyone would do exactly what he told them to do. Despite his never using the term "or else", or mentioning horrible consequences for failing him, the message was quite clear.

First, he explained, if this Major Highcross were to reappear at Fort Royal while Wallingford was away, he was to be detained until Wallingford got back. How? Bardley was handed a letter, written by Captain Wallingford, that would, in turn, be given to this major. In this letter Wallingford wrote that General Tindale ordered Highcross to remain at Fort Royal until Wallingford returned. That would hold him here. Bardley then would tell Selkirk to have Rawley start his fire.

"What fire," asked Selkirk?

"Never mind 'what fire', Rawley knows what to do. If Highcross reappears, you tell Rawley to get that fire started," Wallingford snarled. "And if Devonshire reappears back here while I'm gone, I want you to clap her in irons! I want you to take her to the stockade shed behind the barracks; have her put her hands behind her back around the post in the middle of the shed and fasten the irons around her wrists. I want her under twenty four hour guard. I want someone watching her day and night until I return. And yes, as soon as you have her locked in, tell Rawley to light that fire." Wallingford looked back and forth at both men, inviting any questions. There were none. "Oh, while I'm at it. If Smith shows his face back here while I'm gone I want him shot on sight." Both men stared at the captain. "No, wait a minute." Wallingford gazed off out the window for a moment. "No. I want you to lock him in the stable. In irons. Chain him to the anvil, and keep him there until I get back. I want to shoot him myself."

After once more going over the instructions to both men, he turned to Selkirk, "No settlers are to be allowed to travel west of here until I return. No one! Tell them there's Indian trouble. No one goes west, understand?" Both men nodded. "And you and the rest of the troop are restricted to the fort until I return. Except for Rawley and the men I told to help him. Restricted! Do you understand?" Captain Wallingford did not want anyone wandering around out in the frontier while he *attended to business.*

Selkirk saw his chance of getting whatever reward was being offered for Devonshire vanish in a flash. Common sense told him there was no point in arguing. Disappointment was evident, and Wallingford saw it. He leaned closer to Selkirk, "Restricted," he whispered.

A disappointed Selkirk was then dismissed by Wallingford, and sent back to the fort. Wallingford waited until Selkirk was out of the house before leaning toward Bardley and poking him in the chest with his forefinger, "Keep an eye on that sneaky bastard while I'm gone. Under no circumstances trust him with anything. Do . . . you . . . un . . . der . . . stand?"

Bardley smiled weakly. "Where are you going?" Bardley finally asked. "How long will you be gone?"

Wallingford shook his head at his business partner, he understood nothing. "I've got to go stop that Major *before* he gets to Dubious. If he gets there and sees . . .? Sees what? Sees nothing? Our little game is up. All those supplies; all those provisions we've ordered for the troops there; all that merchandise from the warehouses in New York and Philadelphia supposedly going to Dubious, but instead being sold, and the cash winding up in our pockets! That all comes to a halt! And when he tells the authorities back east about what we've been up to . . . . Well, I don't think it will go too well for us." Wallingford made a sickly smile. "Do you know what good King George does to people who steal from the Royal Treasury?" He again made that smile. "Sometimes he just hangs them; but sometimes . . . sometimes – if he's in a sour mood – he gives them a good flogging before hanging them."

Bardley thought he might be getting sick. He felt the muscles in his neck tightening. "My God," was all he was able to say.

"I've got to find him, and get him turned around and headed back here. He cannot be allowed to reach Dubious."

"What if he won't come back? What if he insists on going there? He's a major; you can't order him around, he outranks you." Bardley was beginning to sweat. "And even if he comes back, how long can you delay him?"

The captain was surprised how quickly Bardley had seen this problem. He was right. The major could not reach Dubious. That was out of the question. And he was also right that the major would not allow himself to be detained at Fort Royal indefinitely. Phillip Wallingford smiled at Josiah Bardley, "I have no intention of allowing him to reach Dubious. And I have no intention of allowing him to return to Fort Royal."

For a few seconds Bardley did not comprehend what Wallingford's plan was. He just looked back at the captain with a faint smile and nodded. Then the smile disappeared; his eyes widened; he asked, "You're going to kill him?"

Wallingford ignored the question, and began to explain the scenario he thought was likely as he pursued the party west. When he caught up to them, he would send Sho-Taka, Shea and the Virginian on their way, before circling back with Devonshire and Highcross. And if they, as a twosome or individually, somehow turned around and headed back to Fort Royal, slipping past him, Bardley and Selkirk had their instructions.

Bardley's head was swimming with the different plots afoot when one thought suddenly arose. "What are you going to do with Devonshire while you're taking care of Highcross?"

"The warrant for her says 'Dead or Alive'," Wallingford said. "I think handling her will be so much easier once I put a musket ball through her black heart."

"Oh my God," Josiah muttered.

Chapter 10 – "The Lives of the Saints (and Sinners)"

Walk a mile in my shoes, or so the saying goes.
Road's been tough - paid my dues, and had my share of woes.
I have had good days too; there have been real great times.
Wine? Women? Songs? Yes! True! Sunny days, balmy climes.
In hindsight I would say, when all is said and done,
Yeah! I would push "replay". All-in-all, it's been fun.

It was after dawn, but there wasn't much light because the heavy rain clouds overhead blocked whatever light the sun was providing. The rain had continued all night and, although the rocky overhang had protected the six of them from the rain, the air was very damp.

One by one they woke up and began shuffling around the campsite, each preoccupied with his own tasks. And much like the way last night had ended the conversation was minimal, and whispered.

Shea warmed up some of last night's leftover rabbit, and made a pot of porridge. She boiled some water to make tea, as a special treat. Mrs. Devonshire observed how quiet everyone was being, and did nothing to change it. Tyson ate some breakfast, but skipped the tea. When he had finished he went to work on the wagon where some canvas had pulled loose during the night and allowed one small corner to get thoroughly soaked by the rain. Sho-Taka, who also passed on the tea, ate in silence and then returned to work on his rabbit skins soon-to-be-moccasins.

Falwyn moved about as if in a trance; ate little and sipped his tea. He was still annoyed that he had been unjustly maneuvered into walking by himself out in front of the wagon yesterday; needlessly risking his life. And as he mulled that injustice over in his mind he recalled that he had never received that promised cup of Sho-

Taka's home brew for taking that river bath. He was feeling very much the victim of cruel fate.

The major was more chipper than any of the others, but noticed the subdued atmosphere. He wondered why. Unable to get a conversation going, he went off by himself in the far back of the overhang.

An hour later Shea was sitting by the fire preparing bread. Tyson sat across from her soaking the salvaged buckskin in a large tub. Mrs. Devonshire came over and sat down. "What are you going to do with the skin?"

Tyson looked at her and said, "I don't know. Make something with it." She seemed surprised by his answer. He explained that he always skinned anything he killed. "You can always find a use for something like that." Very little was discarded when he killed a deer. Because he was travelling he wouldn't make total use of the carcass, but when he got settled in his new home in Kan-tucky he would try to make use of every part of the kill. He assured her that there was a use for every part, from the hoofs to the brain. "Skin, bones, meat and sinews! They all have uses. Nothing goes to waste if you have the time and space to take care of it all." Sho-Taka, working a few feet away, agreed without saying anything.

The conversation consisted of Mrs. Devonshire asking questions (as she usually did) about what some of those "uses" were and Tyson answering. Shea and Sho-Taka listened in, while Falwyn daydreamed about the home brew. The major, they all noticed, was off by himself in the far corner of their camp. He was sitting under a low hanging rock reading his bible.

Tyson was listing some things he had seen people make from the leg bones of deer when he stopped in mid-sentence. He was facing out into the open space beyond the outcropping rock; Mrs. Devonshire had her back to it. When he stopped talking, and slowly stood up, she looked at him and noticed his attention was focused on something behind her. She too rose and turned around. Shea and Sho-Taka, who had only been half listening, became aware of the sudden silence and movement and looked up. Then, they too, rose. The four of them stood silently staring into the surrounding woods.

It took a moment before Falwyn became curious at the silence and followed their gaze. He struggled to get out from underneath his blanket, and staggered to his feet.

"Don't do anything rash," Tyson warned, "Everyone just stay calm."

"Stand still," Sho-Taka ordered Falwyn, who had started inching toward the wagon.

Mrs. Devonshire whispered, "The one on the right looks like a boy!"

"The one on the left has a musket," Tyson countered.

The two Indians had come out of the woods into the clearing deep in conversation. The younger one was angry, and complaining that the older brave had gotten them lost. "You said you knew where the river was. That all we had to do was follow the river. But you can't find . . . "

They both froze when they saw the pilgrims sitting around their campsite.

The Indians and the pilgrims stared in silence at each other from a distance of twenty yards.

Major Aaron Highcross read his bible every Sunday, and had since he was a little boy. There wasn't any section of it he hadn't read ten times already. He had memorized many parts of it, but his favorite section was the Book of Psalms. It was poetry and music to his ears, and always made him feel better. He was totally engrossed in it at this moment, and did not notice the sudden deadly silence enveloping the camp.

Shea tried to get his attention by clearing her throat, twice, and then coughed. He went on reading for a moment, and then glanced up at all of them for only a moment before returning his attention to his bible. He read for five more seconds before he realized what was happening. His eyes suddenly bulged open, and he leapt to his feet.

He was over six feet tall when fully erect. The rock above his head was just a shade more than five feet from the ground. His head hit the stone overhang with a force that turned his knees to jelly. He muttered something like "Ow!"(It might have been "ouch"?); took a step to the left, and went down.

The pilgrims didn't see him hit his head, but they heard it. Everyone turned in time to see him crumble to the ground. The two women rushed to the prone major's side. Tyson and Sho-Taka both grimaced, but then returned their attention to the two intruders.

The younger Indian asked his companion, in a whisper, "Did you see that?"

The older replied, again in a whisper, "That must have really hurt."

The younger one suddenly focused on the uniform of the unconscious Major Highcross. "Look at the fallen one;" he said to his companion, "He is a soldier. He is an English soldier."

"We should run," said the taller Indian.

The younger brave gave a withering look to his companion, but before he could say anything the man by the fire began to talk.

Tyson, turning only slightly in Sho-Taka's direction said, "Tell them we are just passing through. We are going far to the west. We mean them no harm. We are not trappers." He spotted his rifle propped up against the wagon's wheel. He calculated he could get to it and get behind the wagon before the taller Indian could fire his musket. But his companions would still be exposed. He stood still, and returned his attention to the Indians. He then realized Sho-Taka had said nothing. He glanced at him, and said, "Go on, tell them what I said."

Confused by Tyson's instructions, he gave him a puzzled look.

"Go on," was all Tyson said.

The others (except Highcross) looked at him. Sho-Taka shrugged and began, "We are only passing through. We are not . . . . "

Tyson interrupted him, "Not in English! Talk to them in their language. So they understand." Tyson shook his head.

"What language do they speak?" Sho-Taka asked.

The question confounded Tyson, "I don't know! What do you think they are, Shawnee?"

"More likely Lenape," offered Falwyn.

"I don't speak Lenape," Sho-Taka sadly admitted.

"It don't matter. Lenape or Shawnee, they talk the same. It's Algonquin, I think," Tyson thought he knew. "Talk to them in Algonquin," he suggested.

Sho-Taka gave them more bad news. "I don't speak Algonquin either."

"Try Iroquois! They've been living alongside them forever. They might know some of that." Tyson was starting to feel desperate.

"They might understand Iroquois," whispered Sho-Taka, "But I don't." Tyson turned and looked at Sho-Taka in disbelief.

"What are they whispering about," asked the young brave to his companion? The older one, who spoke no English whatsoever, just shook his head.

Tyson looked out at the two Indians, waved his hand in their general direction, and tried another option, "Do you understand English?"

The two Indians looked at each other. "What did he say?" asked the older.

The younger Indian was the son of his village's chieftain. His father had negotiated with English soldiers and traders on a few occasions. He had heard English spoken before. "I think he wants to know if we're English."

That made no sense to the older brave; how could they think we're English? But he wasn't about to argue with his young friend. He had gotten them lost, and his standing was not very high with the chief's son right now. Both Indians turned back toward the people under the rock, and continued to stare.

Shea, although listening to the conversation, had gotten a wet rag, and was gently rubbing the major's head. He began moaning. Everyone turned their attention to him.

"I hope he jumps up again. I've never seen anything like that before.' whispered the older Indian.

The younger brave shook his head at his companion, but remembered seeing Moakinah, his cousin, run into a tree in the dark one night. His cousin was never the same afterward.

"They're whisperin' somethin' over there. I think they're up to somethin'!" confided Falwyn. "Let's grab our guns and let them have it."

Tyson was about to shout "No" at Falwyn when Mrs. Devonshire started to speak – in French! It had occurred to her that the French Army and trappers had been here for many years; these two might know some French. "We mean you no harm." Everyone (except Highcross) turned to her. She continued speaking softly. "We are passing through, and going far to the west. We are not settlers. We are not trappers; we are not here to steal your furs."

The two Indians had lived most of their lives with French soldiers stationed at various posts in the territory. Contact with these soldiers hadn't been constant, but frequent enough that they understood some of the language. The end of the French Indian War had seen the French depart, but the younger brave still retained some knowledge of the language. He didn't understand everything she said, but he did understand enough, and relayed the gist of it to his companion.

Mrs. Devonshire asked them, again in French and using gestures, if they would like to get out of the rain, warm themselves by the fire, and if they were hungry, to share some food.

The older Indian hissed, "It's a trick! They mean to kill us."

"Why do you say that," the other wanted to know?

"I have seen the English tricks before. They will kill us the first chance they get." He was sure.

"I am cold. I am wet. I am hungry, and I am lost. I would rather die at the hands of my enemy than freeze, drown, or starve. You can stay out here if you want." When he stopped talking he began walking toward the fire, and his wary companion glumly followed him.

It took some time before all parties began to relax in each other's company. The conversation, in hesitant French, started with the Indians' concern for the unconscious major. They took the offered food (after seeing Shea eat some) and wrapped blankets around themselves when they were provided. The younger Indian, Sho-Taka, and Mrs. Devonshire were the only ones conversant in

French, so all questions and answers had to be relayed to the others in their native language.

The younger Indian was named Kaniawassa and the older, Otekinaya. It took all participants several minutes to come close to proper pronunciation of all their respective names. Major Aaron Highcross did not participate.

Kaniawassa was shy at first, but soon warmed up to the company. After some initial hesitancy, Otekinaya ate everything that was put in front of him. They explained they had gone on a hunting trip as part of Kaniawassa's education and approaching adulthood. Unfortunately they had become confused in the forest, mistaking several landmarks, and had become disoriented. Kaniawassa was not pleased with his supposed tutor's efforts, and Otekinaya knew it. He was not looking forward to their return to their village, where Kaniawassa's father would be furious.

The two Indians asked several questions about various locations as they tried to re-establish their bearings. As the party of pilgrims had only Falwyn as a long standing native of the area the answers to the questions were muddled. They were unable to point in the right direction for some answers, and disagreed on the direction for others. The one thing they could agree on was the location of Fort Royal. That, to their surprise, was a spot the two Indians had no interest in at all. The Indians said they did not want to go anywhere near that English fort, and were asked why.

"The English chief there is evil. He is not honest. He steals from Indians everywhere. He steals land. He steals furs. He steals corn. He steals everything. He does not speak the truth."

Falwyn broke the silence, "They talkin' about Captain Wallingford?"

No one answered; they all knew. But Falwyn, Shea and Sho-taka – who knew the Captain – weren't really surprised by the Indians appraisal. Mrs. Devonshire's instincts about the man had proven accurate too. Only Tyson wondered about the officer he had never met.

"Maybe things will change now," Sho-Taka said. "This man here," he gestured back toward the Major, "Will be the new chief of all the English soldiers now. He will be in charge of all the men; and Captain Wallingford too."

It took a few minutes for that message to be re-translated so that both Indians understood what he had said. They both looked at Sho-Taka strangely. Then, as the idea settled in his head, Otekinaya's eyes widened as he leaned far to his right so he could see around behind Tyson, at the reclining Major. Kaniawassa did the same. The prostrate major with his bandaged foot, half opened eyes and wet cloth on his head was not inspiring to either Indian. Kaniawassa returned his gaze to Sho-Taka. He wasn't sure how to take that news. He began an extended conversation with Sho-Taka and Mrs. Devonshire. None of them stopped to translate what was being said.

When they had finished they turned to their companions and explained. Sho-Taka spoke to Tyson, Shea and Falwyn. He told them the Indians wanted to know how the major had hurt his foot. They had spotted the bandage. "I told them he hurt himself hunting." They then asked if he hurt himself often. They asked that if he kills himself will Captain Wallingford be back in charge. "I told them the truth. I said that he would."

Across the fire the two Indians were talking. "Then things here will not get better," Otekinaya said, "Because I don't think this major will last until the first snow." He shook his head, and then added, "Did you see how hard he hit his head?"

Kaniawassa couldn't argue with him; he was probably right. "All the English are like that captain. We will all be pushed out of our homes under their rule. I think we will all end up like the Wackentutes." He was referring to a clan of the Susquehannock Indians, called the Wackentutes, who had originally lived on a large tract of land stretching from the Fort Royal area southwest toward what later became known as the Shenandoah Valley. After the French had left the Wackentutes had lost their lands, and were being transplanted by the victorious British and their allies, the Iroquois, to a stretch of land in the far reaches of upstate New York. Their land here had been sold or stolen piecemeal until there was nothing left. The Captain at Fort Royal had cheated them out of everything, and that wasn't his only crime against them. They hated him.

It suddenly occurred to Tyson to turn the tables and ask them the obvious question. He told Sho-Taka to ask them if they knew where Dubious was.

"Do you know where the other English fort is? The one that was French," Sho-Taka translated into French.

Kaniawassa didn't know, and passed on the question to Otekinaya.

"What other fort?" Otekinaya asked Kaniawassa.

The younger brave couldn't answer that; he knew of no nearby forts. He turned to Mrs. Devonshire and asked, in broken French, "What do you mean? There is no French fort. The French have gone."

"No, not French. Was French, but is now English. With English soldiers," she said.

"No English Fort here. Just the one with the evil chief." He said, almost as if apologizing.

"Wait!" Otekinaya interrupted. "The English have that big fort . . . "he paused a moment to look around. Deciding that he knew the right direction he pointed off to the north, "The big fort by the rivers. You have never been there," he said to his young friend. "It took many days to go there. I went two summers ago. With your father. Many of us went."

"With my father? After the peace came?"

"Yes, it was to make peace with the English."

"The one where the big rivers meet?"

The party remained quiet as the two Indians spoke with one another. Finally Kaniawassa turned again to Mrs. Devonshire, "You want to find the big fort with many soldiers; by the rivers?"

She turned toward Falwyn, "Is Dubious located on the banks where there are big rivers? Are there many soldiers there?"

No one noticed him but Major Highcross shook his head. He didn't know the exact number but he thought that Dubious had less than 20 soldiers there.

Falwyn didn't know how many soldiers were there either. He said nothing. Everyone looked at him as they waited for an answer. "I don't know how many there are," he answered. That was a safe answer.

"You don't know how many of *what* are there? Rivers or soldiers?" Sho-Taka asked. His long running suspicions were getting confirmed.

"I ain't gonna say how many soldiers are there. These sneakin' Indians may be just trying to figure out how many savages they need to attack it," Falwyn said defensively.

"How many rivers are there at Dubious," Tyson tried?

Falwyn looked at him, and said, "What?"

"How many rivers are at Dubious," Tyson asked again?

"One? Or maybe two," he guessed weakly.

"One or two? At the big English fort?" Sho-Taka asked the young Indian again. He, in turn, asked his older friend. And be sure, he instructed.

Otekinaya declared with absolute certainty that there were three rivers there. He told Kaniawassa that two came together to make three. That each one was large; that a brave would need a canoe to cross them. This was relayed to the group.

Major Highcross attempted to sit up at this point, and nearly toppled over. Shea helped him regain his balance, and he groaned as he felt the top of his head. All attention was on the Major as he tried to understand what had happened to him. While he was brought up to speed, he sat quietly listening. It would take him a while to recover.

Once more Tyson asked the two Indians a series of questions, translated by Sho-Taka and Mrs. Devonshire, about what they knew of that large English fort. No one asked Falwyn anything. The last shreds of credibility that he had were gone. Finally Tyson heaved out a long sigh, and said, "They're talking about Fort Pitt, up on the Ohio . . ."

Otekinaya blurted out, "Pitt!" he was nodding, "Pitt . . . . Pitt!" He spoke to Kaniawassa for a minute.

Kaniawassa turned to Sho-Taka and Tyson again, and said, "Yes, that fort is named Pitt. He heard that said many times. He remembers now. It is called Pitt by the English."

In the next five minutes Sho-Taka and Devonshire explained to Kaniawassa that Fort Pitt wasn't the one they were looking for.

They were looking for a much smaller fort; it was also an English fort., but smaller than Pitt. Then they added that the fort they were seeking had once been a French fort, but the English took it.

A glimmer of recognition lit in Kaniawassa's eye, but there was still doubt. "There is a fort that was French. But French no more. No soldiers there. No French. No English." And then after a pause he added, "No fort."

"What is the name of the fort," asked Sho-Taka. The Indians didn't know.

"Do the English there call it Fort Dubois?"

The Indians looked at one another and then said, "There are no English there. There is no one there."

"Where is it?" Tyson suddenly asked.

The question was repeated to Kaniawassa, and he in turn began a question and answer conversation with Otekinaya. They agreed, and disagreed, a number of times. There was pointing in different directions. And despite talking in their own language, several times Devonshire and Sho-Taka would recognize the usage of French. The Indians seemed to agree on "*trois frère*".

Kaniawassa turned back again to Sho-Taka and began a discourse in French. Sho-Taka and Mrs. Devonshire listened carefully to the hesitant French of Kaniawassa. Several times they nodded in agreement, or signifying that they understood. The major seemed to be listening too, and understanding some. Tyson, Shea and Falwyn just sat and watched.

When Kaniawassa stopped talking, both Devonshire and Sho-Taka smiled and nodded. They turned to their companions and said, "There was a small fort, but it was French. And no one is there now. But it is not too far away." Sho-Taka turned to Falwyn, "What do you remember about Dubious?"

"What?" said Falwyn.

"What do you remember about Dubious? Anything at all?"

"I don't know. I never saw it. Never told you I did." The look Falwyn saw on the faces around him told him he better say something more. "Captain Wallingford told me where it was."

"Okay. What did he say about it? What was it like? Its walls? How big? What was around it? Where did the fort get its water? Anything?" Falwyn just looked back at Sho-Taka with his mouth open. Annoyed, Sho-Taka tried once more, "Where is it from here? What direction?"

In a rare bit of insight Falwyn remembered the Indian pointing off in the direction of the road during his discourse with Sho-Taka. He gambled, and did the same.

Sho-Taka had no idea that it had been a lucky guess. He was, in fact, amazed that Falwyn was approximately right, so he went on, "How far is it?"

Falwyn was lost. He obviously had no idea, and was trying hard to come up with an answer that would be reasonable.

The silence lasted too long, Sho-Taka said, "Never mind," and waved his hand at Falwyn. He turned to his companions, "They say that the old French fort is only two days away, at most. They keep saying no one is there; but they haven't been there in a long time. So maybe there are troops there now. So maybe that is Dubious!"

Knowing they were close and that it might be Dubious made everyone feel a little better. "Two days away? That's a relief," sighed the major.

Sho-Taka wanted to make sure he had understood what had been said, so he turned to Mrs. Devonshire who spoke better French than he did and asked, "They said we follow the river that's south of here?" Devonshire nodded. "And we follow the river southwest . . . past the rapids . . . and then when the river turns to the south we go west. And continue out to the plain. That's where it is. And watch for the three large mountains to the south line up. That's why the French liked to call their fort '*trois frères*."

"That's right," said Devonshire, "He said that we would see mountains . . . three of them. And they would be in a line. And the front gate of the fort would line up with those mountains.

"That's right. Three of them." said Falwyn to no one; nodding to himself.

The others just turned and looked at him. He didn't notice.

By noon the Indians were warm, dry and fed. The rain had tapered off to a fine mist, and they decided it was time for them to resume their journey. They wanted to get back home to their village. They were given some dry powder for their musket, and left. They headed southeast into the forest, and couldn't wait to get home and tell the story of the new English chief who nearly knocked his head off.

An hour later the sky was still dark with heavy gray clouds, but the rain had stopped. Tyson and Sho-Taka had resumed working on their skins. Falwyn was wrapped in a blanket, and staring up at the rocky ceiling. The major sat quietly looking out at the surrounding forest; his only movements were long slow blinks. Shea and Mrs. Devonshire had just returned from a berry picking foray to some bushes Shea had spotted earlier in the morning light.

"Are they okay to eat? You've picked them before?" Devonshire asked Shea.

Before Shea could answer Falwyn spoke up," There's a way you can tell if they're all right to eat." He nodded around to the group. He was about to offer some frontier expertise and that caught everyone's attention. "There's this poem you can say that lets you know if they're poison, or not." He smiled at them, and then recited, "If they're sweet – go ahead an' eat. If they're sour - yer dead in an hour." He nodded again, sure they'd be impressed.

Sho-Taka looked at him with a sad smile on his face. "How does that help? I mean if you have to eat one first, before you know . . . how does that help?"

"What?" Falwyn said.

Frustrated, Sho-Taka answered him, "How does that help you if you have to eat one before you know if it's poison?"

"It don' matter because I don't eat berries anyways. They always give me the . . . . "He caught himself before he said it.

Shaking his head Sho-Taka suggested that Falwyn make himself useful. "Go tend to the horses while it's not raining."

"Why do I have to do it? Why don't you go tend to the horses? Or even Tyson can do it; it's his horse." In a rare display of compassion he exempted the major.

"Because," Sho-Taka explained, "You don't have anything else to do. Your job as a guide is over. We don't need you anymore." He paused a minute and then said, "Thank God."

Falwyn shot back, "Well, we don't need you any more either. Now that we know you can't speak to no Indian. Said you could speak in five languages. Ha! What tribe you from, anyways?"

Everyone at the fire was turned and looking at Sho-Taka; including the major. "You wouldn't know it if I told you," he finally answered. "Besides, I left it when I was little."

"You were stolen?" Falwyn guessed.

For a moment they all remained quiet, waiting for Sho-Taka's answer. He gave none. "Why did you leave your tribe? Your home?" asked Mrs. Devonshire. She knew what it was like for a child to leave home early. "You ran away?"

"No. My mother did," he paused, "She caught a terrible disease, and left the tribe when I was just a baby; she took me with her."

Several listeners straightened up; but hesitated to ask about his mother's "*disease*". Only Falwyn possessed less tact than the major, but he was too busy imagining the worst to ask the question. The major leaned in, and softly asked, "What was it, Sho-Taka? Smallpox?" he guessed.

Not to be left out, Falwyn offered, "Yella fever?"

Sho-Taka looked at each of them and shook his head. "No, something worse than those two combined." He looked around for a minute, raised his eyebrows and said, "She caught something more sinister . . . more consuming than any of those. She caught religion."

Their reaction to his words differed from one to another, but no one spoke.

He went on, "I was told a traveling preacher came to our village and was going on and on; raving and roaring about this and that; and my mother just got caught up in it." He said that the preacher was the well-known theologian Jonathan Edwards who was preaching near Boston at the time. Both the major and to a lesser extent, Shea, had heard of him and his work with what became known as the Great Enlightenment that occurred during the 1730's. The others didn't know the name at all.

"She got caught up in the excitement of it all, and finally left our village to move into the English settlement, and went to work for a preacher there. She couldn't convince my father to go with her; he didn't want anything to do with the English, or their religion. And he wouldn't let her take my two older brothers. They didn't want to go with her anyway." He shook his head, acknowledging that he was sorry it had worked out this way, "But I was too young to make a choice. I wasn't even a year old yet. So off we went, my mother and me, to live among the English."

"And that's why you don't speak Algonquin, or Iroquois, or anything else?" Tyson asked.

Sho-Taka nodded, "But I didn't lie. I do speak, or at least can read or understand, five languages."

"Really?" asked the major. The sound of his voice caused everyone to turn in his direction. But when Sho-Taka began to answer they turned once again to him.

"Well, you know I speak English, and this morning, as you heard, I was able to speak in French." There were no objections, so he went on, "I can understand and read Spanish and Italian. I'm better at Spanish than Italian, but I can do both."

The group just sat and stared. Mrs. Devonshire smiled to herself, "This is a man of many talents." She was pleased because she had suspected he was from their very first meeting.

"What else," Shea asked? "You said five."

"I admit I have trouble understanding the spoken word, but I can read Latin."

The major was astounded. Wondering if the blow to his head this morning was affecting his hearing he asked, "My God, man! You sound as if you've been to Oxford. Where were you educated?"

The reticent Indian told his story. It took some time and many questions to hear it all. Sho-Taka told them that he was raised under the roof of a local preacher, the Reverend Ivar Coote. His mother was a servant in his house. Although she slaved away for the preacher for almost no wages, mother and son were both given their bed and board at the reverend's house. And when the reverend thought he was the proper age, although he was *just an Indian,* he was sent to the local schoolhouse.

His early years at the school were harsh. His schoolmaster and schoolmates thought him inferior because he was an Indian. He was treated as many "outsiders" are treated. The schoolmaster ignored him. His schoolmates did not. He was tormented and bullied. Classmates and older boys often initiated fights that he couldn't win. He learned the value of being a faster runner then his attackers. And as the years dragged on he became faster than them all. But he also grew bigger than most of them too. In time he no longer feared them individually. They, in turn, feared him. No longer did any of them attempt to take him on one on one. Yes, there were times they outnumbered and cornered him, and he suffered the consequences. But he did not forgive and forget. He bided his time, and retaliated when the opportunity presented itself. As he got older, and bigger, the conflicts escalated until they were ambushing him in large numbers. Also escalating was the nature of the fights. What had started out as fistfights had turned into something far more sinister. Some of the other boys who realized that he was too big and too strong to be taken on began using bats and sticks (some sharpened) to fight him. He defended himself in kind. The preacher and elders, aware of the conflict, did nothing to stop it. Not surprisingly they heaped the blame for the trouble on the "**savage**". He was singled out and forbidden to carry a knife. Sho-Taka's mother, still awash in religious reverie, told him that if he prayed more fervently it would resolve itself.

Early in his thirteenth year he was ambushed on his way home by a fusillade of rocks thrown by the some boys. It was then that he began learning the art of throwing stones. It was, at first, practicing self-defense. It would, in later years, become so much more.

"Yes, but the languages? Where did you learn Spanish and Italian," the Major wanted to know?

"The Reverend had a library full of books in his house. He collected them. He used to read them to us . . . everyone who lived there. He and his wife didn't have any children, but my Mother and I and two other servants would all sit down after dinner and he'd read. He'd read to us from the Bible, but sometimes he'd read from one of the other books he had. *The Odyssey, The Iliad,* Chaucer's *Canterbury Tales;* I remember him reading that more than once. He had some books that were in Spanish, or Latin, or French. I remember he said that if you read Dante's *Divine Comedy* in anything but Italian you would miss so much. I asked him to teach me what these books said, and he did. I guess I took to it pretty well because it seemed I learned to read those books pretty quickly. It just kind of came easy to me. Instead of going to school where there would always be trouble, I would take one of his books and go out into the fields for the day. That was always better than going to school."

Falwyn asked, "He teach you how to make whiskey too?"

"After I stopped going to school the Reverend wanted me to start learning a trade. He thought I should apprentice myself out to some tradesman, so I might earn my keep. Well, there weren't many folks around that wanted to take me on, because all they knew about me was what they heard their children say; that I was a "trouble making savage!" I didn't want any part of them either. So, for a while I just kept to myself, staying out in the woods doing some more reading, but also learning how to hunt and fish.

One day I met up with a hermit named Ezra that lived far out in the woods. Most people in the settlement knew about him, and kept their distance. They thought he was demented, and maybe possessed by the devil. The day I found him he wasn't either of those things. It seems he had taken a fall, and he was just lying on the ground bleeding and in terrible shape. I got him back to his shack, and took care of him for a spell. I wasn't sure he was going to make it, but he did. We became friends. He's the one that taught me how to make whiskey. He taught me how to do many things. He could hunt and trap and fish and skin and cook. He could grow stuff, and build stuff, and make stuff out of practically nothing. He knew about all kinds of things.

A few years later my Mom died, and I moved out to my own shack near Ezra. He helped me build it. I was staying out there most of the time anyway. I learned just about everything from Ezra. What he couldn't make or grow he traded for. Come harvest time he'd work picking apples for a neighbor, and instead of cash money, he would keep a couple bushels for himself as pay. With those apples he'd make a batch of hard cider, and then bring it into Boston and trade it for some pigs, or sheep. He'd keep some, but trade the rest for something else, and then keep on trading, and trading, and keep on going and before you know it we'd have enough food and supplies for the whole winter."

Sho-Taka paused in his story, and Tyson asked, "Sounds like you liked it there fine. Why did you decide to leave?"

"When Ezra died," he said without feeling, "Didn't see any reason to stay. Massachusetts has two things I don't like. Cold winters and Englishmen." The major made a face. Mrs. Devonshire smiled. "That's why I'm going southwest," he said. "I'm going south because I hear that it's warmer, and I'm going west because there aren't any English out that way. Been around them too long."

"Amen," whispered Mrs. Devonshire.

The conversation thinned out for a few minutes as the people around the campsite tended to small matters. But the major was starting to rally, and wanted to talk. "Falwyn," he said, "Where were you born? Have you lived in Fort Royal all your life?"

With his most sincere, most puzzled, dumbest look, he answered, "What?"

"Where were you born?" the major repeated.

A suspicious Falwyn asked, "Why you want to know?"

"Just making conversation, that's all." This seemed like a good way to pass the time to the major, and after all, they weren't going anywhere.

"It's my business where I was born. I don't need any of you poking into my personal business." That attitude surprised the major. Before he could answer, Falwyn continued, "Why ain't you askin' Tyson, or Shea about where they was born. Or even telling about your own self!"

That was, apparently, all the encouragement he needed. Highcross launched into his own personal history. "Very well, if you insist," he smiled. No one had.

For an hour he relayed the story of his life. And for reasons only he knew he left nothing out. Although it was not a life without its ups and downs, he seemed to relish every bit of it. The listeners were surprised by how well he accepted his bad luck and occasional setbacks.

He was only interrupted once, when he was finishing his tale of his time in Europe and his subordinates had sabotaged the food of Major Graham. He was explaining the difference between the enlisted men's commissary and the officers'. "Now the men in the ranks are fed from huge tubs and pots, prepared by the cooks drawn frequently from their own ranks. But the officers, especially the senior officers, often have their own personal cooks travel with them to prepare their meals. Whereas the captains and majors may pool their resources and have their meals prepared for them by a genuine chef. You may find any number of very good cooks at headquarters. My God! If you keep your ears open there are wonderful things you can learn from them all. There are Italian, French, Spanish, Portuguese recipes and techniques everywhere!" He wasn't stopping to inhale. "I learned about sauces and gravies; I was taught by masters how to prepare fowl and beef in ways I had never dreamed of! Spices I never knew existed. And pastries! They were made with creams and fruits and sweeteners beyond my imagination."

It was at this point that Mrs. Devonshire asked, "Why are you a soldier?"

The question caught the major off-guard, "I beg your pardon?"

"Why are you a soldier? It seems to me you are more interested in cooking than being a soldier."

The major looked at her for a minute, trying to determine if he was being teased. "I told you. My grandfather secured this commission for me. It's not something one can turn down when offered. It's a very sought after profession."

"But you would prefer to cook?"

"I do like to cook; but that's not a profession compared to being an officer in the British Army. There is no comparison between the two. There was no other choice I could make." He thought about that for a moment, and then added, "There was no choice! An officer's commission has been borne by a member of my family for generations. It is a great privilege and an honor to serve King and Country."

Mrs. Devonshire wouldn't let it go. "There was no other choice you could make?" she repeated. "Why is it you do not get to choose? There is no one else in your family who could serve in your stead? Brothers? Uncles? Cousins? Why you?"

"I have no brothers or uncles. And my cousins already have positions and careers of great promise. The military post fell to me."

She decided that she would not disparage his family legacy; but it seemed to her that he had somehow drawn the short straw. "You are the son of a baker. You said she was an excellent baker. I think perhaps you might lead a more contented life as a baker than a soldier."

No one disagreed; and the major just shrugged.

Later, when the major had finally finished his story, he turned to Falwyn again and asked about his background. And again Falwyn declined the invitation to tell his story. Mrs. Devonshire dismissed the possibility of her telling her story. She reminded them that she had already done so the first night she joined them. That was partly true, and no one objected.

Tyson, after much prodding, told his story. His start in life had not been a happy one. He had been found in a wagon on a country road by workers of a nearby farm. His mother was deathly ill with a fever. That fever took her life a day later without her ever regaining consciousness. At least this was what Tyson was told when he was older, by his adoptive father who owned that farm.

That man was named August Haupt, and he was a widower with two sons of his own. They were twelve and fifteen years older than Tyson, and that age difference, as well as not being blood relatives, kept them from being close. When Mr Haupt died his substantial estate was divided primarily between his two sons. The eldest inherited the farm and all its property, while the younger continued his career as a lawyer, politician and land speculator. What was left over was a 24,000 acre tract of land in Kan-tucky that the father had been awarded because of his service in the Virginia militia. It was deeded over to Tyson when his stepfather died because neither of his stepbrothers wanted it.

"Why ain't your name Haupt then, if you was his son? How come your name's Tyson?" Falwyn wanted to know.

"When they found me and my Mom in the wagon no one knew who we were. Or where we came from? But in the wagon they found an old bible. On the first page someone had written, in big letters, 'TY'. They figured that must be our name or, at least, our initials. So I must be TY's son. Tyson!"

Tyson finished telling his tale by explaining that he had travelled to Philadelphia to certify some deeds for the property before heading out to his land. He repeated that he knew how to farm; he knew how to build; and he knew how to hunt. And he couldn't wait to start his new life in Kan-tucky.

Shea started and finished her tale before anyone could say a word. She had been born and raised in New Jersey on a small farm owned by her family. Her brother and his wife had it now because her father had joined the army, and had gone west. According to what she had learned he was now stationed at Fort Dubois. Her mother had become ill, and Shea was going to find her father to tell him that, so he could return home before she passed.

Without speaking out, Major Highcross had some reservations about her tale. He doubted that men could enlist in the army here in the colonies. But he cautioned himself that he wasn't sure how they did many things here in the colonies, so he remained silent. And he had never received an official roster of the soldiers stationed at Fort Dubois (he was told that that would be provided by Captain Wallingford), so he could not say with certainty that her father was there at Dubious, or if he could be granted leave to return home to his sick wife.

Shea didn't care what the major's reaction was. In fact the only reaction she cared about was Tyson's. She kept shooting him glances as she spoke.

It now fell to Falwyn to tell his story, and he wanted no part of that. Only when he was advised that he could either tell his life story or *take another bath,* did he begin. Answering long questions with short answers his life unfolded. He had been born in Scotland, and had travelled with his mother to New York when he was very young.

"What happened to your father? Why didn't he come?" someone asked.

"He died when we was still in Scotland."

"How did he die?"

"He was a mason, I think. Maybe not a mason, but a mason's helper, anyways. They was buildin' a building . . . or a wall, I think my mother said. And I s'pose they weren't doin' it too good, because one day the damn thing fell over on his head. Killed him dead."

"Good Lord!" said the major. The others grimaced in varying degrees.

It took more coaxing to get Falwyn to continue, and when he did he said that after that his Mom couldn't make a go of it where they were so she decided to sign up as an indentured kitchen maid in the New World. "And that's how I got to come to New York."

"Any brothers or sisters? They come with you?" the major asked.

"None I can remember. Just me and my Mom." The major could identify with that. Falwyn went on. "But my Mom didn't like the kitchen work so much. Matter of fact she didn't like anything about the place at all. The owner of the place was an old lady named Mrs. Dillon; and she was as mean as a wet cat. Mrs. Dillon was old and bony; she liked to poke people with a stick, especially me. My mom tried running away a few times, but we never got too far. We got caught each time, and when they brung us back my ma would get a beatin'." He shook his head at the memory. "Mrs. Dillon's nephew would be whuppin' ma with a rope, or broomstick, or somethin', and old Mrs. Dillon would be cheering him on. How my ma would howl! But that didn't stop her from trying again. She and this other servant, who worked out in the stable, took a shine to each other and decided to try to make another escape. Only this time she figured, because I was slowin' her down every time she took off, she would have to leave me behind. Well, I went to sleep one night - I was mebbe five or six - and when I woke up the next mornin' she and that stable hand were gone! And they was gone for good. So I guess takin' me along was slowin' her down. Anyways, never seen hide nor hair of her since."

"Your mother left you there?"

"She deserted you?"

"Always thought she'd come back for me someday; but never did."

Everyone in his audience felt a tinge of pity, but that hadn't been his intention. Feeling sorry for himself was a luxury Falwyn hadn't allowed in his life for years. Mrs. Dillon was a mean and harsh taskmaster who resented that Falwyn's mother had run off. Had it been left to her she would have thrown the six year old out into the street to fend for himself. But the other servants who worked at the Dillon estate took his part and convinced the mistress to allow the youngster to stay. He made his keep by doing any little job that came up. And often the other servants helped him do it. It left no time for schooling or play. Almost as an aside Falwyn added, "It had been her who began to call me 'Falwyn'."

"He started to call you that? What were you called before?" asked the major.

"You mean that's not your name?" asked Sho-Taka. "What is your real name?"

"Falwyn's my name. I been usin' that since I was real little. I can't hardly even remember what my old name was."

"Oh, don't tease us," said Mrs. Devonshire, "tell us your real name." Of all the people there she was most likely to appreciate an alias.

He tried to steer the conversation off in another direction, but they would have none of it. Finally relenting, he said, "Fitzmorris." There was general agreement that that was a solid Scottish name, and then somebody asked what his first name was.

Again there was hesitation. His waving his hand at them did not change their minds. They continued to press it. "Morris," he finally said.

"Morris Fitzmorris? That's your name?" someone asked.

"That's a good name," added another.

"I don't like it. Don't start calling me that." said Falwyn.

"What's wrong with it? It's a good strong Scottish name," chided the major.

Falwyn shot right back, "I don't like it. I don't wanna be called Morris! And I don't wanna be called Fitzmorris either. And not Fitz most of all!"

"What's so good about Falwyn? Why is that better than Fitzmorris?" Shea asked.

"Why 'Falwyn' anyway? Where'd that come from?" Sho-Taka wanted to know.

The conversation halted while Falwyn just stared at Sho-Taka. It was a noteworthy occasion when Falwyn considered a question stupid. His raised eyebrows and pursed lips conveyed the sentiment to all the rest.

"Well?" innocently repeated Sho-Taka.

"Whaddya think? It ain't that hard to figure. Least it shouldn't be for someone who can speak five languages!" Falwyn answered sarcastically. The others were puzzled, and looked around at each other to see if anyone understood. No one did. Letting a silent moment go by, Falwyn decided he had to explain. "Falwyn?" He looked around. First he looked at Sho-Taka, who just stared back. Looking at the major he saw only the officer's blank face. He turned to Tyson.

Tyson looked back and almost imperceptibly shook his head, "What?"

"Fal . . . . . . wyn," said Falwyn in a whispered voice. There was no reaction by Tyson. Falwyn tried again, "Fal . . . . .wynn"

Tyson tried to mimic what he heard, "Foll . . . . wynn?"

Falwyn smiled.

That smile told Tyson he was on to something, but he had no idea what. He pursued, "Foll win? Foul win?"

"FOUL WIND!" said Shea.

"Foul wind?" Sho-Taka repeated instantly. But he wasn't sure what he had just said.

"Foul wind," asked Shea, not knowing what she had right. "She . . . what was her name? Oh yes, Dillon – Mrs. Dillon called you 'foul wind'? Why did she do that?"

More embarrassed than he had been in many years Falwyn explained that Mrs. Dillon did not care about the cleanliness of her stable hands. The work that Falwyn did, and the place where he did it contributed mightily to his *aura!* Dillon did not provide washtubs for the bodies or clothes of those servants in the stable. They were never permitted in the house. They were never permitted near her family. That was okay with Falwyn because he soon learned that every time he got within close proximity of one of the Dillon family they felt it their right to hit him with whatever they had handy. This was especially true when they wanted to go riding. Already holding a riding crop when he would bring them a horse to go riding, he was as likely to be struck with that crop as the horse. They invariably found this hilarious.

Because the name "Fitzmorris" uncomfortably reminded the Dillon family of the indentured servant who had run away they slowly gravitated toward the new name for her son. He became "foul wind", or "Falwyn" to them all.

Falwyn went on to tell them that his chief benefactor was a liveryman named Myles, who worked in the same stable. Myles looked after him, and saw to it that he got fed and was clothed. They became inseparable. Many years later Myles had finished his term as an indentured servant, and was free to go. For reasons known only to him he longed to travel west, despite the onset of the French Indian War in the Ohio Valley. Falwyn, who was not bound to the Dillon household by any indenture, went with him. Six months later they had gotten as far as Fort Royal. And there they stayed. The war had heated up and the French Army, with their Indian allies, was making travel west a very dangerous proposition for English speaking people. Myles and Falwyn made Fort Royal their home.

For the next several years the two did what they could, where they could, when they could, to get by. Their life was far from opulent but they were happy. But then Myles died.

"Just went to bed one night, and never woke up," Falwyn explained. Without Myles and the oversight and wisdom he provided, Falwyn's life once again began to slowly spiral downward.

There was silence after Falwyn told them of Myles death. They could sense that Falwyn hadn't thought about this in a long time, and was wishing he wasn't thinking about it now.

Shea was the first to speak, "I can't call you Falwyn anymore. Now that I know what I'm saying." Sho-Taka agreed, but said nothing.

"I know several good men named Morris. It's a good name," asserted the major.

"NO! I ain't gonna be called Morris by no one." Falwyn was determined not to let this go any further.

The topic became a dispute. The three men and two women tried to convince Falwyn that Morris Fitzmorris was far better in every respect than Falwyn, or Foul Wind. They even stopped pronouncing his name "Falwyn", but instead said it distinctly as "Foul Wind".

They reminded the defiant ex-guide that the name was given him by that wicked tyrant Dillon. That the name was no longer valid, now that he was bathing regularly. ("Okay, so you only have bathed once, but you will again soon." He wasn't so sure.) He was reminded that the Fitzmorris name was the proud name of his blood relatives, and of all his ancestors. He countered "that whole bunch of them ain't done nothin' for me since the day I was born." The major began to make some point about the name, and then somehow lost his train of thought and stumbled into silence. Sho-Taka tried to make him realize that the name was demeaning, and he should revert to his old one as a matter of pride.

"And what does Sho-Taka mean?" he retorted. "Betcha you don' even know! You don't speak Indian, do you? Could even mean 'foul wind', couldn't it?" Falwyn nodded as if he had just won a court case against the Chief Magistrate!

It was becoming heated. The Major and Sho-Taka continued to argue the point with Falwyn. Shea and Tyson joined in sporadically, so when Mrs. Devonshire spoke it surprised everyone, and they all became silent.

She looked directly into Falwyn's eyes, and said softly, "I am sorry, but I agree with them. I, too, cannot call you Falwyn anymore. It is beneath you." Her voice tranquilized him, and he couldn't take his eyes off her. In the low light beneath the rocks provided only by the flickering campfire her face was as pretty as any face he ever saw. "And your birth name belongs to the person you no longer are." He was too enthralled to even nod. "I cannot speak for the others, but, with your permission, I will call you Myles."

It took about ten seconds of absolute silence for the thought to take hold in his head. And then the newly named Myles broke into a huge grin. They all did.

Chapter 11 - Tally Ho, Captain Wallingford

A rain like BBs
Fired from low hanging clouds
Pelting everything

Farmers have always had another word for "sun-up". Because of who they are, and what they do, they refer to that time of day as *mid-morning*! By way of explanation for their still-dark start of each and every day they will say, "Hey! Someone has to wake up the roosters!"

Captain Phillip Wallingford was up with the farmers today. He was not normally a late sleeper, but today he was extra early. He had a very full agenda. He was greeted by heavy rain that had apparently started later in the evening. It hadn't stopped, but was beginning to taper off. That was good news. The bad news was that all that rain had probably washed away most of the tracks he had hoped to follow today.

He thought he should just go on ahead straight on ahead to Dubious, and waylay them there. It would be easier and quicker to get there because he knew precisely where it was. And arriving before them would allow him to choose the exact location of where to stage his confrontation. He thought it was far and away the better choice.

The only flaw was Falwyn.

With that idiot leading them they may never arrive at Dubious! Hell, he thought, they may wander around in the forest for months before he accidently found it! And Wallingford didn't have months to spare.

It was true, the washed out tracks would now be more difficult to follow than he had hoped, but he still had his ace-in-the-hole. He consoled himself with the fact that tracking a party led by Falwyn would not be too difficult under any circumstances. He put his densely woven, nearly waterproof, gray cape on over his uniform and headed out.

His first stop was Philyaw's. As expected he had to wake him up, and get him to open up his tavern earlier than normal. Wallingford wanted to eat a full hot meal before setting out. It was likely to be his last for the next several days. The reluctant Philyaw was finally coerced into getting out of his warm dry bed, and getting his kitchen going.

Wallingford did not sit around waiting for the meal to be prepared. He circled back to the fort's stable and began preparing the two horses he was going to take on his trip. The first horse was the best of the fort's five horses. This mare was bigger and stronger than most of the stallions in the area. This was to be his mount. The second horse he was bringing was to be his pack horse. For this job he chose the horse he had recently, and that poor animal was still suffering from the effects of the exhausting trip from Philadelphia the day before. And because it was a stolen horse, and could be used as evidence against him on the odd chance someone would show up at Fort Royal looking for it, Captain Wallingford had no intention of bringing it back to the fort. It was to be another *casualty* on his trip back to the fort after he had waylaid the major and re-acquired Devonshire.

After finishing at the stable he began heading back to Philyaw's. As he walked through town he was intercepted by Ludlum. "Oh, Captain Sir. A moment of your time, if I may," said Ludlum from a darkened doorway.

The startled captain turned toward him. It took a moment to recognize the man in the dark. Wallingford's hand rested on his sword. "Ludlum. What is it?" he asked with an impatient sour look. He wasn't looking for conversation.

Neither was Ludlum, "Captain, I'm glad I caught you before you run off again. I need to bring a matter to your attention."

"Go on. I'm in a bit of a hurry this morning."

"Your prisoner stole a horse from my stable to make her escape, and . . . well, because she was a prisoner of the Crown, I think it's up to you – as the official representative of the Crown – that you make good on my loss. I think you ought to replace the horse I lost." There was a pause, and then he added, "With one of yours."

The captain just looked at him. The silence started to grow louder.

Ludlum could hear it, and decided that perhaps he should offer an alternative. Something more to the captain's liking. "Or, if you think it fitting – because Bardley was the one who was supposed to keep her confined, and he didn't . . . then you should tell him to make it up to me, and pay me full value –and the horse she stole was my best – then he should pay me for it." They may be partners, Ludlum thought, but this was about money.

It annoyed the captain that his plan of restraining Mrs. Devonshire was now, apparently, common knowledge, but he could deal with that at some later date. It took him only seconds to take care of Ludlum and his stolen horse problem. In his mind he immediately ruled out any personal liability. And just as quickly, he ruled out any involvement in assigning responsibility to Bardley. There was no proof that she had stolen the horse; but even if she did, that was between her and Ludlum. He then came to the conclusion that this conversation was wasting his time. He looked Ludlum square in the eye and said, "No." He turned and continued on his way back to Philyaw's.

There wasn't anything Ludlum could do. The Captain was the sole authority for the entire area. Ludlum, like all the other settlers in the area, were totally dependent on his favor. The Fort Royal area was an absolute monarchy, and King Wallingford ruled the roost. Ludlum would spend the rest of the morning trying to devise a way for him to be reimbursed by someone, by anyone, for his loss. He decided that Bardley was the likely target. And "Damn Falwyn", if he had been sleeping in the stable like he always did, instead of running around the countryside trying to find Dubious, he would have heard that French bitch stealing his horse, and stopped her. Maybe?

Once back at Philyaw's Wallingford complained about his food not being ready yet. Philyaw tried to explain that his careful preparation took time. Any other customer who made such complaints would have been thrown out into the street. The only consolation Philyaw had been the knowledge that as he prepared the captain's meal he had spit into it.

At the very faintest hint of light in the eastern cloud leaden sky Captain Phillip Wallingford was already underway. Riding the mare the troops called Acorn, and leading the overloaded pack horse he had named "Gus" (after the Commanding General in New York), the captain was approaching Kelly's Crossing. Alternating between a fine mist and a light rain the weather was not smiling on the good captain's mission.

The conversation between the Wallingford and the ferryman, Kelly, was brief. The officer told him that the territory west would be closed for the next few days, and that Kelly was not to allow anyone to cross over the river until he had returned. To make sure that instruction was obeyed Captain Wallingford told Kelly that he would pull himself across the river by the tow rope, and tie up the ferry on the other side. The ferryman mentioned that his only income was from ferrying people back and forth across the river.

When Wallingford didn't respond Kelly just stared at him. Wallingford finally noticed the stare; stared back, and then said, "Yes, I know." He knew, but he didn't care.

Once across the captain disembarked (and untied the tow rope from the ferry so it could not be pulled back over until he returned) and began following the only path going west. The tracks on the trail were nearly obliterated by the previous day's rain. But the wagon that had made them had been heavy, and some traces remained. The captain moved along slowly, watching for traces of the wagon wheels. Sometimes they were clear. Sometimes they disappeared without a trace. The captain gently urged on Acorn, often bending over in the saddle peering down at the wet muddy ground trying to see the signs to follow. He was frequently jerked upright by the halting pace of the following less-than-enthusiastic Gus.

"Damnit, c'mon," he yelled as he jerked the rope attached to Gus's halter.

Time and time again the tracks vanished into the mud. Wallingford spurred on his mount in the direction he thought he should head. Time and time again he found himself hitting a dead-end. The trail sometimes led to a steep ravine, impassable to a wagon. Other times the false trail led to impenetrable woods or a stream too wide or deep for the wagon. Sometimes the trail just went too far without any sign of the tracks reappearing. Sometimes he would cross ground under dense tree coverage, sheltered from the hard rain, which should still have tracks, and see no sign of them. At these times he would reluctantly accept the probability that he had lost the trail. Cursing Falwyn, and Devonshire, and anyone else who came to mind he would backtrack to his last sure sign, and try again. And while he struggled to follow the trail the intermittent rain fell on him. As the morning wore on the cloak he wore became heavier and wetter. His complete focus on the tracks was interrupted by the cold chill of the rain, and the frequent yank of the packhorse's leader. The overloaded, sore legged Gus was stopping every time he could. Poor Gus was not enjoying this trip any more than Wallingford was. When darkness fell that evening Captain Wallingford had lost the trail once again. He was tired, and had been wet and lost most of the day. And by this time Gus was refusing to take another step. Wallingford relented and made camp. He made his way to the highest ground he could see in the fading light, and found an alcove among some rocks that was somewhat covered, and would keep most of him dry for the night. He grudgingly fed the horses, not because they needed the food, but because he knew he would need them tomorrow. He ate some of his own food, but not very much. He was more tired than hungry.

Captain Wallingford was not the only British officer aware of the foul weather in central Pennsylvania on this day. Far to Wallingford's east General Augustus Fothingill saw the storm clouds approaching as he was riding westward from New York toward the outpost called Fort Royal. He was leading a 50 man detachment of British regulars. These were hardened, battle tested veterans of the Battle of the Plains of Abraham (Quebec), and more recently the Battle of the Thousand Islands (Montreal).

There wasn't anything lackadaisical or hesitant about these soldiers, despite it being the seventh day of this march. Their relentless pace caused even the general to spur his horse in order to stay ahead of their rapid tempo. They were oblivious to the approaching rain, and were living proof of the old military adage that "It doesn't rain IN the army. It rains ON the army." Even one glance by an untrained eye would reveal that these fellows meant business.

The rumor mill back in New York had informed them that this march was going to lead them to the apprehension of the infamous "Mad Madam of Montreal". While they had all heard stories about her (what British soldier in the colonies hadn't?) more than a few of them had overpaid for their acquaintance with her which had resulted in both financial and personal hygiene misfortunes.

The genesis of this mission had occurred one week before in New York City. General Fothingill had held his usual Monday morning meeting of all senior officers in New York. Every Monday morning these officers trudged into headquarters for three hours of mind-numbing minutiae. There was rarely, if ever, a legitimate reason for the meeting or positive result from it. But Fothingill was not deterred, and attendance was mandatory.

In the course of some chit-chat during a break for tea General Fothingill overheard the Chief Magistrate say to another officer he was "looking forward to hanging her."

The General inquired, "Who?"

Jeremiah Roose, the Chief Magistrate, suddenly aware Fothingill had heard him, responded offhandedly, "Some harlot from Montreal. Uprooted by the French collapse in Montreal. Scurrying around, trying to evade capture. Has a list of charges against her that would make a pirate blush. Can hang her for any number of them! Quite a reward out on her, I should say. That young captain out in the frontier snared her, and is going to be rewarded handsomely."

When he finished talking he realized everyone in the room was silent, and looking at him. He had violated a sacred protocol held dear at these meetings. He had said something interesting to the general, and that usually resulted in prolonging these proceedings.

The general spoke up, and as he did so the other officers in the room glared at the magistrate; "Tell me more." No one was going to help him. No one was going to bail him out. They would all sit there, each as quiet as a tomb, and leave him to talk one-on-one with the general. And they would not look for a moment at the general for fear of making eye contact; instead they would look only at the magistrate with hard blank faces.

"What young captain? What's his name?" Fothingill asked. Those were just the first two questions the commander asked.

Mr. Roose glanced around the conference table one time, saw no help anywhere, and plunged on. "Captain Wallingford, I believe his name is. Commander of some small outpost between us and Fort Pitt. I don't recall the name. Told me he spotted her the minute she arrived at the settlement. Had his sergeant-in-arms place her in custody, and raced back here to confirm who she was."

"Wallingford?" the general asked no one. He turned to his aide, seated behind him against the wall, "Who is this Wallingford, Forbisher. Do we know him?"

The Sergeant nodded, "Yes Sir. He is the commander out at Fort Royal, Sir. You remember . . . Sweet Lizzie . . . the McGinty Brothers."

By God, of course! Young fellow. Light hair. All of it still there. Yes, I do remember. Wanted a cannon." He laughed. But then the general went silent. And there was silence around the room. A few moments passed before the general wondered aloud, "He never mentioned her in his report." He went silent again, and no one in the room interrupted his thoughts. "Why didn't he just bring her back with him?" he asked Roose.

Roose hadn't asked that question, or he didn't remember the captain's answer if he had, so he guessed. "Told me the situation out there was becoming a bit unsettled. Didn't want to reduce his already small force by assigning any of the men to escort her back to New York. He had her under lock and key; she wasn't going anywhere. So while he made sure of his prisoner, he would allow things to settle down out there. He assured me he'll be bringing her in shortly." In his mind he congratulated himself on a very fine answer.

"What's her name? This prisoner?"

For an instant there was panic. Roose was drawing a blank, but then in a flash it came to him. "Dellie d'Argent," he smiled.

To some at the table the name meant nothing. But to the others it was a shock. Most leaned forward with open mouths, while others broke the silence.

"d'Argent?"

"d'Argent!"

"He's got d'Argent. He has her in custody?"

The general watched the people around the table show more animation than he had ever seen. The name that had caused that commotion was vaguely familiar; he raised his voice for quiet. "Who is this d'Argent?" he asked.

In no particular order the men around the table relayed misadventures they had heard or read about concerning Dellie d'Argent. A few even admitted to personal involvement with her, but obviously omitted some details.

With each tale the general seemed to become more alarmed. He finally put an end to it by declaring that he had heard enough, and he was not going to jeopardize the safety of this "young captain out in the wilderness with this murderous villain." He declared that, "A company of fifty men, led by me and . . . and you too Major Tuite, will start out tomorrow for Fort Royal in order to provide Captain *Waddafer* (?) with a sufficient force to escort this prisoner back to New York and justice." Then he quickly added, "Roose . . . you'll join us."

Both Mr Roose and Major Tuite rolled their eyes; and then looked at each other; and then back at the general. Elsewhere around the table there were restrained smiles. The distance to Fort Royal was well over 100 miles, and a trip there and back would likely mean the absence of the general for a minimum of two weeks. In the minds of most of the officers there the phrase "two *glorious* weeks" repeated itself over and over again.

Early the next morning, Tuesday May 3rd, an eager General Fothingill led a troop comprised of four wagons, Chief Magistrate Roose, Major Tuite, Captain Pickering, three lieutenants, four sergeants, three cooks, and a company of 50 regulars. He could not be dissuaded from bringing along a cannon.

The General Fothingill led detachment of British troops marched due west from New York toward Fort Royal with zeal. Fatigue and foul weather, may have slowed them down at times, but nothing stopped them. Only when it became painfully clear to the normally obtuse general that the men were succumbing to the relentless pace did he allow them some rest. Every day of the march, from sunrise to sunset, the soldiers were pressed westward. Ignoring suggestions to ease up, General Fothingill could only focus on rehearsing the tale he would tell of how he captured the Mad Madam of Montreal.

General Tindale of Philadelphia was not of like mind. By ten o'clock Monday morning (May 8th) General Tindale had been leading his Philadelphia based troop of 60 soldiers northwest, through a driving rain, since 7 AM. They had left Philadelphia at 8 AM yesterday, and had only stopped to rest horses for a few overnight hours since. His eyes gleamed into the distance as he fantasized about what he was going to do to Major Aaron Highcross when he got his hands on him. Or maybe it was Captain Wallingford, as Captain McLayne suggested, who was the culprit in the abduction of his Audrey?

Forty eight hours ago Captain Phillip Wallingford had been only a minor character in the life of General Godfrey Tindale. They had been riding together in the outskirts of Philadelphia discussing the newly assigned commander of Fort Dubois. Tindale remembered the apparent confusion of the captain concerning the whereabouts and assignment of this new arrival. He remembered he took great pains to explain it to the captain. Now General Tindale had to consider that Wallingford may have been intentionally deceitful in his charade of ignorance. The general seethed in fury at the possibility that the captain may have known all along who this Major Highcross was. Wallingford also may have known all along about the new major's assignment. And if so, he may also have known, as they rode along side by side, what the major's vile intentions were concerning his own sweet daughter! This progression of logical deductions was leading General Tindale to levels of fury he had never reached before. He vowed to himself that both Wallingford and Highcross would be drummed out of the service for these deceitful transgressions. That was instantly dismissed and replaced in turn by "flogging" . . . "hanging" . . . "execution by firing squad". "No," he thought to himself, "Too lenient." His inner debate ran on.

All had begun to unfold about noon the previous day. Or rather the first sign something was amiss was at breakfast earlier. Tindale had an early appointment to ride with Wallingford, but was running late. He and his wife had delayed the start of breakfast as they awaited their daughter's arrival. When she hadn't come down to breakfast by 7 AM they sent a servant up to get her.

When the servant returned she did not have Audrey in tow, but rather a small scented envelope addressed to the general's wife. Lady Tindale opened and read it, and then turned to her husband, "She says she's staying at Joy Chilton's house for the weekend, and will not be back until late Sunday night." Lady Tindale made a sour face, and commented, "That's odd. She told me nothing about this last night."

General Tindale knew the Chiltons. George Chilton was a very wealthy merchant who owned a large home on the western outskirts of Philadelphia. The general began thinking more about his delayed breakfast than his daughter's oversight. He moved toward the dining room, and instructed the servant to bring his breakfast. "She's like you, my dear, and a bit flighty at times. Probably decided to go at the last minute."

"I'm not the least bit flighty, Sir. I don't know where you get these ideas." She said, as she too moved toward their morning meal.

Thirty minutes later the General and Captain Wallingford began their ride together. Before the next hour had passed Captain Wallingford had learned of the arrival of this Major Highcross, his destination, and his mission and that had rocked his world. He was well on his way back to his lodging in Philadelphia trying desperately to organize his thoughts on this newly discovered crisis. General Tindale, on the other hand, decided that there was nothing he could do about Highcross until Wallingford reported back. His more important current problem was trying to appease his daughter and wife at the same time concerning Audrey's desired trip west. Audrey had been mooning over the missing Highcross since his arrival in Philadelphia weeks ago. When he continued on his way west she began insisting she go visit him. Her mother, of course, said an emphatic "No!" That frontier, she insisted, posed far too many dangers for the young lady. Audrey's father didn't disagree with his wife, but his daughter pointed out that as Commanding General of the entire colony he had the resources available to provide adequate protection. The mother insisted it would be unseemly for the young lady to go charging after the young man. Her father reminded his daughter that the soldiers under his command had other pressing duties that didn't allow for personal missions such as this. Audrey countered every point with logic and/or tears. It had been going on since Highcross had left in late April.

After Wallingford's hasty departure, the general rode along the quiet road in the tranquil countryside north of the city and began to feel a relaxation he had not enjoyed in some time. The pressing responsibilities of command, and of fatherhood, seemed to slip away as he rode on. The sounds of chirping birds, the warm sun and cool breeze, and the rhythmic motion and hoof beats of his horse soon had him in a trance.

This idyllic Saturday began to crumble almost imperceptibly when he returned to his residence in mid-afternoon. He walked in through the kitchen in the rear, and was told immediately by the cook that "Your wife and Lieutenant St John were anxiously looking for you." He decided that they could both wait until he had a chance to unwind. He would seek out his wife first because he detested St John.

The general considered the young lieutenant arrogant and presumptuous. Virtually everyone did. If he hadn't been the youngest son of one of the wealthiest men in all of England, and who was also one of the king's closest personal advisors, this young man would have been assigned to duty in the far northern reaches of Canada. There, hoped by all those who dealt with him, the frigid cold and bears the size of Conestoga wagons would reduce him to a memory in short order. But that, much to General Tindale's chagrin, was not the case. Lieutenant Jeffrey St John had been assigned to his staff, as assistant to Lieutenant Crosly.

The general had made it clear to Lieutenant Crosly that St John was to be kept as far away from headquarters as possible. He was to be assigned any duty that put him far away; the longer it took and the farther away the better. If he did come to headquarters he was to report only to Lieutenant Crosly. The news that Lieutenant St John was nearby, and had not followed the strict chain of command by bypassing Lieutenant Crosly, was enough to immediately sour the General Tindale's mood.

The lieutenant had left instructions with everyone in the house that the general was to be advised immediately upon his arrival that St John needed to speak with him immediately. The general nodded acknowledgement and went upstairs to change clothes. He would get to St John at his leisure.

He hadn't even gotten his boots off when there came a firm knock on the door. He exhaled deeply, but before he could say a word the door swung open. "There you are, Sir," boomed the young St John, "Didn't they tell you I needed you the moment you returned?" He shook his head, and went on, "I'm going to have to speak with the staff here. You are far too lax with them."

The general held his tongue. He had no choice. He told himself to calm down, took a deep breath and asked, "What is it, St John that you find so compelling that it is necessary for you to barge into my dressing room?"

The rebuke went over the lieutenant's head. "Captain McLayne is here to see you on a most important matter."

The general didn't allow him to continue. He threw up his hand and said, "Can't this be taken up by Lieutenant Crosly. Have you spoken to him first?"

"He's gone. On leave. Didn't you know that? He won't be back for a week. I'll be standing in for him until he returns."

"Where's he gone?" the general asked. The realization that St John was to be his aide for the next few days did not sit well with him. How could Crosly make such an arrangement when he was very much aware of the general's distaste for St John?

"'Personal business' he said. Said he'd be back in a week's time. I told him "No hurry', I would see to things here while he was gone."

The prospect of having St John as his personal aide for the next week turned General Tindale's stomach. He asked himself why Crosly hadn't asked him about this. And the answer came to him instantly. Crosly knew the general wouldn't approve of having St John as his stand-in. And to prevent it from happening General Tindale would probably forbid Lieutenant Crosly from ever taking a leave as long as St John was his backup. Nodding to himself, General Tindale thought that young Crosly was a shrewd one, all right.

"What is it that you needed from me? What is the pressing problem you cannot deal with yourself?" He thought that was a nice little jab at the pompous little twit.

"Captain McLayne is here to see you. It appears he has had a bit of a row with Captain Wallingford." With as sincere a face he could muster he went on, "It appears he got the worst of it."

General Tindale rose and went to the door to show the lieutenant out. He told him to take Captain McLayne to the office and wait for him there. He would be down shortly. "Remain with him," he added.

Walking out the door the lieutenant couldn't resist saying, "He's been here since shortly after noon. I'm sure he would appreciate your earliest attention to this matter."

A cup of tea was brought up to the general's quarters as he changed out of his riding clothes. He wasn't in a hurry to go downstairs and mediate a disagreement between two officers. Wallingford, he thought, is off on an important mission, and won't be back for perhaps two weeks. And as for McLayne, the general reminded himself, he didn't like him very much. "But that's not fair," he thought, "I hardly know the man."

As he changed his clothes he mulled over the scant information that he had. He had spent most of last night and this morning in Captain Wallingford's presence. He had seen the young officer race off back to Fort Royal when he became aware of Major Highcross's disappearance. At no time did Wallingford indicate, by word or action, something unsettling had occurred. When did this dispute between the two captains occur? And what was the dispute about? The two men hardly knew each other. He vaguely remembered the two men might have been sitting next to each other at last night's dinner. And in the garden later, they may have been standing near each other, but there have been no signs of antagonism between the two.

He thought this over, reviewing it several times and then came to the conclusion he could put this off no longer. He went downstairs.

He opened the door to his office and went in. Both men there jumped to their feet. Lieutenant St John was far faster than Captain McLayne. St John had been sitting in the general's chair behind his desk, McLayne sitting opposite. St John slid slowly to the side of the desk as Tindale starred at him.

"Be seated," said the general. He sat down in his chair and looked at McLayne. The slightly balding, overweight captain had sloping shoulders. His face was round, as were his other features. His mouth was topped by a moustache that was sparse. His eyebrows were bushy, and one was longer than the other. He was quite a sight to see. Tindale took stock of him as the captain gently lowered himself back into his seat. His hair was mussed as if someone with sticky fingers had tousled it. His heavy lidded eyes were bloodshot, and watery. There was beard stubble in some places along his jaw and chin. Around his head was a white linen bandage with a blood stain near the front. There were speckles of blood on the front of his waistcoat, which was also dirty and torn. The right sleeve of his uniform was ripped, and several buttons were gone. Both the uniform jacket and pants were smeared with dirt. Because of the bandage he could not see the large knot on the side of his head and several black-and-blue marks on his arms and legs that were the result of the barman's disappointment after finding only a few coins in his pocket when it was pay-up time last night.

"Good God, man! What happened to you?" asked the general.

"I told you he was beat up," nodded St John, as if acknowledging a profound truth.

No he hadn't in fact, but that was irrelevant. Tindale turned toward the lieutenant and told him to sit down and be quiet. "Very quiet," he added.

"Go on." The general leaned forward toward McLayne.

Captain McLayne swallowed hard, and placed his hands on the arms of his chair. He was going to use them to prop himself up straight. After two seconds of pushing he realized he didn't have the required strength. He returned to his slouched position. Sitting on the front half of the seat, he leaned his back against the rear of the chair. His forearms rested on the chair arms and his hands and fingers pointed at the floor. His knees spread far apart and his head declined so that his chin nearly rested on his chest. He half closed eyes looked up and searched for the general. He began his sad tale.

As he did, a door outside slammed and seconds later the office door flew open and Lady Tindale came roaring in. The sudden flurry made General Tindale and St John jump to their feet.

Lady Tindale's day had begun with a delayed breakfast with her husband after learning their daughter would not be joining them. After breakfast she had written some letters, and checked with servants about household chores. But she kept wondering why her daughter had been less than candid about her plans last night. By noon she couldn't stop thinking about it.

She decided to pay a social call at the Chilton residence, and while there she planned on questioning her daughter face to face. Her arrival an hour later was welcomed, but somewhat unexpected. Her daughter wasn't there. And Miss Joy Chilton had no idea where Audrey was. She said that she and Audrey had made no plans for the weekend.

Lady Tindale started to panic. She returned home and immediately dispatched servants to find her husband, who was "out riding". Lady Tindale went out and began making the rounds of the homes of her daughter's friends. She became progressively more agitated as one after another of these friends told her that they neither knew where she was, or who she was with. Her imagination began to get the best of her as she conjured up one possible horrible scenario after another.

Between her fifth and sixth stop (and by now completely manic) one of her husband's staff intercepted her with the news that the general had returned home. She had her carriage driver race back to her house, and roared into the general's office.

"OH MY GOD! OH MY GOD!" she yelled. "GODFREY, OH MY GOD!" she yelled again.

Servants and staff members all over the house heard the commotion and converged on the room. They were dispatched to fetch cold cloths, and a cool drink, for the hysterical Lady Tindale. Her husband got her seated and tried calming her down.

"General, is there anything I can do?" Lieutenant St John innocently asked.

"LEAVE!" screamed the bulging eyed general.

It was all too much for Captain McLayne. At the roaring appearance of Lady Tindale he, too, had jumped to his feet. The commotion, the yelling, the physical exertion of struggling to his feet had a crushing effect on the suffering captain. He took a step toward the door, but instantly knew it was futile. He bent over at the waist; supported himself by clutching the arm of the chair, and threw up.

Ten minutes later some order had been restored in General Tindale's office. A cold cloth lay across Lady Tindale's brow as she regained her composure and lay prostrate on the room's settee. Captain McLayne was back in his chair with a cold cloth on his head too. Two servants were busy trying to clean up the mess he had made on the rug. With calming encouragement from her husband Lady Tindale relayed the day's events to him. He didn't stay calm long.

Philadelphia in the early 1760's was no longer a small village. It was a city with over 150,000 residents. A search for the missing young lady would not be an easy matter. The chaos of organizing that search mounted in the General's office with various officers and aides being summoned and dispatched.

Amidst all this chaos Captain McLayne sat in a chair in the corner and slowly recovered from his own recent misadventures. He watched as Lieutenant St John listened in on every conversation taking place. He watched as the worried parents patted each other's' hands. He was starting to feel a little better. He credited that to the unfortunate but somehow curative regurgitation. Surprisingly he was starting to feel a little bit hungry. He watched as servants brought in some plates of food, which no one but him touched.

General Tindale was talking to some officer about sending a troop of mounted soldiers off to block the river south of the city when the Chiltons unexpectedly arrived. Mr and Mrs. Jehoshaphat Chilton arrived shortly after 4 PM. They had their daughter Joy in tow. With a very stern face Mr Chilton told his daughter, "Tell General Tindale what you told us. Word for word!"

Joy Chilton stared at the carpet, and after a long pause spoke in a whisper. Both the general and his wife gave her their complete attention. "She never told me where she was going. Really, she didn't." The young lady, after much prodding by both her parents and the Tindales, went on to say that Audrey had told her she was "going off on a mad adventure. I am going to follow my heart. I have found my true love."

Lady Tindale let out a low cry, "She's eloped!" and collapsed back onto the settee. The general's eyes bulged.

Joy swore that Audrey hadn't told her with who, or where she was going. Lady Tindale didn't hear her, she was swooning. The general barked at an aide, "Get her a brandy," as he gestured toward his wife. He stood up, and the room went silent. Everyone could see he was deep in thought.

The room was dead still. The only movements were the eyeballs of each person in the room as they shifted left and right. The general finally whispered, "Highcross!"

Only the sound of the ticking grandfather clock could be heard. Everyone was peeking at the General except McLayne. He was watching the aide with the brandy decanter, and looking to see if there was another glass in the room.

Slowly the general turned toward his friend, Jehoshaphat Chilton, and with a look of desperation and resignation said, "He's just a major!" It seemed that the General had set his sights a few grades higher for his daughter's nuptials.

The silence was broken when Lady Tindale began moaning and crying. The brandy would go straight to her head, and fifteen minutes after finishing her glass she would be asleep. Not so the general, he began making preparations for his daughter's retrieval. She wasn't going to marry some 'goddamned major who hasn't shaved yet!"

The Chiltons left. The servants returned to their various jobs. Lady Tindale went to lie down. Only the general and his various officers were left in the office, and that included the uninvited Captain McLayne. He was sitting in the chair by the window with the decanter of brandy and a glass he had obtained from who knows where. The conversation was about where the general and accompanying soldiers would dash off to once the sun was up tomorrow. He was going after his daughter, and "whoever the snake was that has seduced the poor child."

Watching the brandy swirl in his glass McLayne said to no one, "I'll wager Wallingford had his hand in this." And purely by chance when he said it, no one else in the room was saying anything. Everyone heard him. Everyone turned toward him. The general was surprised he was still here.

Tindale was the first to speak. "Why did you say that? Why would he take her?"

The captain shrugged his shoulders, "Well I'd say he's got a hand in all this, somehow. Last night he couldn't stop asking me one question after another about your daughter. Couldn't get enough information to suit him, I tell you. He even dragged me out to some wretched alehouse last night after the festivities here so he could continue his interrogation. I, of course, was discreet and left him flat as soon as I could make my escape. That, I assume, is why he attacked me this morning. He shook his head and let out a sigh, "I wouldn't be a bit surprised if he isn't the one she's run off with!" McLayne then waved his hand toward St John, "He told me she's been pestering you about going out to see Highcross, correct? Isn't that where Wallingford was going? And I might add he was in a godawful hurry to leave when I last saw him."

Tindale turned toward St John, "You spend your day discussing the private affairs of my household with other officers?" St John opened his mouth, but nothing came out. Considering the general's current state of mind there was nothing to say. Lieutenant St John smiled weakly. The general made a mental note to forbid Crosly from taking any leave in the future.

The officers in the room stood quietly while Tindale decided what to do. It didn't take him long. "Prepare to leave tomorrow morning at sunup," he said to one officer. "We'll take your entire company." He went quiet again as he thought this through.

"All the men, Sir? How should they be provisioned?" the officer asked.

"All your men. Full provisions. Enough for a week. Fully armed," barked the General.

"Where are we going," asked St John?

The General looked at him in disbelief. "To Fort Royal, you idiot!" The kid glove treatment of the privileged young man was over.

"To arrest Wallingford?" Captain McLayne asked hopefully.

The general turned to him. He was confused. "Why am I going to arrest Wallingford?"

"He might be the one that's run off with your daughter." McLayne's mind was working fast. He wanted Wallingford locked up. "He and your daughter might have been using Highcross to throw you off their trail." It sounded plausible to McLayne.

"Ah, a clever ruse," mused the nodding Lieutenant St John. He, unfortunately, mused out loud, and Tindale heard him.

If Tindale had had a weapon of any kind in his possession at this moment St John would not have seen his next birthday. The general glanced at his desk in hopes of seeing a letter opener, or anything of that kind.

McLayne spoke up, and distracted him. "Captain Wallingford has a long, well known reputation as a lecherous ladies' man. It wouldn't surprise anyone if he had designs on your daughter."

"My daughter and Captain Wallingford," said General Tindale thoughtfully. He turned to McLayne and dismissed that possibility by saying, "Good God man, he's only a captain."

An almost indignant McLayne shot back, "Then arrest him for assaulting me. He used a bottle to club me in the head, Sir. He broke it."

"Your head?" The general had not been told about the details of the confrontation, and with his mind preoccupied with his daughter's departure, this information was new.

An incredulous McLayne answered, "No! The bottle! Blood spurted everywhere."

"From the bottle?"

McLayne drained his brandy glass. "No Sir. From my head!' He paused and started over. "General Tindale, Sir," he started to explain slowly, "Captain Wallingford assaulted me with a bottle. He crashed it on my . . . ."

Tindale didn't let him finish, "You come with us. We'll straighten all this out at Fort Royal."

The General issued orders around the room. Plans and logistics needed to be ironed out and made final. They would leave Philadelphia at sunup tomorrow morning. He never considered taking a cannon.

Chapter 12 – Morning Rush Hour

I gotta go, I gotta go!
I gotta get my ass in gear.
There's things to do, places to see
And they, my friend, ain't here.
But most of all there's folks to find,
And these people I need to see.
To some say, "Hi", others "Goodbye"
The last two? "R. I. P."

There were a great many people traveling the rain soaked roads of central Pennsylvania on this Monday morning May 9, 1761.

Farthest west were the six pilgrims on their way to Dubious. And for the first time since they had left Fort Royal, thanks to those Indians, they knew about where they were, and the approximate location of what should be their destination.

Heading toward Fort Royal from the southeast was General Godfrey Tindale. He was accompanied by Lieutenant St John, Captain McLayne, a Captain Castlewich and his company of 60 soldiers of Applewood's Light Dragoons. This entire detachment was on horseback. This hard charging mounted troop was followed in the distance by their four wagon supply train.

Independently, just heading out of Philadelphia for Fort Royal were the three wagons of supplies that Captain Wallingford had requisitioned the previous week from General Tindale. Hitched to the rear of the third wagon was Captain Wallingford's brand new cannon. They would not follow the more direct cross country path that General Tindale was taking, but rather go north to intersect with the Western Road and head west from there.

The resupply column of five wagons (the last one pulling the new cannon) from New York had been on the road for the last eight days. The Western Road they travelled was fairly straight and level, so with the exception of the recent rain, the trip was progressing quite nicely and they felt no need to hurry. That was until they were overtaken by the contingent of marching troops led by General Fothingill rushing west to the aid of Captain Wallingford.

All the officers with Fothingill were on horseback, while the sergeants and 50 regulars marched behind to that relentless beat of the drum. In the rear came the four supply wagons for the troop; the last towing a cannon. General Fothingill could barely contain his excitement about being on the march. The captain and three lieutenants, as well as the sergeants and enlisted men, had been on forced marches before – many of them. There did not share the general's enthusiasm. Major Tuite and Magistrate Roose sided with the troops. The men in the ranks, who at first looked forward to going out to arrest the infamous Montreal Madam, had lost their enthusiasm by this seventh day of forced march; especially the part of it done in the pouring rain. As they trudged along the grumbling in the ranks was becoming louder and louder.

There was also the anxious, but stationary, contingent of soldiers already at Fort Royal who were trying to figure out a way of safely disregarding Captain Wallingford's orders to stay at the fort. But they knew – at least Selkirk knew – that there was money to be made if they could catch up to Mrs. Devonshire and bring her back.

By ten o'clock this morning the troops from New York had already been marching for three hours. Esprit de corps was becoming rarer than dry feet.

In the fourth supply wagon a sergeant was berating the driver. "If you had gone and done what I told you to do we wouldn't be in this fix, I tell ya!"

"Ya never told me. You said nothin'. I thought maybe ya told Allerton to do it. But ya never told me!" They went on arguing, but speaking softly. They did not want to be overheard.

"This is the bloody arms wagon, isn't it? Why in bloody hell would I tell Allerton?" the sergeant hissed. "He's got nothin' in his bloody wagon you could shoot except peas, yer damn fool!"

The driver offered, "They probably got some in the supply wagons. We can always get some there if we need it."

The sergeant scoffed, "What? Ya gonna tell the bloody captain ya left the ammunition back in New York? Ya gonna tell him you did not bring any? He'll bloody well hang ya from the nearest tree." He wasn't finished, "And supposin' they don't have any in those bloody resupply wagons? Whaddya gonna do then? Spit at the Frenchies?"

"If we can get to Fort Royal without running into any trouble we'll be all right." The driver nodded; assuring himself he had it right. "We can grab some of theirs at Fort Royal . . . and everything will be right as rain. Hell, we probably won't even need it; this is all safe country. There aren't any whitecoats out here anymore." He kept thinking it through, "And once we're back . . . who'll know the difference?" The driver had convinced himself and snapped the reins again. The sergeant continued thinking it through, "But if we do run into trouble . . . ya gonna get court-martialed. Geez they'll hang you as sure as blazes."

"Me? You wuz the one that forgot to bring it. You gonna be the one whose feet will be swingin' in the breeze." The conversation went on and on. Neither man giving in.

At this very same moment the troop from Philadelphia was riding hard. The 60 men of Applewood's Light Dragoons were racing to keep up with General Tindale as he led them northwest toward Fort Royal. He was leading the troop not to the more circuitous, but safer and flatter Western Road, but on a more direct cross country route. He wanted to get to Fort Royal in the shortest possible time. His daughter's honor hung in the balance, and the general wasn't going to allow some major, or even worse, some captain to stain the Tindale name.

Riding hard was what the general needed. On those occurrences when they stopped to rest the horses he had time to think. As various thoughts circled round his head each one made him angrier than the last.

"That idiot Highcross! Thought it a good idea to marry my daughter after knowing her all of ten days! Good God!" Tindale shook his head, then switched gears, "Or maybe it wasn't him? If it was Wallingford I'll shoot him myself. Why in God's name would he think it proper to run off with my little girl? That snake! And here I am out in these goddamn woods . . . in the goddamn rain . . . with this little shit St John constantly yapping in my ear. . . . and this repulsive McLayne too – who never stops whining . . . ." These thoughts just circled through the general's head time and time again. The worry, the weather, and the weariness from the hard riding were making General Tindale a less than congenial travelling companion.

Far to the west, the camp of the six pilgrims was starting to come alive. It was going to be a good morning as the rain clouds were gone. The sun was peeking through the trees in the east, and a light spring breeze was reminding everyone it was May. But as nice as the day promised to be there was a cloud forming over the group. It slowly dawned on each of them that their days together were coming to an end.

True, they had not been together for a long time, but it felt like that to them. Sho-Taka and Falwyn – or rather Myles – had been acquainted since last summer. And they had spent a great deal of time together since then. Sho-Taka, with a seemingly unending array of skills, always seemed to have a job to do, and more often than not he had invited Myles to help him with it. Shea had arrived at the Fort Royal settlement a little bit after last Christmas. She had been working at Philyaw's almost from the day she arrived, and had become an everyday fixture to most of the inhabitants of the settlement. Tyson and Highcross had only recently arrived on the scene, but were the reason they were all here together. Of them all only Mrs. Devonshire seemed to stand apart.

The morning progressed as usual. The cow was milked and the chickens fed; the breakfast was prepared and eaten. It was all done in silence. Blankets were rolled, and the wagon carefully loaded as they went about their tasks wondering how many more times they would do this as a group.

Sho-Taka and Myles gently attached the frames holding the stretched animal skins to the side of the wagon. "When are my moccasins goin' to be ready?" Myles asked.

"Soon" was the one word reply.

Tyson tended to the horses, and Major Highcross followed him around. "I'm walking much better, don't you think," he asked Tyson.

Tyson answered by asking a question, "How's your head?"

"Oh, just a small bump," he said. But Tyson noticed he was bareheaded. The major would wear nothing on his head for the next few days; there was a bump on top the size of a walnut.

They chatted about their respective futures. And if you listened carefully there was a difference in the tone of their voices. Tyson spoke of his future as a farmer with enthusiasm. He had plans . . . definite plans. He spoke about building a home, and what it would look like. His barns and corrals would be placed just as he imagined them. He knew how his fields would look, and what would be grown where; and when. Major Highcross seemed to be more reserved. He was looking forward to the prestige of assuming command of his post at Dubious, but less so as to what that would entail. He envied Tyson's certitude, and wished he had it about the duties he was about to undertake. When they were finished Tyson took two of the horses back to the camp to hitch them to the wagon. Highcross brought the other horse back to camp and saddled him. He mounted it, and rode off a little distance to the south "to look over the area". What he wanted was some time to himself to think some things over.

Shea and Mrs. Devonshire busied themselves with packing pots, pans, and food. After a long period of silence, Shea whispered to her, "What are you really running away from?"

Mrs. Devonshire looked at Shea for a long minute, and then asked, "What do you really want to find at Fort Dubois?"

"My father," she answered. Devonshire smiled, and then shook her head. "I do," Shea insisted, "I want to tell him that we, my brother and me, need him back at the farm. That Mother's awful sick. She hasn't got long, and there's no time to spare."

Once again Devonshire looked long and hard at Shea. "You're not a farm girl. I can tell." She smiled again, "Oh, I don't think you're the Duchess of Kent, either. But you are not a farm girl. You know your way around a kitchen. You know that much and you can take care of yourself. I heard that much about you too."

Amused, Shea asked, "What else do you know?"

"Well, I don't think you've got a brother and his wife back on some dirt farm in New Jersey. Do you?"

Still amused Shea asked, "Why?"

"As I said; you're not a farm girl. You're hands and nails . . . especially those nails . . . aren't those of a farm girl. So there is no dirt farm. And as for your brother . . . well every time you tell a story about him you change his name." They both laughed.

Shea wasn't sure she should argue the point. Her heart wasn't in it. She did not like being deceitful even though it was necessary for her to accomplish her goal. The truth was that she hadn't worked on a farm since she was eight. When her father had deserted mother and daughter after nine years of stormy marriage her mother sold their worthless piece of land and began working for a large landowner nearby. The mother and daughter worked for the man cooking, sewing, tending to household chores, and even working in the fields, on occasion, for the last ten years. Her mother was still there, content with her lot in life. Shea, on the other hand, grew weary of toiling for the benefit of the insufferable landowner. She was also growing weary of fending off the unwanted advances of, among others, the man's son. Saving and scrimping for a year and a half, she left one morning to "find her father". It was as good an excuse to leave as any other. Her mother wished her well, but had no interest in its outcome. She didn't care where her husband was. "If you find the bastard, don't you dare bring him back here," was her only comment. Some vague promises were made by both the landowner and his son to get her to stay, but they were empty; and she was gone.

Mrs. Devonshire interrupted Shea's reverie, "Is your mother even sick?" Then she corrected her question, "Is she even still alive?"

"As healthy as a horse," Shea said without thinking. She smiled; her secret was out. She looked at Devonshire and was going to ask for her silence, but was interrupted.

"Your secret's safe with me. I'm good at secrets," Devonshire said. Then added, "I'm *really* good at secrets."

Shea believed her immediately, and wanted to tell her the truth. "If I do find my father at Fort Dubois," she paused here for a moment, "I'm going to cut his treacherous little heart out!"

Devonshire cemented the friendship by saying, "I'll help you."

With a new found camaraderie the two women chatted on in subdued voices. Shea divulged far more of her personal "secrets" than Mrs. Devonshire did, but it wasn't one-sided. At one point Shea asked, "Why are you really running from the authorities? What did you do?"

Devonshire made a motion like waving away a bothersome mosquito. "They are charging me with everything they can think of! They are accusing me of every criminal act committed in New England colonies in the past ten years," she laughed. "If I had done what they say I've done I would be richer than the Queen of France."

"What will they do if they catch you?"

"Well, I presume under the law I will get some sort of trial. But that will just be for show. I will most likely be found guilty of every charge. And I suspect that will take less time to decide than it will take them to decide on whether to put me in front of a firing squad or to hang me."

"Oh dear!" Shea said.

"I suspect they will choose hanging. Men consider a firing squad so much more honorable than hanging, and besides it's over too quickly for their murderous hearts. No, I think those vengeful bastards will hang me." She said it in such a soft and winsome way that it took Shea a moment for the meaning to sink in.

"Oh my goodness! How terrible. How are you going to escape them?"

"I have to go southwest. I have to stay away from settlements where British soldiers are. If I can evade the authorities at Fort Pitt

. . . if I can get to the Ohio River, I will ride that to the Mississippi. Once I have made it that far I can float down that mighty river to French New Orleans. I will be safe there."

"That's so far. So dangerous! So many miles through the frontier."

"I have already travelled many miles. I escaped Montreal after it fell, and made my way to the coast. I thought if I could reach Acadia I would be safe. But I was wrong. The Acadia I knew is no more. It had fallen to the English; they changed everything. They call it Nova Scotia now. I barely got away with my life. I was smuggled in a wretched little scow to Boston. And there I searched for a vessel that would take me to the Caribbean . . . the French Caribbean! Or Spanish even. But I was betrayed to the authorities, and they began closing in. I narrowly escaped. I can no longer go to any of the big cities on the coast. New York, Philadelphia, or farther south . . . Baltimore or even Charleston. They are looking for me everywhere. Soon they will look for me at Fort Royal. I must get past Fort Pitt to the Ohio before they know where I am."

The conversation petered out as each woman began to focus on her own pressing issues. For Shea time was running short before she would have to decide what she was going to do when she finally met up with her father. She had never been sure when that crucial moment arrived whether she would embrace her long lost father, or plunge her knife into the chest of the man who deserted his wife and daughter. When she had left her mother and home back in New Jersey she was partial to the option of assault, and assault without hesitation or regret. But now, as she drew closer, she was starting to have her doubts.

Devonshire had a different problem. In fact she had two. She believed eluding the major's attempt to arrest her and return her back east would turn out to be very easy. That problem was small. But she wondered if she could convince Tyson to take her further into the frontier and find the Ohio River. If she could reach the Ohio she was sure she could make it to New Orleans. If his land in Kan-tucky was on, or near, the Ohio River her task would be far easier than getting him to go far out of his way. Her budding friendship with Shea might prove to be an advantage to her for this because she saw that there was something blooming between those two.

And there was one other thought she kept returning to. Last night, as he told his life story, Sho-Taka had said, "That's why I am going southwest; it is warmer, and there are no English there." He was, as far as she knew, supposed to be an assistant guide to Myles, and one might presume that upon reaching Dubious, would turn around and return back east with Myles to Fort Royal. But it had sounded to her that he was saying that he was going southwest, and was going to *keep on going southwest!* This was, to her, very good news. He was a man of many talents that would be a great advantage to her if she could steer him into going all the way to New Orleans with her. And steering men into doing what she wanted was something she was quite good at.

When the major came riding back into camp from his short scouting foray he assured them all it looked "quite clear up ahead". They all shuffled around checking once more the campsite and the loaded wagon, and then started south to find the river that would lead them southwest to Dubious. The mounted Major led the group with Tyson walking beside him. The wagon followed with Shea driving and Devonshire sitting alongside. With the information provided by the Indians yesterday it was no longer necessary for Myles to pretend he was leading them; so Myles and Sho-Taka took up the position at the rear. And although none of them felt that any hostile attack was likely, Myles felt much better walking in the rear than the front.

The steady pace set by Tyson was the result of the beautiful spring weather that had returned this morning. And added to that was the good feeling he had that for the first time since leaving Fort Royal he was very confident that they were heading in the right direction; thanks to the guidance of the two Indians yesterday. The good feeling did not however lend itself to much conversation between him and the major. In fact, it was quite sparse. The major, feeling quite chipper this morning, had tried several times to start a conversation with Tyson, but got little or no response at all from the seemingly distracted Tyson. When he finally gave up he found himself easily distracted, and mesmerized, by the beauty of the woodland surrounding him. He daydreamed in the saddle about the command he was soon to have.

Tyson, on the other hand, wasn't daydreaming in the least. He also thought that the scenery around him was beautiful, but did not forget for a second that danger was ever present in this frontier. He remained vigilant, and constantly aware of maintaining a southerly course.

Twenty feet behind the major and Tyson was the wagon, and twenty feet further on was the duo of Sho-Taka and Myles. They had been walking in silence since they had started off this morning. Sho-Taka, much like Tyson, remained aware of their surroundings and direction; Myles was lost in thought.

"How long should we stay at Dubious?" he said glancing at Sho-Taka. The question interrupted Sho-Taka as he was trying to keep a landmark in sight. He was using it to make sure their route remained consistently to the south. He turned for a moment to Myles, but as he had done so often since meeting Myles, he ignored him and went back to checking his direction.

Myles had been giving this some thought and realized there was no hurry in getting back to Fort Royal. It had occurred to him that Ludlum probably wouldn't do any of the dirty work he usually had Myles do, so it was probably piling up (no pun intended) back at the stable. It had also occurred to him that Captain Wallingford – who was never very pleasant to Myles – might be angry at him because he had led this party to Dubious. And Captain Wallingford topped the list of people at Fort Royal that Myles did not want to cross. Several of the soldiers he had spoken to about Dubious's location had vague feelings that the Captain wouldn't like anyone going out there without him.

Unwilling to let it drop, once more Myles asked, "We don' hafta go back right away, right? I mean, we can stay at Dubious for a few days or weeks; to rest up, and resupply before we go back. Can't we?"

Distracted once more, Sho-Taka turned to his companion and just looked at him for a minute. "I'm not sure I'm going back."

This wasn't the answer Myles expected to get. "What?" He stopped walking and stared.

Sho-Taka just shrugged and kept walking.

Myles caught up, "Whaddya mean? You goin' to stay at Dubious? What for? Why?"

Sho-Taka hadn't thought this through yet so he didn't answer and kept walking.

"What's there? Why you wanna stay there?"

Sho-Taka shook his head, "I didn't say I was going to stay there. Maybe I'll stay, but maybe I'll just move on. Head up to Fort Pitt. Got to be over a thousand settlers up near there by now. Must be plenty of work to do."

"You know anybody out there? You been there before?" Myles was astounded.

Again, Sho-Taka shook his head, "No. No I don't. But there are lots of people there, and more are heading there every day. And there's plenty of work for anyone willing to take it on, too!" He hesitated, and then added, "A man could do well there."

"Yeah," Myles jumped in, "But all them people there are whites. Thought you didn't want nothin' to do with them Englishmen?"

"It don't have to be at Fort Pitt where I settle down. There must be thousands of empty square miles out there waiting for someone to come along and put down stakes."

"What! You gonna cheat some Indian out of his land just like the white man does. Even though you say it's wrong . . ."

Sho-Taka cut him off, "Who says I'm going to cheat him out of his land? I'll pay him cash money. Fair and square. I won't cheat anyone."

Myles dismissed him, "You gonna live way out there surrounded by Indians? They'll take your scalp just as quick as they'll take mine. First chance they get; I tell ya. Won't make no difference how quick you tell 'em your folks was Indian. They'll take one look at how you're dressed . . . one listen to the way you talk, and *slish-slash* (he wiggled his hand in the air) . . . your hair is gone!" Myles laughed out loud.

Sho-Taka did not want to discuss his unmade plans with Myles. He waved his hand at him, and went back to checking his landmarks.

Myles accepted Sho-Taka's waved hand as his acceptance of defeat in their debate, and went back over the conversation in his mind. Where was Sho-Taka thinking of going? It couldn't be Dubious. No. And going to Fort Pitt and being surrounded by hundreds, maybe thousands, of Englishmen didn't make sense either. Would he head out into the frontier by himself to farm? He could, but he had never shown much enthusiasm for farming back at Fort Royal. The thought that maybe he would partner up with Tyson in Kan-tucky occurred to him. But he don't like farming he repeated himself. Maybe he's just giving me a hard time? He sure likes doing that! Myles finally decided that Sho-Taka was going to go back to Fort Royal, and had just said what he said to rile me up. That's all.

In the wagon there was little conversation. And what talking was being done was being done almost entirely by Devonshire. In a very short time it became apparent that Shea was preoccupied with other thoughts, and Devonshire began using the silence to begin solving the problems she was facing in the near future.

She had to be prepared for the eventual attempt by Highcross to arrest her. She had to decide what she was going to do to avoid that; preferably without violence. She had to decide how to approach Tyson about having him accompany her all the way to the Ohio River where she could catch a riverboat to the Mississippi. Or, she thought, she could approach Sho-Taka to see if he wanted to join her all the way down to New Orleans. Opportunities abounded there for a man with his varied skills. Perhaps they could even be partners in a venture she was planning to initiate after she got settled there. She wouldn't fail to mention to him that New Orleans never got as cold as Massachusetts, nor were there any Englishmen down there. (She was a very good listener.) Either of these scenarios would serve her purpose, and both were a distinct possibility. But first she would have to deal with Highcross.

Shea watched the countryside go by. It was a beautiful spring day with the foliage coming into full bloom. A gentle breeze and warm sun made the surrounding silence hypnotizing. Only an occasional bounce by the wagon or bird's cry broke the spell. When she wasn't looking around, she was watching Tyson in front of her. And today, for the first time, she was aware that she was watching him. She wasn't sure why?

Tyson wasn't wearing anything different, or acting any different, or talking different. He was exactly the same as he had been since they met at Fort Royal. From her rear view he was unremarkable in almost every way. Only when she remembered his grey-blue eyes and quiet demeanor, did she think of him as unusual. But as the morning wore on she thought more about him than her surroundings. Thoughts were scurrying in and out of head like mice in a barn. He wasn't bad looking. He was pretty good with his rifle. He knew all about farming. He had land, and a plan!

This recitation went on in her head for longer than she would have imagined. After a while she was becoming dizzy with it as it went on without stop, and seemed to be accelerating. She finally caught herself, coughed out loud to clear her throat and head. Think about something else she told herself.

Feeling the nearly midday warmth she took off her shawl, and raised the sleeves on her dress to bare her arms. Devonshire turned her head toward her for a moment when she did, but said nothing. Shea noticed that, and when she did she also noticed that Mrs. Devonshire was still wearing her cloak.

"Aren't you hot under that thing?" she asked. Devonshire, lost in her own thoughts, didn't understand and made a face. "Your cloak," explained Shea.

Devonshire nodded her understanding, "I feel the cold easily. I like to keep it on."

Shea thought about that in silence. As she did it occurred to her that Mrs. Devonshire hadn't taken her cloak off since she arrived in their camp four days ago. She even reminded herself that she slept in it. Or, at least she kept it next to her as she slept. Well, she thought to herself, some people just feel the cold more than others. She allowed her mind to drift back to Tyson.

As the sun reached higher into the sky some of the pilgrims began thinking about taking a break for a noon time meal. They all had other thoughts in their minds too. Major Highcross was hungry but was willing to continue their trek as they grew ever closer to

Dubious. Myles was wondering how he could arrange to ride in the wagon; he was tired of walking, and riding a horse was out of the question. Sho-Taka continued to consider the options he had beyond Dubious. Shea had the fate of her father in mind if . . . IF . . . he was at Dubious. And Devonshire had the major, Tyson and Sho-Taka to manipulate. And although manipulating men was something she was quite adept at; all three would be a tall order.

The only one not thinking of lunch was Tyson, and he did not hear the major talking to him from atop his horse. It took Highcross several questions to get Tyson's attention, and each one was louder than the previous one.

"What are you thinking about? Can you hear me?" he shouted.

Tyson turned up to him, "I'm sorry. What did you say?"

"What are you thinking about? You were in a trance."

No, I thought I . . . . Listen. Do you hear it?"

Major Highcross looked around in silence, and then said, "Sorry. I don't hear anything unusual." There were some noises, but it sounded to the Major like ordinary sounds from a forest. The wagon behind them made a sound as it bumped over a tree branch on the trail. Tyson raised his arm to stop the wagon. The two women in the wagon sat still as their eyes went from Tyson to the surrounding woods. Sho-Taka noticed the halt immediately and walked quickly up to the side of the wagon. He, now too, looked from Tyson to the surrounding woods.

Suddenly beside Sho-Taka, Myles whispered, "What?"

Sho-Taka, looking in all directions, walked slowly up to where Tyson stood. Tyson asked him, "Do you hear it?"

"Hear what?" the major asked.

Myles had joined the group, "Stalkers?"

"No," Tyson grinned at him. When Myles began to say something else Sho-Taka shushed him. Major Highcross said nothing, but watched Tyson and Sho-Taka stare off into the woods left, right, and center.

"We've been going south; straight and steady, right?" said Tyson.

"I think we are, yes," agreed Sho-Taka.

They remained silent for a time, when finally Tyson broke the silence and said, "It sounds like it's over there," pointing to the right side of the trail. "Off to the west, right?"

Sho-Taka nodded, and the major asked, "What's 'over there'?" He didn't want to guess.

"The river," said Tyson.

It the next few minutes it was agreed that the major (who couldn't be stopped) and Sho-Taka would venture out to their west and see if they could find the river they thought they heard. The others would remain on the trail with the wagon, give the horses a rest, and prepare a lunch.

The two scouts returned only ten minutes later with the news that they had found the river they had been looking for. Everyone was excited because this was supposed to be the last signpost before reaching Dubious. The Indians had told them that all they had to do now was follow the river southwest until it turned south, and then they should continue due west ("toward the setting sun"). The fort they were looking for was only a half day's walk from there.

The Major's enthusiasm had him urging the group to continue on, "We can eat as we go," he said.

The others convinced him there wasn't any need to hurry. They still had to "follow the river southwest, past the rapids, until it turns south". And they reminded him that they still had a half day's walk after that. They would not reach Dubious until tomorrow afternoon at the earliest; there was no need to skip a lunch break. He sat in the saddle for another ten minutes arguing with himself before he reluctantly dismounted. The others had spread out around the wagon, each occupied with something or other.

Sho-Taka and the Major were asked about the river.

"How far off is it?"

"Is it big? How wide?"

"Did you see any rapids?"

"Is there a trail alongside? Will we be able to follow it?"

Highcross gave very animated answers to all the questions, and Sho-Taka explained them afterward. The discovery confirmed that they were closing in on their destination. And although it did not excite them all equally, it was a relief to them all. Arrival at Dubious meant different things to each of them. But it also meant that they would be safer there than out in the forest. It would provide some rest and hot meals, and a chance to relax.

For Shea and Major Highcross it was the final destination they had set out for so many miles ago. For Sho-Taka and Myles it meant that a fateful decision could no longer be put off. For Mrs. Devonshire it meant time was running out, and she had to solve some pressing problems. But for Tyson it meant only a stopping off point on a journey that still had many miles to go. It would seem it meant less to him than any of the others, but he was the most reflective.

It didn't take very long for Shea to notice that Tyson was saying very little. And she quickly came to the conclusion that his reason was that Dubious meant less to him than anyone else. The talk whirled around their circle, but now it was both Shea and Tyson saying very little.

Mrs. Devonshire soon noted that Shea was quiet and watched her. In no time at all she saw that Shea was shooting glances at Tyson every few seconds.

One by one they all grew less animated and quieter until finally Myles, who was saying something about how sure he had been that under his guidance he would lead them to Dubious, stopped mid-sentence.

". . . so I knew from then on . . . What?" He looked around.

No one said anything until Shea broke the silence, "Are you sorry we made it to Dubious?" she asked Tyson.

He hesitated a bit before answering, "Well, we haven't made it yet."

"We're close. There's no denying that," said Highcross. His optimism was suspiciously close to wishful thinking.

"I'm not so sure," was all he said.

"What!"

"Wait a minute!"

"Why do you say that?"

Tyson raised his hand, and everyone got quiet. He glanced back and forth at Sho-Taka and Mrs. Devonshire, "You two were the only ones who talked to Kaniawassa?" They both nodded. "In was all in French, wasn't it?"

"Hold on! I speak . . . or rather I understand some French. I heard him," said the major.

"All you heard wuz bells ringin'," joked Myles. "You were just lyin' there."

The major nodded agreement, and Tyson spoke up, "Otekinaya didn't say much in French either. He spoke to Kaniawassa mostly in their language. It was just Kaniawassa and you two talking, right? What did he say? What were his directions?"

Sho-Taka and Devonshire exchanged glances, and then looked back at Tyson. Sho-Taka deferred to Mrs. Devonshire, "She speaks better French than I do." He looked at Devonshire, "Tell him."

She thought about it for a minute, and then said, "They told us to go south until we found the river, and then follow it southwest, past the rapids, until it turns south. Then we should go west for a half day. That's where it is."

To her right, Sho-Taka nodded, "That's what I heard him say, too."

Devonshire spoke up again, "They said there was a small lake, or pond . . . I'm not sure of the word he used . . . on a plain. It was fed by streams from the north. And to the south there were three mountains, or hills, that lined up in a row pointing at the fort's front gate. That's why some soldiers called it '*Trois Frères*' instead of Fort Dubois."

"Yes! Yes, I heard that too. That's what Kaniawassa said," said the major. Sho-Taka was also nodding in agreement.

"But Kaniawassa was never there. Was he?" asked Tyson. "All he said came from Otekinaya." They others just looked at him.

Then they started to question Tyson about his hesitation to accept the directions they had gotten from the two Indians.

"You think they lied to us?"

"Why would they lie?"

Myles asked, "Do ya think they're tryin' to steer us into a trap?"

"Wait. Wait a minute," Tyson said, raising his hands. "I think Kaniawassa was telling us the truth . . . as he knew it. But he never saw Dubious. Only Otekinaya saw it; and that was years ago. Maybe he's confused about where it was; or maybe he forgot some details?"

Devonshire prided herself on being a good judge of people. She didn't say it out loud, but she felt that Kaniawassa had told her the truth, and she had done most of the talking with him. She was also fairly sure that Otekinaya had not lied to his companion, although she did not know their language. "Why don't you believe them?" she asked Tyson.

"Something's wrong," he simply said.

Confusion reigned supreme for next five minutes as they asked Tyson, and each other, many questions. And most times they did not wait for an answer. Tyson was the man-in-the-middle of the hubbub, and as a result didn't have time to answer a question before another was thrown at him.

It took some time, but they finally settled down. Questions didn't stop, but they slowed down.

"You think it's a trick?"

"You think we may be going the wrong way?"

"You said something's wrong. What's 'wrong'?" Devonshire asked.

That made everyone pause and wait for his answer. "You two were the ones Kaniawassa spoke to; you know what he said." Tyson looked at Devonshire and Sho-Taka, "He said to go south to the river, and then follow it southwest past the rapids until it turned south. Then we should leave it and go west right to the fort." They both nodded. "We did go south; and we did find the river." There was no disagreement by the listeners. "And now we will follow it. It is flowing southwest."

Sho-Taka and the Major looked at each other to see if they agreed. "It looked like it was going south to me," Sho-Taka finally said.

"Yes," said the Major.

Sho-Taka decided to add, "But I looked downstream, and it was bending west. So I think it is going west or southwest up ahead."

Major Highcross wanted this river to be what he was looking for. He wanted it to be the river that the Indians had told them about. He wanted it to go southwest, past rapids and then turn south. He wanted that very much. "Rivers don't flow in straight lines. They bend and turn. Is that why you're doubting we're in the right place? Because it isn't flowing southwest?"

They all turned to Tyson, who was looking right at the major. "No, that's not the problem. Of course I know that rivers twist and turn. The problem is . . . ." He stopped talking, and looked back at Sho-Taka and Devonshire. "We're on the wrong side."

The five people looking at Tyson were dumbfounded. They didn't know what to make of what he said. A couple began to talk, but nothing came out.

It was Mrs. Devonshire who spoke first, "What do you mean? How are we on the wrong side?"

Tyson took some time to explain what he meant. He started by explaining that the river to their right was flowing in the direction somewhere between south and west.

"Okay," said the Major, "That's what they said it would be. Flowing southwest."

"And they said we should follow it as it flowed in that general direction . . . past the rapids . . . until it turned due south."

"Right!" chimed in the major again.

"And when it does we should leave it and travel due west."

"Right," said the major once more, "And continue due west to Dubious."

His five listeners were quiet, and stared at Tyson. "To do that we have to *cross* the river." Tyson looked once more at Sho-Taka and Devonshire, "Did Kaniawassa ever say anything about having to cross the river?"

While none of them were cartographers, they all knew the points of a map. In their minds they saw a river running southwest; they saw that they were currently to the east (right) of that river. And one by one they saw that to go west (left) of that river; they would have to cross it.

"Do you remember Kaniawassa ever saying anything about having to cross the river?" Tyson asked Sho-Taka.

Mrs. Devonshire answered, "No. Never said anything at all about having to cross that river."

"I didn't hear him say anything about that," Sho-Taka agreed.

Optimism was not to be denied. Highcross laughed, "So what! We'll cross it when we come to it.

"With a wagon you have to be real careful where you cross," Tyson advised. "A lot of things can go wrong."

Once more Highcross looked for the bright side. "There's got to a ford somewhere. A shallow spot. Why I remember someone once telling me that a ford can usually be found just below rapids.' He wasn't finished. "And we've got to travel downriver past the rapids anyway, so we can worry about crossing it then if we find no place suitable before we get there."

There was nothing to be gained by sitting around arguing about whether they were on the right side, or not. They decided to get back on the trail, and begin following the river for the rest of the day. Myles, again denied a place in the wagon, joined the major out in front. And as Myles continued to grumble the major kept his eyes far to their front. He almost expected Dubious to pop up at any moment. Shea, who said she needed to stretch her legs a little bit gave up her seat in the wagon and joined Tyson who was walking between the wagon and the river. Tyson kept his eyes on the river, watching for a place to cross. He was also paying attention to how fast the river was flowing. That current would vary depending on different factors, but he was worried because he never saw a place where it slowed down to a speed where he felt would be safe for his wagon to cross. And the wagon, with all his earthly possessions in it, held the promise of Tyson's future.

And Devonshire had Sho-Taka all to herself in the wagon.

"They never said anything about crossing the river," Devonshire said to Sho-Taka. She wanted to start a conversation.

"No, I didn't hear them say anything about that either," he agreed.

"Maybe Otekinaya said something to Kaniawassa, but he never repeated it to us." Sho-Taka just nodded. Silence wasn't in the cards; she tried another topic. "I don't think Myles should go back to Fort Royal, do you?"

"I don't know. He can do what he wants," Sho-Taka shrugged.

"If he goes back to Fort Royal he'll just become Falwyn again." She paused for a minute, "You're his friend. You don't want that for Myles, do you?"

Sho-Taka wasn't comfortable thinking of him as "Myles" yet, so he just shrugged and said, "He isn't going to take my advice no matter what I say. Never has."

She knew she could convince Myles to accompany her to the Ohio, just by batting her eyes. But would Sho-Taka be more willing to accompany her if she had Myles join them? Or would he be less likely to do it if Myles came along? She spent some time thinking this over.

With the cow tied to the rear of the wagon it had to be driven slowly. The mounted major, in his eagerness, allowed his horse to expand the distance between them and the wagon behind. Myles slogged along somewhere in between.

In the wagon Mrs. Devonshire once more spoke up, "And you? You aren't going to go back there, are you? Back to Fort Royal?"

Sho-Taka paused for a moment, and then said, "No."

"Where then? Not Dubious surely; that's probably even drearier than Fort Royal; and smaller!"

"Maybe Fort Pitt."

"Fort Pitt? Why that's Fort Royal, only with more English!" She let that simmer for a bit, and then added, "Have you ever thought about traveling on ahead with Tyson? Maybe do some farming in Kan-tucky like him?"

He thought about it for a moment, and then shook his head, "No, I'm no farmer. You work from sunup till sundown all year long . . . and then some storm comes along and wipes it all out. It's all for nothing. No, that's not for me. Besides, I think I'd like to live in a city for a change. I'm done with small towns."

This was music to her ears. She had to hide a smile. But be careful, she warned herself, go slowly. "Have you considered going down to New Orleans? It's big and getting bigger. Filled with Spaniards and Frenchmen; no English. And it never gets cold." She watched him as he glanced over at her. "After I go back east with

Major Highcross and clear my name, I plan to travel to New Orleans and settle down. Perhaps start a business of some kind. There are so many opportunities there for someone with skills and energy."

He smiled at her, "You're not going back east. Not with Highcross or anyone else. I'm not sure what you are going to do; but you are not going back east."

"Why do you say that?"

Sho-Taka started to explain, "Mrs. Devonshire . . ."

She cut him off, "Please! Call me Dellie. All my friends do."

"Okay," he said, "Dellie, I know the English, and what they call justice in their courts. And if I was facing what you're facing . . . , I don't think I'd be too anxious to wait around for the outcome. They can be sort of one-sided when it comes to people who aren't one of them."

Unwilling to open up to this man yet, she asked, "And what would you do if you were me?"

"Now don't get me wrong. I like the major. I think he's a good man. But he is an officer in King George's Army. He'll do his duty, and arrest you. But if I was you; after we get to Dubious; the first time he turned around I would get on my horse and disappear." He raised his eyebrows and dipped his head. "I figure he will be so busy taking over his command that he won't even notice you're gone. At least not right away. But like I said, "the first time he turns around" I'd be gone. He might slap you into the guardhouse right away, so you better be quick about it." He looked at her waiting for a reaction, but there was none. He took a deep breath, and then went on, "Tyson will only stay at Dubious for a few days, and then head out on his way southwest. You could wait for him out there in the woods; latch on to him when he makes his way by. You did that with us when we left Fort Royal. You know how that works." He smiled at her.

"You know him. You think he would take me to the Ohio?"

"I don't know whether he would, or not. But I do know he has a soft spot when it comes to ladies in distress."

"Why do you say that?"

You weren't there, but at the shooting match back at Fort Royal," Sho-Taka paused, "He fooled with the target so Shea could come along with us. Duped nearly everyone."

"But not you?"

With a crooked grin, Sho-Taka shook his head. Tyson, like so many others in the human race, wasn't nearly as slick as he thought he was.

"Are you going to lay over for a few days when we get to Dubious?" Shea asked Tyson.

For a few days, sure," he responded. "Rest my horse. He's going to be doing all the hauling from here on, all the way to Kan-tucky. And let my cow get a good feedin' before we start off again."

Shea had already decided that if she found her father at Dubious . . . and she decided *absolutely* . . . to kill him, she wouldn't do it until Tyson had left. She didn't want him to think of her in that way for the rest of his life. "Tell me more about your farm," she asked.

For an hour they walked and talked about Tyson's proposed farm. No other topic under the sun would have distracted him from watching the river as did his farm. They chatted about where it was; what it would look like; what it could produce.

Her history with a small farm in her youth would have lead one to think that she really wasn't interested. And, at first, she was just looking for conversation, but as the talk wore on she became more interested. It surprised her when she realized it. Her glances in Tyson's direction were becoming more meaningful.

The major came around a small bend in the trail back toward the wagon. He had a huge smile on his face. Nearly breathless, he began shouting while still 50 yards away, "The rapids! The rapids! They're just up ahead. I just saw them. Come on! Come on." He waved his arm, and then wheeled his horse around and went back the way he came.

This, of course, caused quite a stir among the others. Shea and Tyson hurried back from the river edge to the wagon. Sho-Taka had the presence of mind not to get caught up in the excitement and snap the reins on the two horses pulling the wagon. That would have made them bolt ahead and make the wagon spurt.

While it was unlikely that that spurt would have caused either Sho-Taka or Mrs. Devonshire to tumble from the wagon, it would have played havoc with the nose ring on the taciturn cow tied to the wagon's rear.

A quarter of a mile further down the trail the trees opened toward the river and an expanse of thundering rapids came into view. The noise and rush of the water kept everyone silent. It was an impressive sight. They all stood and stared at the spectacle.

After a few minutes, without saying a word, Tyson began making his way down river; looking all around. He stopped two times to gaze out at the river; trying to see its depth. He did not see what he wanted to see; a place to cross.

The major and Sho-Taka followed him down, and stood next to him.

"Can we cross here?" asked the major.

"No. It's too deep out there in the middle. The wagon's heavy, even if we unload it and pull it across empty. If we get it out that far and the wheels get stuck in the soft bottom we'll never get it out."

"The horses can't pull it across?" he asked.

Tyson shook his head, "It's too heavy to pull, even if the water was lower. The horses can swim across. I'm not worried about them getting across. Up above the rapids there's a place that's narrower than here; and the current is slower. It's too deep for the wagon, but they can swim across there."

Sho-Taka spoke up, "But the wagon? That's the problem."

"Yes."

The three men stood looking up and down the river in silence. Finally Tyson broke the silence, "Let's head on down a bit, and see if we can find a better spot. We have to be looking for a spot where it isn't too deep and the current slows down." He stood staring at the water, and then said, "If we have to we can build a raft and float the wagon across. May take some time, but we can do it. We still have plenty of daylight left."

"The horses too?" Highcross asked.

"No, just the wagon. Horses might get a little too skittish on a makeshift raft. And like I said the horses can swim across."

An hour later they had travelled another few miles along the river without seeing a place that Tyson felt confident they could cross with the wagon. The conversations centered on what they could do, and how they could do it. But all their conjecture depended on them finding a place suitable for crossing, one way or another.

They saw the bend in the river from a hundred yards away. The deep banks of the river ran almost straight for those one hundred yards. "That's got to be it," said Sho-Taka. "That's the turn south."

"That's it, all right," Tyson said looking up, trying to position the sun.

When they arrived at the bend, they all examined it carefully. Walking up to the edge of the bank they looked up and down the river and over it to the other wooded side. "Why don't we camp here, and deal with the river crossing in the morning?" suggested Mrs. Devonshire. She had plans to finalize before reaching Dubious.

Major Highcross, on the other hand, was the most eager and disagreed. "Why wait? We have hours of daylight still. Let's get ourselves and our things to the other side so we can get an early start in the morning."

There was some discussion, and disagreement, but it was finally decided to try to cross the river then. The sun wasn't high but as the major had said, there was still several hours of daylight left. Tyson immediately took the lead. He issued orders to everyone.

He told Myles to unsaddle the major's horse, and then unhitch the two horses pulling the wagon. The women unloaded the wagon; everything out. There was only Tyson's ax for the tree cutting so they took turns gathering the trees that would become the raft. After his turn at chopping, Tyson and Myles ventured half a mile upstream and then downstream looking for a suitable place for crossing. They succeeded in finding a good place for the horses to swim cross, barely forty feet wide. And as an added bonus there was a place, not too far away, between three boulders that would serve as a place for them to bathe with privacy. During the brief conversation concerning it Myles was apparently stone deaf.

The five trees selected for the crude raft were bound together with rope from Tyson's supplies, and reinforced by vines they had found nearby. Tyson felt they would hold the raft together for the very short time that it would be needed.

The plan was simple. Tyson, with a rope tied around his waist, would ride a horse barebacked across the river allowing it to swim at the deeper part. Once across he would tie the horse up; anchor his waist rope to a tree and return, holding onto the crossing rope, to the eastern side. The major, observing Tyson's trip over and back, insisted he too could do it. There were two more horses that had to be ridden over to the other side. He insisted on riding one of them. Despite some genuine concern by the others he insisted, and to his credit he did not fall off his horse until he was in the very shallow water on the western side. On his trip back, going hand over hand on the crossing rope, he probably swallowed two quarts of water.

With the horses safely across, it was time to utilize the raft. Daylight was starting to fade, and they still had work to do. Tyson explained to them what the plan was. The method would be simple. A rope would be tied to each end of the raft. One of those ropes would be stretched across the river to the west side to be pulled by two men to draw it across. The other rope would be held by the men on the east side slowly letting out the rope as the raft crossed the river, thereby stabilizing it. They did not want to overload the raft on any one trip. After some discussion it was decided that three trips should do the job. The first crossing would involve the lightest load, to determine if their raft was up to the job. It would include their possessions. And, as dear as they were to each, they were only possessions, and if disaster struck they could always resupply at Dubious.

The second load involved the livestock. The cow and chickens would, if settled and secured properly, would not be much heavier than the possessions were and should go across as well as the first load.

The third crossing caused them the most worry; it would be the wagon. The first two loads would be centered on the middle of the raft, which would minimize the risk of it tipping over. On this third crossing the wheels of the wagon were to be on the four corners of the raft, and this load would be heavier than the first two. There was a nagging voice in Tyson's head saying that this was going to end badly.

When Tyson began assigning the men their jobs Major Highcross objected. "You and Sho-Taka are on the other side? Why are the two of you together, and I am . . . ." He almost said "stuck on this side with Myles." But he didn't. He felt the effort required to do the job would not be fairly shared between them.

"Major, all you're going to have to do is pull the empty raft back across. Me and Sho-Taka are going to have to pull a loaded one across; all you'll have to do is let out the rope and keep the back end steady. And don't forget to anchor it."

It sounded so simple, but that was not to be the case.

The tree trunks making up the raft were finally pruned down to their satisfaction and bound together tightly. And then the raft was pushed and pulled into the water so that only a few inches of it still rested on the bank. The possessions were loaded onto it and secured. Ropes were tied to the front and back. Tyson and Sho-Taka made their way to the other side (with difficulty) with the lead rope tied around Tyson's waist. The current looked docile from the bank, but when he was in the water Tyson realized how swift it was.

The two women, who had bathed in privacy up the river, and had crossed, very carefully, at nearby rapids stood off to the side. Sho-Taka and Tyson gripped the rope, that was anchored behind them to a tree that stretched across the river to the front of the raft on the other side. Aaron Highcross and Myles stared back at them from behind the loaded raft on their side. The men grew silent and tense as the ropes slowly became taught.

"All set?" Tyson called out.

"Ready?"

"Almost there!"

"It's almost in the water!"

"Jassus!"

The raft's edge slipped the last two inches into the water and was floating free. The two men on the western side began pulling the rope hard. The tow rope leading to their side straightened up out of the water.

"Let loose some slack!" one of them ordered. They strained to pull it over.

On the other side the veins in Major Highcross's forehead bulged. "Let it loose a little Myles!"

"I am! I am!" came a scream.

Sapping strength they didn't know they had Tyson and Sho-Taka pulled the raft to the western side while Highcross and Myles tried to keep it steady. Coordination came slowly, but it came. It didn't cross over the river in a straight line, but it made it. The raft didn't tip but splashing water soaked much of their possessions.

Realizing that time and daylight were limited the two men, with Shea and Mrs. Devonshire, hurriedly unloaded the raft. Shea and Devonshire began hanging up clothes to dry on every branch and bush around. When the raft was unloaded Sho-Taka held the rope on his side as Highcross and Myles pulled the empty raft back to their side.

Again the process of carefully loading the raft began. The chickens in their crate commented without stop about the process. The cow took one look at the raft, looked back at Highcross who held its lead rope, and apparently had misgivings. It might have proved a larger problem if Myles hadn't taken over for the major. Myles, who had dealt with livestock most of his life, was the far more experienced hand. He may have had a healthy respect (fear) of horses but, as he would say, "I don't take any shit from cows."

The animals were loaded and secured, and the cow was blindfolded. The raft was again pushed toward the edge of the bank. All parties confirmed their readiness, and while shouting instructions and encouragement, the raft was once again afloat.

While coordination of give-and-take between the two sides was attained quicker on this trip, the current also seemed more rapid. It dragged the raft further downstream, despite the efforts of Highcross and Myles to keep the route a straight line. If they had timed this trip they would have seen that it took twice as long as the first one. Their aching arms and backs insisted it took four times as long.

Tyson secured the raft the instant it touched solid ground on the west side. As he and Sho-Taka unloaded the animals he thought that perhaps it would have been a better idea to do the heaviest load first, when they had the most strength. But it was too late for that now.

As the emptied raft was pulled back to the eastern side by Highcross and Myles they both came to the happy realization that this was the last time. They were worn out. It took tremendous effort to secure the raft to the bank. Then they realized that they still had to manhandle the wagon onto the raft. They struggled to get it centered on the raft. But then a wheel slipped off an edge, and became hopelessly stuck. Neither Highcross nor Myles, nor both of them combined, possessed the strength to lift that corner of the wagon back up onto the raft. And it was getting darker.

As a last resort Tyson came back over to their side. The three of them managed to lift the errant wheel back to its proper place. They secured it as tightly as they could, and then the three of them edged the raft as close as they dared to the water. Tyson swam as fast as he was able back to the western side, and took up the rope. Sho-Taka joined him as they pulled on it to take up any slack.

"Are you ready over there?" Tyson yelled.

Highcross waited a moment for Myles to grunt his readiness, but Myles was too tired to talk. Highcross turned around to see what was wrong. Myles was just standing there, slope shouldered with the rope in one hand. "Better anchor that rope, this last load is the heaviest," said the major as he took one deep breath and turned back around to start pushing the wagon laden raft into the water. "Here she goes!" he called out to Tyson and Sho-Taka.

Behind the major Myles had readjusted the end of the rope so it was looped around a tree and then around his arm; he then bent his knees awaiting the tug of the load hitting the water. The last thing he remembered doing was looking down and being unconcerned by the 10 feet of slack that lay between him and the major.

Major Highcross remembered that one second he was pushing the rear left corner of the raft off the last three inches of solid ground into the water, and the next second two boots went flying past him. And he may have glimpsed a strangely familiar hole in the sole of one of them? He may have also heard, "YIEEE!"

His immediate reaction was to turn and ask Myles if he had seen those boots too. But, of course, Myles wasn't there; he was in those boots . . . heading downstream . . . now underwater.

Myles had seen the raft hit the water . . . catch the current . . . and accelerate exponentially. The raft's explosive departure included the rope tied to its rear corner. And that rope's other end – after becoming taut and circling the tree – was "anchored" around Myles' left arm. The flight (making Myles arguably the first man on the North American Continent to achieve Mach 1) around the tree and into the river would always be a blur in Myles' memory, but he would explain in the future that this episode was the reason his left arm was longer than his right.

The departing rope had left scorching burn marks on the palms of Major Highcross's hands, who had let go of it a nanosecond too late. But lucky for him, he hadn't "anchored" it. It took a second, or two, for the burning sensation in his hands to register with the major, but when they did he noticed! His solution to the handfuls of brimstone he apparently held in these hands was to dance on one foot screaming, "Oh my God – Oh my God!" Then another possible solution popped into his mind, and he dropped to his knees and stuck his hands in the river at his feet. Good idea, but done without agility. Losing his balance he plunged headfirst into the shallow water at the edge of the river.

By this time the raft was off and running with the current down the river, and but was secured only to the west side of the river. There were two men holding it on that side, and fortunately the end of their rope was tied securely to a tree behind them. The raft speeding down stream caromed off a large boulder sitting in midstream, which slowed it down. This reduction in speed wasn't enough for the two men holding the rope to bring it to a halt It disregarded the efforts of those two men but halted midstream when the slack in their secured rope ran out. Miraculously the rope did not snap. Two feet below the surface Myles did.

Neither Sho-Taka nor Tyson were aware of Myles' dilemma, it was too dark and played out too quickly for them to realize what had happened on the eastern shore. But they did know in an instant that the raft's very valuable cargo of the wagon was in jeopardy. Tyson raced down along the bank to where the river was pushing the raft. He dove into the water and swam a few strokes to the bobbing raft. He somehow knew that he needed to get the rope from the other end, and get it to shore and secure it. He moved quickly to the downstream end of the raft and found the rope. Grabbing it he began swimming hard toward the shore. It occurred to him in this fog of activity that it was harder to pull than it ought to be. He hoped the rope wasn't snagged on the bottom. When he reached shore Sho-Taka was waiting for him. The two men hauled on the rope bringing the battered raft to the near shore. Once grounded the out-of-breath Tyson and Sho-Taka fastened the rope to a tree. The Indian began hauling in the slack to make sure the raft was securely tied up. It was unusually heavy. An exhausted Tyson dropped to his knees as Sho-Taka pulled the last few feet of rope out of the water. As he did Myles broke the surface of the water and was dragged onto shore. He was still clutching the rope!

Tyson was only able to stare at the prostrate Myles lying a few feet away at the water's edge, as still as a stone. Forty feet away, Shea stood next to a pile of wet clothes, her mouth and eyes wide open. In a voice so low no one could hear her, she asked, "Myles?"

Mrs. Devonshire, who was closer and could see Myles clearly, could say only, "*Merde sainte*!"

Sho-Taka saw Myles clearly too, but he was wondering, "Where'd he come from?"

Oddly enough it was Myles who moved first. He began gagging and spewing water, and also thrashing about in the six inches of water he was in and then, quite suddenly, was in a sitting position. Ten feet in front of him was Tyson, and they locked eyes.

"What?" Myles said.

Sho-Taka secured the raft to the tree by the bank, and then went to help Myles. Tyson had him back up on his feet, and was holding him by his arms. Tyson looked down and noticed Myles still gripped the rope in both hands. "You can let go of the rope, Myles."

"Yer damn late with that suggestion," he muttered.

Tyson looked at Sho-Taka, "Take Myles back up to the camp. Where's the major?

"Heard him flopping around in the water over on the other side. Says he's all right."

"I'll fetch him. You go on ahead."

Ten minutes later the major and Tyson made it back to the western shore. The major held up his hands and showed off his mementos of this evening's misadventure. He received some sympathy from them all, except Myles.

The group sat around a fire trying to get warm. Most of their clothes had gotten wet on the river crossings earlier, and their food had gotten spoiled or lost. Only the women had dry clothes. The men, in wet clothes, sat beneath damp blankets. They were wet, hungry and tired, and mostly quiet.

Myles, in a very foul mood, finally broke a long spell of silence and asked the major, "Why'd yah let the rope go?"

Somewhat apologetic and shrugging the major said, "It was in my hands . . . and then . . . it was gone." That explanation might have sufficed for some, but Myles was having none of it. He grunted and shook his head in disgust. The major displayed the palms of his hands again, showing the rope burns he received, "Just look at these hands."

Shea chimed in, "We'll keep a wet cloth on them tonight. They'll feel better in the morning."

Myles listened to her, and then turned back to the major, "You want me to take off my wet clothes so you can wrap them around yer hands?"

Highcross didn't recognize the sarcasm, and said, "No, I think . . . Wait!" A look of shock came across his face. "Where are my boots?"

A sullen Myles shot a thumb over his shoulder at the river behind him, "Away back there somewheres . . . I don't know zactly where they come off."

"You lost my boots?"

"You let go of the rope!"

"You were supposed to anchor it."

"I DID . . . kinda. Whaddya let go of the DAMN rope?"

"OKAY! OKAY! Everybody calm down." Tyson barked. "I think we've all had a long day. Let's get some sleep. With any luck we'll be in Dubious tomorrow night. In warm dry beds." Tyson turned to Sho-Taka and said before he turned in he was going to go back down to the raft to see what damage had been done to the wagon.

The others spread out and tried to get comfortable for the night. The fire would be low because they hadn't had time to go collect enough firewood before it got dark. Most of them wore damp clothes. And there had been no dinner. The last one that said anything that night around the campfire was Myles. Just before they closed their eyes and went to sleep his grumpy whispered voice drifted over the camp saying, "And I ain't takin' no bath, neither."

As Tyson moved off a soft voice behind him said, "I'll go with you." He didn't break stride as Shea shuffled up next to him.

They started down toward the river bank where the raft was tied up. As usual Tyson was silent, and Shea was surprised to find herself suddenly lightheaded as she walked along beside him. Say something she told herself. "That was a very brave thing you did. You could have drowned."

Tyson, thinking she meant his saving the wagon, turned to her to explain that he absolutely had to have that wagon if he was going to get to Kan-tucky with the supplies he needed to homestead. She was referring to his rescue of Myles. The different interpretations of his motive were never uncovered. He was two steps in front of her, so he stopped and half turned to her. He was about to explain how indispensable the wagon was but he became distracted when he saw her face in the pale moonlight.

She was pretty.

After a moment he corrected himself, she was beautiful.

This wasn't new, he had thought so the first time he saw her back at Fort Royal. And he had confirmed his opinion many times with quick glances at her since their trip began. But at this place, this time, in this light, he was stunned. It was like he was seeing her for the very first time. He opened his mouth to speak, but had neither the breath nor the words to say anything. She said something else, but he didn't hear her.

She had continued walking before noticing he had stopped. She turned toward him when she got no answer and saw him standing still, and staring at her. His disheveled hair and damp clothes clung to him. His mouth was open, but still. Did I say something stupid, she wondered? Was it insulting? What did I say? She couldn't remember. Why doesn't he talk? She took another step, and then stopped too. They looked at one another, and knew.

When the sun came up the next morning whispered voices stirred Major Highcross from his sleep. Once awake, he lay still for a minute trying to think where he was. Yesterday's events came slowly back to him, and under his blanket he flexed his hands. Opening and closing them they began to sting. He tried to sit up without using his hands, and awkwardly succeeded.

"How do you feel, major?" came Tyson's low voice from somewhere.

The major twisted around to see where Tyson was.

"How are your hands?" whispered Shea.

The major saw them sitting on a fallen tree, under a shared blanket, a few feet away. "They hurt," he said flexing them again.

Lying a few feet away under a blanket was Mrs. Devonshire. Her eyes were fully open and she asked, "How is your head?" and sat up.

The major, distracted by the question and Sho-Taka's sudden rise, felt the top of his head, forgetting his sore hands. "Oh, it's fine."

"How's yer toe?" snarled a curled up Myles in a pile of blanket. He had slept in damp clothes (refusing the advice that taking off his wet clothes would be a better idea than sleeping in them), and that along with yesterday's river crossing episode, had him wake up this morning a smorgasbord of aches and pains.

All but Highcross recognized the sarcasm and remained silent. And one by one they noticed the pair sitting under the blanket.

Myles took two deep breaths, and then barked, "Nobody gonna ask me if my arm hurts? Think I busted a rib too!" If he had been asked he would have recited the ten or twelve places on his body that he felt were bruised, battered, or maybe even broken.

If he was looking for sympathy, Shea provided it. "We're thankful you're still alive. You could have easily been killed."

Sho-Taka thought out loud, "How long were you under that raft? Underwater?" Myles didn't understand that he wasn't really looking for an answer.

Myles was about to shoot back a comment that he was too busy drowning at the time to keep track of the time when Major Highcross said, "Thank God the rope was wrapped around your arm, and they were able to grab it and pull you out."

Myles began to shake as he turned slowly toward the Major, "And if you hadn't let go . . ."

"HEY!" shouted Tyson clapping his hands. "We've got work to do. I've got a wagon to fix. We should see if we have any food left. We need some fire wood to cook it. Someone should go collect some. Let's hang up anything that's still wet, or even damp. And maybe someone can go out and get us some fresh meat? We don't need much; we should be in Dubious by tonight."

That seemed like enough to keep everyone busy, and one by one they got up and began making themselves useful. Even a very disgruntled Myles was soon up and about, albeit slowly, collecting firewood.

Two hours later, what little food they had salvaged had been consumed. Shea and Dellie Devonshire had been repacking dry clothes and blankets, and readying supplies for the wagon.

Devonshire, after a long silence, said, "You know there's nobody at Dubious. Not your father or anybody else." Shea nodded agreement. "Then why are you going there? Why are you travelling all this way?"

"I don't know," Shea said. "I've come this far; I suppose I just want to see for myself."

Neither woman said anything for a few minutes before Devonshire spoke up. "I saw you with Tyson," she said flatly. She turned toward Shea and looked at her for a moment. Then she broke into a beaming smile. Shea tried not to smile back, but failed. "I'm happy for you. I think he may be a good man. And those are hard to find."

Shea finally said, "I think so too." She resisted the urge to list the thousand or so things she loved about him.

"You'll go to Kan-tucky with him?"

"If he asks me," Shea nodded.

"He'll ask," Devonshire assured her. "I think he'll beg if it comes to that," she added with a smile.

"He won't have to."

Devonshire was now thinking that the possibility of Tyson escorting her to the Ohio River was more likely with Shea on her side. "You know that I do not want to go back east. I don't trust them to treat me fairly. I think the major is a good man, but I do not trust the rest of them."

Shea looked at her, but said nothing.

Dellie Devonshire laid down her cards, "I will not go back east, and I will not allow the major to arrest me. As you continue on, will you allow me to accompany you as far as the Ohio River?"

Shea's first thought was that she should have seen this coming. But, then again, she hadn't really seen Tyson coming either! She wasn't even sure that Tyson was going to take her along! "No, of course he will," she thought. And then to Devonshire she said, "And if I go, I will ask him to let you come along."

"I have seen him look at you. I know that look. If you asked him to walk across that river, he would do it."

Meanwhile Tyson was reinforcing the battered wheel, and Myles was tending to the livestock. Sho-Taka and the major had gone off to hunt. At the campsite they heard two gunshots in the distance, and hoped it meant they would eat fresh meat today.

To the northeast of that campsite was a drenched, tired and very irritated Captain Phillip Wallingford. He hadn't slept long or well or dry. Not quite eleven miles distant a rumpled Wallingford sat on a rise scanning the horizon for any sign of smoke. He had been there since the first hint of sunrise. His position did not afford him a complete and unobstructed view of the entire area, but it was the best he could find late last night. The morning broke sunny and still; exactly what he wanted. He looked for the smoke of what he hoped would be their breakfast campfire. Not wanting to betray his own position he had not ignited his own, and had to settle for water and raw vegetables for his breakfast.

He scanned the horizon around his own position because he glumly realized that they, being led by Falwyn, might be anywhere within 50 miles radius of where he was. Peering through his telescope on this bright Tuesday morning he looked for any wisp of smoke. The wind was calm, and so he was hopeful. He thought to himself that they do not know they are being pursued, so they would not be careful about diffusing their campfire smoke. And only this man called Tyson was any kind of a woodsman, and would know about being cautious with telltale smoke in the frontier. He had convinced himself he would see it if he just kept on looking. It would be far easier for him to catch up to them by spotting their smoke than going back and trying to find their trail.

Wallingford was right, only Tyson had given any thought last night about revealing their position by campfire smoke. But yesterday's near catastrophe crossing the river, and more importantly, the blinding effect Shea now had on him made this morning's campfire smoke invisible to him

However Wallingford never saw it, either and wasted two hours of morning daylight looking for it. Cursing his luck, hungry, and tired from a poor night's sleep he packed up his gear and headed out once more to track the pilgrims.

It was almost midday when they once more began travelling west. A bareheaded Major Aaron Highcross, sans boots, led the way on his horse. The reins were held by thumb and forefinger. The hands were wrapped in wet rags. He had however recovered some dignity earlier when he had returned to camp with fresh game. Sho-Taka had applied the *coup de gras* to the deer, but the Major had initially brought it down.

Myles, not to be denied again, lay in the back of the wagon, grunting with every bump. Tyson and Shea sat in the front without much conversation. His only complaint was not knowing what she intended to do once they reached Dubious. He was afraid to ask.

Her arm entwined with his, she thought only of what she would do if her father was at Dubious. She wished they would circle around Dubious and continue on to Kan-tucky. She wished that Tyson would say clearly that he wanted her to join him. She wished that he'd allow Dellie to join them.

As Highcross rode alone at the head of the group he had time to think to himself. He was excited about finally reaching his post. After setbacks and interminable delays he was nearly there. He thought his appearance wasn't what it perhaps should be, but it wasn't the uniform that demanded respect; it was the man. Lacking boots, bandaged foot and hands, and a head bumps that wouldn't allow for a hat, may not present a dignified image for a Major in the service of King George, but time (and a new pair of boots) would heal all wounds.

But the more he tossed these thoughts over in his head the more another problem surfaced. He wasn't as excited about his prospects as he thought he ought to be. Upon returning to England he had badgered and tormented headquarters to issue him his orders. After the frightful trans-Atlantic voyage and arrival in South Carolina some weeks ago, he had charged up the coast to Philadelphia. Once there he had eagerly made his way to Fort Royal. After some delay there he had been meandering through the Pennsylvania colony. Now he was just miles away from his ultimate destination, Fort Dubois. And, surprisingly, he was no longer as anxious as he once was. He was puzzled by this.

"Have you decided what you are going to do?" Devonshire asked Sho-Taka as they walked along behind the wagon.

"What do you mean?" he asked. "About what?"

"About where are you going next. About taking Myles along with you. What we talked about."

He continued walking, and didn't answer right away. Out of the blue he said, "Why aren't you thinking about what you're going to do. We're getting very close to Dubious, and once we arrive you're going to be placed in irons. And I think we both agree that that is not going to end well for you. I would think you'd be more concerned with that than where I'm going."

She wasn't sure how much she could tell him, so she said nothing. If the possibility of Tyson and Shea taking her to the Ohio hadn't looked as promising as it did, she would have confided in him. But as it now stood she held that in reserve. Her real concern was not knowing how far off Dubious was, and therefore how much time she had to set things up.

Her reverie was interrupted when he asked, "Aren't you warm under that cloak?" There were small beads of perspiration on her forehead and she wondered if that had prompted the question. "Do you want to put it in the wagon?"

"No, I'm fine thank you. I always feel the cold."

It wasn't remotely "cold", and she noticed that he held his gaze on her longer than necessary.

She quickly changed the subject. "Do you think about Ezra much?"

He was surprised she recalled the name. "All the time," he whispered.

"What would he do if he was with us? What do you think he'd do in your place?"

He thought that over and finally shook his head. "I don't know."

"Well, I certainly can't speak for him, but I would wager that he'd do what he wanted to do. I think he would go where he wanted to go. Somewhere he felt comfortable, and not surrounded by people he didn't like." She warned herself to be careful and not too obvious.

It was late afternoon, and they still had no signs pointing to the whereabouts of Dubious. Whatever enthusiasm Major Highcross had had earlier was now gone. He had thought they would have found it hours ago. He rode alongside the wagon, mostly staring at the ground.

Sho-Taka and Mrs. Devonshire had traded places with Shea and Tyson two hours ago. The difference was only that now they walked in front of the wagon, not behind.

Shea occasionally asked Tyson something about his family, or his home in Virginia, or his plans for the farm in Kan-tucky. The reason she did was because he smiled every time she spoke to him. She loved that. And he loved her questions, her voice, her face.

They came to a vast open space as the forest on their left faded off to the south. The trees on the right continued due west along the ridgeline. Crossing over a small rise they spotted a lake off to the left in front of them. Tyson immediately started looking to see if it was fed by any flowing water. He did not want to deal with more river crossings. The others barely noticed. He thought there was a brook flowing down from the ridge to the lake, but he wasn't sure. He couldn't see the ground nearest the lake but the water was visible coming out of the woods. He followed it down the slope almost to the lake before losing sight of it. He began to gauge the brook, and look for the best possible crossing place. He didn't want to have to detour around the distant southern tip of the lake. His view to the south was no longer blocked by a nearby tree line.

Tyson looked at the open space to their left, and then back to the right. He slowed down, and Shea noticed. She followed his gaze to the left, but saw only the retreating woods. "What is it?" she asked.

He said nothing, and turned to look to the right. After only a moment he looked back to the left; and then again to the right. "What's that?" he asked her, pointing to a copse of trees off to their right.

"Where?" She looked in the direction he pointed, and saw only some bushes and trees. Tyson turned back to the wagon and motioned Sho-Taka to halt.

It took only moments for them all to gather around Tyson. They asked questions, but he remained silent. Shea watched his eyes darting back and forth, and then turned trying to see what he was seeing.

"That's it?" she said. Then asked, "Can that be it?"

She and Tyson exchanged smiles. Tyson pointed to the copse of trees to the right, "That's it there." He pointed back up to the left, above the receding tree line, "There's the three mountains. Lined up. And there's the water," he said now pointing to the lake. "And there's . . ." he paused before gesturing to the cluster of trees, bushes and brambles to the right, "There's what's left of Dubious."

"There's nothing . . ." Major Highcross started to say, "Those trees?"

"Myles? Is that it?" Mrs. Devonshire asked.

One by one his silence caused them to turn toward him. "What?" he finally said.

"Let's go see," said Sho-Taka.

They made their way the several hundred yards farther to reach the thicket stretching down the plain. As they approached it they moved more cautiously, as if they expected an ambush. And as they got closer reality set in.

Small trees and bushes camouflaged the remains of burnt walls and scattered trash. The logs used in the construction years ago were rotted and strewn about like old burnt matchsticks. Looking through the scattered vegetation one could see the remains of a building corner here, a hitching post there.

The reaction of each person came sporadically, and differed. Mrs. Devonshire and Tyson came to the same conclusion, but with different reactions. Dellie Devonshire thought that Highcross's plan of arresting her was now the last thing on his mind. She hid her smile. Tyson wasn't smiling either. If there wasn't any Dubious, there wouldn't be any source of supplies here either. He hadn't been counting on those supplies, but he would have felt better knowing that some were available.

Shea and Sho-Taka had different reactions too. Sho-Taka had never had much faith in the existence of Dubious. Nobody who spent much time at Fort Royal did. If it had been here it presented an option as a destination for him. But, as he thought that over, that chance was rather remote. In truth, it was very remote. The idea of moving on to New Orleans was starting to take root. Shea was, at first, disappointed. Dubious wasn't here. Therefore, neither were soldiers in general or her father in particular. As that crossed her mind a large smile came across her face. Her father had vanished with the fort. Who cares? She was now free to abandon that deadly pursuit. She was now free join Tyson. She was now free to live her life.

Myles was neither surprised nor disappointed at his arrival at Dubious. He thought to himself, "If it isn't here, maybe it's somewhere else?" The possibility of more getting more money for additional service as a guide occurred to him. "No," he reasoned, "Sho-Taka seems to think this must be the old Fort Dubois, and he's usually right." As he poked around at the mixture of fresh vegetation and rotted wood he wondered why Captain Wallingford was always coming out here. He had heard Selkirk, and the other soldiers as well, talk about the battle with the Frenchies way back when. He always wondered why none of them got wounded or killed, if that battle was as fierce as they said. It suddenly occurred to him that he had succeeded! "Hey!" he said out loud, "I got you here. No one thought I could do it, but I did! I guided you all the way to Dubious!!!" He turned to the major to ask for the balance of his fee, but stopped short when he spotted him, and went quiet. The others turned to look at the triumphant Myles, and noticed his change of demeanor right away. They followed his gaze toward the major.

Major Aaron Highcross sat on a log with his head in his hands. It almost appeared as if he was crying. At first no one knew what to make of it. Were those tears of joy? They all moved closer, quietly, wanting to console their friend.

Devonshire walked up to where he was sitting and sat down on the log next to him. "What is it, major? What's the matter?" He shook his head, but didn't look up.

Tyson walked up slowly and crouched in front of him, "Maybe this isn't the place. Maybe it's further on?"

The major glanced up at him, and shook his head again. "No, this is Fort Dubois. This is my post." His head fell again into his hands. They all felt the need to say something to him that might make him feel better; but there was nothing to say.

Sho-Taka and Tyson moved off together, out of the major's earshot. "We're starting to lose daylight," Sho-Taka said to him, "Think we can camp here? Or would it be better for the major if we found someplace else?"

Tyson looked back at the major and shook his head. Making a quick decision Tyson spoke up so all could hear, "Let's get our things and go find someplace to camp tonight."

The major stood up, "No! No need to go any farther. This place is as good as any." Pointing off to the south he said, "There's water right there; and there's shelter right here. This is good. I'll tend to the horses." And nodding to them all, off he went.

With little conversation they all got busy. Myles and Dellie Devonshire cleared an area in the middle of the thicket for the wagon and their campsite. Firewood was collected, and Shea began getting the dinner prepared. They had some deer meat left from this morning's hunt, but Tyson and Sho-Taka went out again to see if they could add to the larder. It was a very good spot for that because in less than an hour they were back with several rabbits.

The silence lasted through an early dinner. What was said was said quietly. The major said nothing at all. Sho-Taka remembered that he still had some homemade liquor with him, and brought it out. Out of respect for the major he did not say it was to celebrate reaching Dubious. And with the surprising appearance of the alcohol not even Myles felt like celebrating. In fact, at one point he sidled up to the major to tell him (quietly, of course) that he forgave him for letting go of the rope. The major nodded acknowledgement, but said nothing.

From early evening until dark they sat around the campfire in silence enjoying the beautiful spring weather. The weather, the arrival at their destination, the bountiful dinner; all combined to create an atmosphere of peace and contentment they had not had in some time. It was felt differently by the various parties. For Tyson and Shea the journey was not over, but they had found each other. For Mrs. Devonshire the path to the Ohio River now seemed closer than ever, and wide open. Sho-Taka sat thinking that about where he would go and, for the first time, the somewhat agreeable thought of bringing Myles along with him.

It was only Major Aaron Highcross who was morose. He replayed in his mind the long arduous trail that had brought him here. He thought back to his difficult youth, with only him and his mother fighting the ever-present wolf at the door, despite their wealthy relatives. He considered his unwelcome, yet life-saving, career opportunity in the military a mixed blessing at best. His assignment in France had barely begun when he received word from home about his mother's new found involvement with the widower. He now knew that the man was a pig farmer; and he, his pigs, and his five children had moved into the simple little cottage back home with mother. There was no going back there now. And, of course, he thought about the near disastrous episode with the cooks in France. When he received the assignment to Fort Dubois he thought his career . . . his life . . . had taken a giant leap forward.

This was the chance to make something of himself. But, no! The journey here had been one disaster after another. The delays had been interminable. The missteps had been innumerable. The sea voyages had been nightmares. From bouncing into the South Carolina coast, to Philadelphia, to Fort Royal, to this . . . God forsaken patch of nowhere . . . with no fort . . . with no troop . . . with no command! He was distraught.

One by one the alcohol, the relief of finally finding Dubious, and the full dinner took their toll on the pilgrims, and they drifted off to sleep. Shea and Tyson were the last to bed down. Shea's last thought that night was to wonder if she would ever stop smiling.

But as miserable as Major Highcross felt, another English officer not ten miles away, was feeling elation for the first time in days. Sitting on his horse, with his pack horse in tow, Captain Phillip Wallingford was making his way southwest in the general direction of where he had spotted a plume of smoke earlier.

He had been travelling through heavily wooded areas for most of the day, and therefore had not had the opportunity to see any great distance. He had given up any hope of following the wagon trail, and shrewdly thought that going to Dubious and lying in wait for these pilgrims was the better (the only!) strategy. As late afternoon came he broke into a wide open field which offered a rise in its middle. Spurring his mount, and dragging his pack horse along behind him, he raced to the top of the hill. There he saw the telltale smoke immediately.

"Could that be them?" he asked his horse. The rhetorical question was mostly disbelief. The smoke seemed to be coming from the general vicinity of where he calculated Dubious to be . "Falwyn found it?" This was inconceivable to Wallingford. "Falwyn couldn't find his asshole using both hands and his nose," he whispered as pure fact. But it was smoke all right, no doubt about it. The daylight was beginning to fade but he saw it all the same. "No time to waste," he said out loud, "I've got to get there before morning." Had either of his horses, who were now both completely worn out, understood English they would have objected vehemently to this plan, but alas . . . .

As a bright moon crossed the cloudless night sky Captain Phillip Wallingford pushed himself (and his poor horses) to the southwest . . . to Dubious.

At Dubious the six weary travelers slept soundly in rolled up *dry* blankets, with a cozy fire still burning. By three AM the burning embers of their fire hissed a white noise to them all. They were oblivious to the sporadic sounds around them.

On the evening of their seventh day of marching the New York contingent of English soldiers under General Augustus Fothingill was bedding down. Their only consolation was that they knew they were, at most, only two days from their destination of Fort Royal.

General Tindale's hard charging cavalry force from Philadelphia was also only two days away. But unlike Fothingill, General Tindale was going to keep his men in the saddle for another two hours. Over those next two hours the General would curse the souls of Wallingford and/or Highcross no less than 23 times.

While back in the Philadelphia area hundreds of military personnel and civilians were still looking for Miss Audrey Tindale. And although no one was looking for them, the exact whereabouts of Lieutenants Smith and Crosly were known only to themselves.

Chapter 13 - Dubious Ft Dubois, I Presume?

It's no more Mister Nice Guy,
It is time I kicked some ass.
And that's the truth - that's no lie.

She robbed my stuff on the sly,
So excuse me if I'm crass.
It's no more Mister Nice Guy.

Want my stuff back, don't ask why,
I'll not listen to back sass.
And that's the truth – that's no lie.

She took it all, on the fly.
She stole it all, bold as brass.
It's no more Mister Nice Guy

She'll return it or she'll die,
I'll not allow this to pass.
And that's the truth – that's no lie.

I'll speak to her eye to eye,
My things she cannot amass.
It's no more Mister Nice Guy,
And that's the truth – that's no lie.

It was barely daybreak, and a morning mist hung over the surface of the lake. The only noise came from a tree a hundred yards away that was full of birds doing their morning calls. That cacophony woke Sho-Taka, and stirred two of the others. Sho-Taka lay still in his blanket, not quite ready to get up. The others rolled over and attempted to go back to sleep.

BANG!

The sound went through the camp like a clap of thunder right above them. Sho-Taka and Tyson bolted upright, while Shea and Myles buried themselves in their blankets. Mrs. Devonshire flinched, but then kept absolutely still. Major Highcross tried to struggle out of his blanket, but became hopelessly tangled in it.

"NOBODY MOVE!" barked Captain Wallingford, as he laid the spent pistol on the wagon wheel and replaced it with a loaded one from his belt. "NOBODY!" he repeated.

Heads involuntarily turned to the sound of the voice. A man in a military uniform stood just at the outer circle of sleepers; he held pistols in both his hands.

"I am Captain Wallingford, of Fort Royal. I am here in service to King George, and I will shoot dead anyone who doesn't do exactly as I say."

"I'm Major High . . . "

"QUIET!" Wallingford loudly interrupted. "I know who you say you are." His eye caught the slightest motion from a blanket close to him. "If you move one more time d'Argent, I will shoot you where you lie." He let that settle in for a moment, and then added, "The warrant for your arrest says 'Dead or Alive". And I certainly don't have a preference over which one it's going to be."

He reached over and pulled the blanket off Mrs. Devonshire. She lay on the ground staring up at him. The other five were hardly breathing. "Stand up, d'Argent," he ordered. Keeping his eyes on her as she rose, he spoke in a louder voice to the others, "As soon as I have this traitor confined, you will have your freedoms back. Remain where you are, and do not move. Please allow me to do my duty, for your safety and my own."

As he spoke, Mrs. Devonshire watched him very carefully. If he diverted his eyes from her for even an instant she was going to go for her lap bag which held her pocket pistol. But he didn't, therefore she couldn't. The group gave each other glances, and then returned them to the Captain and Devonshire.

"Drop that cloak," he instructed her.

She started to object, "I feel the . . . ."

"DROP IT!" he shouted. He wanted her hands in plain sight. She untied the cord from around her neck, and placed the cloak at her feet.

It took a few minutes, as all the others watched, as he led her to a tree. He had her sit down with her back to the tree. Then he had her place her arms behind her around the trunk of the tree, and then he bound her wrists in irons. "If you make any attempt to escape I will place irons not only on your wrists, but also on your ankles and you will have to hobble on foot back to Fort Royal." He said it loud enough for all of them to hear. But he also whispered something else to her that they didn't hear. "I would gladly shoot you dead for the slightest reason." But he wasn't finished. He smirked at her and said, "Or for no reason at all."

When he was done shackling Mrs. Devonshire, and double checking his efforts, he returned to the circle of pilgrims. "Where are her things?" he asked them.

Tyson was the first to start to rise. Sho-Taka quickly followed suit, and kept his eyes on the captain. When Tyson was standing he began looking around.

The captain noticed, and said, "If you're looking for your weapons I placed them all on the far side of the wagon." He smiled, "I have to commend you all. You are all very sound sleepers." He purposely did not put his pistols away. "I thought it best that you remained unarmed because my arrival needed to be cautious. Yes, my friends, when dealing with this d'Argent woman one must be ever so cautious."

"Why are you calling her 'd'Argent'?" Major Highcross asked. "Her name is Devonshire. She is our companion."

"You have all been deceived by that French whore," barked Wallingford. He quickly painted a very dark picture of her, and finished with, "You are not the first good subjects of King George she has lied to but, hopefully, you are the last. I have come to arrest her, and turn her over to the authorities in New York." Glancing repeatedly over at Devonshire, he went on, "Now why don't the rest of us become better acquainted so we all feel more comfortable? I am, as I said, Captain Phillip Wallingford. I am the commander of His Majesty's forces at Fort Royal." He paused here, but then added, "And at Fort Dubois."

Several were going to ask him if this place wasn't Fort Dubois but Highcross spoke up, "I am Major Aaron Highcross. And I am now the commander of Fort Dubois." And changing his tone, and gesturing about him, he asked, "Isn't this Fort Dubois?"

Wallingford was prepared for this. As he rode last night he had finalized his scheme. He assumed that they had reached the ruins of Dubious, and would have to be told the real Fort Dubois was somewhere else. But, he would say, that too was now abandoned. He would tell them that a recent outbreak of hostilities by a large rogue band of Indians had made it too dangerous to remain manned. Settlements and farms throughout the area had been attacked and burned. All forces in the area had been ordered to concentrate at Fort Royal. "Major, you will assume command of all forces once we return to Fort Royal."

As Highcross listened to the explanation he had some doubts. While delayed at Fort Royal he had heard nothing about any outbreaks. And he glanced around at the ruined remnants of the old structure that had been here, and thought this had to be Fort Dubois. But when Wallingford had mentioned that Highcross would "assume command of all forces" his mind latched onto it.

Tyson and Sho-Taka both had doubts about the news of an uprising for the same reason as Highcross. There hadn't been any talk of it at all at Fort Royal. And no assumption of command distracted them.

"Is it safe for us to continue on? Toward Kan-tucky? Southwest?" asked Tyson. He was heading into the far frontier, and needed to aware of what he might face. This was the first he had heard of any hostile Indians between here and his destination. Something was wrong, he sensed.

Wallingford, continually glancing at the seated prisoner he had manacled around the tree, said offhandedly, "Sure." Then he added, "Sooner the better."

Sho-Taka had known Wallingford for a long time, and experience had told him not to trust him. Myles didn't trust him, and he didn't like him either. But he said nothing because he was afraid of him. Shea wasn't paying any attention at all to Wallingford; she was looking at Devonshire sitting in the dirt bound by hand irons to a tree. In her heart she wished there was something she could do.

"But until then," Wallingford went on, "You'll have to allow me to do my duty, and that duty is to lead you back to Fort Royal; and to also escort the prisoner – the very dangerous Dellie d'Argent - back to Fort Royal for transport back to New York to face justice for her crimes."

The pilgrims had heard her side of the story, which differed considerably from Wallingford's version. Each of them wanted to believe her. They thought that over in silence until Highcross spoke up. "She has been a boon companion to us all since she joined our party. I think you may be judging her a bit harshly . . . ."

Wallingford cut him off, "Don't let that pretty face fool you, major. She's as wicked as any depraved soul in this part of the world. I cannot even list the crimes she's committed, or the misery she has caused. Trust me," he nodded, "you would do well to save your sympathy for a more deserving soul. I assure you that your cooperation in helping me return her to the authorities back at Fort Royal will not go unnoticed."

Highcross looked over at her, and to avoid eye contact with her, he looked back at Wallingford immediately. Sho-Taka was puzzled by something Wallingford had just said. Who was Wallingford going to hand her over to "in Fort Royal"? Lieutenant Smith? Private Selkirk? That made no sense.

He was about ask "To who?" when Wallingford asked, "Where are her things?"

"I'd like a drink of water, please," Devonshire said.

Everyone turned toward her. The Captain was about to say "No" when Shea said, "I'll get it."

"NO!" Wallingford yelled.

Highcross spoke up, "Oh Captain we needn't be so harsh. She's restrained and completely under our control. There's no reason not to be civil. I insist. I'll take full responsibility."

Wallingford was thinking fast. What the major insisted on, or didn't insist on, was soon to be of no consequence to Wallingford but he was not yet ready to confront him; he wanted to hold off on that until Tyson, Shea, and Sho-Taka were well on their way. "Very good, Sir, as you wish. But, her hands are to remain shackled. And

Miss Shea, before going near her I'll have to insist you give me that knife of yours. We wouldn't want that to accidentally fall into her hands." He was smiling, "Just to be safe."

She stared at him for a moment, and then silently agreed. As she approached him his own hand rested on the butt of the pistol he had in his belt "Here it is," she said as it suddenly appeared in her hand.

Everyone's attention was focused on Shea as she gave her knife to Wallingford, and then as she went to fill a cup with water for Devonshire. That is everyone but Tyson. Tyson used the distraction trying to see where Wallingford had put the guns he had collected in the dark last night. He didn't have an unobstructed view of the wagon, but their guns were nowhere in sight. He wasn't sure why this made him feel uneasy.

Shea brought the cup of water over to Mrs. Devonshire. Shea felt sorry for her, and almost felt as if she should somehow apologize to her for the mess she was in. She started to say something as she knelt down and brought the cup to Devonshire's mouth.

"Get my cloak and put it with your things. Don't ask why. Just do it," Devonshire hissed in a whisper. Because she was talking, and not drinking, the water from the cup spilled down her chin. Shea had expected her to drink, not talk, so the request surprised her. She wasn't sure what she had just heard. She looked at Devonshire, and Devonshire glared back. They stared at each other.

"Just water, Miss Shea, no conversation, if you please," instructed Captain Wallingford.

Shea stood up and turned toward the group. Had the captain heard Devonshire whisper? Shea wondered if she had heard Devonshire correctly? She glanced back down at Mrs. Devonshire, who was still staring at her. She then moved back toward the group.

"Now, once again . . . and I hope for the last time, where are her things?" asked the captain. Someone said "wagon" and Highcross pointed to it. "I'll need to go through what belongings she's got with her." He paused for a minute conjuring up some justification for it. "She has stolen some valuable documents, as well as an official seal belonging to the Crown. I have to see if they are still in her possession." Assessing the group, he thought the major the most gullible and easily managed, "Show me her baggage, if you will, major."

Sho-Taka watched them go to the wagon. Myles, who hadn't said a word since the captain appeared, remained a wallflower. Tyson was trying to feign interest in the proceedings, but was also scouring the ground around the wagon looking for the weapons.

Shea spotted the cloak on the ground next to where Mrs. Devonshire had slept, and where Captain Wallingford had told her to drop it. She nonchalantly moved closer to it.

Major Highcross stepped up on a wagon wheel to get a better view of its contents. The captain noticed something odd, "Major, what happened to your foot? And where are your boots?"

The Major waved away the questions, "Long story, captain, I won't bore you with it." He stretched his neck this way and that way and then proudly pointed to a bundle in the corner, "There it is. That's her belongings there."

"Get them for me, will you major. And bring them over here." His eyes constantly moved from one person to another, but most frequently he looked back at Devonshire. He was also constantly on the move positioning himself so he kept everyone in view. The major's retrieval of Devonshire's baggage captured Wallingford's attention for a moment, and Shea took her chance. She was standing right next to the fallen cloak, and when the captain seemed occupied with the major handing him Devonshire's baggage she reached down and snatched it up. It was unusually heavy.

For the next few minutes Wallingford rifled through Devonshire's things. Pulling them out and tossing them away one by one. He was looking for something, and by his demeanor he wasn't finding it.

Throwing a lace shawl to the ground, Major Highcross finally objected, "Now see here, Captain Wallingford, be a tad more careful with her things. We aren't savages, you know."

Wallingford didn't respond as he continued his search, and alternately looking up at them and Devonshire. Captain Wallingford held off responding until he had gone through all her things. With her belongings strewn all over the ground, and with him obviously exasperated he turned to Highcross, "Major, she is an enemy of the

King. She doesn't deserve your slightest consideration. Nor mine," He barked. "I'll thank you to let me do my duty as I see fit." His frustration was showing. He let out a long breath of air, and then spotted the pots around the fire. "Falwyn! Get me something to eat." The order frightened Myles, and made him jump. Shea wanted to tell Wallingford not to call him Falwyn anymore; his name was Myles. But she didn't, she did not want to call attention to herself while she held Devonshire's mysterious heavy cloak. Sho-Taka noticed Shea holding a cloak, and it somehow seemed odd to him. He wasn't sure why. Highcross was becoming embarrassed by the boorish behavior of his fellow officer.

As Myles scurried around the pots of cooked rabbit, Wallingford continued to survey the group. He got up and walked over to where Devonshire had slept. He did this without taking his eyes off the group. He bent over and picked up her lap bag. Examining the contents he removed the small gun. He looked over at Devonshire and shook his head at her disapprovingly; but with a smirk on his face. He started to turn away but stopped and turned back to Shea, "That isn't yours, is it?" he asked, pointing to the cloak.

"Where are our guns?" Tyson interrupted.

Without looking at him the captain said, "Why?"

"Because they're ours. I want mine back."

"While you're here, with me, you are under the protection of His Majesty's forces. You don't need them. When you leave to go off to wherever it is you're going I will gladly return them to you." He added, "If you're in such a hurry to get them back, why don't you climb up on that wagon, and take whoever is going with you, and head out now. What's keeping you?"

"I'm got to rest my livestock here for a day, or two."

Wallingford was sorry to hear that, an extra "day or two" was not in his plan. He then turned his attention once more to Shea, "I'll take that cloak, Miss." It wasn't a request.

Shea stood still, not offering him the cloak. His left hand was outstretched toward her, his right held Devonshire's little pocket pistol at his side. She cringed inside that she had given him her knife earlier.

Major Highcross broke the silence and tension, "I *will* take my pistols back," he paused for a second and then added, "*Captain.*"

Wallingford looked over at the major, and smiled sadly. It was not playing out as he had wanted it. His plan had been quite simple. He would have goaded Tyson, Shea and Sho-Taka to resume their journey west as soon as possible. And suggest they take Falwyn with them; he was excess baggage in Wallingford's mind. If Falwyn insisted on returning to Fort Royal with them, it would only be a minor inconvenience. He would have then started back to Fort Royal with the three of them. At the earliest deserted spot along the way he would dispatch the Major (and Falwyn too), and then begin negotiations with d'Argent. He would trade her freedom for the return of the contents of his black box. Upon the return of his goods he would renege, of course. He would then proceed directly to New York. A few hours away from New York d'Argent would be shot dead "while attempting to escape". His report would state that d'Argent and a few unnamed associates had killed the major before he caught up with them.

Exasperated, frustrated, and getting progressively angrier Captain Phillip Wallingford threw his plan away. "SIT DOWN . . . ALL OF YOU," he shouted while raising the pistol and pointing it at Shea's head. It happened too fast for any of them to stop it. The muzzle of the small pistol was only feet from her head. They all froze. "SIT DOWN!" he repeated, as he drew one of the larger pistols from his belt "Sit down now, or I'll put a ball through her head."

Myles was the first to comply, and Sho-Taka followed right away.

The Major was indignant. "Captain! I am ordering you to stand down. You could be court . . . "

"SHUT UP! MAJOR. Shut up and sit down!" He was pointing the larger pistol at Major Highcross.

The captain exhaled deeply through parted lips. "Major!" Tyson yelled, "Do as he says." Highcross turned toward Tyson, and Tyson sadly nodded to him. Reluctantly, Major Highcross sat down. Tyson couldn't come up with any alternative in the three seconds Wallingford allowed him to think about it, so he sat down too.

Only Shea was still on her feet, and it seemed the proximity of the gun muzzle to her face had struck her deaf. She stared at it with a look of horror on her face. It surprised him when he turned toward her, and found her still standing, he roared, "I SAID SIT

DOWN!" In the excitement he had forgotten about the cloak. It was lying at her feet.

It took only a few minutes for him to keep them at bay while he got rope from Tyson's wagon. He had Tyson, Sho-Taka and Highcross sit in a circle with their backs against the bark around the base of a tree. Under his close supervision he had Myles tie them together, as well as looping the rope around their hands. He then had them spread their legs and manacled their ankles to each other. At the edge of the camp he placed Shea and Myles back to back, with a sapling between them, and then manacled their hands to each other. He told them all they were not to talk.

When he was sure everyone was secured he went to Devonshire. "Where are my things?"

"What things?"

He wet his lips and said, "It's a long way to New York, especially if you have to walk all the way there without any food or water."

She didn't reply; she just looked at him with a faint smile.

"Suit yourself, bitch, but you'll be whistling a different tune before we're halfway there."

He checked the constraints once again, and then he began going through the wagon, swearing non-stop, looking for the possessions that he knew d'Argent had stolen from him. While Wallingford was tossing things hither and yon from the wagon, the pilgrims grimaced when their particular items were thrown about. Their protests were answered with threats of all kinds if they didn't keep quiet. Tyson had some crates and trunks filled with things he would need to establish his homestead in Kan-tucky, they were opened, inspected, and thrown to the ground. The captain marveled at metal coils he found in Sho-Taka's pile. He asked what they were for, and Sho-Taka said something about a religious practice. Wallingford shrugged and threw them away.

He kept at it for a time, and then realized he did not have to hurry. He broke for a long delayed breakfast. He helped himself to some leftover rabbit, as well as the biscuits that Shea had made the night before. He drank water freely, and at times threw some on the ground. He knew they had to be getting hungry and thirsty, and were watching.

By midday it had gotten warm. They began to ask for some water, and something to eat, and to be allowed to use the privy. He told them that when d'Argent returned his property he would be more amenable. After many more requests and her continued silence his responses shrunk to a simple "no", or he ignored the request altogether. Things were becoming desperate for them. They told him so. His response was to walk over to where Devonshire was and crouch down in front of her. "Do you hear them begging me for water? Begging me to let them go piss? Why don't you be a good girl and tell me where my things are."

"I don't know what you're talking about," she replied.

"They're your friends. How can you let them suffer like that?" Her only response was a blank stare back at him. "Let me tell you something," he said, "You give me back my things, or tell me where they are, and I'll let you all go on your merry way." Again, she only stared at him. "Oh," he said, "I know what the problem is! You've hidden your stolen loot from Canada in with mine, and you're afraid I'll take the whole lot, right?" He paused here to watch her face, but it revealed nothing. "Honest to God," he swore, "All I want is what's mine. That's why I came after you. I just want what's mine."

In her mind she knew that if she did tell him he would indeed take it all. And she also surmised that after he had it he would not leave witnesses. The only reason she, and probably her friends, were still alive was that she had not revealed the whereabouts of the booty. Her only question was how long she could hold out.

The conversation, or rather the one way discussion, lasted another ten minutes with the same results. He'd promise; she'd say nothing. He'd offer deals; she would only stare back at him. He began to threaten physical violence, cruel and crude treatment, and other dire consequences for her continued refusal to cooperate. He even suggested that he would begin by harming "all these good friends of yours".

"Let them go first, and then we'll talk."

He stood up and kicked the ground right next to her. He had nearly hit her. He was now getting very angry. Letting her friends go was out of the question. They weren't going anywhere; he couldn't afford to do that. If he let them go he was sure some stupid sense of loyalty would have them circling back to save her. Even if he released them without weapons he did not want to deal with 5 other hostile people despite how harmless they might be. Another reason was that Wallingford thought he could use them as bargaining chips. Physically harming them, or worse, might pressure her into revealing what he wanted. She may be able to stand up against him, but would she allow him to mistreat them all as she was forced to sit and watch? She, of course, could not be threatened. If he killed her his fortune would be lost with her. No, he needed her alive. He knew it, and so did she. And so she also knew he was not about to release her friends. He stormed off to sit in the shade of the wagon.

The return of Wallingford to Mrs. Devonshire's spot at the tree was repeated several times throughout the day. Each time he would offer some new inducement to her, and each time she would remain silent. He would color his offer, and she would refuse. He would ultimately get angry and storm off once again. He couldn't make her talk, and he couldn't kill her. And he didn't know how to solve his dilemma.

Several times the prisoners requested water, or some time out of the sun, or a chance to stand up. But Wallingford as adamant, he had to think of some way to use these people as bargaining chips with d'Argent.

"Jassus, Captain," Myles pleaded, "I gotta go bad . . . ."

"SHUT UP!" came Wallingford's reply.

Another time, the Major cried out, "Captain Wallingford! I am ordering you to release . . . ."

"Piss in your damn pants, major!" said the unsympathetic captain.

By 6 PM the Captain was no closer to solving his dilemma. He began once more to rummage through the campsite. He was looking for something to eat, and came across the last remnants of Sho-Taka's home brew. He couldn't have been more delighted; he was like a child on Christmas morning. He polished off the last of the rabbit meat, and finished the home brew. He tried once more to get Mrs. Devonshire to reveal her secret (to no avail) and checked the restraints on his prisoners again. As the last daylight faded

Captain Wallingford, under the influence of a full stomach and just enough whisky, and with no sleep in the last 36 hours, faded also. He sat down under a blanket, leaning against the wagon, and promptly fell asleep.

"Is he asleep?" whispered Sho-Taka a half hour later.

"I can't see him," responded the Major, who was facing the other direction.

Tyson turned his head to see, but warned, "I wouldn't trust him when he's awake, or asleep."

"I think he's asleep," Sho-Taka said, still whispering.

They both spoke quietly to each other speculating whether the Captain was asleep, or not. They spoke about whether he was trying to trick them, and they spoke about whether it made any difference to them. They were securely tied to each other around the tree, and fastened by manacles on their ankles. The Major was twisting and turning trying to see for himself, and frustrated that he was facing the wrong direction. Several times Sho-Taka or Tyson shushed him as his squirming around and questions made too much noise.

After one particular loud grunt by the major after accidently banging his injured foot, Wallingford stirred. They all froze. The Captain sat up straight for a long moment, and then slowly lowered himself to the ground and laid still. None of them moved for a long time, until the captain snored and then rolled over; his back toward them.

"Be quiet over there," came the quiet, yet strained, voice of Shea. The three men turned their faces toward her (and Myles) manacled around the sapling fifteen feet away. They all shushed each other.

"I told you, even if we had a knife and could cut the rope, we still couldn't get the manacles off," explained Tyson once again to the major. If nothing else, what Tyson said stopped the major's squirming. The three men sat there trying to think of some way to escape.

Fifteen feet away Shea was whispering to Myles to please stop wiggling, she was trying to think. "I really gotta go make piss," he apologized.

She was going to tell him that they all did, but kept quiet. That information wasn't going to help any. But to his credit he tried to sit still, and she went back to thinking of some way to solve their predicament.

Meanwhile, the major was whispering a possible solution to the other two men. "I'd wager that Mrs. Devonshire could pick these locks if we could get over to where she . . . ." He voice trailed off when he realized how utterly ridiculous his solution sounded when said out loud.

The minutes ticked by, and became hours. The moon, the only source of light, sailed across the cloudless sky and finally disappeared. Shortly thereafter a faint light could be seen in the eastern sky. Shea was sitting straight up with her back not touching the sapling. Over and over again she tried to think of any scenario where she could get one of her hands free of the manacle and then they'd be free of the sapling holding them stationery. Her wrist was rubbed raw from her trying to twist it free. She and Myles had tried to snap the sapling's thin trunk. They had stood up and tried to use their combined might to do it, but other than making too much noise they had achieved nothing. More than an hour ago Myles had leaned his back against the sapling, and fell asleep. She had continued trying to solve their problem. Sometime during the night it had dawned on her what Tyson, Sho-Taka, Mrs. Devonshire, and maybe the Major already knew; their fate depended on getting free. Occasional random noises came from the three men sitting by the other tree, and assured her they hadn't given up. And then Myles tickled her hand.

"Stop that!" she insisted in a whisper, "I'm trying to think." She shot a quick glance over left shoulder, as if her angry expression would end his foolishness in an instant. Distracted for a minute by his completely inappropriate gesture, she shook her head and smiled. It was so out of character she thought and . . . .

And then the tickling happened again! She whirled around ready to bite his head off, but before she made a sound her eye caught sight of something on the ground between them and the bush a foot away. For a nanosecond she thought was that it was a fat snake. But she caught herself again before she screamed. It was an arm!

Chapter 14 - Meanwhile, back at the fort . . .

Two generals blew in from the East
Seeking Dellie d'Argent and "that beast"
But their jaunt was for naught
Neither one would get caught
The old boys weren't pleased in the least!

Thursday, May 12th was a day not soon forgotten by the residents of the Fort Royal. The arrival at 11 AM of the General Fothingill contingent of soldiers from New York came as a complete surprise to the residents. The ridges and rises and the forests surrounding the settlement obscured the drum beat accompanying them. General Fothingill led his troop of soldiers past a thicket of trees, around a bend and then down the main thoroughfare of the Fort Royal village. The drum beat, the footsteps, the unusual noises coming from a large group of marching soldiers brought people out of every doorway and alley. Stunned at the sudden appearance of this military unit the locals, at first, said nothing at all.

With the possible exception of Captain Wallingford's maniacal display last Sunday the people of Fort Royal hadn't seen spectacle like this ever! Slowly at first they began whispering to one another about who these soldiers were. Where had they come from? Who was that officer out front? Why were they here? And look! They brought a cannon!

General Fothingill absolutely basked in this limelight parade. Ramrod stiff in his saddle he rode his horse at a crawl toward the front gate of the fort at the end of the street. Magistrate Roose and Major Tuite rode right behind him. All three of them expected Captain Wallingford to emerge from that gate before they reached it. Surely one of the soldiers at the fort had spotted them approaching and ran to tell him of their arrival. Had they knew more of the Fort Royal regimens and protocols they would have thought differently. Of the six soldiers currently at the fort (the other four were up in the woods collecting dry wood for the signal fire) five were still asleep. When the New Yorkers arrived at the front gate, it was only the guard, Private Bloodworth, who stood there to greet them. And he was in shock.

The high ranking officer in front slowly approached and, with a face like an eagle, stared down at him from his horse. The other officers grimly looked at Bloodworth too. The stern man in civilian clothes among them was perhaps the most frightening of all. He was dressed completely in black . . . a very dusty coating over that black . . . but black nonetheless. Behind this intimidating array stood soldiers five across and there must have been 10 to 15 ranks of them. Bloodworth didn't count them. There were drummers and wagons behind them, he could see parts of them and the drivers standing up and looking. And up and down the street he could see the residents of Fort Royal standing and talking and pointing.

He caught himself before he foolishly said "Good morning!" That, of course, would be inappropriate. He thought quickly (definitely not something in his skill set) and snapped to attention. He couldn't think of what to say. His mouth was totally dry, yet he felt the need to swallow, and say something. So he swallowed, and went with "Good morning", simultaneously. That was wrong on two counts. "Good morning" wasn't appropriate, and swallowing and talking simultaneously can't be done. General Fothingill saw the lips move but heard nothing. And he could have sat there on his horse until dark before it occurred to Bloodworth to salute. He spurred his horse, and moved past Bloodworth into the fort. Roose followed him immediately, but Major Tuite paused a moment to give orders to the officers behind him before following the other two inside.

When he joined Fothingill and Roose in the courtyard of the fort there were five men partially dressed in army uniforms stumbling out of their quarters toward the general's horse.

Fothingill leaned slightly toward them and asked, "Where's Captain Wallingford?"

All five, as if they were a precision drill team, shot their right arms up and to their right, and pointed west. Fothingill turned his head in the direction they were pointing, saw nothing but the wall of the fort and so turned once more to them. After a moment, he too pointed in that direction and asked, "What's that?"

No one said anything at first, and the non-response made Private Finlay nervous. He blurted out, "That's west, Sir."

General Fothingill was out of patience (this quickly!) and snarled, "Who's in charge here?"

Again, with admirable precision, four of the five men redirected their pointing arms at Selkirk. He didn't notice at first, but then from the corner of his eye he saw one, then another, then all of the others pointing at him. He wasn't pleased. Being in the crosshairs was never good.

"What's your name, soldier?"

"Selkirk, Sir. Albert, Sir. Private Albert Selkirk, Sir!"

Someone behind him whispered, "Albert?"

The general tried again, "Where is Captain Wallingford, Private Selkirk?"

Selkirk looked around at his fellow troopers and hissed, "Put your arms down!" He then turned to the general and caught himself before he said "West." For any enlisted man conversations with officers were fraught with danger, the higher the rank the more dangerous. Tread carefully he told himself. He had to remove himself from the crosshairs. "He went looking," and resisted the urge to point, but rather tilted his head in the correct direction and said, "That way for them people that left last week . . . Sir!"

"When will he be back?"

Thinking as fast as he could he looked for an out. What an idiotic question. How could Wallingford possibly know how long it would take him to find Highcross? Selkirk started to shake his head. He wet his lips, and sucked in air. Whirling around his faced his fellow soldiers, "Did he say anything to you boys?" He congratulated himself; he had redirected the officer's attention to them. They stared back blankly. He thought to himself, "Don't turn around and make eye contact with the general. Hopefully he'll turn his focus to one of these idiots." But it was not to be.

"Selkirk!" the General Fothingill's voice rang out.

Damn! Selkirk turned back to Fothingill. "Yes Sir?"

"When did he say he would return?"

Selkirk looked the general in the eye, and shook his head from side to side, "Never said a word to me, Sir." He turned to the other five, and asked again, "Did he happen to mention to any of you men when he'd be back?" He knew that answer before he asked the question. Captain Wallingford didn't make a habit of confiding with the men.

Then an idea hit home. A brilliant idea. A BRILLIANT IDEA!!! Selkirk spun back around to the General, "You know, Sir, who you might ask?" This was a great idea. The general raised an eyebrow. "You know who might know? Mr. Bardley. Josiah Bardley." Selkirk wasn't finished. He let this bit of information simmer for a moment, and then added, "His *partner.* Mr. Josiah Bardley. Lives in that great big house with the broken fence, down at the end of the street." He wasn't done. He looked around at his fellow soldiers. They were nodding, and giving signs that what he said might be true. "They had a very long private talk the night before he left. I know that for a fact, Sir. I was in the room with them for the early part of the discussion, Sir, before they sent me out." he said hoping this would be the coup-de-grace. Selkirk tried very hard not to smile.

"His partner? What do you mean 'his partner', Private?"

"Those two, Sir," Selkirk smiled, "They're as thick as three in a bed, Sir. Pardon the expression, if you will. Always goin' about whisperin' to each other. Confidin' all the time. I'd say if anyone knows the whereabouts and schedule of Captain Wallingford, it'd be Mr Bardley for sure, Sir." Selkirk turned to the other soldiers and saw them nodding back and forth to each other in agreement. He was sure he had sidestepped this predicament, and had neatly placed Josiah Bardley squarely in the bullseye.

That was until General Fothingill turned to the Major and ordered him to go get "this Bardley fellow" and bring him back to the fort's office. He then told Selkirk to join him and Mr. Roose in that office. Selkirk was shocked. But he wasn't any more shocked than the other four soldiers when Fothingill told them, in disgust, "And you four! For God sakes, go put your uniforms on!"

Slowly they made their way back to their quarters grumbling to themselves. They weren't on duty; why did they have to get into uniform? And they would have taken all day to do it if Major Tuite hadn't ordered one of his sergeants to escort them back to their barracks to spur them on.

General Fothingill, Magistrate Roose and Private Selkirk went into the fort's office. The General took the chair behind the desk and Roose opted to stand in the corner. Selkirk looked around but was afraid to sit in the empty chair opposite. He wasn't sure he should stand at attention either. He was uncomfortable.

Outside Major Tuite ordered a lieutenant to take a look around. "I want you to report back to me after you give the place a thorough inspection. See if they have anybody in irons. Particularly a woman!" Another lieutenant was sent to see to the men that were still in formation out in the street. "Have them fall out, but not wander off anywhere. Tell them to stay on the main street." He began to stride out of the fort where he would take a squad with him and find a local who knew where this Bardley lived. Passing Bloodworth at the gate he relieved him, and sent him back to join the others.

Inside the office the General continued to question Selkirk, without getting very far. Since the age of seven Albert Selkirk had treated every conversation he had with any authority figure as one would treat a minefield. The three overriding principles that governed every answer he ever gave were *brevity, uncertainty,* and *vague.* He couldn't spell them, but he knew what they meant. He had become quite good at it.

"So Wallingford went west? Why did he go?

"To find those pilgrims, Sir. The ones with Major Highcross."

"Who is Major Highcross?"

"I think someone said he's to be the new commander at Dubi . . . at Fort Dubois."

"Really?" This surprised the General. "On whose orders?"

"I wouldn't know, Sir."

"Is that where this Major Highcross is now? Fort Dubois?"

"I don't know where he is at the present time, Sir." With Falwyn as the guide it made no sense to Selkirk to hazard a guess as to where Highcross was right now.

"Where is the rest of the troop? Are they with Captain Wallingford?"

Can't feign ignorance here, he warned himself. "No Sir. The four other soldiers from here are up on the ridge by the river; preparing the signal fire."

"What signal fire?"

The answer to the general's question required four more questions to explain that Wallingford had wanted a signal fire prepared if Highcross returned. Then the General returned to a previous statement, "Only four soldiers?" The General did some quick addition. "And the six I have already seen here makes ten. Where is the rest of the troop? And where is the junior officer; the lieutenant? And the sergeant?"

Apologetically Selkirk answered, "We haven't got a sergeant here, Sir. Haven't had one in over a year. The former one – he retired - is livin' comfortable up near the New York border, I believe. And as for 'the rest of the troop'," he repeated the General's reference, "There ain't any 'rest of the troop', Sir. We only got the ten you seen, or told you about."

"How many soldiers are at Fort Dubois?"

"I don't know, Sir." Selkirk thought that his next statement should pack quite a wallop. "I've never been there." This wasn't actually true, but he had only been there once – on that "historic conquering foray" – and that had been a long time ago.

General Fothingill stared across the desk at Selkirk. His mouth hung open. Roose, in the corner, was trying to process what he had just heard.

The general finally broke the silence, "Your sergeant isn't at Fort Dubois with ten soldiers?"

Selkirk was starting to enjoy this. "Well no, Sir. The sergeant that used to be here is up near New York now. And he don't have no ten soldiers with him. And I can't tell you what's at Fort Dubious, er, Dubois, because like I said, I have never been there."

Fothingill was having trouble getting this into his head. "You have *never* been to Fort Dubois?"

Selkirk shook his head. "And the other troops here; have they been to Fort Dubois?" Again Selkirk, burying a smile, shook his head. Fothingill went on. "And there's no 'ten other soldiers' . . . and no sergeant . . . and no lieutenant?"

"Oh no Sir, we got a lieutenant. Lieutenant Smith." Selkirk pronounced it properly.

"Where is he?"

"I don't know, Sir. Disappeared last Sunday."

Frustrated by Selkirk's non-answers, the general allowed Magistrate Roose to take over. The lawyer, based on his long experience, considered himself quite adept at interrogation and cross examination.

"Do you know the whereabouts of Mme. d'Argent?" Roose asked out of nowhere.

Selkirk shifted on his feet. Never be in a hurry to answer a question he reminded himself. He was looking at the floor, but then raised his eyes to Roose; then at the ceiling. "Dar Junt?' he asked slowly. He started to shake his head, "No Sir. Don't know anyone with that name, or where she might be." It was true, he had never met anyone who identified themselves as "d'Argent", but he had a pretty good idea who Roose was asking about.

"Captain Wallingford hasn't placed anyone under arrest recently?"

"Under arrest? No Sir. Not recently." He was good; he was on solid ground.

Roose gave it one more try. "A French mademoiselle? Rather attractive, some say."

"Oh-oh," Selkirk thought. "Do I acknowledge that a woman calling herself Devonshire, and having a slight French accent, went through Fort Royal recently?" He made a face as if he was thinking hard; shifted his feet again. "Pretty women don't come through here every day; I should acknowledge her. But, let me put Bardley back in the crosshairs." He raised a smiling face to Roose and said, "You know . . . there was a very pretty woman here last week, or so, that sounded a little like a "Frenchie", but she was English, I think her name was Devonshire. That was her name I heard someone say. I never spoke with her. Josiah Bardley did; she stayed at his house."

Without a trace of satisfaction on his face Selkirk thought to himself, "Well done, Albert old boy, well done!"

A moment later there was a knock on the open door. They all turned to look. Josiah Bardley stood in the doorway with Major Tuite standing right behind.

"Mr. Bardley?" the general asked. Bardley stood there stone-faced, Major Tuite, behind him, nodded, and then gently nudged the man into the room.

"Come in," said Roose, "Sit here."

Bardley, who had heard what Selkirk had just said, nodded to the officer and Roose, and then turned his gaze to Selkirk. "Been entertaining the general, Private? Won't Captain Wallingford be ever so grateful?" He smiled, but only with his mouth.

Roose took the lead and instructed Major Tuite to escort Selkirk out.

In the time it took the three men to make proper introductions Bardley was furiously arguing with himself as how he should handle this. He was not nearly as accomplished as Selkirk at evasive answering, and was wondering what Selkirk had already told them. With the exception of Captain Wallingford, and on rare occasions his wife, he had not been intimidated by anyone in years. He was intimidated now. The sudden arrival of these officials had caught him off-guard.

He had been doing some inventory work in the large barn that served as his warehouse in anticipation of the two supply trains that Wallingford had told him were on the way. That was when his wife raced in to tell him of the commotion in the street. He was unsettled by anything out of the ordinary, and a parade of senior (at least senior to Wallingford) military personnel with 50 soldiers marching down Main Street certainly qualified as that. He made his way into his house and went to the front window. He peeked out to see the soldiers marching by. He began debating with himself over which course of action he should take. There were many ways he thought he could deal with this unexpected development. Be calm; be decisive; meet it head on; be evasive; be proactive; try to anticipate any and all outcomes. But one plan kept circling through his consciousness every few seconds. "Go out to the stable, and saddle and mount my best horse. Start riding west and go as fast and as far as the beast will carry me." This plan fell apart when Major Tuite, arrived unobserved, posted his squad around the house, and banged on the front door. Josiah Bardley wasn't going anywhere.

These two men could ruin everything he had worked for his entire adult life. He cursed to himself that Wallingford had run off into the frontier and left him alone to deal with these two intruders. And damn Highcross for compounding all the fuss. And Damn Devonshire – that French whore! And, of course, DAMN Selkirk for running off at the mouth. Oh, Wallingford would make him pay for that in due time! And Damn Smith! He ought to be around here to deal with these two; not me!

He suddenly realized he was being spoken to by the general. "Where has Captain Wallingford gone off to? I am told you are the one to ask."

He smiled, "Me? I believe you've been misinformed, General Fothingill. I never involve myself in Captain Wallingford's military affairs. It wouldn't be my place," he turned his gaze to Roose. "In the first place, Captain Wallingford wouldn't allow it." Well done, he thought to himself, put some distance between myself and the good captain.

Roose asked, "So you do not know where he's gone, or how long he'll be away."

"Haven't the foggiest notion, Mr. Roose."

Roose shot right back, "Then what were you two discussing at the private meeting you had with him the night before he left?" Roose wasn't accusing him of anything, but was still totally confused about the goings on at Fort Royal. "Private Selkirk told us you are "partners. Was it business you were discussing?"

Bardley smiled at them both, "Selkirk? You'd be better served not listening to a word that man says." Despite the smile on his face, he was seething inside. "He is a known liar, and a man of little merit. He has barely managed to remain in the King's service despite repeated brushes with regulations."

Roose persisted, "He said he was there while you discussed Wallingford going off to look for this Major Highcross. Not so?"

"Careful, Josiah," he thought, "There's a witness." Bardley waved his hand as if dismissing them both, "Now he might have said something about having to go out and locate this officer – what did you say his name was? Highcross? Yes, but he was talking to Private Selkirk, not me. It was a military matter. My conversation involved a stolen horse. It seems that someone from the fort may have – I'm not saying this is proven – but may have, been involved with stealing a horse owned by a local merchant named Ludlum. Mr. Ludlum asked me to intercede with Captain Wallingford for recompense; him being the local representative of the law, you see." Bardley was thrilled with his version of the conversation. He had made most of it up as he went along. He was feeling quite good.

"Do you know Mme. d'Argent?"

The blood drained from his head. He felt faint, and had trouble with his breathing. He looked at the general, and then at the magistrate. The room was moving. He tried to say something, but nothing came out.

"You may have known her as Mrs. Devonshire, perhaps? She was your houseguest." Mr. Roose said quietly.

Selkirk would pay for this. Oh, he would pay! "Why yes," he said in a voice an octave higher than normal. He cleared his throat while trying to clear his head. "She was a friend . . . if I'm not mistaken of Captain Wallingford's. I may have that wrong; I didn't hear him clearly. He asked if I could offer her lodgings while she was here at Fort Royal. I think he felt the local facilities were a bit below her standards. But I'm not really sure. I don't know her."

Roose and General Fothingill exchanged glances, and then Roose asked, "Where is she?"

"I don't know," he answered in wide-eyed innocence.

There was suddenly a commotion outside that interrupted the conversation. A panting sergeant ran up to the door, and called out (and not for the last time would this be said in the New World) "BRITISH ARE COMING! BRITISH ARE COMING!"

Again the General and Roose exchanged glances, and then moved to the doorway. The out-of-breath sergeant reported,

"There's a whole troop of mounted regulars racing toward the village, Sir."

The General, Magistrate Roose, and several of their accompanying officers looked out at the roadway and then at each other in confusion. They were more confused than alarmed because, after all, those advancing troops were British and as such weren't a threat. But hard charging cavalrymen would make anyone nervous, no matter whom they appeared to be.

The 50+ horses and riders raced into the village down the main street, and just as suddenly came to a halt as the lead officer reined in his horse at the fort's gate. Dust and noise and commotion overwhelmed the onlookers, both foot soldiers and residents.

"WHO IN BLAZES IS THAT?" Fothingill kept shouting at Major Tuite. Major Tuite kept staring at the arriving officers, with his mouth open.

As General Tindale raced through the town he couldn't help but notice all the soldiers standing around. He was confused by their numbers as he tried to remember how many troops Wallingford had here at this post. His memory, although uncertain, told him that it wasn't more than 20.

He slowed his horse as he went through the front gate, and stopped it in the middle of the yard. He dismounted and began striding toward the gawking officers in the office doorway. As the dust settled Fothingill recognized the advancing soldier.

"GENERAL TINDALE! Godfrey you old windbag! How are you? What are you doing here?"

Ten paces from the doorway General Tindale suddenly realized the officer in the doorway was not the expected Captain Wallingford, but General Fothingill from New York.

General Fothingill had been a general longer than Tindale, and therefore outranked him, but why was he here at Fort Royal? This fort was under his command. "Augustus?" he asked, not believing his eyes. "What are you doing here?"

It took them a few minutes to shake hands and pat each other on the back, and then move back into the office. Roose joined them, as did Philadelphia's Major Castlewich, and Lieutenant St John (of course). Captain McLayne was still in the process of dismounting; he was so saddle sore he was unable to do anything quickly.

Josiah Bardley had considered taking advantage of the distraction Tindale's arrival had created and thought of exiting through a back door while they had gone out front. That didn't happen when Bardley looked around and saw there was no back door. He did, however, spot a rear window. Debating with himself whether his legs had the resolve to allow him to stand up and carry him to that window, and further still did he possess the flexibility to fit out that window, took too long. They were back inside, and he was still sitting on his bench.

Things were happening. There was widespread confusion and commotion in the village. This was opportunity with a capital "O" thought Selkirk. "I have to get out there," he said to the five other soldiers in the barracks with him. But the sergeant who had escorted him back to the barracks stood at its front door pinning them all in.

Several months ago Selkirk had thought that having an alternate access to and from the fort would be beneficial. Something other than the main gate and something out of the sight of the officers and residents of Fort Royal might prove quite useful under certain circumstances for him . . . and the others too. He had settled on making a knee high hole through the rear wall of the barracks that would be hidden behind a gun rack. The door would open into a small alley behind the barracks, two feet from the fort wall. There he would cut another small hole through the wall into a rarely used stable on the other side. A new fence, or better yet some barrels filled with dirt would seal off the alley, and an old crate could hide the hole in the stable. He had spent much time selecting its location and planning its design. It was to be out of sight and easily used. Until he could decide on whether to let his fellow soldiers in on the plan he delayed construction. But one thing after another had delayed the implementation of the plan, and today it was no nearer completion than the day he thought of it. He glumly thought how valuable it would be to him today if he had gone through with it.

"Damn!" he said out loud to himself. Thompson heard him and, without knowing what it was, agreed. "Damn," he repeated.

Back in the office it took one and all a minute or two to settle down. "What are you doing here?" General Tindale finally asked Fothingill.

"I'm looking for Captain Wallingford – the commander here." Then, with a furrowed brow, he asked Tindale the same question.

Tindale's was, at first, perplexed because it wasn't necessary for Fothingill to identify who Wallingford was. But his overriding concern was his daughter's disappearance, so he said, "I'm looking for . . . ," his voice trailed off. He gathered some resolve and went on, "I'm chasing after my daughter. I'm afraid she may have run off. And she may have very well run off with Captain Wallingford." Fothingill raised an eyebrow, and peeked over at Roose. Tindale continued, "Then again maybe my Captain Wallingford is guiltless. It just may be that Major Highcross is the guilty party. I don't know. That's why I'm here; to talk to the both of them."

Fothingill thought the phrase "*my* Captain Wallingford" odd, but he too had a more important quest. "Have you seen a woman named d'Argent, or Devonshire, in your travels?"

"Or D'Arnay, or even Dubonne," Magistrate Roose added.

"No, those names aren't familiar to me. Are they all one in the same? Who is she?"

"She's the most nefarious criminal on this side of the Atlantic. I can't believe her name isn't familiar to you; magistrates from all over have warrants out for her arrest." Fothingill said.

Tindale gave a slight shrug. This was something his staff would normally handle. "Is that what you're doing out here? Chasing after some felonious Frenchwoman?" This seemed odd to him because he thought it was below standards for a general to chase after some common criminal. But his concern quickly returned to his own daughter. Getting back to what he cared most about, Tindale asked, "Where's Wallingford? Is Highcross here?"

Roose crossed his arms across his chest and, although talking to General Tindale, he stared down at Bardley who had been sitting as quiet as a church mouse this whole time, "Getting information here is far harder than one would imagine possible." He turned to an officer at the door and instructed him to go get Selkirk and bring him back in here. And have the other five Fort Royal soldiers fall into formation out in the courtyard. "Let's get to the bottom of this."

In the barracks the officer asked Selkirk if he preferred "to step lively, or would you rather be placed in irons and dragged across the yard?" Selkirk opted to step lively. As they left to return to the office the captain yelled at the five others sitting on their bunks to "FALL IN!" The two lieutenants there repeated the order, "FALL IN. FALL IN!" A sergeant, not to be outdone, bellowed, "FALL IN!" Even Private Thompson, caught up in the excitement began saying, "Fall in . . . Fall in." With a haste they had not displayed in a very, very long time the soldiers from Fort Royal assembled five abreast outside. Private Tilden, arthritic and wheezing, was the last to arrive.

While Selkirk was retrieved Roose brought Tindale up to date on what they had so far learned. That hadn't taken very long because the information from Selkirk had been sketchy, at best. They were exchanging recent news from "Mother England across the sea" and tidbits of news from their home bases when the office door opened.

The pleasantries stopped between the two senior officers as Selkirk was ushered back into the room. Both generals stared at him as Selkirk was marched in and told to sit on the opposite end of the bench Bardley was on. They were back to back.

The two generals sat at each end of the desk in the office. A coterie of six different officers (including the bowlegged Captain McLayne) stood against the walls. Roose stalked around the room firing the majority of the questions.

The generals asked, "When did Wallingford get back here? Was he alone?"

Bardley nodded, but Selkirk said, "Last Sunday, Sir. He rode in alone. He didn't seem to have anyone with him."

"Where did he go? And who went with him?"

Fothingill quickly added, "And don't say 'west'."

Selkirk thinking quicker, turned toward Bardley to await his answer. Bardley realized it and stammered, "He . . . Captain Wallingford . . . went after . . . to find Major Highcross." He paused for a moment, and then thought it best to tell all. "And he thought Mrs. Devonshire might be with them."

"Who is this Major Highcross?" General Fothingill asked no one in particular.

"Who is this Devonshire?" Tindale counted.

Roose ignored them both and continued his interrogation.

Misleading and conflicting answers to repeated questions led often to mind numbing confusion. Contradictions arose as often as obvious lies. Both generals fired questions at the two men on the bench, and Roose was at the top of his game. Private Selkirk was dodging and flinching like a nude man in a hail storm. Josiah Bardley was wilting.

General Fothingill wanted to know if the captain had ever had the elusive Mme. d'Argent in custody. General Tindale, on the other hand, wanted to find out if Wallingford had made off with his daughter, or was it Highcross? Had anyone there seen his daughter? And after only a short time it was apparent something wasn't right at Fort Royal. And as both generals happened to be the Commander of Fort Royal – although neither knew about the other one – each was bound and determined to get to the bottom of it.

Due primarily to the very nimble Private Selkirk the truth took longer to ooze out than they all expected. The first part of it was the fact that Fort Royal had been getting supplies from both New York and Philadelphia.

A puzzled General Fothingill leaned back in his chair and looked at Tindale, "Godfrey, why are you supplying Fort Royal?"

"I might ask you the same question," Tindale replied.

Their conversation then excluded everyone else in the room as they unwound the intrigue. "My God," Fothingill whispered, "He's reporting to both of us!"

Fothingill continued questioning Selkirk, but the private was nimble. And Selkirk, for the very first time, was glad he was not part of the double dealing (except the excess pay – should that come up - which he felt he could easily explain away). It occurred to him that at the first opportunity he had to make sure these officers understood that.

What began to emerge slowly was Bardley's admission to "a certain cooperative understanding with Wallingford in regard to excess supplies".

"How much *excess* is there?" Tindale asked.

"Quite a bit I would imagine," barked General Fothingill, "He's not only getting supplies from both of us, but he getting supplies for 23 . . . or is it 24 men? I don't even know! He's receiving supplies for 40 some odd men. And, Godfrey, he has only 10 enlisted men here. No sergeants and one missing lieutenant. That's the whole lot! And unless I'm badly mistaken there isn't a single soldier at Fort Dubois." He was nearly out of breath when he finished.

General Tindale stared at him wide eyed. "I say," he said.

Both Generals were speechless. Roose stepped in after a quiet minute, "Private Selkirk, what does he do with all these excess supplies?"

In a flash, Selkirk responded, "I wouldn't know, Sir. Captain Wallingford keeps all matters pertaining to the commissary to himself." He shifted around so he could see Bardley, and said to Roose, "Maybe Mr Bardley knows? He got a barn full of them 'excesses'."

All eyes turned to Bardley. What could he say? He didn't know the exact numbers Wallingford was feeding them. And this had been happening monthly, he thought to himself, for close to two years. He needed to say something; no matter how weak and flimsy. "Good God, Selkirk! You don't know the first thing about being a merchant trader. Of course, I have an inventory. You're an idiot." He turned to the generals behind the desk, "You are both educated men, you understand about buying and selling. Trading. Commercial business." He stopped before he began to stutter.

Roose saw him weakening and jumped in, "Do you buy and sell with any of the soldiers at Fort Royal or Fort Dubois?"

Bardley, with his mouth open, stared at him. There were papers – bill of sales, receipts, contracts; attesting to transactions with both forts. There were sales of livestock and feed; livery and equipment; foodstuff and cloth; powder and ammunition. Wallingford had handed every one of them in so they would be reimbursed by New York and/or Philadelphia. And Josiah Bardley's signature was on every one of them. No one in the room except Josiah Bardley could hear the world crashing down around his ankles.

The silence in the room did allow them to notice a disturbance coming from the street. The disturbance seemed to be growing louder, so Tindale dispatched Lieutenant St John to find out what was going on. The lieutenant didn't want to miss what was going on in the office, but reluctantly obeyed.

When he exited the fort gate into the street, he looked around to see the dragoons still mounted on their horses in the middle of the street. Up and down the street the foot soldiers lined the sidewalks. Each group seemed to be chanting at each other. The irregular tempo of both sides made it impossible for St John to understand what either side was saying.

"What's going on here, Sergeant?" St John asked the non-com.

"Oh it's just the boys giving each other a bit of a razz, Sir. Nothing much."

"What on earth are they saying?"

The sergeant smiled and explained that infantry and cavalry had engaged "in a friendly rivalry since there ever was an infantry and cavalry". He said that the infantry disparaged cavalry, and vice versa. So that being the case the infantry liked to say that cavalry forces lacked resolve, and would likely relent as soon as they were pressed. "So you see lieutenant, that's why those foot soldiers there are saying, 'Light dragoons - are macaroons'." The lieutenant made a face. "What they mean, Sir, is that those cavalry forces are filled with nuts and crumble when pressed."

"And the dragoons are responding what, Sergeant?"

"Well, as you might expect, Sir, the dragoons naturally are always looking down at the infantrymen – being up on a horse and feeling superior anyway - so they chant, 'The Foot Guard - smell odd.' It seems to please them, Sir."

It made little sense to St John. "Tell them to stop. It's disturbing the General. (He didn't say which one.) Changing topics he instructed the sergeants to have the dragoons make camp on the west side of the fort, and for the foot soldiers to set up camp on the east side. "No mingling! Restrict everyone to their camp."

Sergeants began yelling at the two groups of soldiers, telling them to be quiet and to begin making camp in their respective locations. Lieutenant St John took one last look around and then turned to return to the office. He was intercepted on his way back to the office by an officer from the New York troop.

Ten minutes later Lieutenant St John slipped back into the office. The questioning was still going on. Josiah Bardley was explaining that the many transactions he had done with Fort Dubois had all been through Captain Wallingford. He had never been there. The heavy sigh and heading shaking signs of exasperation were duplicated by the two Generals. General Fothingill took it a step further and dropped his head into his hands.

It came as a flash to General Tindale. "Good God Almighty!" he moaned. "Augustus, he's been collecting a payroll for almost **50** men!"

Lieutenant St John was moving around the room, attempting to catch General Tindale's eye.

He succeeded. "What is it, St John?" General Tindale barked.

"Important information, Sir." Everyone in the room turned their focus to him.

"Well, let's have it!" again barked Tindale.

"Privately, if you please, Sir. It's about your daughter," answered the Lieutenant

Alarmed, the general jumped to his feet and moved quickly toward the door. He grabbed a handful of St John's coat on his way out.

Once out in the courtyard; still with a grip on St John's coat, he passed the five Fort Royal soldiers who were standing in formation. A few steps further out of their earshot, the general turned to his lieutenant "What is it?" He immediately noticed St John had another lieutenant in tow.

"Sir, this is Lieutenant Jeremy Daniel. He's an old chum from back at Pipperwich." St John turned to the other Lieutenant and smiled, "What times we had there, eh old boy!" They both laughed. Tindale had no idea what or where Pipperwich was; he didn't care. "Yesyeshownicegladtomeetyoulieutenant," spewed the General in a flash. And then turning back to St John, he asked in a far more reserved manner, "What about my daughter?" Jerking his thumb at Lieutenant Daniel, he added, "And does he need to hear this?"

Lieutenant St John went on, "Actually he does, Sir. He's the one that has the news." He explained, "Lieutenant Daniel is attached to the infantry force accompanying General Fothingill." St John had no intention of being the bearer of bad news - messengers sometimes get shot - so he sidestepped out of the way between the Tindale and Daniel, and said, "He best tell you, Sir."

The general now turned to Lieutenant Daniel, "Well, out with it. What do you have?"

The lieutenant was tall and very thin. He looked down at the general, "I may know where your daughter is."

There was a pause. The general stared at him with wide expectant eyes, the blurted, "Well go on! Go on!"

"Two months ago I received a letter from an old friend of mine who's at Philadelphia. He wanted to know if I still owned that little seaside cottage over on the shore in New Jersey."

"And . . . ."

"I wrote back, and told him I did. He then wrote and asked if he could borrow it for the second week in May."

"Go on, man, go on!"

"I told him 'Of course, you can; take for the month, I told him. The man was my best friend back at school. He practically carried me through. He said he wanted it . . . for his honeymoon . . . with his new bride, Sir."

General Tindale leaned in a little closer, "Did he call her by name?"

"He only called her by her first name, Sir. And that's why when Lieutenant St John here and I were chatting, and your daughter's disappearance came up, I took notice."

In the flattest possible voice the General asked, "What was the name of this bride?"

After a momentary hesitation the Lieutenant said, "Audrey."

The General's first reaction was furor. He gritted his teeth and squeezed the handle of his sword. But then a sudden thought occurred to him. Audrey was not necessarily a common name, but by no means was it rare. There were hundreds – maybe thousands – of Audreys throughout the colonies; and no small portion of those thousands were located in the New York/Philadelphia area. This young bride could be any one of them. Another question popped into General Tindale's head. He tilted his head toward the lieutenant and asked slowly and quietly, "Who is this friend of yours? What's his name?"

Lieutenant Jeremy Daniel offered, "John." But he instantly knew that was insufficient, and corrected his answer to, "Lieutenant John *Crosly*, Sir."

General Tindale mouthed the words, "Lieutenant John Crosly?"

Lieutenant Jeremy Daniel nodded. Lieutenant St John smirked. General Tindale smoldered.

He hadn't used the word in several years. He wouldn't use it again for several more. But never in his entire life – from cradle to grave – did he say this word with more vehemence, with more visceral hostility, than he did now.

"**A *FOKKING* LIEUTENANT**," he bellowed. "Sainted Mother of Christ," he wept.

This was beyond anything he had imagined. He was ricocheting between rage and abject misery. For the past several days, as he had thundered across Pennsylvania toward Fort Royal, he had pondered what he was going to do to either Wallingford or Highcross. Whichever officer was responsible for the stealing, and possibly the deflowering, of his beautiful innocent daughter was going to beg for mercy. And General Godfrey Tindale had long ago resolved to show no mercy whatsoever. But now those two particular officers were erased from his mind. No, now there was only one thing on his mind. Crosly! I'm going to kill him! It was now General Tindale's only goal in life. A lieutenant! A Goddamned Lieutenant!

Whirling back around toward Lieutenant Jeremy Daniel, he hissed, "Where's this cottage of yours?"

"In New Jersey, Sir. I told you."

"Where in New Jersey, you idiot. It's a big place."

"Middlesex County; just south of the mouth of the Raritan River in a beautiful little village called Morganville. Right by Cheesequake Creek. You can see Staten Island and the village of Brooklyn to the north from the beach there."

The General turned away from them and started back to the office. "It won't be so beautiful after I get through with it," he muttered. As he stomped across the yard he continued to mutter, "A Lieutenant! A GODDAMNED LIEUTENANT! NOT A DUKE. NOT AN EARL. NOT A LORD OF ANY KIND. NOT AN MP. DOCTOR. LAWYER. NOT A GENERAL OR A COLONEL. NOT EVEN A MAJOR OR A CAPTAIN. A LIEU . . . ." He couldn't finish the thought.

General Tindale stormed back toward the office in a straight line. That line carried him through the rank of Fort Royal soldiers still standing in formation in the courtyard. They had been standing there for a long time, and that was something they were not accustomed to doing. They were tired and sagging. As the general pushed his way between two of them they stumbled to the side and knocked into the others there. Private Tilden at the end of the line was knocked off balance and fell in a heap to the ground. He momentarily scrambled into a sitting position. The sergeant assigned to watch over them felt some sympathy for the worn and weary soldier and offered a hand to help him to his feet.

"Nah, that's okay. I'm good here," he said as he remained seated.

Tindale made his way back to the office door and asked General Fothingill and Roose if they would step outside for a moment. Once the three were outside he begged Fothingill's indulgence, but explained he had to leave immediately to go back east. "To New Jersey," he spit.

They discussed a few details, but Tindale's heart wasn't in it. He wanted to go, and go now. Fort Royal was in the Pennsylvania Colony, which was Tindale's jurisdiction, but Fothingill had seniority in rank. Tindale, eager to leave, was only too glad to defer to that seniority and said he would leave the resolution to General

Fothingill's good judgement. And he would leave with only a lieutenant (NOT St John) and ten cavalrymen. The rest of the Philadelphia contingent would remain here with General Fothingill's contingent until all matters were resolved. "I am also going to take along your Lieutenant Jeremy Daniel. I need him to lead me to the where he says my daughter is."

Within only another ten minutes and virtually no additional conversation, General Godfrey Tindale and 11 other riders were on their way to the New Jersey shore.

Lieutenant St John slid back into the room after glumly waving goodbye to General Tindale. Captain McLayne, who had never left the office, had a bad feeling when he saw that General Tindale had not returned with St John. Was his chance at bringing retribution down on Wallingford's head riding out of town? He sidled up next to Lieutenant St John and whispered "Where is he going?" The pained expression on his face would have made one think his toes were being nailed to the floor. The look on St John's face wasn't much better after having been in close proximity to McLayne's bad breath.

St John blew air into McLayne's face and then said, "New Jersey." He then motioned him to be quiet.

In the office it had been established that Bardley did extensive business with both forts. But he had insisted he had no direct knowledge or contact with Fort Dubois. Roose knew he was lying, and moved on.

He was firing questions at Bardley and Selkirk, and sometimes not waiting for an answer. "Wait one minute! WAIT ONE MINUTE!" Roose suddenly yelled. "Let's get something straight here. There are how many soldiers here at Fort Royal? You said ten soldiers, a lieutenant and Captain Wallingford. That's 12, correct?"

Surprisingly, Selkirk offered an answer, "Well, Mr Roose, the lieutenant is gone. So as of this morning the real count would be 11."

"Gone? Gone where?" Roose shot back.

"I don't know," said Selkirk. Then he turned and looked inquiringly at Bardley.

Roose did the same. "Mr Bardley, do you know where he is?"

Josiah Bardley had last seen Lieutenant Smith racing for his life into the woods near his house. Wisely he decided to keep that fact to himself. He shook his head. If he had to he could explain it away as a military matter, and not his business.

"Okay, there are only 11 soldiers here, Captain Wallingford included." General Fothingill said. "How many are there at Fort Dubois? Let's get that straight. Ten? And who is in command out there?"

Bardley, tired of being beaten to the punch by Selkirk and left to answer these questions, leapt into the lead to answer, "Don't know," he nearly shouted, "I've never been there."

Selkirk having no desire to be the center of attention instantly added, "Neither have I."

Fothingill was the first to respond, and asked Selkirk, "Captain Wallingford reported to me that he ran joint operations with the troops here and at Fort Dubois against hostile Indians on several occasions. Did you join forces with the Fort Dubois troop last January to keep the peace in . . . ?" He couldn't recall the locale that Wallingford had used in his report.

Selkirk's brain was on high alert. "Sir? Last January? If I remember right last January was awful cold and there was lots of snow. I don't think we left the fort from New Year's Day until late February. We sure didn't meet up with any troops; not from Fort Dubois or anywhere else."

Roose gave up this line of questioning and began asking about the whereabouts of Wallingford, Highcross or d'Argent. The answers to this line of questioning were pretty much the same as they had been to last line of questioning.

The repetition of "I don't know" or "I've never been there" answers by both Selkirk and Bardley was finally brought to an end when General Fothingill and Magistrate Roose gave up, and ordered them both into the guardhouse. Both immediately began howling about this injustice. While Bardley was professing his innocence of any crime and Selkirk was professing his ignorance of any crime, the jail door slammed behind them.

General Fothingill and Magistrate Roose next went on to interrogate, one by one, the remainder of the Fort Royal troop. If possible, these men knew less about Major Highcross, Captain Wallingford and Fort Dubois than Private Selkirk. When the very last soldier to be interviewed (Private Tilden) shuffled out of the office (that lasted longer than his interview) a stunned, frazzled, and despondent General Fothingill dropped his head into his hands.

Magistrate Roose suggested that they huddle, and make some sense out of all this. All the other officers were ushered out, while food and a pitcher of cool water were brought in. Fothingill and Roose waited until they were alone in the room before beginning to discuss the situation, and what must be done. Both men wanted to find out how this could have happened. They both wanted to find out more about Wallingford's double dealing thievery. Who had been involved? How much had gone on? For how long? General Fothingill wanted to get his hands on Captain Wallingford (preferably by the neck) as soon as possible. Reporting this back to London was going to be a catastrophe and cause a scandal.

"Let's review what we know," Roose said.

"Good idea," agreed Fothingill.

"Let's list the facts as we know them. What do we know?" Roose said looking at the general.

"There are twelve men stationed here at Fort Royal," stated Fothingill.

"Eleven," corrected Roose.

"Right! Yes, just eleven."

Roose asked, "How many men at Fort Dubois, general?"

"We don't know that . . . exactly."

They paused and looked at each other. Roose broke the silence and said, "Why don't we just keep to things we do know."

"Capital idea," concurred the general.

Roose re-started, "I think we know that Captain Wallingford has been submitting false or misleading action reports, undetected by you . . . for an extended period of time."

"That's true, I'm afraid. But don't forget – General Tindale has been hoodwinked by the scoundrel too."

"He has also been submitting inflated supply and equipment requisitions, not to mention exaggerated payroll numbers."

Almost to himself, Fothingill mumbled "Don't see how Tindale's going to explain that away."

Roose didn't understand that remark, but went on, "And how long has all this been going on?"

"I don't think we know that, do we?"

They sat in silence for a few minutes until Fothingill said, "I wish Tindale hadn't run off so abruptly. He might have been able to fill in some of these blanks."

Roose wouldn't say this out loud but he suspected Tindale's departure had more to do with this colossal scandal than his daughter's supposed disappearance. "Perhaps it would be more constructive if we listed the things we don't know," Roose finally offered, "So we'll have some idea of the questions Wallingford will have to answer when he returns."

"Why not," sighed Fothingill.

"You have been authorizing supplies, equipment and payroll for Fort Dubois for the past year? Or two years? How long??"

"I don't know exactly," Fothingill said. "But," he brightened up, "I will find out. And so has Tindale! I'm not in this boat alone."

Roose was talking again, "You are unaware of the extent of the quantity of supplies fraudulently procured over your signature for this, possibly, fictitious unit."

The general paused a moment to think that over. "Right again," he finally agreed.

Roose went on, "Let's focus on Fort Dubois . . . now we seem to be a little unsure of where it is, or if it is manned. And if it is, by how many men? And who they might be, or who is in command?"

Fothingill acknowledged that, "That's a certainty, I'd say. We don't know." He was thinking that explaining the bloated payroll . . . for a troop of soldiers . . . not technically under his command to his superiors in London was going to be a problem.

"You said that you don't know *exactly* how many men are stationed at Fort Dubois, do you have an official roster?"

"No. I don't know if anyone has," Fothingill's was beginning to waver.

"You don't know why both you and General Tindale are supplying that fort, do you?"

"Haven't the foggiest," he whispered, "No."

"Do you know where it is? Could you find it on a map?"

"My God," mumbled Fothingill.

Roose was starting to feel sorry for the old man, "Let's move on to another subject." He cleared his voice and poured himself and the general a cup of water.

"There is no Mme. d'Argent here at Fort Royal."

That's a fact thought General Fothingill, suddenly remembering that he had sent out a dispatch before leaving New York crowing that she was in his custody. It had been sent to all posts under his command, and to London. That, he now thought in hindsight, was perhaps a tad premature.

"Yes, that's God's honest truth."

"So if she's not here," Roose wanted to know, "Where is she?"

General Fothingill started to answer three times, also making small hand gestures, and eyebrow twitches, before finally saying hoarsely, "No one knows."

"We can't even be certain that she has ever even been here, can we?"

The general just looked at Roose blankly and shook his head.

"So . . . in effect . . . you ordered some 70 men to march 125 miles based on something *you were told Captain Wallingford had said*?"

Roose was slyly making the point that perhaps the Commanding General was not attuned to the vague subtle differences between credible, factual testimony and bullshit. What Fothingill was attuned to was the fact that Roose was starting to distance himself from this catastrophe.

"Once more, let's move on." Roose straightened a paper on the desk. "Aaron Highcross. A Grandson of Lord Nunch; a nephew of some very important people in London, and a major in His Majesty's Army. You've met the man?"

General Fothingill whispered, "No."

"But you know who he is?"

"I do now."

"But you don't know where he is now, do you? Or where he can be reached? Or even when he may come wandering back out of the frontier, do you?"

"No."

"Do you know who sent him, or where he's going?"

"I think he's heading to Fort Dubois to assume command."

"And how do you know that?"

"I believe Selkirk told us that a little while ago." Fothingill was hoping for joint confirmation on this.

Roose, clearly showing he was now jumping ship, shook his head sadly, and then leaned in closer to the general, "May I make a recommendation, Augustus?" He didn't wait for an answer. "I wouldn't tell the Inquiry Board that Private Selkirk is your source of information on that, or any other matter under discussion. I don't think they'd find that . . . er . . . prudent on your part."

The word "Inquiry" took Fothingill by surprise. "You think there'll be an Official Court of Inquiry called on this matter?" he asked Roose despite already knowing the answer.

Roose cocked an eyebrow at him and said, "Oh Sir, I am sure they will. You know how all those sycophants and parvenus surrounding King George like nothing more than harping on any little aberration they think may have done by those in service far from home. False reports, dereliction of duty, misappropriation of the King's property, theft of royal funds, need I go on? I expect they'll call for one quite quickly when this gets back to them. But I'm sure, given time, you'll have answers for all the questions they ask." Fothingill wasn't so sure. "But why don't do you look on the bright side," Roose went on, "Perhaps Captain Wallingford will re-emerge from the forest. And at the Official Inquiry, amid the barrage of their accusations, he may very well be able to produce more revelations than those contained in Holy Scripture, and explain away these goings on to everyone's satisfaction!"

Just then there was a knock on the door and it opened. Captain McLayne stuck his head in and smiled weakly. "Begging your pardon, Sir, for the interruption, but I was wondering if I could have a word with you." He didn't wait for an answer because he was so nervous. He had just confirmed that General Tindale had ridden off into the night for New Jersey and wasn't coming back. McLayne was adamant about not letting Wallingford off the hook for his transgressions. As a matter of fact he had just had a few "quick ones" at Philyaw's to bolster up the courage he needed to make this intrusion. "I'm Captain McLayne, Sir, from Philadelphia, and I'd like a moment of your time to discuss a problem I've had with Captain Wallingford and . . . ."

McLayne never saw it but the pitcher of water missed his head by mere inches and smashed into the wall behind him. Besides being startled by the loud noise of the crash, bits of clay and droplets of water hit him in the back of his head and neck. He thought someone was shooting at him, and he thought the water was his blood. His initial reaction was to leap into the room and slam the door behind him. Then he turned toward the General and Mr. Roose for confirmation. He saw the general picking up a large bench with both hands and putting it over his head. His intentions were clear. Captain McLayne's instinct for self-preservation had sharpened appreciatively over the past several days, and he was out the door in a flash.

With the possible exception of his marriage, this was the worst week of his life.

Chapter 15: Second Battle of Fort Dubois

(But we know it's really the first!)

Twas talk of bloodshed and carnage,
At the scene of Fort Dubois.
But we know it never happened,
That whole story's just bushwah.

But now we hear of the second;
A war 'tween men hand-to-hand.
They used guns and rocks and arrows.
The end? A flash in the pan!

Looking back it's just history;
And no one died in the fray.
There was one who got just deserts.
While others went on their way.

Somehow, Shea caught herself before screaming. The initial shock of thinking it was a snake; the relief in realizing it wasn't; and the surprise of seeing an arm all rendered her incapable of making a sound. It took her a moment to collect herself. Myles had been jerked awake, and was starting to say something. She hushed him. Peering down behind her right shoulder she saw an arm reaching out from under the bush to her manacled hand. In the very faintest light of dawn she was barely able to see that the fingers on the end on this arm held a key, and it was trying to find the keyhole on the manacle. "Myles," she whispered, "Keep very quiet. Very, very quiet!"

"Click" came the sound, and the manacle loosened on her wrist, and then slid off. She didn't hesitate for a moment before reaching with her free hand to grab Myles' still manacled wrist. "Don't make a sound. Don't even move," she ordered.

"Who is that?" he asked.

"Ssssshhh!" she ordered again.

The hand put the key into Shea's hand and then slowly disappeared back under the bush.

Shea watched in wonder as it retreated, and then shrugging, she turned to look through the darkness at the reclined Captain Wallingford. "Is he asleep?" she asked herself? "If he is I can free myself, and then free the men. If he isn't, I'll have only seconds to free myself from Myles, and get away." She felt Myles stir. "Don't move," she whispered.

She twisted around to her left as Myles twisted around also to face her. Again she motioned for him to be quiet. She put the key in the other manacle and wrapped all the folds of her skirt around it to muffle any sound as she unlocked it. She was now free.

She motioned to Myles to sit still, and remain quiet. Moving slowly and quietly she made her way over to the three bound men. As she approached them they sat there wide eyed, questions all over their faces. Motioning for them to remain quiet, and moving cautiously she undid the knots in the rope. Then, with extreme care and caution, she went around them one by one unlocking the manacles from their ankles. Everyone gave everyone else the hand sign to be quiet, several times. Any flurry of action, any false step or snapped twig could awaken the sleeping captain. And they were well aware that although they numbered six to his one he was the only one who was armed. He had several pistols, and her knife. And they were out of sight.

Mrs. Devonshire had noticed the activity and continually peeked off in Captain Wallingford's direction, eagerly awaiting her turn. As the men continued to unwind the rope from around them and the tree, Shea moved off to free Devonshire. She had unlocked one manacle from her wrist and was about to unlock the other when she heard a hissing sound. The men did too, and were looking all around trying to see its source.

Major Highcross was the first to find it. He threw a pointing finger at the woods between the men's location and Mrs. Devonshire. They others stared off at the place he indicated. They all could see Myles urinating.

"WHA . . ." came a loud voice. "WHAT THE HELL IS GOING ON?" Wallingford was sitting up looking at them all. The men bolted to their feet and scrambled into the woods. Their flurry distracted the Captain as he ransacked his bedroll trying to locate one of his pistols. That allowed Shea and Devonshire to get up and run too.

When Wallingford finally found a pistol, his targets had disappeared. He decided not to chase them, and searched again for his second large pistol, and Devonshire's small one too. He could see the dawn was breaking, and he would soon have enough light to track them down; or Devonshire at the very least. "They're on foot and unarmed. They won't get too far," he assured himself. He lied back down and assessed the situation. "How did they get loose?" It didn't matter. The original plan hadn't worked at all, but he had a new plan. Kill them all. "They're all scared little rabbits. They may have scattered when I woke up, but they'll all cluster together before long. If I find anyone's tracks, they will lead me to the rest." he smirked. He wrapped the blanket around him again and went back to sleep.

He was right. Before the sun had climbed above the horizon they had reunited. Tyson and Sho-Taka had had to move slowly because their companion, Major Highcross, was still nursing a sore foot. Myles had caught up to Shea and Devonshire, and the three of them moved off in the direction they thought the men might be. In twenty minutes they were proved right.

In a thick cluster of bushes and trees they sat around breathing heavily from their mad dash, and plotting their next move. They still spoke in hushed whispers. "There's six of us, and only one of him," said Highcross.

"But he's armed. We're not, remember that," Tyson said.

"He has his two pistols, and a musket, I think," offered Sho-Taka.

"And my pistol too," Devonshire added.

"He has all our guns too."

"And my knife! I can't believe I just gave it to him." Shea was angry.

"You had no choice," said someone.

"He's got plenty of powder and balls in the wagon."

There remained silent for a time, each lost in their own thoughts about different things.

"We've got to go back." Tyson declared. "He has the horses, food, weapons, and my wagon. We have no choice."

They looked around at each other for a time, and then Major Highcross, out of nowhere, asked Shea, "Where did you get that key?" Everyone turned to her.

She sat still for a moment, and then shrugged her shoulders, "Someone handed it to me from under the bushes."

"Who," asked Myles?

She shook her head, and everyone remained silent.

They sat for a time in silence, and then one by one drifted off to their own private privy, except Myles. Someone said they were thirsty and the rest agreed they were too. Sho-Taka said he thought that the brook feeding the lake came down through these woods, and if they moved – cautiously – to the west they ought to find it.

"He'll be watching it," cautioned a woodsman, stepping out from behind a tree. He was wearing a leather shirt and black linen pants. He wore no hat, and had a bow and quiver across his back. And, as Sho-Taka noticed first, he wore moccasins on his feet that were embellished with different colored beads on them. It took them all a long hard look to recognize who he was. And it would have taken even longer if it hadn't been for the man's incessant blinking.

"Lieutenant Smith?" the shocked major was finally able to say.

People began to talk and ask questions, and then some reminded the others that they still had to be quiet. With whispering resumed they asked if it had been him who rescued them. He said it was. Someone asked him why he did it, and he responded that he knew what Captain Wallingford's plan was. "I was sitting under the open window the night he told Bardley what he planned to do." When no one said anything he went on, "It wasn't right what he planned to do to you, Mrs." Smith looked over at Mrs. Devonshire and said,

"He wasn't going to bring you back alive. You either, Major. I couldn't abide it." She just smiled at him. He had come to save her, and she was once more amazed at what a little kindness can do.

The major wasn't smiling, "What!" he snapped. This man was insinuating that a fellow officer was plotting murder?

Smith cut him short. "I'm tellin' the truth, major. He was going to do you in too. He and Bardley couldn't have you interfering in their business." Smith went on to tell them that he believed Captain Wallingford was a very bad man. He also said he was afraid of the captain, and always had been. That was why he had spent most of his time at Fort Royal out in the frontier, away from the Wallingford and the troops. Asked about having a key for the manacles he told them he had worn one around his neck for the past five years, since the troops had left him locked up in the guardhouse for three days as a practical joke. He and the troops hadn't ever really gotten along, and Captain Wallingford had never seen fit to interfere, so Smith spent most of his time in the forest. He had learned many skills over time, and had made many friends among the local tribes. They hated Captain Wallingford and so, he admitted, did he.

They began to discuss the plan of turning the tables on Captain Wallingford. It was noted that while Wallingford had the guns, they had superior numbers, and the captain didn't know that Lieutenant Smith had joined them. And while Lieutenant Smith had no firearms, he did have a bow and arrows, and a small knife. With the bow, he told them, he was a "good shot", but not "deadly". And he only had three arrows. And, most troubling of all, he admitted he had never shot at a man. And by the sound of his voice he didn't appear to be looking forward to it.

As the daylight came up, the plan developed. The two women would remain here, as would the major. It was explained, over his objections, that his injured foot limited his mobility and running fast might be a crucial factor. Myles would also remain with the women. (He didn't object as vociferously!) If the plan went bad someone would be needed to lead the women back to safety.

Further debate on this aspect was cancelled when Tyson insisted the daylight was coming on and they needed to get going.

The plan unfolded with Lieutenant Smith, Tyson, and Sho-Taka moving back toward the camp. Lieutenant Smith, in the middle, would approach as silently, and as closely as possible, until he spotted the captain. Then he would remain motionless, and out of the captain's sight. Sho-Taka would move toward the camp on the left flank; again as closely and silently as possible. And Tyson would do the same on the right flank. "You and I," Tyson said to Sho-Taka, "Should try to get as close to him as possible without revealing our position. And, we both have to be ready; as soon as you or me are close enough to rush him . . . then we jump him. The two of us together ought to be able to handle him."

They debated for a time about any method they could use to lure him closer to the fringe of the camp. Lieutenant Smith was told to be ready at a moment's notice to shoot one of his arrows. Neither Sho-Taka nor Tyson put much faith in Smith's accuracy, but at the very least it could provide a momentary distraction to Wallingford, and that might be the difference between subduing him or not. Tyson added that before they confronted the captain he would first work his way around the wagon, to try and find their guns. If he was successful the confrontation with Wallingford wouldn't be so one sided.

Finally, Sho-Taka asked Lieutenant Smith if he was any good at throwing his knife. The lieutenant shook his head, "It's too small for throwin'." Sho-Taka wiggled his fingers asking for it, and Smith gave it to him without comment. Sho-Taka weighed it in his hand for a minute, and then returned it.

"Unless we find our guns, it looks like Lieutenant Smith's arrows will be our only weapons," sighed Sho-Taka.

There were a few final words about what the remaining four should do if the plan failed. Smith was reminded not to reveal himself to the Captain, no matter what. He was to shoot his arrows only if the captain was looking away. If Sho-Taka and Tyson failed, he was to return to the hideout and lead the other four to safety. That spoken possibility had a chilling effect on Shea. Highcross again protested not being included, but his slowness on foot ruled him out. He wished them well. Devonshire did too; shaking Tyson's hand, kissing Smith on the cheek, and reminding Sho-Taka to be careful - she would need a man like him when she got to New Orleans. Myles tried to smile at them but couldn't. And Shea just stared at Tyson with tears in her eyes. "I'll be right back," he told her. And off they went.

"Go slow." "Watch where you step." "Be alert." These were only some of the instructions they gave each other as they moved from their hideout south toward their camp. When they had gone what they thought was more than half way they silently split up. Sho-Taka moved off to the left (east) flank, Tyson off to the right (west) flank, and Lieutenant Smith slowly continued straight. There was still no sighting of the camp, or Wallingford. They had told each other to move slowly, and they did. Tyson would take two crouched steps, and remain still for a moment. Other than a few forest sounds there was no noise. Sho-Taka listened more than he looked. Smith was using the skills he had honed in these woods over the last ten years. He sat in a squatting position and moved his hands forward one over the other on the ground in front of him. Once stretched out he would bring his legs back underneath him. He knew he had the shortest distance to travel, and so he went very slowly.

Lieutenant Smith gingerly moved around a large huckleberry bush and surprised himself when the camp appeared just 15 feet in front of him. He remained frozen, as his eyes darted left and right. Seeing no one he backed up behind the bush once more. He remained still listening to hear any movement from the direction of the camp. As he listened intently he saw a flat rock half buried in the ground ten feet to his right. He remembered crawling across that rock as he stealthily approached the manacled Shea last night. He knew where he was. He slipped the bow and quiver from his back and placed the notch of one arrow on the bow's string. He then took another arrow and pushed it through the leaves on the bush in front of him until he had a small tunnel of view into the camp to the front, and watched.

Sho-Taka had given the camp a wide berth as he approached. A narrow alley of trees allowed him suddenly to see a small section of the campsite. He remembered its setup. The fire had been in the middle of the roughly circular clearing, with the wagon just a bit on its south side. The bedroll blankets had been scattered around the fire in semicircle on its north side. Sho-Taka could see the rear of the wagon, with clothes and possessions strewn around on the ground. The campfire had to be just out of his sight to the right. From this vantage point he saw no sign of Wallingford.

Tyson had managed to get behind a thicket of ferns off to the west of the campsite. Bobbing his head in all directions he got unobstructed glimpses into the camp. There were the clothes and possessions all over the ground. The camp fire was dead. There was no sign of Captain Wallingford.

He made little movement, but sat and looked, trying to see something that wasn't there. The best way to spot subtle movements in the woods was to look at one place, and let your peripheral vision pick up whatever movement occurred. And for that patience was required. Tyson got into a comfortable position, and began to watch. He put off going in search of the weapons until he knew where Wallingford was.

Minutes ticked by and the three men held their positions and remained patient. They had warned each other before splitting up that Wallingford might do one of two things. Most likely he would set out tracking and looking for the group. He would be on horseback, and he would be heavily armed. He needed to find them, and prevent them from ever reaching safety. They felt the less likely thing he would do is head back eastward, and lay in wait for them, perhaps as far back as the ferry point, as they attempted to reach safety. The last thing Sho-Taka had said to the foursome left at their hideout was "Stay quiet, and stay still. Be patient."

The sun was well above the horizon now, and the three men continued to peer into the pieces of the camp they could see. It was the unlimited patience of Sho-Taka that kept him still. Lieutenant Smith did not possess unlimited patience. However he had unlimited fear of Captain Wallingford and that is what kept him motionless.

There was no sign of Wallingford anywhere; maybe he had already gone off in search of them thought Tyson. He finally decided that this stalemate had gone on long enough. He rose slightly and began making his way to the edge of the clearing. Off to his left, on the fringe of the clearing, was the white oak tree that he had been tied to last night. He slipped behind it, and peaked out at the entire campsite. He wondered if Smith and Sho-Taka had seen him. He really wondered if Wallingford was looking at him this very minute.

He was.

As the dawn had begun to break earlier this morning Captain Wallingford had decided not to chase off after the prisoners. Where could they go? They had no food, no supplies, no weapons, and no horses. Their own horses still had the shackles on their fettles that the pilgrims had placed on them last night to prevent them wandering off. And they certainly didn't know where Wallingford had left his own mount and pack horse. He had collected their weapons with the nimbleness of a ballerina as they slept last night, and had hid them nearby. And everything else they had was right here in camp. Oh no, he wasn't going to go chasing after them in the dark.

When he awoke this morning the second time the sun was fully up. He scrounged around the camp looking for breakfast. He found a little, but consoled himself with the thought that it was altogether likely that before noon he would have the re-captured Shea making him lunch. He was preparing his things for that recapture when he heard noise from the woods, and quickly jumped out of sight. He had to admit he hadn't thought they possessed the gumption to come back after him. He clutched his two pistols and musket close, and smirked at the irony that he also still had Devonshire's pistol and Shea's knife.

From behind the tree Tyson looked out at the camp. It was empty, he thought, Wallingford must have gone. He stepped away from it.

"DO NOT MOVE!" Wallingford shouted as he stood up in the bed of the wagon. But Tyson hadn't waited for him to finish his order. He spun around and jumped back behind the tree.

BANG!

The tree was just wide enough to shield Tyson, but the bark splintered and flew off. Wallingford dropped the musket and drew out one of his pistols, "COME OUT FROM THERE, OR I'LL KILL YOU WHERE YOU ARE!"

Tyson didn't doubt he would be shot either way, and hesitated. Wallingford waited for him to step out from behind the tree as he pointed the pistol in his left hand. He had every intention of shooting him dead the minute he emerged. As Tyson wondered what he should do, the captain pulled his second pistol from his belt with his right hand, and pointed that too.

Sho-Taka, who was thirty feet to the right of the captain, could see that Tyson was trapped. Although he knew he was too far from the captain to be accurate, he tried anyhow. The rock whistled by the head of Wallingford close enough to get his rapt attention. The startled captain screamed in anger, "Who's throwing rocks?" and whirled around trying to spot its origin. As he turned he saw a figure moving . . . and fired.

BANG!

Only after firing the shot did he realize it was Sho-Taka. He didn't know if he had hit the ducking assailant, and stood there in the wagon with his outstretched right arm still pointing the spent pistol. Remembering suddenly about the threat on his left he pointed the still loaded second pistol back at Tyson. It was at this same instant that Lieutenant Smith stood up and fired his arrow at the captain standing in perfect spread-eagle silhouette up in the wagon. The arrow whistled through the air with nary an inch of deviation either left or right of the target. But it was too low! It hit the side of the wagon one inch below the top edge; four inches below Wallingford's crotch. Instantly understanding what might have occurred had that arrow been a smidgen higher, he went into a rage.

His eyes instantly shifted to the direction the arrow came from and spotted the shooter. "GOOD GOD!!!" It was Lieutenant Smith! Unable to control his anger he fired in desperation at the lieutenant.

BANG!

He instantly regretted wasting the shot. But Wallingford was a fast thinker and postponed that shock and regret for a later time. He was down to his last weapon – Mrs. Devonshire's Queen Anne's gun. He knew he needed more firepower, and he knew where to get it. He was off the wagon in a flash and racing to the southwest fringe of the campsite. The wagon blocked the view of Sho-Taka and Smith, but Tyson could see him clearly; and in an instant he could see where he was going. There between two rocks was a tree branch with ever-so-slightly withering leaves. It was camouflage for the hiding place of the guns. Tyson bolted for it, but Wallingford was closer. To clinch his victory Wallingford fired a wild shot . . .

BANG!

. . . back over his shoulder at the trailing Tyson, who naturally flinched. The ball missed him, but the race was over. Wallingford threw the branch to the side, which revealed Sho-Taka and Shea's knives, Tyson's long rifle, Myle's and the major's muskets, as well as the major's two pistols. Grabbing the one on top he wheeled and pointed it at Tyson.

Sho-Taka and Smith came around the corner of the wagon a second later. "Don't move!" he hissed in a whisper. He was breathing heavily.

"He only has one shot," said Lieutenant Smith, finding some courage in the face of Captain Wallingford that he never thought he had.

Tyson looked at Wallingford curiously. Sho-Taka warned Smith not to move.

Thinking, as he would, that no one is that brave, Wallingford snarled, "Who wants to die?"

Five seconds ticked by as Tyson looked carefully at the captain.

"I DO!" he suddenly said, and took a quick step forward. The movement surprised Wallingford, and his reflex reaction was to redirect the muzzle at Tyson and pull the trigger.

Myles' "rusty piece of shit musket" exploded in Captain Phillip Wallingford's face.

By late afternoon that day they sat around the fire. "How did you know it was Myles' musket?" someone asked Tyson.

"I could have seen that rust from 20 paces. The barrel was even bent," Tyson smiled. "I'm surprised Wallingford didn't notice it."

"He was too busy trying to kill us," Sho-Taka said.

The group around the campfire, including Lieutenant Smith, now numbered seven. The camp had been cleaned up, and their possessions were once again collected and put away in the wagon. Several noticed that the first thing Mrs. Devonshire did when she returned to camp was to retrieve her cloak off the ground.

Supplies were reclaimed and even some thought lost were salvaged. The discovery and recovery of Captain Wallingford's pack horse provided some extra food, while a hunting foray in the afternoon yielded a rabbit and a boar.

The food, as well as the elimination of Wallingford's threat, allowed spirits to rise as conversation around the fire was light. The only one not enjoying the evening was the one not sitting by the fire. Captain Phillip Wallingford, was off by the oak tree, restrained by his own manacles. Those were obviously necessary; just as necessary was the blindfold he wore. He wasn't objecting, it was for his own good. The exploding musket had burned his face, and the blindfold was to protect the skin around his eyes. Shea had seen something like this before and remembered that the victim's sight returned after a time. But for the time being the Captain would be as docile as a sleepy two year old.

"Will you be heading off to Kan-tucky in the morning?" the Major asked Tyson.

"No, I think I'll give my horse another day's rest. He's got a heavy load to pull, and a long way to pull it yet."

"Why don't you take one of Wallingford's horses with you? As a gift to help pull the wagon. Wallingford's not going to need it anymore," smiled the major.

Without saying anything, Tyson had to agree that that would be a great help. He nodded his head "yes" to Highcross.

"How will you take him back to Fort Royal, Major," Sho-Taka asked? "You are going to take him back, aren't you?"

"I suppose I must. He'll have to answer for the things he's done." The major was right that Wallingford had crimes to atone for, but he had no idea how extensive they were.

"How about Mrs. Devonshire? You're not gonna have to take her back too, are yer?" Myles wanted to know.

The major and Devonshire looked at each other. He half-smiled and said, "No, I'm afraid she escaped during all the excitement. Completely disappeared." She smiled at him.

"I can help you bring the captain back to Fort Royal, major, but only as far as the ferry," Lieutenant Smith announced.

"Why? Why only to the ferry?"

"Because I don't want to go back there anymore. I don't want to be a lieutenant I don't want to be a soldier even. There's nothing there for me. I just want to be out here in the woods; living my life the way I want to live it. Bothering nobody and no one bothering me; doing as I please."

"They may come looking for you, lieutenant. They might not let you be," warned Highcross.

"He can come with me," said Tyson. "To Kan-tucky. I have plenty of land he can get lost in. They'll never find you." Lieutenant Smith . . . now once more Wilbur Smith . . . smiled and blinked at Tyson.

With a touch of remorse in his voice the major said, "Well, I have to go back. Someone needs to bring Wallingford to justice."

"Do you really have to go back, major?" Devonshire wanted to know. "New Orleans needs people who can cook. I'm going to need a good chef!"

"Someone has to bring him back," Highcross smiled, "Wallingford needs to be brought back to answer for what he's done."

While none of them were sorry for what was in store for Wallingford, they did feel somewhat sorry for the major's fate. It seemed his lot in life.

"Maybe you don't have to go back either, major" Smith said.

"Of course I do," insisted Highcross, "Someone needs to bring Wallingford to justice."

"Well," Smith paused, "You don't really *have* to go back, you know." Again there was a pause. "Suppose we gave Wallingford to the Wackentutes. They would love to get their hands on him. We could make them a gift!"

Smith got hit with a barrage questions; about the Wackentutes; about what they would do; and why? He quieted the questioners down and explained that the Wackentutes were a clan in the Susquehannock Tribe. They had originally lived in this area but had not backed the British in the recent war. They were a peaceful clan who wished no one any harm, and as a result hadn't backed the French either. When the war concluded the English, in the person of Captain Wallingford, and their allies, the Iroquois, took over the Wackentutes land. The Wackentutes were to be displaced to a lakeside valley far to the north in the New York colony. They were moving there en masse in the next few days. "They blame him for the re-settling they have to do." But there was more, and Smith told it. "They also resent him for cheating many of them out of their possessions. And with the aid of whisky they blame him for several liberties he took with some of their young women." Smith let that sink in for a moment. "They will take him, and treat him harshly, but not kill him. They'll treat him better than he treated them. He will be forced to work as he has never worked before. Cleaning up after any of the livestock; providing wood and water to their village; being the target in any rock throwing contests the children have; they'll keep him busy. He will be fed, but probably not something he is partial to. He won't like it but he'll be treated better than he deserves to be treated."

"He's pretty tricky. I wouldn't be surprised if he escapes before a month is gone by," said Sho-Taka.

"Not if we give him to them with his manacles around his ankles, and the chief keeps the only key," smiled Smith.

The discussion continued around the fire over the pros and cons of giving Wallingford over to the Wackentutes. Suddenly Devonshire interrupted them all. "Major, if we give him over then you can come with me to New Orleans. You don't really want to be in the army, do you?"

He didn't answer.

Devonshire turned to Sho-Taka, "And you'll come with me too, right? What a partnership we will be. You," she said pointing at Sho-Taka, "Know how to make things. To build things. And you can bring Myles along." She turned to the staring Myles, and said, "You'll come with us, won't you?" And not waiting for an answer she turned to Highcross, "You can cook things. And bake things. You know all about food! And I? I can run things. I am very good at that. Imagine what a partnership we can have!" She stood up and took off her cloak, and then turned it inside out. "In the lining here . . . my fortune . . . my dowry! All I have been able to earn, and to keep." (She failed to mention at this time that Captain Wallingford had contributed to this fund recently.) She went on, "I have precious stones and gold. I even have English and French money, thousands of it. I can pay for whatever we need to start." She looked around the circle with expectant eyes. There was a long silent pause.

"Well," she finally said, "are you ready to follow a dream?"

Smiles started to show on Sho-Taka's face. Myles quickly followed suit. Devonshire smiled at Highcross, and then, he smiled back.

Tyson looked at Smith and said, "You want to follow your dream to Kan-tucky? You'll be welcome." Smith broke into a wide grin.

Tyson now turned to Shea, "And you, please say yes, will you follow me to Kan-tucky too?"

"Yes."

Epilogue: All's Well That Ends…

Well, some roses are red,
And some violets are blue.
I hope some of these things
Never happen to you!

Tyson and Shea went to Kan-tucky and built a cabin . . . a farm . . . a home . . . a family. He worked every day of his life to make them better, and loved it. She lived every day of her life with him and their family. She loved that.

Wilbur Smith moved with them to the virgin frontier of Kan-tucky. He lived in the woods, and associated with more animals than humans for the rest of his life. He never regretted it, not even for one minute.

Dellie d'Argent and Aaron Highcross made their way to New Orleans and, under their new assumed names – Delia Delon and Joshua Calvary - opened a restaurant, a saloon, and a boarding house. And then they opened several more. And then they bought land – shrewdly. That made them very rich. For a time she was the richest woman in the south. He was the happiest chef.

Sho-Taka and Myles followed them to New Orleans and had earned enough money in ten years to retire. They gravitated to the French island of Martinique in the Caribbean where they made rum and drank rum, and never wore a coat again.

With Wallingford spirited off to the oft frozen climes of the soon to be named Wackentute Valley, it was assumed by command that he had perished in his pursuit of the wayward (and also missing) Major Aaron Highcross. For that his transgressions were overlooked, and he was posthumously promoted, with his pension benefits redirected to his long neglected wife and two daughters in London.

Josiah Bardley was convicted of a dozen crimes against the Crown, and was sentenced to ten years of hard labor. His wife found the stash of gold he had hidden in the barn "for hard times", and lived quite comfortably while he served his time. During those ten years of incarceration Josiah lost 90 of the 250 lbs he weighed on the day he went behind bars. So, at least, that's good.

Private Albert Selkirk was not charged with anything, He adroitly denied and dodged responsibility for any and all crimes committed in the Fort Royal area since the Pleistocene Era. But although he avoided the hammer of the court's justice he was still subject to the whims and will of the King's Army. And the sad truth was that King George III was not currently accepting resignations from the ranks. Private Selkirk was, as were the other nine men of the Fort Royal troop, transferred to a newly established military outpost on an island in the far northern reaches of Baffin Bay, Canada. On that remote island there weren't any hostile (or otherwise) French, or women, or taverns. And although it was a peaceful place, it was also cold. It is rumored that in high summer the temperature could soar up to 40 degrees Fahrenheit. Not often, but sometimes.

General Godfrey Tindale frenetically made his way to the New Jersey hamlet of Morganville where he located the cabin of the elopers. Arriving at 6 AM he found his daughter cooking breakfast for her still snoozing husband. Blasting into the room he began swearing vengeance on the man and total absolution for the young lady. He was into a long tirade about what was in store for the licentious lieutenant when his daughter was finally able to get a word in edgewise. It was the argument, the rebuttal, the discussion ending words that daughters have used to countermand fatherly admonitions since before recorded history.

"Oh Daddy," she said. And whenever he paused for breath she repeated it. About the sixth, or seventh, "Oh Daddy" he ran out of steam and slumped into a chair, his head on his chest, and was silent. She advised him, in her gentlest voice, that any further tantrums would lead her "to never speaking to you again" and then offered him some breakfast. Had he a white flag, he would have waved it.

Within a week the young couple was back in Philadelphia, and the toast of their social circle. Lieutenant Crosly was soon *Major* Crosly. Why? Because, as General Tindale bellowed, "I'll not have a lieutenant as a son-in-law!" The fiasco out at Forts Royal and Dubois was piled mostly on Fothingill's doorstep, yet Tindale was sent a special Inspector General to oversee all matters under his command for the foreseeable future. The inspector's name? Colonel Sydney St John, Lieutenant St John's snotty older brother.

General Augustus Fothingill made his way back from Fort Royal to New York far slower than the trip out there took. Upon arrival Magistrate Roose wasted no time filing the proper reports to his superiors. Fothingill reluctantly followed suit and sent official reports concerning the mission and the goings on at Fort Royal/Fort Dubois back to London. And as an example of the long believed, though unconfirmed theory that the only thing faster than the speed of light is the speed at which bad news travels, the response from London seemed to arrive the next day!

Fothingill was summoned back to England for an Official Military Court of Inquiry. While none of his answers to the court were any more enlightening than Selkirk's and Bardley's had been, at least he didn't directly quote either one of them. The judgement by the Court of Inquiry was not a condemnation of the general, as he had fully expected. As a matter of fact it was lenient, finding the general almost as innocent as a new born babe. He was unaware of it but the real cause of the leniency had to do with the batting of his daughter's eyes, in the presence of King George, at the speed of bad news. This same king would be married within a year, and all the batting in the world would not have saved her dear old dad if the trial had happened then. In any case, General Fothingill was not charged with any crimes; nor sacked nor demoted. He was, unfortunately, reassigned to a post in Ireland. He promptly retired.

Before he left Fort Royal to return to New York, Fothingill appointed Captain McLayne as commanding officer of Fort Royal. He appointed Lieutenant St John as second in command. Needless to say this was a volatile mixture, and did not end well.

Philyaw? His wife returned to the tavern full time, and became "fully involved" with its operation. He would later say that that was when he began drinking heavily.

Ludlum never got his stolen horse returned, or Falwyn's cheap labor. He spent his remaining days mucking his own stalls and, much to his surprise, missing the little guy.

The missing Fort Royal guides Edward Twibbleton & Horace Simpson . . . & Rhoda? Your guess is as good as mine.

www.ingramcontent.com/pod-product-compliance
Lightning Source LLC
Chambersburg PA
CBHW050905250626
47155CB00001B/106

* 9 7 8 0 9 9 0 5 6 7 9 1 2 *